MORTAL GRACE

Also by EDWARD STEWART:

ORPHEUS ON TOP

HEADS

ROCK RUDE

THEY'VE SHOT THE PRESIDENT'S DAUGHTER

LAUNCH!

THE GREAT LOS ANGELES FIRE

BALLERINA

FOR RICHER, FOR POORER

ARIANA

PRIVILEGED LIVES

DEADLY RICH

EDWARD STEWART

MORTAL GRACE

Delacorte  **Press**

Published by
Delacorte Press
Bantam Doubleday Dell Publishing Group, Inc.
1540 Broadway
New York, New York 10036

The trademark Delacorte Press® is registered in the U.S. Patent and Trademark Office.

ISBN 0-385-31132-X

Manufactured in the United States of America
Published simultaneously in Canada

BVG

For Bunny Dexter—because this time she didn't

ONE

I t was dark in the confessional. Cold. Staying awake was an agony. *If only I could sleep,* Wanda Gilmartin thought. It seemed she had never closed her eyes in all her sixteen years.

"Is there anything else, my child?" The priest was an ash-colored stirring on the other side of the grille. "Make a full confession."

Her head slammed groggily into a wood panel. "I stole some stay-awake pills from a friend."

"Have you taken them all?"

She sneaked one into her mouth. "I have two left."

"You must give them back and admit what you did."

"Yes, Father."

"Anything else?"

"No, Father."

The priest pronounced the formula of absolution. "Ten Hail Marys. Ten Our Fathers."

Wanda groped in the dark for her crutches. She found a wobbling balance and stumbled out of the confessional. Her ankle ached as though a spike of ice had been driven through it.

The priest led her to the altar rail. The crutches clacked to the marble floor. She knelt. White and gold vestments slid through light and shadow. A voice intoned.

Wanda turned her head. The church was a vaulted, echoing emptiness behind her. *Why aren't there other people here? Why is it so dark? So cold?*

"The body of Christ." The priest laid the wafer into her cupped hands.

She had been cold and alone, justifying herself to strangers, going through other people's rituals, for all the sixteen years of her life.

"The blood of Christ." The priest tipped the chalice toward her lips.

She felt as though she were falling into the wine. She realized she still had a buzz on from all the drugs—especially that pink pill. She could no longer follow what was happening.

Hands helped her up onto her crutches. Helped her along an endless aisle. The cast on her left ankle weighed like a concrete block. Hands helped her through a door and up into a van.

A voice was asking her questions, oily with caring. "Tell me, my child, how long have you been a runaway?"

Wanda didn't know what answer was desired. *Always give the customer what he wants.* "A long time."

Now they were driving. On the other side of the windshield bloated flakes of snow drifted weightlessly in and out of the headlight beams. Her fingers played with the gold chain she had braided into her hair.

"Tell me, my child, how long have you been prostituting yourself?"

"A long time. Since I was eleven."

The van passed through iron-barred gates and into a garage. Hands helped her out of the front seat and up a narrow flight of stairs. Her crutches thumped on each creaking wooden step. She reached the top and had to rest a moment to catch her breath.

A parchment-shaded lamp clicked on. She saw a small apartment with Gothic-lettered mottoes hanging up on the walls:

Bring me young sinners.
Suffer the little children to come unto me.
My kingdom is not of this world.
The kingdom of God is within you.
You must become again as a child.
He who dies with forgiveness of sins . . . wins!

The air carried a suffocating reek of incense.
"I need the bathroom."
"Right in there."
Wanda propped her crutches against the cold white tile wall.
She knelt at the toilet and tried to throw up. Her throat could
produce nothing but empty retchings.
She hobbled back into the other room. Darkness was coming at
her in waves. She had to force her eyes to stay open.
The priest stood lighting incense in a small copper bowl. "Tell
me, my child, how long have you been taking drugs?"
"I don't know—a long time. I'm sorry, Father, I'm fogging out.
Could we finish this talk later? I really need to sleep."
"There's just a little bit more of the ceremony."
Something in his face was wrong. Something in the moment
was bent. It was as though time had taken a right-angled turn.
"I thought the ceremony was over," Wanda said.
"Almost. This is the last part. You'll feel better if you atone."
"I thought I did atone." *Christ, I've been atoning for one per-
son's sins or another's since I was born.*
"No, my child, you confessed. Now you atone."

Father lifted off his pectoral cross. He kissed it and laid it with
a soft thunk on the table beside a highball glass that was still half
full. Ice cubes rattled as he raised the glass. He took two long
swallows. The rum sent a chilled, 150-proof sting down his
throat. He stood a moment, savoring the sensation of icy heat.
Then he removed his embroidered stole and draped it neatly over
the back of the chair.
The zipper of the black cassock required care: it had been stick-

ing the last several times he'd worn it. With patient, coaxing tugs he finally freed himself. He arranged the cassock on a hanger and the stole over the cassock, adjusting them so there would be no wrinkles. He hung the vestments in the closet.

Now he took the transparent waterproof smock from its peg. He slipped into it.

He returned to the table and swallowed the rum remaining in the glass. He poured a fresh drink from the bottle. The young girl, leaning back in the peach-colored leather chair, watched him with a drowning gaze. She did not make the obvious comment about his drinking.

The second glass went stinging down the hatch. He wiped his lips with the back of his hand.

The smock squeaked as he bent to lift her. She moved easily into his arms. He centered her weight on his shoulder and made sure she wasn't going to slide. Walking sideways, he carried her carefully down the narrow stairway.

She gave a little bounce at every step. Faint puffs of air parted her lips, and with each puff the smock sent out a mousy little squeak.

He crossed the cellar and laid her in the galvanized laundry tub. He moved the braids away from her pale, high-domed forehead. Her dark eyes showed surprise, flecked with something else.

He closed each eye, kissed each eyelid, kissed her lips. She did not flinch from the rum. The inside of her mouth had the salty taste of a spent firecracker. He gazed at her, stretching the small, personal moment.

"God loves you, Wanda," he whispered. "So do I."

He slipped a tape of Maurice Duruflé's ineffably beautiful *Requiem* into his Walkman. He put on his earphones.

The "Kyrie" surged into his head. He started the electric saw, braced himself against the vibration, and began his work.

Kyrie Eleison.
Christe Eleison.

Two hours later he had finished one bottle of rum and begun another. Wanda lay neatly arranged in a basket—large pieces on the bottom, smaller pieces on top. He took a deep, slow breath and pushed the basket up a steel ramp into the rear of the van.

He drove slowly into the glassy New York night. The sky overhead had the color of an old bruise. He sat slightly hunched at the steering wheel, squinting, keeping the city streets in focus. Singing along with the "Agnes Dei," he swung into Central Park.

The looping half-lit roadways were deserted at this hour. He ignored the PARK PERSONNEL ONLY sign and eased off the main road, driving around a sawhorse onto an unlit service road. Fifty yards up he pulled into the shrubbery.

Twigs snapped and bare-limbed bushes trembled. He cut the motor.

It was a peak moment and he sat there, losing himself. The "Sanctus" surged through his earphones. A powdering of snow drifted down through the air. The silent city was asleep.

He took the flask from his breast pocket and sat sipping rum. *Work to be done,* he reminded himself.

He screwed the top back on the flask and reached behind the seat for the pickax.

TWO

On a small outdoor stage, a group of young clowns and ballerinas were dancing for the crowd. Their movements took on a sassy snap as the Dixieland band kicked into the final bars of "New York, New York."

Arms linked. Feet fell into smartly synchronized step. Legs high-kicked à la Radio City Rockettes.

A-one. A-two.

Top hats and canes arced into the air.

A-one-two-three-four.

Sock-it-home kick-spin-kick jump-split-leap-spin hold-it-absolutely-still take-a-deep-sharp-bow. Two thunks on a cow bell.

A current of excitement fused the crowd into a clapping, screaming applause machine. The air jingled with we-love-you vibes.

Twenty bows later, the dancers exited the proscenium.

Behind the canvas drop, Johanna Lowndes pulled off her Columbine cap. She stood near the corner of the wooden stage, catching her breath. She leaned her head on the shoulder of her Pierrot. He wordlessly slipped an arm around her.

She listened to the cheering, whistling ovation that wanted to go on and on. "You hear that sound, and you realize there's nothing else in life that matters."

Well, *almost* nothing else. She could feel a familiar craving in her nerves, a need for that certain boost that only a toke on the wow-pipe could give her. "How long do we have till the next set?"

Pierrot consulted his watch. "Ten, fifteen minutes."

"Be right back." Johanna kissed him and hopped down from the stage. It had been set up ten feet from the woods of Central Park. Peering into the trees, she could see all the way through to Fifth Avenue, past silhouettes of fellow dancers relieving themselves in the bushes.

Not there, she decided: *privacy is required.* She had only half a nickel rock left in her sock, and she was in no mood to share. *After all, a dancer needs all the energy she can muster.*

She made her way through the crowd. The Vanderbilt Garden had been closed for three years due to a city budget shortfall—but now, thanks to a grant from the Port Authority Foundation, it was being reopened with a gala ceremony. Everyone was here: socialites, celebrities, Rockettes, Guardian Angels, hand-picked street kids from Harlem and the South Bronx, print people, radio people, TV people, clergy, laity, the whole world. And more were pouring through the wrought-iron gates that once had guarded the Vanderbilt mansion.

Music boomed: marching bands; rock bands with vocalists yowling into hand-held mikes. What roaring! What thumping!

Johanna's heart soared.

Minicams scanned, still cameras flashed, faces and hairdos and flowers bloomed. There was Bianca Jagger!

Johanna smiled.

And there was Tina Vanderbilt, the unofficial doyenne of New York society!

Johanna waved.

And *there* was Sheena Flynn, the blond news anchor, shouting orders at her TV crew.

Johanna blew airkisses. "Hello!" she sang out. "Hello!"

At the south edge of the garden, she peeled off from the crowd, lifted aside a lilac branch, and sneaked behind the rhododendron bushes. Bracing herself against an elm, she bent down and retrieved her smoking paraphernalia from her leotard.

Step one: Center the precious rock in the pipe bowl. *Step two:* Hold the flame of the Bic against it till the crystal pulses. *Step three:* Place pipe in mouth, pull the hot gases into your lungs, and count to ten.

She sat on the ground and shut her eyes halfway. Filtered through the trees and through her eyelids, the garden became a blue and pink and bright yellow shimmer. The leafy shadows seemed to wear a smile. The roar of the celebration seemed a light-year away.

A squirrel sped past, ripping the mood like a gunshot.

Johanna dropped her pipe.

She gave a dismayed yelp. Her eyes scanned tangled vines and underbrush, searching. She got on her hands and knees and pawed through dead leaves.

Her hand struck something solid, smooth, man-made. She pushed back the leaves and uncovered the lid of some kind of hamper.

She frowned. She felt a prickling of curiosity.

She lifted the lid.

"Who found it?" Lieutenant Vince Cardozo, NYPD, asked.

"I found it." A young woman stepped forward from the group of witnesses. She was dressed in blue-and-white striped tights and matching ballet skirt. Her cheeks and the tip of her nose bore circular splotches of clown's blue. The makeup had run.

Cardozo could see that the shock had poleaxed her and she was still reeling, unable to control her crying or her shaking or her breathing or anything else that was happening to her body.

"And your name is?"

"Johanna Lowndes." Her voice quavered like a child trying very hard not to bawl.

"How did you happen to be in those woods?"

"I was one of the dancers. Columbine." She nodded toward the small wooden stage that had been set up twenty feet away, but her eyes stayed on him. "I needed to . . . you know . . ."

"I'm not sure I do know."

Shock had brought her down to her naked reflexes, and he realized that those pale staring eyes were paying him a compliment. Flirting. Playing the save-me card. No longer a permissible card for a politically aware woman, but still permissible for a teenage girl.

Cardozo knew he was no pinup—he was well into his forties, and though he was tall and had kept himself in shape, he'd always tended to stockiness. But his hair and mustache had started showing flecks of gray and he'd noticed that younger women had started looking at him just the way this girl was looking now.

"I needed to take a pee," she said.

He could see the poor kid was embarrassed. Mentioning peepee was a kiddie taboo, and right now she didn't know what age she was.

"And there's no bathroom, so I went into the bushes."

Cardozo's eye measured the distance from the stage to the bushes where the body had been found. She would have had to force her way to the far side of the garden through a crowd of three hundred to reach those lilacs. On the other hand, bushes grew equally dense directly behind the stage and afforded at least as much privacy.

"Did you choose those bushes for any particular reason?"

Confusion flickered in her face. "I'm sorry?"

"Is there any reason you didn't use the bushes in back of the stage?"

She stared at him openmouthed, not answering.

"Perhaps I can help," a voice behind Cardozo said.

He turned. A brown-haired man in a neat gray business suit stood smiling at him. The smile was not social, but political: I-want-your-vote-but-I-don't-have-time-for-your-shit. "I'm David Lowndes—Johanna's father. I'm the attorney for the sponsors of today's event."

"And?"

"I find it horrific that this sort of thing should happen in a civilized community."

Like the daughter's voice, the father's conveyed a sense of privilege even when it was complaining. Unlike his daughter, the man had a good working mastery of the nuances of intimidation.

Cardozo flicked the message out through his eyes: *Buddy, you're wasting your nuances on this cop.*

The smile evaporated from Lowndes's smooth, evenly tanned face. "If you wish to interrogate my daughter, I'll be glad to act as counsel for her."

"I'm not booking your daughter."

"I'm grateful."

If that's a thank you, you're welcome. But it wasn't. Sarcasm had a thousand accents in New York, and Cardozo recognized 999 of them.

He retraced the journey Ms. Lowndes claimed to have taken. He wedged his way as gently as possible through the swarm of guests. Some of them posed. Some chatted. Most waited sullenly in line to give their names and addresses to the police.

He moved aside lilac branches and stepped into the deep shade of the woods. The air hung humid and motionless. The trees seemed to push the sound of traffic far into the distance.

The crime scene squad had dug around the container, disturbing the earth as little as possible, and raised it from its three-foot hole. Cardozo stood for a long time gazing into it. His finger touched the edge of his brown, beginning-to-gray mustache: it was an instinctive impulse to cover his mouth, just as instinctively suppressed.

The skull was recognizably a skull. The rest was harder to distinguish. Time and worms had done their work. There were bones, there was earth, and there was something else that was not quite one or the other.

Lou Stein from the lab was crouched down beside the box with a measuring tape. "This container was built for shipping."

"Shipping what?"

Lou stood. He brushed dead leaves and twigs from his slacks. He removed his near-vision glasses and slid them into his shirt pocket. His naked eyes radiated blue energy from under a cap of blond-fringed baldness. "Perishables."

Cardozo reflected. A strong man could have carried the container, but not easily or inconspicuously—so assume for the moment it had to be brought here by vehicle. How would a vehicle get to this spot?

Cardozo surveyed the woods.

Ten strides north brought him to the bushes at the edge of the garden. He ruled out that approach on two counts: a vehicle driving through the garden would have been stopped—and it couldn't have gotten through without crushing the shrubbery. At the moment, the bushes formed an unbroken wall.

Oak and pine grew to the east of the gravesite, too closely spaced to allow any vehicle but a bicycle to pass.

Which cut out half the compass.

Cardozo walked unhurriedly to the south, almost meandering. The ground dipped steeply to a depression that had filled in with undergrowth and brown leaves. He noticed something white poking through the dead vegetation. He pushed the leaves aside with the edge of his foot.

Newspapers, plastic cups, cartons, and bottles had formed a decade's worth of landfill.

He took a dead branch and poked it down. The stick slid through compacted slime. He found a ravine three feet across and three feet at its deepest, running in a ten-foot arc—possibly the bed of an old stream—just wide and deep enough that a vehicle's wheels would have gotten trapped in it.

Which ruled out every direction but west.

The trees were fewer, much wider spaced. There were mostly bushes and brush. Ten feet along, Cardozo saw that this had once been a section of dirt road. He shifted leaves and overgrowth and saw a number of tracks that could have been animal or human, a few that might even have been tire prints. He doubted that any could predate the most recent rain.

The dirt road curved past oak and pine and petered out a yard or so from a one-lane service road surfaced in asphalt. A shallow gutter edged the asphalt—but it was nothing tires couldn't get across.

Cardozo began building a scenario in his mind, a rough sketch of what might have happened. Whoever left the body brought it by car or truck, pulled off the service road into the bushes. Certain types of vehicle would not be noticed here. Not if they seemed to be park maintenance. As for a man or woman walking or even digging here any time of day or night—who would bother to challenge or even notice? Especially if that person was wearing a park service uniform—or if they looked homeless or dangerous. This was New York, after all: no one noticed anything anymore—certainly not in the park.

"Hey, Vince—look at this." Lou Stein was examining a shoulder-high branch of a dogwood tree. It was the only dogwood among the oaks and pines, probably a distant relation of the dogwoods planted in a horseshoe marking the boundary of the garden.

The sharpened points of several twigs projected downward from the branch. They had all been torn in the same direction and in the same way—a narrow rip on the upper side had stripped off two inches or more of bark. Young bark had grown back, pale compared with the old.

"Were they cut?"

Lou shook his head. "This wasn't done with a blade. They were snapped off in winter when they were brittle. Something went past and caught them." He took out his tape and measured the height of the snapped twigs. He jotted figures in a notebook. "Could have been a vehicle of some sort."

"Last winter?"

Lou studied bud scars along the twigs. "Winter before."

Cardozo's gaze traveled past the dogwood to the overgrown dirt road that branched off the service road. A lot of leaves had fallen since the winter before last. "Any tire tracks in that dirt?"

"A few tracks—hard to date." Lou began snapping flash photos of the twigs. "We'll see."

Cardozo tried to visualize this spot in winter. Leafless. In the gaps between trees, he could see out to the garden and the Vanderbilt Gate. Intermittently, he could see beyond to the high rises across Fifth Avenue.

The view was obstructed now, but in winter months it would be clear. From a vehicle in the trees you'd be able to see the buildings. And from the buildings, depending on the time of day and the light, you might be able to see a vehicle in the trees.

Another of Lou's flashbulbs went off.

An unexpected glimmer of color from the underbrush flagged

Cardozo's attention. He stopped. He looked back slowly along the bushes but he couldn't find it.

The faint indentations of his footprints were still visible in the leaves. He retraced his last three steps, placing his feet exactly where they had walked before.

He came forward again and this time he saw it.

Five feet from the dogwood, no more than six inches above the ground, a red-tinged object dangled in the shade, suspended from the branch of a bush. It was the slight swaying motion combined with the curious color that enabled him to see it now.

He stepped closer. At first he thought that strands of spiderweb might have wound together. He hunkered down and moved a leafy branch aside.

It was a piece of thin red string.

He took a ballpoint pen from his pocket and stuck the tip of it into the loop. He drew in a careful breath and slowly eased the string free of the branch.

He saw now that it had twisted into a figure eight. A bunch of dead twigs had caught in the lower loop. Or rather, the string had been looped around the twigs three times.

He counted twigs.

There were twelve, almost straight, almost the same ten-inch length, held almost parallel by the twisted string.

"Hey, Lou—would you come over here a minute?"

Lou grunted and rose, brushing a dead leaf from his trouser cuff.

Cardozo pointed to the bundle of twigs. "What would you say these are?"

"Twigs have been clipped." Lou made a thoughtful face. "Looks like the remnant of a mixed bouquet." He tipped his glasses at an angle. "I'd take a wild guess and say lilacs, lilies, some kind of rose."

"That seem odd to you?" Cardozo said. "A grave there, a bouquet here?"

"When you put it that way, doesn't seem so odd." Lou slid the remnant into a plastic evidence bag. "Bird could've moved it. Doesn't seem odd at all."

THREE

The medical examiner's office occupied the northeastern corner of Thirtieth Street and First Avenue. Structurally and architecturally, it was the southernmost building of the University Hospital complex. Administratively, it was a separate entity.

The redheaded woman at the subbasement one reception desk was filling out a receipt for a cop who'd dropped off a hit-and-run. Cardozo flashed his shield and signed the log.

As he hurried down the stairway to subbasement two, the temperature seemed to drop three degrees with each step. His breath vapor glowed in the overhead fluorescent light. He pushed through a heavy steel door with a green rubber jamb. A smell of formaldehyde and eight flavors of human decay floated up like ambient tear gas.

All the tables in the cutting room were taken. Green sheets covered two of the cadavers. A woman doctor was working on a third, a white female. Cardozo still had trouble accepting this as woman's work.

As he watched, she reached plastic-gloved hands into an open chest cavity and lifted out an enormous, glistening gray liver. She loaded it onto a scale suspended from the ceiling and slid a poise along the fine adjustment beam. The faint *boom-boom* of music leaked from her headphones.

At the fourth table, Dan Hippolito was closing the rib cage of a young black male. He saw Cardozo and lifted his Plexiglas face shield. "Hi, Vince. You're just in time." He wiped his hands with a downward sweep over his rubber apron and finished the job on his surgical smock. "She's over here."

He led Cardozo to the wall of stainless steel body lockers. Their footsteps clicked across wet cement. Dan fitted a key into the latch of 317 and swung the door open. Darkness seemed to *whoosh* out. He bent down and gave the body tray a nudge. It rolled out on silent ball bearings.

"It's a young female." Dan lifted the green nylon sheet that covered the body. "She was sawed."

Cardozo gazed. Slow leaden shock pulled him down. She looked as though she had been buried by Cro-Magnons and unearthed fifteen thousand years later. Her bones lay black and encrusted on the thin rubber mattress, separated into groups that corresponded roughly to limbs and trunk. Each group had been placed in its approximately correct anatomical relation to the others, as though a paleontologist had arranged them for easy reassembly.

Her skull rested on a thin pillow, the kind airlines give you on overnight flights. Her eye sockets, staring up with black, dignified stillness, seemed to pulse. The facial skin that remained had darkened unevenly, giving her the look of a shrunken head that hadn't shrunk at all. Hair still clung to the scalp, twisting around her noseless face in two long braided clumps.

"Probably a high-power rotary meat saw."

"Professional butchering job?"

"A professional wouldn't saw into the joints." The heavy latex forefinger of Dan's glove pointed to the splintered gaps. "This was done by a guy with a fair amount of time and no knowledge of the anatomy of the larger mammalian vertebrates."

"How much time?"

"Took him a good hour to do this." Dan Hippolito's hairline had receded halfway up his skull, lending his dark eyes a grim prominence. "A professional could have done it in fifteen minutes."

"How did she die?" Cardozo prayed to God she had died before any of this butchery had started.

"She wasn't exactly preserved for posterity in that Styrofoam box. Most of the soft tissue is gone. What we've got here is mostly bones and teeth and they don't tell us how she died."

"So what do we know?"

"We know she didn't die of a fracture. We can see she was out in the park twelve, fifteen months. She's got the femurs and the pelvis of a woman fifteen, sixteen years old, give or take a year on either end. Skull indicates she's Caucasian, possibly northern European ancestry. She has no cavities, no dental work at all—so she could have grown up in a state that has fluoridated water—or she could have been a conscientious kid who brushed her teeth and flossed after every meal. Don't know how many decent meals she had—these bones are borderline calcium-deficient, unusual in a person her age. But she did eat shortly before death. She's got bread mold on her teeth. The bread mold is weird—there are no yeast cells, dead or alive."

"What does that tell us?"

"She could have been eating matzo."

"And so were two million other girls her age. You're not giving me much, Dan."

"Stick around, there's more. Look here at her third rib . . . it's been broken—twice—and healed twice. Not as well the second time, though."

"What would have caused that?"

"Bare fist could have done it—or a frying pan, steam iron—anything heavy and compact."

"So someone hit her."

"Hit her hard when she was eight or nine and harder when she was eleven or twelve."

"I don't remember Sally getting—"

Dan Hippolito finished the sentence for him. "Getting a rib broken?"

"Not twice." Cardozo frowned, trying to remember. "Once I might have forgotten, but not twice."

"From what you've told me about Sally Manfredo, I doubt this is her. I'll have to check, but I very much doubt it."

Cardozo didn't know whether he felt relief or pain. His niece had vanished six years ago, and every time an unidentified female teenager turned up dead he had that instant of black dread: this time it's Sally. "Would you check, Dan? Just to keep my mind at ease? I'd appreciate it."

Dan picked up a bone from the lower leg and for one surrealistic moment Cardozo thought Dan was going to ask him to touch it, feel it, get to know it.

"Now, this is her left ankle and *this*"—Dan's finger ran along an uneven inch-long fissure—"is a bad fracture . . . happened no more than eight weeks before death. Hasn't healed . . . she should have stayed off it, but obviously she didn't. She probably got it set by a doctor, then she started putting weight on it, which is how it developed this seventeen-degree twist that you see here. Safe bet she was taking painkillers."

"This girl led a rough life."

"That's understating the case." Dan pointed to an area above the break. "There's a fair amount of skin tissue still adhering to the tibia—and these things here are leather particles."

Cardozo squinted. There was a layer of dark matter stuck to the bone, and he couldn't see which particles Dan was talking about. "Leather?"

Dan's dark eyes met Cardozo's. He nodded. "Commercially treated and tanned and dyed black. Hard to see without a microscope."

"What's leather doing on her shin?"

"It could be someone secured her bare feet with a belt."

Cardozo frowned. "How soon before death?"

"Put it this way: between that belt and death, no shower intervened." Now Dan pointed to the rib cage. "Exactly the same thing goes for these patches on the sternum, the clavicle, the seventh rib—her skin's been preserved."

Cardozo could see the patches, gray against the intermittent ivory of the bone, but he would never have recognized them as skin. "Preserved how?"

"With wax."

"I don't get it."

"Somebody most likely lit a candle and dripped it on her. Probably while her feet were tied with that belt. Most people wouldn't hold still for hot candle wax." Dan's hand made an arcing gesture toward the arm bones. "If any of the tissue around the radius or ulna had survived, we might have found that her forearms had been secured too."

Dan walked around to the front of the body tray.

"I've cleaned her hair a little—wanted you to see the way this is woven in." The gloved hand lifted one of the girl's braids. Something foreign glinted through dully, something that wasn't dirt or dead cells or decayed vegetation.

Cardozo could make out a series of tiny metal links. "Looks

like a jewelry chain." Or a dime-store key chain that had been pressed into service as jewelry.

Dan nodded. "She didn't do it herself—someone helped her." He reached into the pocket of his rubber apron. "I found one other piece of jewelry on her person." He placed something in the palm of his outstretched glove. It was a tiny, very tarnished metal ring.

Cardozo frowned. "That's too small even for a pinkie."

"It's not a finger ring. It was in her left nipple—preserved in wax. The nipple was pierced four, five years prior to death. The other nipple didn't get the wax treatment, so we don't know if she had a pair of rings. I didn't find any other ring with the bones. The lab may have found something in the hamper."

Cardozo shook his head. "Not yet."

"The maggots left a little marrow in the right femur—possibly I can liquefy some blood cells. Don't get your hopes up, but sometimes even a few cells can tell us what infections she was carrying, what drugs were in her system."

Cardozo was still for a moment. He was aware of a desolating flow of sadness inside his chest. It was an old sadness—he had been handling it for six years, he would handle it now. He wasn't going to let sadness keep him from doing his job.

"What's your feeling, Dan? What's her story?"

"I hate to extrapolate from the condition this body is in." Dan's gloves smoothed down his surgical smock, leaving ashen tracks. "But I get a feeling she was a teen hooker—with a heavy s/m sideline."

FOUR

As Cardozo came up the precinct steps, he saw that one of the two green globes flanking the doorway had been shattered again. He shook his head. If it hadn't been the station house, the five-story brick building would have been run off Sixty-third

Street for pulling down the neighborhood. Broken panes had been patched with duct tape. Half the iron bars over the windows had rusted and the nineteenth-century facade was caked with grime that dated from the era when Teddy Roosevelt had been police commissioner. Since World War II, city hall had been promising to rebuild. It had never happened.

Cardozo stepped inside, where peeling industrial-green paint maintained the level of shabbiness. The female lieutenant on duty at the complaint desk was trying to calm down a hyperkinetic blue-haired lady.

"Razors!" The lady waved two purseless blue leather straps. "The kids had razors! *White* kids! We pay your salary and you let that happen to us!"

Cardozo tossed the lieutenant a sympathetic nod and took a deep breath. He had a two-story climb. He dodged a pizza delivery boy barreling downhill and bypassed two shouting lawyers on their way up.

A century of tramping feet had worn a dip into the marble stairway. Weekly moppings had preserved only a narrow central channel of the original gray-brown grain.

On the second floor, a white skinhead was cursing as three sergeants shoved him into the holding cage where a black man sat reading an old issue of *U.S. News & World Report*. Two steps down from the third-floor landing, a woman was sitting trying to quiet a screaming child.

Cardozo said, "Excuse me." He wondered how she could sit there. The sides of the steps were caked with built-up gunk that had the color of unprocessed petroleum.

"Anyone belong to that madonna and child out there?" he shouted as he came into the detective unit squad room. Phones were ringing. Voices were hollering. A fax was beeping and a PTP radio was sending out soft rock music with bursts of static.

"She's mine," Sergeant Henahan called out. "She witnessed a shooting."

Cardozo had to turn sideways to squeeze between crammed-together metal desks and wood tables. "You're deposing the baby too?"

Henahan was filling out a form, hunting for the keys on an old typewriter. "She couldn't get a sitter."

Cardozo shrugged. "What's one decibel more or less."

He crossed to his office, a small one-windowed cubicle off the main room. He shut the door. It didn't keep any of the racket out, but he felt better knowing he had tried.

Departmental paper had a way of piling up on his desk. He could swear it was an inch higher than when he'd gone out. He sat down and cleared enough space to open the case folder on the girl in the basket.

CASE UP61 #11214 OF THE 22ND PRECINCT, DETECTIVE VINCENT R. CARDOZO, SHIELD #1864, ASSIGNED.

He turned pages. The facts were still alarmingly few: JANE DOE, CAUCASIAN, HOMICIDE BY MEANS UNKNOWN.

In 80 percent of homicide cases, the important breaks came within the first forty-eight hours, or they didn't come at all. Ms. Basket Case didn't look like she was going to get her break.

In the space where a passport-sized photograph of the dead girl's face would ordinarily have been stapled, a photo of the skull had been stapled instead. It looked like an artifact from a museum of primitive art.

The spaces for time and place of homicide were still blank. Description of crime scene, still blank. Victim's name and employment, notifications made, all empty.

The spaces for names and addresses of persons interviewed were beginning to fill up. So far, detectives had questioned over thirty guests from the opening ceremony and twelve doormen from the apartment buildings overlooking the garden. Cardozo skimmed their reports.

None of the guests had had anything useful to say. None of the doormen could recall seeing any kind of truck or van inside the garden during the last sixteen months—except for park department vehicles.

Cardozo sighed. The sound of the air conditioner washed over him.

He slipped a cassette into the VCR and pressed the *play* button. Unedited TV footage of the garden ceremonies came up on the screen. This wasn't the first time he had viewed it and he knew it was far from the last.

Actors from *Sesame Street,* dressed up in their animal costumes, cavorted on a specially built stage. Celebrities and socialites mixed with a mob of Guardian Angels trying for a comeback and carefully selected, nonthreatening ghetto kids.

The camera wandered past brown and tan and yellow faces till it picked up another cluster of whites. Cardozo recognized the faces from newspapers and TV—Samantha and Houghton Schuyler, premier Manhattan party givers and partygoers, chatting with Tina Vanderbilt—the aged First Lady of New York society. The gaunt-looking man holding Mrs. Vanderbilt's left elbow wore an obvious yellow wig.

There was a knock. Cardozo didn't turn. "Come in."

"I just got off the phone with the National Register of Runaways." A woman stepped into the cubicle.

Now he turned.

Detective Ellie Siegel's dark eyes gazed at him out of a fine-boned, honey-skinned face. "They estimate they have over twenty-one hundred possible matches."

"They always say twenty-one hundred possible matches. Keeps them in business." Cardozo stopped the tape. "Who's that guy with the nonhair product on his head?"

Ellie leaned toward the hiccuping image. Today she was wearing a violet dress that hugged every carefully exercised curve in her body. "According to the columns, his name is Whitney Carls and he's Mrs. Vee's walker."

Cardozo sat tapping a pencil on the arm of his wooden swivel chair. There was little to absorb sound in the dimly lit space: no curtains, no carpet. In places, the linoleum had worn down to the wood flooring. The furnishings were City of New York standard issue: a battered steel desk; a seriously abused steel filing cabinet; a straight-backed steel chair that visitors rarely opted to sit in.

"Can we narrow our description of the dead girl?"

Ellie pushed a waving strand of light brown hair away from her eyes. "Not yet we can't."

"How about the X rays?"

For the last forty-eight hours four detectives had been combing emergency room records for fractured ankles, female, fourteen to seventeen years of age, occurring one to two years ago.

Ellie shook her head. "Nothing so far."

Cardozo looked up at the sound of knocking on the open door. Detective Greg Monteleone was holding a notepad in one hand

and a toasted bagel in the other. At six-foot-one, two hundred five pounds, he was definitely an overeater. He mumbled something.

"Swallow your food," Cardozo said. "Please."

Greg swallowed. "Styrobasket of Kalamazoo."

"What about them?"

"They made the meat container. It's the institutional size—the largest. The sales department says they sell over eight hundred thousand a year. There's no serial number, so individual Styrobaskets are untraceable."

"How many dealers handle them in the metropolitan area?"

"Over three hundred. They're faxing us the names."

"Mazel tov," Ellie muttered. "How long was it in the park?"

Cardozo dug through the papers on his desk and found the lab report. "At least fifteen months. Which is in the same ballpark as the broken dogwood branches. The only tire marks in the immediate area were made by a four-wheel-drive vehicle—but they can't be dated because leaves don't fall in discrete layers. Lou found a narrow indentation in the earth four feet from the grave —it could have been made by some kind of loading and unloading ramp. . . ." He thumbed through sheets of computer printout. "Which suggests we're dealing with a van."

"Hallelujah," Greg said. "There are only about three hundred thousand of those in Manhattan."

Cardozo flipped a page. "A pair of Levi's and a T-shirt were in the basket with her."

Ellie grimaced. "That's not adequate clothing, not for the time of year she died."

Greg sighed. "Try to get a kid to dress right."

"Greg." Ellie glared at him. "Shut up."

"The lab has found bits of acrylic gray shag carpet sticking to the blue jeans." Cardozo skipped over the chemical analysis. "It's an inexpensive variety—Monsanto—designed for office buildings and hotels."

"And motels." Greg licked cream cheese from his fingers.

"There's a powdery residue in the fabric—incense. All-purpose, bottom-of-the-line variety. The big users are churches."

"I take it back," Greg said. "She was a good girl after all. But do good girls have pierced nipples?"

Ellie glanced up. "She had a ring in her nipple?"

Cardozo nodded. "A tin ring. With a thin gold plate that's practically worn through. It's a cheap item. They make a lot of them in Taiwan."

"We seem to be hearing the word *cheap* a lot," Greg said.

"It's all generic—the clothes, the carpeting, the incense, the nipple ring." Cardozo dropped the report onto the desk. "Even the girl. Generic unidentified young female." He sighed. "And somewhere there's a generic mother worrying about her—going crazy because she doesn't know whether her kid is dead or alive. She can't figure out whether to close the book or keep hoping. Hope can be a poison."

He pressed the *start* button on the VCR. On the screen, figures broke again into plastic joie de vivre. Heads tipped back merrily. Hands gestured grandly. Drinking glasses danced.

He reached a hand to boost the sound. Chatter and laughter from another dimension rose above the growl of Fifth Avenue traffic, and above it all two miked voices were singing *We are the children of life, we deserve laughter, we deserve joy.*

A girl's voice screamed.

The image on the screen whited out for just an instant, and then the camera panned crazily toward a bank of lilac and rhododendron. Two young men in clown suits were struggling to tug a mud-covered basket out from the bushes onto the lawn. Socialites and ghettoites clustered to gawk.

Cardozo pushed *reverse.*

The image froze, then sped backward. The clowns pushed the muddy mess back into the bushes. The camera panned away. The screen went blank.

"What's that flash?" He pushed *forward*. The girl screamed. The screen blanked out for just a half instant. The camera panned. He ran it again. Scream. Blank. Pan.

"Are you sure it's not a flaw?" Ellie said.

"The sound carries over," Greg said, "so the tape's not flawed."

"It's something in the image," Cardozo said. "Something out there in the garden is flashing."

Ellie was thoughtful. "Maybe it's a reflection from a windshield. Go back. Let's see what's happening in the traffic."

Cardozo rolled the tape back and this time ran it forward in soundless slow motion.

The traffic on Fifth Avenue was intermittently visible through shrubs and trees. Slow-moving windshields and roofs peeked above the park wall—cars and trucks, limos and taxis and buses, even the odd van or two.

"The sky's too overcast for any sun to reflect," Greg said.

"Then it's a flash camera," Cardozo said. "It's shooting straight into the minicam."

"Or past it." Ellie's teeth came down on her lower lip. "Who's got the ground plan of the crime scene?"

"You do," Greg said.

"No. Vince does." Ellie lifted a pile of paper debris from the desk. She tugged loose a neatly drawn map labeled *Vanderbilt Garden, 11 May, 2:40 P.M.*

Cardozo watched her, feeling a slight irritation, though he knew he had no right to. "How come you know your way around my mess better than I do?"

"I was married for seven years." Ellie laid a pencil on the map. She placed the eraser tip on the spot marked *stage*.

"So was I. What does being married have to do with it?"

"Everything. You're not as messy as he was." She held the eraser in place and rotated the pencil till it passed through the point marked MINICAM. "Ahem." She smiled as though to say, *Don't I do this well?* The pencil tip was pointing directly at the bush marked BODY FOUND. "That flash could have been someone photographing the bush."

"Why would they photograph the bush?"

"Shutterbug on lookout for photo-op hears scream."

Cardozo frowned. "At the very first scream—before anyone has identified what's going on, or where—the photographer knows exactly where to aim his camera?"

"Maybe they were shooting something else that just happened to be in that direction at that moment. Or maybe they had inside knowledge that there was a body behind that bush. There could be a dozen reasons."

"Inside knowledge like they put the body there themselves?"

"Inside knowledge like we don't know yet."

Cardozo was dubious. "Why would they photograph the discovery if they were involved?"

"All I'm saying is, we've got a whole range of maybes and let's not rule any out without at least looking at them."

"Okay, let's look." Cardozo ran the tape back to the scream, then forward again. Just before the flash, he froze the frame.

"The resolution on this VCR is rotten," Ellie said. "Can you keep the picture from vibrating?"

"This is as steady as it gets."

Her eye scanned the screen. "Our photographer has to be someone looking toward the minicam instead of toward the stage."

Greg's finger tapped a cluster of wide-eyed faces that had turned around to stare out of the screen. "One of these five."

A jolt went through Cardozo. Two of the men were wearing priest's collars, and Cardozo recognized one of them.

FIVE

I t was exactly as Cardozo remembered.

Despite an endowment rumored to be the second largest in New York City, St. Andrew's Episcopal Church gave the impression of Yankee sturdiness rather than Manhattan grandeur. In size and design it resembled the proudly undecorated, tall-spired church in a New England town square—except for two details: instead of white clapboard siding, the architects had used gray granite; and there was no graveyard.

The rectory, by contrast, was a turreted, gabled redbrick curiosity. It must have been the only building on the Upper East Side to boast white marble gingerbread—certainly the only such structure on the tree-lined stretch of East Sixty-ninth between Madison and Park.

And this particular marble gingerbread, Cardozo realized, with its pierced lighter-than-air filigree, looked like something out of the *Arabian Nights*, carved by genies.

He pushed the rectory doorbell. After a moment a young woman with alert green eyes and wavy blond hair opened the door. She was wearing a gray blouse and faded jeans and he didn't recall seeing her the last time he'd been here.

"Vince Cardozo. I have an appointment with Father Montgomery."

She smiled. "I'm Reverend Bonnie Ruskay." She led the way to the waiting room. It was still furnished in the almost opulent Victorian manner that Cardozo remembered—carved chairs, potted palms, beaded lamp shades, table shawls.

"Would you care to take a seat? Father Joe will be with you in just a moment."

Two women were already waiting. Well dressed and striking in a carefully understated way, they were both engrossed in magazines.

Cardozo settled himself in an armchair. He picked up a copy of *Architectural Digest* that was lying on the table. Opening it, he found himself staring at a four-color photo of the very room he was sitting in.

THE HOUSE OF GOD THAT JOE BUILT, a line of bold type announced with fanfare.

Father Joe Montgomery channels the hurly-burly of a thriving Upper East Side parish into good works that really work. Socially impeccable, socially sought-after, and socially responsible, New York's "vicar of the blue bloods" epitomizes the new mix for the 1990s. Is he the paradigm that can hold our fragmented and fragmenting city together into the next millennium? Miranda Lembeck interviews Father Joe of Manhattan's St. A's.

Cardozo leafed through the article. Photos showed a brawny, vigorous, gray-haired Father Montgomery cavorting in shirtsleeves and clerical collar with instantly recognizable female celebrities—tasting oysters with Nancy Reagan . . . directing Sonya Barnett in last season's educational TV award-winning *"Saludos, Electra!"* . . . joining Liza and Lena in a down-and-dirty "Swing Low, Sweet Chariot" . . . joking with Chairperson of the Vestry Tina Vanderbilt.

Cardozo felt mild surprise at the realization that Sonya Barnett —his mother's all-time favorite singing, dancing, emoting actress —was still alive. In the pantheon of American values, Barnett occupied a niche as high and almost as old as the Statue of Liberty and Coca-Cola. Though he hadn't seen one of her movies in years, he liked to think of her as one of her roles—a naughty old ethnic WASP with a Dixie accent.

"Father Joe will see you now."

Cardozo caught resentful glances from the two waiting women and realized he had been jumped to the head of the line. The young woman led him down a corridor to a study lit by the soft glow of a Tiffany-shaded table lamp. The carved marble fireplace and bookshelves beveled in brass continued the Victorian motif of the waiting room.

Father Montgomery came across the oriental rug, hand extended. He looked to be in his mid to late sixties, but he must have worked out daily with weights, because he had the incongruously hefty build of an ex-linebacker. "So good to see you, Lieutenant."

Do you remember me? Cardozo wondered. *It was only six years ago. In this very room.*

Father Montgomery gestured toward an armchair.

Cardozo sat. He was aware of the lady reverend softly closing the door as she left.

Father Montgomery settled himself behind the desk. He struck a match and held up a pipe. "Do you mind?"

"Not at all."

"When it comes to smoking in public, I am pro-life rather than pro-choice. But in the privacy of my place of work, I find it relaxes me." Father Montgomery lit the pipe. "And how can I help the New York City police?" There was a grace note of irony in the intonation.

"Could you identify the people in this photograph?" Cardozo leaned forward to place a small color glossy on the desk top. It was an enlargement taken from a single frame of the videocassette: a sea of heads at the opening day ceremonies of the Vanderbilt Garden and five faces—four men and a woman—turned the opposite direction from everyone else.

Father Montgomery studied the picture. "Well, there's yours truly, obviously." His lips pursed disapprovingly. "I loathe the way I photograph. The woman is my neighbor and very good friend, Sonya Barnett—looking her usual ageless self."

Cardozo's eye moved from Ms. Barnett to her neighbor, a man with a beard that looked as though it could have been a prop in one of Father Montgomery's amateur theatricals. "And the other men?"

"The hirsute fellow is Iman Zafr Mohadi of the West Side Mosque. The chubby-faced rogue is Rabbi Jack Green of the Village Temple. And the other priest is Father Chuck Romero of St. Veronica's, over in Queens."

"Can you recall when that picture was taken?"

"More or less."

"Did one of you take a flash picture?"

"I did. Wouldn't have missed that photo-op for the world."

"What were you photographing?"

"I took a whole roll of my performers—if you'll excuse the possessive. They were doing a knockout tap-dance number. St. Andrew's puts on musicals using young volunteers for talent. You may have heard of our productions."

Father Montgomery waved a beefy hand toward the wall. Elegantly framed posters announced twelve years of annual musicals, written and directed by Father Montgomery. Alongside them hung framed reviews and interviews. The largest and most ornate frame enclosed a citation from Operation Second Chance, honoring Father Joseph Montgomery for *exceptional and meritorious service to the youth of our city.*

"I'm very proud of my talent pool." Father Montgomery opened a desk drawer. He brought out a Brooks Brothers shoe box and set it on the desk. "They're a wonderful mix—Social Register, ghetto, black, white, oriental."

There was something about his expression—particularly when he boasted—that seemed almost juvenile. And then Cardozo realized it was something about Father Montgomery's *lack* of expression: he'd had a lift, and his face was absolutely dead around the eyes.

"We even have one ex-hooker; she's so street, so funny, so divine."

"What about the photo you took of the bush?"

"The bush?"

"When Ms. Lowndes screamed, didn't you turn and photograph the bush where the body was found?"

Father Montgomery blinked and missed a beat. "I'm a garden fiend—I was probably just photographing the flower beds."

"Could I have the film you shot that day?"

"If you honestly think my amateur photography will help you find that poor child's killer."

"You may have caught something that the TV camera didn't."

Father Montgomery lifted the telephone receiver. "Bonnie—be an angel. Do you think we can locate that film I shot at the Vanderbilt Garden opening?"

When he replaced the receiver, Cardozo was staring at him.

"You don't remember me, do you?"

Father Joe smiled defensively. "Should I?"

"We once had a conversation about a relative of mine—a teenager by the name of Sally Manfredo."

"Really? I hope your relative is doing well."

"So do I."

At five-thirty that afternoon, Cardozo got back to the precinct and found himself stuck behind a minor traffic jam: two sergeants were pulling a teenage male Hispanic up the narrow iron-banistered staircase. The kid's scrawny wrists were jerking in handcuffs behind his back. He was kicking, shouting that the cops had confiscated his inventory.

"Take you to the Supreme Court, man, the Supreme Court!"

They dragged him to the second-floor holding cage and threw him in with a half dozen docile-looking deadbeats.

The words *confiscate* and *inventory* echoed strangely in Cardozo's ear as he climbed to the third floor. He went to the lieutenant's desk in the squad room and looked over the sixty sheet—the complaints from the preceding tour.

"What's going on downstairs?" he said. "They arresting vagrants for panhandling or what?"

Ellie Siegel looked up from her desk. Her eyes had a don't-give-me-any-more-nuisance-today look. "Crackdown on sidewalk peddlers selling magazines without a license."

"Last I heard, girlie and porno magazines were free speech."

"New orders from the Puzzle Palace." Headquarters at One Police Plaza churned out so many exasperating and nonsensical orders that cops called the place the Puzzle Palace. "More than eighty percent picture content, and it isn't printed matter."

"That's crazy. The courts'll knock it right down."

"In a year." Ellie came with him into his cubicle. "There's a copy on your desk."

The latest directive from the police commissioner—printed, like all of them, on blue paper—sat on the desk top, anchored by a small plastic bottle of fresh-squeezed orange juice and a plastic-wrapped wedge of prune-colored something. Cardozo picked up the shrink-wrapped something. "What's this?"

"Rice cake." Ellie shut the door. "It's delicious and it's good for you."

Cardozo peeled off the plastic. His nose told him the wedge was sweet. His teeth bit down on corrugated air. He skimmed the directive as he chewed.

It was exactly as Ellie had said, and it had all the thumbprints of city hall. Polls showed that fear of crime was up—and for a very good reason: crime was up. But the mayor—always running for re-election in this city—was putting out stats that crime was down. His figures were cooked: plea-bargained violent crimes were reclassified as lesser felonies. The nonviolent-crime count was padded with quality-of-life offenses like littering and loud radios, so the percentage of violent crimes appeared to decline.

Cardozo felt a hot ball of anger in his gut. The murder rate in this city had soared to an even dozen a day. Armed and violent assaults averaged a daily hundred. Cops nailed perpetrators in fewer than a third of the cases. The D.A. opted to prosecute fewer than a third of that third, and juries returned convictions in fewer than sixteen percent of all criminal trials. Half of those convictions got reversed on appeal.

Thirty-six hundred people were getting murdered a year, the list of the terrorized was going up by a half million annually, and the mayor and his commissioner had decided that the best defense against the human tigers ripping the city apart was a wall of paper.

Cardozo crumpled the directive and sailed it into the wastebasket where it belonged.

"You had a message from Dan Hippolito," Ellie said.

He was still tasting sulfur and he realized it was Ellie's rice cake. His tongue told him, *No way.* "This thing is awful."

"You're running around twelve, fourteen hours a day without a regular meal. You can't live on coffee. You have to put something in your system besides junk."

He knew better than to argue with Ellie. The only way out was to change the subject. "What did Dan want?"

"He says he has good news that he hopes you'll have the good sense not to take as bad news."

Cardozo rewrapped the wedge and tossed it into the wastebasket on top of the commissioner's latest. "I'll stick to junk."

"He says there's no way Ms. Basket Case could be Sally."

When Cardozo looked around, Ellie was staring at him. Her eyes had a slight almond shape and it gave her gaze an oddly personal quality that made you look twice.

"I'd appreciate it if you wouldn't look at me that way."

"Which way?"

"Like you're sizing up a suspect."

"Sorry," she said. "It fascinates me how your jaw tenses when you feel threatened."

"My jaw tenses when I'm trying to swallow the commissioner's prose and a rice cake ambushes my mouth."

"Vince—who's Sally?"

Cardozo uncapped the orange juice, swished his mouth clean of rice treat, and swallowed. "Sally Manfredo. You never met her."

"Your sister's girl?"

He nodded. "She vanished six years ago. Before I knew you."

That look in Ellie's eye sharpened. "And you're still worried about her."

"When something like Ms. Basket Case happens—sure, I'm worried."

Ellie nodded. "I understand." She turned to go. "Oh, there was one other message. Sam Portola."

He tipped his head back and drained the plastic bottle. "Do I know him?"

"A doorman up on Fifth Avenue. He thinks he may have seen something in the garden."

1010 Fifth Avenue, an elegant granite-faced prewar building, stood directly opposite the Vanderbilt Garden. It must have been one of those co-ops where the maintenance had gone so high that the tenants required something tangibly ritzy for their money—which in this case meant a doorman dressed in a full three-piece uniform no matter how hot the day.

And today was hot.

The name tag on the gray-and-gold livery jacket said SAM PORTOLA. He held the door at Cardozo's approach, smiling with cheerfully counterfeit affability.

"Sam, can I have a word with you?" Cardozo flashed his shield.

Portola's face fell. "Sure, but I'm on duty."

"You phoned the Twenty-second Precinct—you wanted to report something you saw in Vanderbilt Garden?"

"Right. A detective was asking me the other day, and I didn't remember. But today is Ginny's birthday—my other kid. And that made me remember. I saw a van in the garden, parked near a light."

Cardozo took out his notebook. "This was inside the garden?"

Portola nodded. "This was inside the garden—back by the shrubs where they found that . . ." He didn't finish the sentence.

A man and woman glided through the lobby in conspicuously tailored clothes. Portola jumped to hold the door for them.

"Do you remember the approximate date when you saw this van?" Cardozo asked.

"It was a year and three months ago. March seventh."

Cardozo had learned to distrust exactness in memory. "How do you happen to recall?"

"There was kind of a smiling sun painted on the side. The smiling sun reminded me to buy happy-face balloons from the balloon factory on West Twenty-first Street. For my other kid. Sammy. March seventh is his birthday. If it hadn't been for that van, I would have forgotten."

"Did you see who was driving this van?"

Portola shook his head.

"See anyone hanging around?"

Portola held his head at a thoughtful tilt and his finger stroked the web of broken blood vessels on his nose. He was silent a long moment before he finally nodded. "Well, there was a guy in the bushes, but I thought he was taking a leak, so I didn't look too hard."

"How long was he taking a leak?"

"I didn't notice him there for long."

"Can you describe him?"

" 'Fraid not."

"How long was the van there?"

"Oh, it was there for an hour, an hour and a half, at least."

"Do you remember anything else about its appearance?"

"It was blue. Looked like a Toyota. It had teardrop-shaped windows in the rear. And there were some words painted under the smiling sun. But there were branches in the way—I couldn't read them all."

"Could you read any?"

"God."

"God?"

"All I could read was the first word—*God*."

SIX

A voice on the speaker softly prodded. "Eminence. You said three-fifteen."

On the sofa, Barry Ignatius Cardinal Fitzwilliam stirred. *So soon?* he thought. "Is he here?"

"Yes, Eminence."

"All right. Send him in."

Cardinal Fitzwilliam got up, went into the washroom, and splashed his face. His nap had not rested him. It never did. He massaged cold water into the mottled, fallen skin around his eyes.

The face in the mirror reminded him of an elderly dog—good-natured, deserving of love, but beginning to fail, no longer deserving of complete trust.

He came back into his office. The high ceilings gave a sense of emptiness and space. A little too much space. Despite the uncluttered, gleaming surfaces, he kept losing things. He frowned, looking for his biretta.

"Hello, Barry. How are you?" Manhattan District Attorney William Kodahl held out a hand. It was a steady hand: the district attorney was twenty-one years the cardinal's junior. His hair was gray, but it was an effective, carefully styled gray: it brought out something electric and determined in the blue of his eyes.

The cardinal's fingertips grazed the D.A.'s hand. One didn't offer one's hand to a cardinal, but you couldn't expect a busy, free-thinking Jew to know that. And did it matter, really?

"I'm looking for my biretta. . . ." It occurred to the cardinal that the D.A. might not know the word. "That cap of mine."

"On the sofa."

"Oh, yes. You have good eyes. Thank you." The cardinal bent down, placed the biretta on his head, and—feeling a little more like a cardinal now—turned. "What have you got for me?"

The D.A. handed the cardinal a State of New York Department of Law interoffice manila envelope.

The cardinal looked for his spectacles. He was surprised, pleasantly, to find them hanging by a cord around his neck. He adjusted them to his nose, crossed to his desk, and spread out the contents of the envelope across the blotter.

The cardinal's desk lamps—a pair of blackamoor women dressed like dancing footmen—had belonged to his mother. They were old-fashioned and politically very incorrect, but quite endearing once you got used to them. He had been used to them a very long time. He turned one of them on and moved a glossy magazine into the lamplight.

The cover showed a skimpily clad entertainer dressed as Carmen Miranda with a platter of tropical fruit on her head. He or she—it was impossible to tell which—was standing on tiptoe to kiss a cardinal in full ecclesiastical regalia. The cardinal, he realized, was himself.

The photo had to be some kind of computer-generated trick. He had never even met a Carmen Miranda impersonator.

His eye went to the name of the publication: *OutMag: A Monthly Journal of Gay and Lesbian Interest.* A bold red headline teased: THE HUSHED-UP SCANDAL OF KIDDOPHILES IN THE CATHOLIC CLERGY—WHO'S FOOLING WITH WHOM?

The cardinal was aware of a slow burning sensation in his head. "Are these people still publishing? Who's funding them?"

"The editor won a lawsuit. She's invested her settlement in the magazine."

"What kind of lawsuit?"

"She accused a man of rape."

Why would a man rape a lesbian? That struck the cardinal as odd, like so much else in the world nowadays. "I don't suppose there's any point in the diocese taking legal action against the magazine?"

"Don't fight freedom of the press. Looks medieval."

"You mean, it looks Catholic."

"I mean, why give *OutMag* the publicity?"

Beneath the magazine the cardinal found a sheaf of police photos and documents. "And these?"

"Those are the bad news. Raw data. Don't discuss them with anyone."

The cardinal looked at the autopsy photos and read the report and slowly shook his head. "Poor lost child. Is it a boy—or a girl?"

"Female. They found the body in a meat container in the Vanderbilt Garden in Central Park."

An unbounded sadness descended on the cardinal. "Then she's another one of our man's?"

"I'm sorry to say she is definitely one of our man's."

"Of course. You wouldn't have brought her to me if she weren't." Still, the cardinal couldn't help hoping this one would somehow be different. "Is there communion wafer in the mouth again?"

"Fortunately, the medical examiners are still calling it unsalted matzo."

"I'd hoped this was all behind us." The cardinal sank down onto a velvet-cushioned chair. "This poor child makes the third. It just goes on . . . and on." The phone on the desk rang. The cardinal lifted the receiver. "I asked you not to disturb me."

"I'm sorry, Eminence, but will you take a call from your grand-nephew?"

"Who? Oh, yes. Certainly." He covered the mouthpiece. "This will only take a moment."

The D.A. shrugged.

Cardinal Fitzwilliam listened to a voice excitedly telling him that he had just become a great granduncle. "Nora's fine—twelve hours in labor, but she's fine."

"A girl or a boy?" The cardinal found himself thinking of that picnic basket in the Vanderbilt Garden. Lately, he noticed, he'd been unable to keep his thoughts in the categories he assigned them to. They overflowed, like water.

"A boy. We're calling him Barry Ignatius—with your permission, of course."

"I'm honored."

"We hope you'll do the baptism."

"And a wise move, because if you dared ask anyone else I'd have you excommunicated."

"Same old Uncle Barry."

The cardinal hung up the phone. He went to the curtained window and stared out at the false Gothic spires of St. Patrick's. They seemed lacy and stunted compared to the sculpted steel towers that soared far above, shadowing them.

"Strange. In Central Park, another young person is senselessly dead. In New York Hospital, another life is brought into the world."

"It happens every day. Barry, you can't take things personally."

"I'm seventy-three. There comes a time when you have to take life personally. There comes a time when you have to wonder." He could feel a dark wind of energy rebounding from the high steel slabs, from the traffic-clogged avenues. A chill went through him. "Are the Hindus right—is destruction inextricably interwoven with creation in the fabric of existence? Are we watching the work of the four hands of Siva?"

"You're picking the damnedest time to turn Hindu."

"We have to find this man. He has to be stopped before he kills any more . . ." The cardinal released the curtain. It fell back, whispering. "And before someone puts it together." He felt unspeakably tired. He was overcome by a yearning to hear music—Mozart, opera. Something that didn't matter.

"We'll find him. We'll stop him. And no one's going to put anything together. Count on it."

The cardinal had doubts. Nothing seemed certain anymore—not even the Lord's mercy. "When we find the killer—if we ever find him—what if he's a Catholic?"

"We live in the real world, Barry. If he's a New Yorker, there's practically a fifty percent chance of that."

"What if he's a priest? What if he's a *Catholic* priest?"

"If he were, chances are we'd have a lead by now. You direct a highly efficient organization, Barry. I wish mine were half as well run. You monitor suspect priests. You know which priests have had breakdowns, which priests have drinking problems, which priests have sex problems. You never allow problem priests to be alone or unsupervised. You require them to make regular confessions and you require them to go to self-help groups or psychiatrists or both. You see their records; I see their records."

"And it's on my conscience." The cardinal let out a long, sighing breath. "Once upon a time confession was inviolable. Now it's been redefined. Like everything else."

"The courts did that, Barry—not you. There's no confessional privilege in a capital case. Not anymore."

The district attorney flashed his come-on-now-we're-both-men-of-the-world smile. The cardinal had to wonder just how confident Bill Kodahl really was beneath the throwaway ease of that smile.

"If the killer isn't a priest," the cardinal said, "then who is he? What is he?"

"Whoever he is, the Church will be protected."

"How?"

"As it's always been protected."

"I'm not unaware or ungrateful—just concerned."

"You have to keep your perspective on this. Right now, we're dealing with one killing—this girl. As far as the media are concerned, the other two are already forgotten. There's no linkage."

"But sooner or later someone in the police department is bound to make a connection."

The D.A. shook his head—respectfully. "The bodies showed up in different precincts—each case has gone to a different detective." His voice was precise and calm. "The detectives don't even know one another, let alone one another's caseloads. Hell, they're so overworked, half of them don't even know their *own* caseloads. In a city this size, with the homicide rate we're running, it's not exactly probable a single unaided detective is going to see the similarities—let alone have the time to dig them out."

"But you can't be sure."

"I'd bet my home on it. The assistant deputy police commissioner in charge of media and information is working closely with my office on this."

A shadow moved across the cardinal's thoughts. "I know cops, Bill. I have two in my own family. Maybe I know them a little better than you."

"Cops are employees. They take orders."

The cardinal felt too restless to stand still. He walked again to the window. "I still can't help worrying."

"Don't. My right-hand man will have a talk with the detective who's handling the case."

The cardinal turned. "When?"

The D.A. angled his wrist to glance at a lozenge of gold. "In about ten minutes."

SEVEN

If Assistant District Attorney Harvey Thoms minded the straight-backed steel chair with no cushion, he didn't show it. "If you release too much to the press," he was saying, "this could be a tough case to prosecute."

"We generally give the media the victim's identity," Cardozo said. "Failing that, a description. Plus time and place of the crime."

"You hold back the M.O.?"

Cardozo considered his visitor. Harvey Thoms was happily working a plastic toothpick through his upper left molars. He had the beefy build and the florid complexion of an ex-heavyweight who had spent twenty years drinking martinis. That last question of his suggested he been drinking them on his afternoon coffee break as well.

Of course you hold back the M.O. Rookie cops know that. Rookie D.A.s ought to know it.

"We hold back the details," Cardozo said. "The idea is, give a general picture so anyone with information will recognize enough to come forward."

"We may want to modify that procedure this time."

"We'll have to. We can barely describe the victim, let alone identify her. We don't know exactly how she was killed, we have no idea where she was killed, and we're not going to be able to fix the time of death closer than a month."

"The easiest thing would be if you don't discuss the case with the media."

"Easy for the D.A., maybe. We're going to need some lucky breaks. Witnesses aren't going to come to us if they don't even realize they're witnesses. We have to let the public know the girl's dead."

"Let the office of the commissioner for press relations handle it."

"They usually do handle it—in their half-assed way."

"What I'm saying is, nothing travels between you and the media. It all goes through press relations."

"I'm not sure that's a great idea."

"It'll simplify your job not having to deal with reporters."

"I'm not sure of that either."

A moist, spring-loaded smile bent Harvey Thoms's mouth. "That's how the D.A. wants to handle it."

You could have said that ten minutes ago, Cardozo thought. "If that's what the D.A. wants, naturally that's what he's going to get. Within reason."

"Within reason is all we're asking."

"So long as you're not putting a gag order on the investigation."

"Hell no." Harvey Thoms rose from his chair and gave Cardozo a playful college-jock punch in the bicep. "Just be sure you don't talk to anyone."

Cardozo ignored the pain in his arm and walked Thoms out through the squad room. At the moment it was mobbed. Voices screamed, telephones rang, faxes beeped, printers clattered.

"Busy," Thoms observed.

"Always."

"Good meeting you. We'll be seeing one another again."

Cardozo didn't doubt it, and right now he didn't want to think about it either. "Thanks for coming by."

Thoms gave an oddly petite wave.

Cardozo turned and bumped into a large, bearded, shambling man who was holding out a sheet of drawing paper.

"What's this?" Cardozo studied the portrait. The girl's eyes had a goofy, glazed stare that was somewhere between moronic and dead. The skin had an unreal, unhuman stiffness. It was the kind of face that would never sweat or smile or cry or scream.

"It's a computer-assisted probable reconstruction of the dead girl's face." Nico Forbes, an artist who specialized in magic realist cityscapes, eked out his earnings by doing portrait work for the police.

"Maybe you should try it without the computer assistance."

Nico shrugged agreeably. He put very little ego into his police work. Maybe that was the trouble.

"Come over here." Cardozo took Nico to the bulletin board. He pointed to the photographs of two recently murdered teenage prostitutes. "Neither of these is the actual kid, but they were both unhappy enough to run away from home, and they were alive when these pictures were taken—not dead like that drawing of yours. People have trouble recognizing a dead face. They remember their friends alive." Cardozo picked the more somber-eyed of the two. "Couldn't you give her more of an expression in her face? Like this one has?"

Nico stood nodding. "Yeah, yeah, there's a feel there."

"See what you can do. ASAP."

Cardozo returned to his cubicle.

"There are only twenty-two." Ellie Siegel had laid out two rows of negatives on his desk and, beneath each negative, the matching print.

"Is that good or bad?"

"Lou says there should be twenty-four."

Cardozo picked up Lou Stein's report and skimmed the dot-matrix lettering. "The prints are taken from a roll of Kodak A-20 —and A-20 has twenty-four exposures. So two negatives and two prints are missing."

"Like I just said."

"He also says the tire prints at the gravesite have the wrong wheel spacing to be park vans."

"The parks department phoned." Ellie threw him a dark glance, outlined in perfectly understated mascara. "They don't have any vans with smiling suns painted on the side. Only maple leaves."

Cardozo laid down the report. "So what about these missing negatives?"

Beneath an avocado blouse, Ellie's shoulders shrugged. "Maybe they didn't turn out."

"Doesn't the company usually return the bad negatives anyway?"

"Maybe this time they didn't. Or maybe Father Joe threw them out."

Cardozo's eye meandered among the prints. Four photos showed Harlequin and Columbine doing the lindy on their little stage. Two showed the lady reverend from St. Andrew's standing with two grinning towheaded kids.

Father Joe had concentrated a dozen or so exposures on the A-list contingent, the rich and the recognizable, dressed and jeweled as if they were camouflaged for a weekend in the rain forest.

It interested him to see what Father Joe had not bothered to photograph: except for one shot of an overweight Curtis Sliwa chatting with Tina Vanderbilt, there were no Guardian Angels. There were no ghetto kids at all, no faces darker than a four-weekend Hamptons tan. Odder still, there were no photos of the Styrobasket being dragged out onto the lawn.

"I don't get it," Cardozo said. "Father Joe turned around when the girl screamed, but he didn't photograph the bush."

"Unless those were the missing photos."

"Then the question is, why are they missing?"

Ellie shrugged again. It didn't seem to bother her. "Were there drag acts in that show?" She picked up a starkly lit shot of a tall, caramel-skinned woman wearing a blond wig and spandex exercise tights and a ratty violet boa.

Cardozo studied the photo. The woman's makeup had a coarse, putty-knifed look. The eyelashes were centipedes that had crawled through a vat of coal tar dye. The posture had a whacked-out wackadoo theatricality—ass jammed back, tits thrust forward, hands up and out and right-angled to wrists, mouth a huge glossy red O like the bull's-eye on an archery target.

But there the staginess stopped. Her shadow fell across a brick wall tattooed with garish graffiti and torn posters. A dark, narrow stain trickled from the wall down across the sidewalk. You could almost smell the urine.

"It may be drag, but it's not part of the garden show. The light's wrong. This was taken at night. And it's not an act. That's no stage set."

Ellie separated the lady in the boa from the other photos. "He photographed her three times."

A second view, from the rear, showed her smiling peekaboo over the shoulder, forefinger cocked in an unmistakable get-your-ass-hither. A third showed her blowing kisses to the wind like soap bubbles at a children's birthday party. In this one she wore a rose over her left ear.

"Funny rose," Ellie said.

"Why funny?"

"Yellow and pink variegated—I've never seen one. Could be an imitation. You know, I get the feeling this lady is definitely a theatrical act. Only her theater happens to be the street."

Cardozo called Greg Monteleone in from the squad room. "Greg, you worked vice. Give us the benefit of your expertise."

Today Greg was wearing a Hawaiian shirt colored like a punch in the eye. The two top buttons were undone, the third button was missing, and two gold chains glistened in a graying nest of chest hair.

He stared a moment at each of the three photos and put on his reading glasses. "She's a transvestite hooker."

"Recognize her?" Cardozo said.

"Not personally, but I recognize the type—and the street. She's working the corner of Hudson and Fourteenth, down in the meat market."

"What the hell is a society minister doing with transvestite hookers?"

"That collar doesn't make him a saint." From nowhere Greg flashed a leer that lit up the cubicle. "What the hell does anyone do with transvestite hookers? You get your rocks off—and your pocket picked."

"Okay, maybe Father Joe plays around with gender-bender hookers. But how could his assistant be so careless and just hand us the photos?"

"Maybe she wasn't careless," Ellie said. "Maybe there's nothing to hide. The church does run an outreach to hookers, after all."

There was a knock at the door. "Anybody in charge of this disturbance?"

Nico Forbes stood there, floppy hair, floppy smile, holding his revised drawing.

"Let me see." Cardozo took the drawing to the window.

Nico had given the girl high-shadowed cheekbones, a slightly asymmetric nose with a hint of an upturn, a gem-quality sadness in the eyes. He had caught the paradox, the mix of gauntness and baby fat.

Looking at that face made Cardozo feel endlessly sad. "You did a good job, Nico. We'll canvas the runaway zones with this."

"What about giving it to the papers and media?" Ellie said.

"We'll give it to the press department."

Ellie frowned, perplexed.

"Slight change of procedure," Cardozo said. "Orders from the D.A."

EIGHT

Cardozo pushed the doorbell of Saint Andrew's rectory. Reverend Bonnie Ruskay answered.

"I'm sorry to trouble you," he said. "Could I have a word with Father Montgomery?"

"He's not here. Today's his day in jail."

"Is he serving some kind of sentence?"

"No—he visits the prisoners. Is it anything I can help you with?"

"If you have a moment."

"I have a moment."

He followed her into the waiting room. "We developed those negatives." He handed her a packet of photos. "They came from a roll of twenty-four. There were two exposures missing."

She dropped into an armchair. "Long day," she said with a sigh. "Have a seat. Please."

He sat in the chair facing her. "Do you know anything about those missing photos?"

She opened the packet and studied the prints. "I'd assume they didn't come out and the lab didn't bother sending them back with the others." She separated one photo from the others. "What a great shot." She held up the picture of the two grinning blond children. "It would make a wonderful Christmas picture for the parish newsletter. I'd love to keep it—could I?"

Cardozo shrugged. "No problem as far as I'm concerned."

"Could you give me the negative?" She hesitated. "It's easier for the printer."

"I'll have to mail you the negative. It's back in my office."

"I'd appreciate it." She looked through the remaining photos. "There seem to be three pictures of a prostitute in that group."

He couldn't tell if the look she gave him was shy or puzzled or both. A moment went by. Through the window behind her, he could see twilight arriving in the courtyard.

"I'm sorry," she said. "Was that a question?"

"Just an observation."

"You mean these three." She was staring at the shots of the hooker with a boa. "Do you expect me to be surprised?"

"Are you surprised?"

"No. Are you?"

Cardozo met her chrome-cool gaze. He studied this neat, quiet-looking young woman with her medium-length blond hair and her pale skin as softly textured as an evening glove.

"I'm not surprised," he said, "but I'm curious. Did Father Montgomery take those pictures?"

"It was his camera. I'd assume he took them."

"Why would he take them?"

"Because he's interested."

"In prostitutes?"

She looked at him with deeply weary eyes. "This city is like a drain—it sucks people in and if they're not careful it grinds them up. Father Joe isn't interested in running a polite little church that serves gospel with watercress sandwiches. He wants to do more than confront prostitution and AIDS through poetry and dance. So he offers the full resources of the church and the parish to those who most need them. He's made that commitment."

Cardozo nodded. "I think I understand."

"Do you? Because an awful lot of people feel he's just another padre with delusions of social relevance. But his bishop and his congregation back him. As do I."

Cardozo wondered if he was being tested. "The prostitute Father Montgomery photographed appears to be a transvestite."

Her eyes went first to him, then back to the photos. Gray-green eyes. Quiet and unreacting. "Saint Andrew's is broadening its prostitute outreach program to include transvestite prostitutes. They're just as much at risk."

"Have you ever seen the person in that photograph?"

"I don't think so, but I can't be sure. They change their appearance as often as they change their name. More often, in fact."

"I'd like to hear about the church's prostitute outreach."

"Why not take a copy of our newsletter?" She went into Father

Montgomery's office and came back with copies of the last four issues.

Cardozo examined them. He saw that the newsletter came out every other month. The photos of prostitutes on and off the job were all carefully captioned PHOTO BY FR. JOSEPH MONTGOMERY, with a little c in a circle signifying copyright.

"We give counseling and legal aid. There's a lot of police harassment—I'm sure you know that." Her gaze rested on him. "We also have a medical team that does blood tests and runs V.D. screens and distributes condoms."

He opened a second newsletter. "Where does the team do all that?"

"In the field—down by the meat market, the Lincoln Tunnel, the chief hooking grounds."

"And who serves on your medical team?"

"Volunteer doctors from the parish."

He came to a photo of two hookers standing on a garbage-strewn sidewalk chatting with the driver of a van. The van had a rising, smiling sun painted on the side. "Do the doctors use a van?"

"Mostly they drive their own cars, but I shouldn't be surprised if they drove a van now and then."

"This van?" He handed her the newsletter.

"Very possibly. It's ours. The sun is our outreach logo. It's meant to be beaming in both senses—shining and smiling."

"Where do you keep the van?"

"In the garage."

"Could I see it?"

She seemed startled but, after a moment, willing. She rose and led him through the rectory dining room and kitchen and down a short, narrow flight of back stairs. Under a blanketing smell of Lysol, a faint sourness hovered in the dark—not exactly a cat odor, but something close.

She opened a door and the scent became fainter. There were two cars parked in the garage: a small green Mazda two-door sedan and a blue Toyota van.

Cardozo examined the van. The blue looked factory-fresh. There was nothing painted or stenciled on either door or side panel. "Your van is new."

"Practically brand-new. We've had it three months. They don't last long, not with the beating we give them."

"The van in the newsletter had a rising sun painted on it."

"That was the van before this. We had to get rid of it."

"Why?"

"The brakes malfunctioned. It shot through a red light—Father Joe was lucky to survive the crash."

"And what happened to the van?"

"We sold it for scrap."

Cardozo's eye roamed the walls. Gardening tools had been neatly hung—rakes, brooms, a hose. The cement floor sloped down to a small covered drain at its center.

"Did anyone drive that old van besides Father Montgomery?"

"Dr. St. Lawrence—he heads the medical outreach; some of the young people involved in our musicals; I drove it once or twice myself when my own car was laid up."

She nodded toward the Mazda. He noticed that a hubcap was missing.

"I'm afraid it's not in very good shape. But I don't need it for much." She was staring at a crack in the windshield as though it hadn't been there yesterday. "I live in an apartment across the street and Father Joe lets me park here."

"Did you ever drive that van in Central Park?"

She smiled. "I've never driven anything in Central Park."

"Do you know of anyone driving it in the park?"

"Not offhand."

He caught another whiff of the smell that wasn't quite cat. It seemed to be coming from indoors. "Where does the stairway go?"

She glanced back toward the rectory. "Those stairs? Up to Father Montgomery's apartment."

"And what's downstairs?"

"Father Joe converted the cellar into a work space."

"Could I look?"

She glanced at her wristwatch. "I suppose we have time for the quick tour."

She flicked a light switch at the top of the stairs. He followed her down creaking wooden steps. A hot-water heater was sighing somewhere. The cat smell was stronger.

"This is the woodworking shop." She pressed a switch beside the door. Fluorescent light sputtered.

The first thing he saw was the power saw with rip teeth mounted on a steel brace. And then the standing power drill. And behind them the eight-foot wooden workbench turreted with vises and clamps. Electric tools had been left on the bench—a circular saw, a saber saw, a hand drill, a sander, cords intercoiled like sleeping snakes.

"What happens here?" Cardozo said.

"Father Joe teaches crafts and carpentry to underprivileged kids. Once a year they build sets for his shows."

"Don't let the fire department see this place. You're breaking three dozen regulations." A wave of cat odor came at him again. "What's that smell?"

"Ammonia."

"Why ammonia?"

"For cleaning tools."

And the tools were undeniably clean: handsaws and jigsaws and hacksaws had been racked in neat, gleaming rows on the walls, and beneath them claw hammers, ball peen hammers, mallets, hatchets, screwdrivers. Even the tools heaped in the well at the end of the bench sparkled: pliers and wrenches, planes and chisels, rasps and files.

"Busy man," Cardozo said. "And multitalented."

Bonnie Ruskay nodded. "Very."

Snowdrifts of sawdust covered the floor. Cardozo's gaze traveled to five jumbo-sized Styrobaskets stacked beside the lumber bin. "And those?"

"They're for picnics."

"Don't tell me Father Montgomery cooks too."

"Every chance he gets. He believes in feeding the multitudes."

NINE

"I'm scared." The pale-faced, redheaded girl pulled at her left pigtail. "What if F-F-Frank f-f-finds out?"

"Who's Frank?" Bonnie said.

The girl had to force her lips apart. "My p-p-pimp."

Bonnie was careful to control her face, to show no reaction. It still shocked her that fourteen-year-old children were prostituting themselves. "How would he find out? You know I'm not going to tell him."

The girl's bright, swollen eyes took a long, considering moment to accept the truth of this.

"Dr. St. Lawrence certainly isn't going to tell him. Doctors aren't allowed to tell. And you're not going to tell him."

"I don't know." The child's voice was suddenly remote. Her fingers bunched the thin cotton cloth of her dress. "I may have to."

Bonnie forgot herself. Her fist dropped to the desk top with the thump of a judge's gavel. "Amy, he gave you this disease. It's curable—but not if you keep going back to him."

The girl began crying softly, miserably. "I don't know what to do."

"You know exactly what to do. You're going to walk out this door to Park Avenue and get into a cab. You have the doctor's card."

The girl looked down at the card in her hand.

Bonnie took a five-dollar bill from her purse. "This is for the fare. Come on now. Dr. St. Lawrence is expecting you."

The girl sat there, helpless in the leather easy chair, clutching the card and the five-dollar bill, staring at them as if she were facing the end of her life. A cry ripped itself from her throat. "If I don't have Frank, who do I have?"

"You have me, Amy." Bonnie rose and pulled the office door open. "Let's go."

She walked with the girl to the rectory door. The girl darted a kiss onto Bonnie's cheek. "Thank you."

Bonnie smiled. "You're more than welcome. And phone me."

She returned to her office. She felt drained. *So many children,* she thought. Tens of thousands of runaways flocked to New York every year—seeking excitement, freedom, fame, success—finding instead abandoned buildings, poverty, drugs, prostitution, disease, and early death. A girl like Amy was only one hundredth of one percent of the problem.

Bonnie fought off a sense of hopelessness. She tried to concentrate on nothing except silence and space.

On the desk, the hands of the little gold Tiffany clock pointed to six-fifteen. End of the workday. No telephone nudged with its well-mannered beep, no parishioner or runaway sat needing her ear, her shoulder, her advice. The moment felt strangely hollow and unreal.

She glanced at her appointment book. Nothing more scheduled for today, no further face-to-face.

"Good night, Bonnie," a woman's voice called from the hallway.

"Good night, Virginia."

She heard the footsteps of the parish secretary going down the hallway, the soft thud of the front door closing. And now she was alone in the rectory.

Her eye inventoried the desk top. Work still needing to be done had sprouted like weeds—letters to be answered, checks to be signed, stacked memos of phone calls to be returned, and names of sick parishioners to be visited.

She began with the checks and worked her way through the phone calls. She was frowning at a contractor's estimate for repairs to the slate roof when the doorbell dingdonged.

The hands of the clock formed a pie wedge at five to seven. *Who in the world?* she wondered.

In the narrow lead-ribbed window beside the front door a man in a black tipped-back cowboy hat was shading his eyes, trying to see inside.

She opened the door. "Can I help you?"

"Where's Talia?" The voice rasped like sandpaper on a blackboard.

"I'm sorry, you have the wrong address."

White eyelashes arched toward an unbarbered blond hairline. "Redheaded kid. Pigtails. Skinny."

She recognized the description, but she felt no dishonesty in keeping her face blank. "I'm sorry. There's no Talia here."

"Talks with a stutter." Two dead teeth dead-centered in a peace-making smile. "I just want to take her home."

"Could you come back during office hours? There's no one who can help you now."

His blue eyes narrowed. "You're alone?"

Don't let him know that, instinct whispered. "Come back tomorrow."

His face hardened like a hatchet ready to strike. "You better stay the hell out of things that don't concern you."

This man is crazy, Bonnie realized. *Or else he's on drugs. Maybe both.*

"Think about it, my woman. I can get you. I can get you anytime I want. Think about it."

Bonnie was thinking about it, not liking the thought. She pushed the door shut. She waited for the sound of his next move.

The cowboy hat appeared again in the window.

She pulled the curtain, blotting him out.

I'm not going to let it bother me. He's on drugs. It wasn't a threat. It was drug grandiosity. All addicts are grandiose.

The idea refocused her. She walked with a calm, unhurried pace back to her office. She picked up the roofer's letter again. With a yellow highlighter she marked his estimate for new copper gutters. He had replaced those gutters eighteen months earlier—she'd have to challenge him.

Quiet had settled on the rectory. There was only the up-and-down throb of traffic on the street, so wavelike in its constancy that she could scarcely distinguish it from silence.

Next she reviewed a bill from the firm that rented folding chairs and china for the Thursday soup kitchen.

Maybe we should buy those chairs. She did a quick calculation on a scratch pad. *With this government, we're going to be feeding the homeless through the end of the century.*

A sharp little arrow of awareness cut in. She lifted her head. Had something dropped on a floorboard, had a foot stepped somewhere?

She listened for an echo in her memory. It eluded her.

Imagination, she decided.

But then it came again. The same unidentifiable sound. Definitely indoors.

A cold, dull premonition closed in on her brain directly behind the eyes.

The air conditioner's turned too high, she told herself. *The room is cold. It's got me imagining things.*

She rose and crossed to the window. Above the garden wall the dark stalagmites of the skyline thrust clear and sharp against the evening sky. She snapped off the air conditioner.

Another layer of stillness dropped. The room seemed smaller.

She heard a faint creaking, the light whispering sound of something sliding against wood. Something on the other side of the hallway.

She went to the door.

The hallway was dim and shadowed. She narrowed her eyes. Through the half-open door to the dining room she could see a figure crouched down near the floor, mixing something in a small bowl.

She took three silent steps forward. Her breathing felt too short, far too rapid.

She saw it was not the man in the black cowboy hat. No hat at all. Someone else, a boy with pale brown hair.

She spoke with a courage that was not completely genuine. "Who are you?"

He straightened up. Gray eyes swung around. "I'm Tod, ma'am."

She detected no menace in the voice, in the gaze, in the fine-boned, slightly angular presence. "What are you doing here, Tod?"

"The baseboard's cracked, ma'am." His left hand pushed soft floppy brown bangs away from an unlined forehead. The right hand held a palette knife edged with a glistening plasterlike substance. "I'm smoothing it out."

"Who asked you to smooth it out?"

The eyes were perplexed, as though she had unjustly accused him. "Father Joe, ma'am. He's paying me five dollars an hour."

The explanation made sense. It was just like Father Joe to hire a teenager to do odd jobs around the rectory. It was just like him, too, to forget to tell her. "How long have you been here?"

"Since two o'clock. I finished three walls."

"I didn't hear you."

"I was here yesterday too. I tried not to disturb you, ma'am." There was something childish about the proud way he was looking at her. "Could I ask you something, ma'am? You're a priest, too, aren't you?"

"Yes, I am."

"Would you be able to talk to a friend of mine?"

"I'd be glad to. I'm here every weekday from ten to six. Sometimes later."

"Her name's Nell." The corners of a smile etched themselves gently in the boy's pale face. "She's afraid to come here."

"Why?"

"She'll be down on West Street. Four-oh-eight West Street, just north of Tenth Street. A little bar by the docks—the Sea Shell. If you go there anytime after eight, you'll find her."

"It's eight now."

"Then she's waiting for you. Just take a table by yourself. Give her a chance to see that you're . . ." He broke off.

"That I'm what?"

"Friendly. As soon as she sees that, she'll come over."

"I have other plans tonight, I can't."

He was silent. There was a quality about his disappointment that was strangely open, strangely innocent. She felt something, she wasn't sure what—apology, as if this were her fault.

"Why don't you ask your friend to meet me another time."

"Nell," he said softly. "My friend's name is Nell."

The front doorbell dingdonged twice. Bonnie and her brother dined together twice a month, and tonight was her brother's turn to pick the restaurant. "That's my date," she said. "I've got to go."

The boy crouched down again and went back to daubing plaster on the baseboard.

She stared at him. "I said I've got to go."

The boy never took his eyes off his work. "Nice meeting you."
"You don't understand. I have to lock up. You have to go too."
The bell dingdonged a third time, impatient now.
"I'll lock up," the boy said.
"I can't give you the keys."
"Father Joe gave me the keys."
The moment embarrassed her. She felt ridiculous with all her
assumptions and prejudices. If the boy had keys, he was all right.
Father Joe wouldn't have trusted him otherwise.
"The upper lock sticks," she said. It was her way of saying
excuse me.
He smiled. His eyes were half-closed. She could no longer see
the gray.
"I know," he said.
Outside, her brother Ben was waiting for her with a taxi.
"We're going to a Thai place." His voice was fast and excited, as
though he had saved up a hundred things to tell her since their
last dinner. "Got a terrific write-up in the *Times* yesterday. Especially the crab marinated in cilantro." Though well into his thirties, Ben had the dark, enthusiastic eyes of a man ten years
younger. "I was lucky to reserve a table."
Bonnie smiled, but there was an uncomfortable undertow to
her thoughts, an uneasiness whose center she could not exactly
locate.
Outside the cab window, the long summer twilight was dying
and darkness was coming. Streetlights and store signs flickered
along Lexington.
"Hope you're in the mood for green tea sorbet," Ben was say-
ing.
"We're going to have to put it off," she blurted suddenly.
"Would you mind horribly?"
In the charged silence of the cab, Billie Holliday was singing
"Lover, Come Back to Me."
"Aren't you feeling well?" Ben said.
"I'm fine."
His eyes fixed on her, large and caring and questioning.
"What's the matter?"
"There's someone waiting for me. A young girl."
"A friend?"

"I don't know her, but it sounds like an emergency."

She tried to explain. Ben was the perfect listener, as always, catching every implication, quick to nod, quick to frown. Quick to pull her up short.

"But you don't know anything about these two people," he said.

"Except that Father Joe trusts the boy."

Ben caught her point. He nodded. "Okay. Do what you have to. The crab cilantro will keep."

"Driver." She leaned forward. "Would you take us to West Street. Four-oh-eight."

TEN

The cab swung west. As Christopher Street brought them to the river, Ben whistled. On the corner of Weehawken, a six-story walk-up had the streaked dark smoky color of braised spareribs. Fire escapes and gutters dangled like caught kites. Amputated furniture parts straddled the window ledges.

"Looks like a force-five hurricane swept through," Ben said, "and no one's gotten around to rebuilding."

The cab turned north onto West Street and slowed. The driver threw a dubious glance across his shoulder. "You said four-oh-eight, lady?"

Number 408 was a six-story tenement, gutted from the third story up. The first two floors were intact and even had glass in the windows. The sign over the door was hand-lettered in red paint, and the hand had not been able to make up its mind between print and script: SEA SHELL. Two words with elaborate Gothic S's.

Ben shot his sister a glance of brotherly concern. "Shouldn't I come with you?"

"Thanks." Bonnie kissed him good night. "I can handle it."

She almost gagged when she stepped through the door of the Sea Shell. The air had a choking smell of cigarettes and hamburgers and whiskey and beer. The L-shaped interior was dimly lit. Smoke drifted through cones of light from imitation Tiffany lamps.

Bonnie took a table. A heavily built man with no hair came from behind the bar and asked what she'd like. She ordered a ginger ale.

An old Frank Sinatra record was playing on the jukebox. She glanced around her.

Men who looked like truck drivers sat in threes and fours. She saw two or three blowsy, heavyset women. Male laughter came in bursts that were almost cruel. In a corner, a man in a plaid work shirt dueled with a pinball machine, driving it into conniptions of bells and lights.

He saw Bonnie watching his triumph and came sauntering over. "Hi. Buy you a drink?"

"Thanks—I'm waiting for someone."

"Have it your way." He shrugged and went back to the pinball machine.

Bonnie noticed a girl sitting in shadow at a corner table. She had pale blond hair and anorectic arms poking out from a loose green tank top. Her hands were playing nervously with a can of Diet Slice. She was observing everything Bonnie did and quietly taking it in.

Bonnie felt something tense in her chest. *That's Nell. That has to be Nell.* She risked a smile. *See, I don't bite.*

The girl's eyelids lifted slightly. Her head was pulled down into her shoulders, as though she was afraid someone might strike her. There was a long moment when she glanced directly at Bonnie. The glance stretched out, became a questioning look. Slowly, the teeth pushed down on the strained, pale lips. A smile crept out across the face.

Bonnie nodded.

The girl got up from her table. She moved with the fragility of a little animal made of glass.

"I couldn't let you wait here alone." It was Ben, dropping into the chair beside her. "The cabbie says this is a terrible place. They had a shooting last month."

The girl stopped two tables away. Her eyes flicked guardedly to Ben and then back to Bonnie. For a moment she stood wondering and staring. Her irises were green, just a shade darker than mint. Abruptly, she turned and ran to the door.

"We've scared her away," Bonnie said.

Ben looked confused. "Who?"

"The girl I was supposed to meet. I'm sorry, Ben—I have a feeling I'd better do this alone."

She hurried outside, hoping he wouldn't follow.

Six lanes of traffic blurred past on West Street, but the sidewalk was eerily unpeopled. She scanned the curb, looking for movement.

How far could she have gone in ten seconds?

Most of the parked cars were missing hubcaps, license plates, headlights—anything and everything recyclable and resalable. Several had been set afire and burned out. A Mazda hatchback was still burning.

Out in the traffic, brakes yelped and angry voices shouted, "Whatsamatta? Wanna get killed?"

A girl in a tank top was weaving jerkily through the cars. Bonnie waited for the red light to change to green, then plunged after her.

The river side of the highway looked like an abandoned car lot. The girl was threading her way through the wrecks. Half of them had been pressed into service for sex, shooting drugs, puking.

A blue-and-white police car slowed to aim its searchlight at a man urinating in the gas tank of a green Chevy. "Hey, you," a cop shouted. "Keep moving!"

Bonnie was afraid she'd lost the girl. Her eye explored beyond the wrecked cars. A dock jutted dark black into the rippling gunmetal-blue of the Hudson. Boom boxes blasted rap. Shadows moved along the dock, and as Bonnie approached, she caught glinting outlines of druggies hungry to score, voguing wannabes in high drag, and gay and straight males and females cruising for sex.

The girl was sitting on the low cement wall, her arms crossed over the tank top that barely covered her adolescent breasts.

"Excuse me. Are you Nell?"

Weary young eyes stared at Bonnie. The expression was calm, nothing showing.

"I'm Bonnie. Your friend Tod said you wanted to talk to me."

"I didn't want to talk to you." The voice had a childlike petulance, an accent that might have been from New England. "It was his idea."

"Why do you suppose he had that idea?"

The girl kept her face blank; closed. Her left arm flexed and she drew a crumpled pack of Marlboros from a fold in her tank top. Keyed-up fingers tapped a cigarette loose, coaxed flame from a blue Bic lighter. A dirt-edged Band-Aid capped the tip of the index finger. She inhaled deeply, held the smoke in her lungs, finally blew out a fine gray ribbon that twisted up toward the moon.

"I'm pregnant." She bit her lower lip. "I don't know what to do."

Bonnie sat on the wall beside her. "What do you want to do?"

"I don't know." The girl's lips trembled and her eyelids came up. "Tod thought maybe you could help."

"Maybe I can. I've helped other girls in your position."

The girl looked down uncomfortably at her cigarette. Silence rose out of her in a tightening spiral. Somewhere down the river a tugboat hooted.

"Tell me about yourself, Nell."

"Same story as everyone else. Just trying to keep alive from moment to moment."

"How old are you?"

"Almost sixteen."

Bonnie wondered if that was a lie. It felt like one. "Do you have a family?"

"My family and me don't talk."

"Any other relatives at all?"

Nell stared at nothing, the way strangers in an elevator stare when they don't want to look at one another.

"Where do you live?"

"Over there." Nell nodded toward the Hudson, upstream. "The next dock. There's a warehouse."

Bonnie could see the outline of some kind of building, a dark unmoving mass against the sparkling blur of the water. "Are you alone?"

Nell didn't answer.

"Are you with Tod?"

"Right now I don't know who I'm with." The hand with the

cigarette reached to smooth down the back of her hair. "I'm in touch with a doctor."

"An obstetrician?" Bonnie said.

Nell's smile had a melancholy weight. "She needs two thousand dollars."

"How soon?"

"Right away. Up front."

"Does that cover prenatal care and delivery and follow-up?"

The eyebrows lowered. "It covers the abortion and twenty-four hours in the clinic."

Sadness descended on Bonnie. She wanted to reach out and soothe the panic and pain in this child. "You don't have to do that."

The girl's mouth moved at the corners as though she had just swallowed. "Don't I?"

"There are programs—you can go away where it's peaceful and have your baby."

"And then what?"

"And then put it up for adoption."

The girl glanced over. She was breathing in a slower and sharper way. "Church programs?"

"Some of them."

"I've heard about those—they question you, make you feel guilty. And you don't get paid if you place the baby through a church." Nell shook her head vehemently. "I'm not going to go through that."

"You don't have to go through anything you don't want to."

The girl lobbed Bonnie a look that said, *What planet have you been living on?*

A light rain had begun to fall, draining the colors from the lights on West Street.

Nell stood up. "I gotta go."

Bonnie ransacked her mind for reassuring words. They weren't there. "Nell, will you please hold off on any decisions? Don't do anything till I have a chance to speak to you again."

Nell was silent, neither agreeing nor refusing.

"How can I get in touch with you again?"

"You can't," Nell said. "You can't get in touch with me again."

Bonnie watched the girl in the tank top walk away down the dock.

That was my chance, she thought, *and I missed it and now it could be too late.*

ELEVEN

"I give two evenings a month to prostitute outreach," Dr. Hillary St. Lawrence said. "The first and third Tuesdays."

"What exactly do you do for the program?" Cardozo said.

The doctor's expression was thoughtful. He took off his steel-rimmed bifocals and probed one of the temples through his brush-cut gray hair. "It's mostly clinical work in the field. I take blood samples, smears, cultures, blood pressure—listen to hearts and lungs. Where it's warranted, I'll take a patient's medical history. I might prescribe an antibiotic or mild antipsychotic. And naturally I distribute condoms and literature and advise on safer sex techniques."

Cardozo noted that the antique table in the softly lit office was stacked with brightly printed pamphlets. One Chinese porcelain bowl brimmed with plain-wrapped condoms and another with individually wrapped sour balls and cough drops. On the wall above, two eighteenth-century cutaway views of human anatomy looked like hand-tinted maps of fantastic continents.

"Do you use the church van on these trips?"

"No, I use my own station wagon."

"Have you ever driven the church van?"

"Never."

Cardozo leaned forward from his chair to hand Dr. St. Lawrence three photos. "Do you recognize this person?"

The doctor moved a jade inkwell to one side and spread the glossies on his desk top. Narrow, pale gray eyes slowly scanned from left to right. Beneath the high-arched nose, thin colorless lips pulled down in a frown. "I can't honestly say I do, except as a type. They're a fairly common sort of prostitute nowadays, God only knows why."

"Has Father Montgomery ever mentioned such a person to you?"

"Not by name."

"In what context, then?"

Dr. St. Lawrence's gaze flattened. "Look, Father Joe doesn't confide his pastoral work to me and I don't confide my medical work to him—or to the police. These prostitutes are my patients. I'm not about to discuss anything they've told me."

"Do you ask them for the names of their contacts?"

"Never."

"Do they ever volunteer the information?"

"That's privileged. But if you're implying that Father Montgomery's friendship for any of these people goes beyond the purely caring, then you're very much mistaken and I very much resent the way this discussion is heading." The doctor slid back a French cuff and grimaced at a gold Rolex watch. "And I have a patient waiting."

Cardozo closed his notebook and slid it back into his pocket. He rose to his feet. "Thank you for your impressions—and for your time." As he was leaving, he turned to ask one last question. "Doctor, are you a specialist?"

A faint smile softened the doctor's face. "Diseases of the middle intestine."

"And you've never driven the church van in Central Park?"

The smile vanished. "Why would I do that?"

"Do you know of anyone who has?"

"Absolutely not."

It was a little after one o'clock in the morning when Cardozo pulled his Honda to the west curb of Ninth Avenue. Across Fourteenth Street, where dozens of refrigerated trucks had triple- and quadruple-parked, flamboyantly dressed transvestite hookers strutted their wares. Out-of-state cars and a few taxis cruised.

Two hookers stood chatting in the light of a flood lamp outside a warehouse door. They both wore imitation leopard-skin minis and red vinyl boots.

As Cardozo approached, they both turned. One of the hookers

slapped a hand on a saucily cocked hip. Her eyebrows arched, subtle as the snap of a burlesque queen's G-string. She had red hair the size of a bushel basket and she wore a fringed cowboy vest.

"Treat you girls to a drink?" Cardozo showed his shield.

"Oh, shit." The hooker dropped her cigarette on the pavement and stomped it out hard. "You busting us?"

"Not tonight. Word of honor. Where's a good watering hole?"

"Forget the drinks. We're on duty—right, bitch?"

The other hooker, a tall transvestite wearing an oversize sombrero, seemed disappointed. "Don't you wish. It's too fucking slow tonight."

Cardozo handed Cowboy Vest two photos. "Ever seen a van like this in the neighborhood?"

She groaned. "I don't believe it. The God Loves You van."

"Tell me about the God Loves You van."

The hookers traded looks. It was Cowboy Vest who finally spoke. "A sad old Japanese sardine can with teardrop windows and a carpet and throw pillows in the rear"—the eyebrow went up again—"just in case."

Her co-worker tipped back her sombrero. "Don't forget that inspirational motto painted on the door—something like God loves you and I love God and you love me and isn't it all a cosmic groove."

"When was the last time you saw this van?"

Sombrero shrugged. "Two, three months ago."

"I don't suppose you happened to get the license number? Or notice what state the license plate was from?"

"Honey, we're not being paid by the Bureau of Parking Violations."

"Who drives this van?"

The hookers rolled their eyes. Sombrero stepped closer to Cardozo. Under the drugstore cologne, she smelled like an athlete who needed a shower. "Would you believe—a priest?"

Cardozo showed them blowups of the two priests from the videocassette.

Sombrero frowned at the grainy enlargements. She tapped a green cathedral-window fingernail on Father Joe Montgomery's face. "Might be this guy."

Cowboy Vest snatched the photos. "You're crazy, bitch. It ain't neither one of 'em."

"I've seen that creep cruising."

Cowboy Vest coughed out a lungful of smoke. "So have I, but he ain't the creep that says we should stop using rubbers and give up hooking. Fat chance in *this* economy."

"How can you be sure he's a priest?" Cardozo said. "Does he wear a collar?"

"He doesn't need to." Cowboy Vest blew out a wriggling jet of smoke. "This business, you get so you can smell a priest on the prowl."

"Anyone happen to know this priest's name?"

Sombrero snorted. "Down here no one has a name. Least not a real one."

Cardozo took out three photos of the hooker in the striped spandex leotard.

"Shit. I do believe . . ." Sombrero strolled to the curb and angled one of the photos to the streetlight. She let out a long exhalation. "It is, it is, it is—our own little Jonquil!"

"No *way*, bitch." Cowboy Vest shook her head with an energy that sent shock waves through her hairdo. "Jonquil may have love handles, but not wider than her hips."

Sombrero hooted. "Feed my pink kitty cat, girl. Jonquil do got love handles wider than a linebacker's shoulders."

"Well, even if she did, she'd never let them show like this."

"Jonquil would show anything she's got if there was a rat's chance of peddling it."

"Mind telling me who Jonquil is?" Cardozo said.

"Island trash. Hawaii." Cowboy Vest handed back the photos. "Haven't seen her around in a few weeks."

"A few months is more like it." Sombrero sighed. "I heard she won some money on the lottery and flew her ass to Miami."

Cowboy Vest let out a mean, crack-fueled cackle. "Her ass'll be back. Trust me."

Cardozo opened his wallet and took out two twenty-dollar bills and two business cards. Bribes to informants were not deductible as a business expense: they came out of his own pocket. "If Jonquil happens to turn up, would you ask her to get in touch with me?"

TWELVE

At 7:55 A.M. Cardozo steered his Honda down the alley beside the precinct building. He saw he had a choice of parking spots: one at the end of the alley, or one halfway back, under the fire escape.

He chose halfway back—it was visible from the street. Though teenage thieves had become brazen about breaking into the cars, they still preferred not to be seen doing it.

He collected his newspapers from the front seat—all four metropolitan dailies—and made sure his windows were up and his doors locked. As he came around to the front steps he was irked to see that the green globe was still busted.

Cops were streaming through the lobby. One shift was ending and another beginning. Voices shouted, radios staticked, telephones jangled. Cardozo gave a few shouts, got a few, slapped a few backs, got slapped, joined the stream heading upstairs.

The noise level was lower in the squad room. Detectives were the gents of the NYPD: they didn't shout, they didn't roughhouse on company time. A group was clustered around the coffeemakers, debating the fine points of last night's ball game.

Cardozo crossed to Ellie's desk. "Anything happening?"

"Robbery in progress." She was dressed, as usual, as though she had a very important tea party to get to. Pale blue today. "The Gap, over on Lexington. Female Caucasian and two male Hispanics seen breaking in."

"What kind of retards would break into a place on a main thoroughfare in broad daylight?"

Greg Monteleone butted in. "Criminals are getting dumb. It's the fault of the fucked-up school system."

"They are dumber," Ellie said, "and it's not funny. A lot more people are getting killed than need to."

Cardozo left Ellie and Greg to their discussion. He frowned

when he saw the fresh paper on his desk: departmental forms, the daily dose of directives from the commissioner, a bunch of updates on ongoing homicide investigations. He cleared a space, dumped his newspapers, and saw that the coffee crowd had thinned. He went to get himself a cup.

Three cups later, he was ready to begin reading.

There was nothing in the *New York Times* about Ms. Basket Case. That was to be expected. The *Times* was more apt to cover a homicide in a former Soviet republic than a shooting on their own street.

Nothing in the *Daily News*. He frowned. He knew they were short of writers, but it seemed odd. No murders at all. There'd been ten killings in town since the last edition, but you'd never know it from these guys.

Nothing in the *New York Post* either—that surprised him. Grotesque killings tended to be the *Post*'s meat—unless they were going vegetarian on their readers.

On page seven of *New York Newsday* he saw the headline WOMAN FOUND DEAD. A real nongrabber. Who was writing their copy, the cardinal?

He read as far as the third paragraph and then realization hit like a punch on the side of the head: it was his case—the girl in the basket. He spread *Newsday* flat, and read the article again, slowly this time.

According to the report, a woman—probably a prostitute, probably black—had been found dead in a ravine in Central Park. The body, showing signs of drug abuse and s/m, had been covered with leaves.

Period. End of report.

He could feel a vein pumping up in his temple. The cup of coffee on his desk was half empty. He took another swallow, trying to hold his annoyance in check. The word *black* repeated in his mind like a bent blade clacking against an electric fan casing.

He propped the autopsy report against the lamp in front of him. A demented fax machine in the squad room was sending out high-pitched squeaks like the signal a truck makes before it backs up over you.

He reached back and slammed the door.

When he had reread the medical examiner's report, he consulted his watch and decided that even over at the D.A.'s office they must have started work by now. He lifted the phone and dialed.

"Harvey Thoms," a voice growled.

"Harvey—Vince Cardozo. I just read *Newsday*. Where did they get that business that the girl in the basket was a black hooker?"

An instant's hesitation came across the line and then Thoms said, "Someone in the press office must have gotten it from the autopsy."

"I'm looking at the autopsy, and I don't see it."

"Well, mistakes happen." There was a kind of dismissive shrug in Thoms's voice.

"Why's there no mention of the Styrobasket? Someone might have seen a basket that size being transported. And why not spell out the exact location of the grave? If we don't give the public something to recognize, how's anybody going to come forward?"

"I'll see if we can get the commissioner to clear that information for release."

Cardozo had an uneasy sense of a bureaucratic snafu in the making—the stuff that internal affairs investigations and mass firings were made of. "From what I'm reading in *Newsday*, this is a murder that took place on Mars. If this is how the press commissioner is handling the case, I'm not surprised the media aren't picking it up."

"I hear you, Vince. You have a point. I'll get right on it."

Cardozo slipped the tape into the VCR and fast-forwarded to the flash. He backed the tape up and froze the frame.

Sonya Barnett gazed at the pulsing image on the screen. "What's so special? All I can see is a nerdy audience of four hundred wannabe celebrities and a tacky little stage with peppermint bunting and an overbuilt Harlequin tap-dancing with an anorectic Columbine."

Cardozo could not see the famous Barnett neck, and that, he realized, was her intention. She had tied a silk scarf around her head babushka-style and knotted it tightly under her chin. The pale blue of the scarf met the pure white of a turtleneck sweater.

"What about the five people facing the camera?" he said.

Her face was heavily caked in makeup, and she was sitting in shadow, but he could see her glance flick up. Her blue eyes narrowed and she laughed. "The divine Ms. Barnett and her four divines—a minister, a priest, a rabbi, and a what-do-you-call-it."

They were seated on wicker armchairs in the living room of Miss Barnett's Tudor town house. Wooden decoy ducks and Uncle Sam mugs and show biz awards lined the shelves. They were drinking tea. Tea had been Miss Barnett's idea, in fact she had insisted, and it was awful stuff—weak and cold.

"Father Joe is such a sixties ecumenist." She paused to sip from her cup. "One of these days he's going to pull a certified witch doctor out of his mitre."

"Why are the five of you facing the TV camera?"

"Because we're all in show biz, darling, and our careers are faltering, and if there's the slightest chance of a photo-op, we'll crawl out of our iron lungs and dance the Charleston."

"But why did you all turn at that particular moment?"

"At what particular moment?"

Cardozo pressed *play* on the remote. The image broke into movement: a girl screamed, there was an instant of whiteout, and the camera panned to the bushes.

"Oh, yes." Sonya Barnett nodded. "*That* moment—the entrance of the party pooper."

"Was it the scream that made you turn?"

"Not bloody likely—it takes more than a scream to get the attention of old monsters like us."

Cardozo reversed the tape and wound back to the flash. "Then what was Father Joe photographing?"

"Let me think." Sonya Barnett took a moment to reflect. "He was photographing the TV crew."

"What was so remarkable about the TV crew?"

"It was just such a relief to see them. We'd gotten all dolled up, but none of us knew for sure whether or not there was going to be TV coverage. And then I looked over my shoulder and lo and behold, there was a five-man crew from NBC. I said, 'Don't look now, fellas, but this little picnic just went prime-time.' "

She was wearing darned gray jogging pants and scuffed track shoes and she had her feet up on a needlepoint footstool. She crossed her legs the other way.

"I don't mean to suggest that Father Joe's *obsessed* with public-

ity. He's a genuinely religious man and it's the Church he's publicizing, not himself. Frankly, I don't believe in a deity—I mean,
look at the state of this world!—but I do respect that sort of
transcendental commitment in others. Which is the only reason I
agreed to be a character witness for Father Joe in that messy child
abuse case."

Cardozo caught her peeking over the rim of her cup at him,
gauging the effect she'd made.

"What child abuse case was that?"

She made a face. "I'd say this tea has lost its pop, wouldn't
you? Shall we tell Ingrid to freshen it?"

"Mine's fine, thanks."

She picked up a small copper bell and gave it a violent shake.
"Ingrid! Come fix this tea, what did you do to it, it's pew-ee!" She
set the bell down and eyed Cardozo thoughtfully. "A female child
in Father Joe's care broke an ankle. You never heard about it?"

"Never."

"Her name was Louisa Hitchcock. It was her own fault. As my
old Swedish mom used to say, if you can't stand up, for God's
sake sit down. Naturally, this world being what it is today, the
parents sued. The father's been involved in some shady Treasury
bond bids on Wall Street. The mother organizes parties for charity
and pockets a percentage. What pigs."

"When did this happen?"

"A year, a year and a half ago. I knew I'd get terrible press if I
stepped into that courtroom." Sonya Barnett sighed. "You'd think
I was advocating child abuse. But I couldn't let Father Joe go to
jail, could I?"

THIRTEEN

Every time Bonnie raised her eyes she saw Nell sitting there in the leather easy chair. But this wasn't Nell, this was Phil, a frightened thirteen-year-old African-American male trying desperately to stay off crack.

"You can't go home," Bonnie said. "Not if your mother's still using."

Silence closed in. The little Tiffany clock on the desk seemed to tick like a bomb. Phil's luminous, lost gaze was like a suction tube draining Bonnie's most cherished assumptions out of her.

"She's not using a whole lot," Phil said softly.

Bonnie knew that was bull. Phil's mother could smoke the yield of a Bolivian coca field in two hours. And using wasn't the worst of her behavior—she was a borderline schizophrenic and in her deluded rages she was beating the boy. New lacerations were visible on his neck and arms and the left eye was swollen shut like a split plum. But Bonnie had never managed to get Harvey to discuss his mother's abuse. That was a barrier for the psychiatrist to scale.

"You can't be around anyone who's using," Bonnie said. "No matter how little they're using. No matter how much you love them."

"But if I . . ." Harvey's mouth twisted. He seemed to be trying to frame a question that was both painful and embarrassing. "If I don't go home, where can I stay?"

"Would you like to stay here?"

He looked away, shyly. "I don't want to be trouble."

"Father Joe has a guest room. Maybe you could stay there till we arrange something. Okay?"

Phil's right eyelid drooped. After a gawky moment he nodded.

"Wait here," Bonnie said. "I'll ask Father Joe right now."

She went and knocked on Father Joe's door. He was at his desk frowning at a copy of the latest diocesan newsletter.

"Can Phil have the guest room for a night?"

"Sure." Father Joe didn't look up. "He can have it for a week."

Bonnie stepped into the office and closed the door behind her. "Where's that boy Tod who was here the other day?"

"He did his work and left." Father Joe laid down the newsletter. "Why?"

"He asked me to help a friend of his."

Father Joe smiled. "Tod has a lot of needy friends."

"This one's pregnant."

"I'm not surprised."

"She doesn't know what to do with the baby."

"And neither would Tod. How pregnant is she?"

"She couldn't be too far along. She looks like a rail."

"Of course, it doesn't show till the twenty-second week or so—and by then it's too late." Father Joe moved a paperweight on his desk. It thunked faintly on the rosewood. "At least it's too late under New York law."

"I wasn't thinking of that."

"But I'll bet the girl was."

"St. Hubert's in Maine says they'll save a bed for her."

"That's a better solution." Father Joe nodded thoughtfully. "Assuming the girl's willing."

"If I can just talk to her again, I know I can persuade her. Don't you have any way of locating Tod?"

Father Joe walked to the window. "Tod Lomax is urban tumbleweed. Goes where chance takes him. Lately he's been with those runaways squatting on the West Side docks."

"I've heard about those docks. The kids are prostituting themselves and doing drugs and eating out of garbage cans."

"Americans in every city are eating out of garbage cans." Father Joe sighed. "You have to know your limits, Bonnie. You're a terrific worker, but you can't maintain an unblinking vigil over all the runaways in this town. No one can."

"I'm not talking about all of them. I'm talking about one frightened, pregnant girl."

Father Joe's eyes were sad. "Then you're talking about all of them."

* * *

The traffic light was green.

Bonnie shifted her purse strap from over her shoulder to around her neck. Her right elbow clamped the purse tightly to her body. Hurrying to catch the light before it changed, she dodged through six lanes of bumper-to-bumper congestion on the West Side Highway.

It was seven-thirty in the evening and somewhere in America a bird must have been singing, but not here on the Twelfth Street pier. The humidity was acrid with chemical discharge and illegal sewage floating downstream on the Hudson. Honking trucks and automobiles added their exhaust fumes to the mix.

A Latino kid was standing in the dying sun behind a rip in the chain-link fence that some city agency had erected, ineffectually, to guard the warehouse. He seemed to Bonnie to be no older than fourteen. Built like a sparrow, shirtless, he watched traffic ooze past as though it was the most thought-provoking spectacle since educational TV. An easy, drugged goofiness played across his features.

Bonnie approached, her best smile in place. "Excuse me. I wonder if you could help me?"

The kid adjusted his flat brown gaze. His left ear was pierced and he had a small ring in it that looked like something from a hardware store keychain.

"Do you know a girl called Nell? She told me she lives around here."

The boy's silence struck Bonnie like a fist. Coldly uncaring eyes examined her. There was a message in those eyes, but she couldn't read it.

"Nell has pale blond hair. She's about fifteen, sixteen—very thin."

The kid's eyebrows curved high as though it were he, not Bonnie, asking the question. She recognized guile and she realized he wasn't going to answer without an inducement. She opened her purse, angling it like a book she didn't want anyone else to read over her shoulder. With a shock, she saw she'd given her last five to the cab driver and had nothing smaller than a twenty.

"Or maybe you know a young man called Lomax?" She held out the twenty. "Tod Lomax?"

The kid took the money without looking at it. He spat and a dust blister rose up on the asphalt. *"No hablo inglés."*

Bonnie changed linguistic gear. *"Yo hablo español un poquito. ¿Dónde están—"*

He tossed a sharp nod over his shoulder, toward the warehouse. "Try in there."

Bonnie's gaze went to the three-story barnlike structure. The wood siding had rotted and weathered to the dead colors of driftwood. Behind it the sun was setting on the New Jersey skyline, bloated and red like an abscessed eye.

She crossed the tarmac, steps slowing.

A door had been boarded up and the boards had been ripped down and thrown on the pavement, six-inch nails jutting. A freshly painted red-on-white NO ENTRY sign dangled like a shop's advertisement. She took a deep breath and stepped beneath the sign. She stood blinking till her eyes adjusted. Right away, her skin told her that she had entered a different universe. A smell hit her with gradual but sickening force, like a simmering mix of garlic and dog excrement.

The last sunlight of the day fell through torn planking and shattered windows, dappling the stagnant, dusty gray air. Half-dressed children had staked out grave-sized plots across the entire warehouse floor. The sound of voices and rap tapes and barking dogs rose and fell in waves.

She felt she needed a mask, not just for the smell, but to fend off the eyes—dozens of eyes, hundreds of eyes like tiny electric insects glowing in a swamp.

She spoke to the nearest child. "Excuse me. Do you know a girl called Nell, a thin blond girl?" She tried to smile, but when she saw that one leg was a kneeless stump she had no smile in her. "Or a boy called Tod Lomax?"

He shook his head. It could have meant *I don't know.* It could have meant *leave me alone.*

She picked her way through bedrolls and furniture rescued from the street, through swollen, ripped-open garbage bags that served as territory markers. It was like losing her way on a checkerboard that never repeated.

"Do you know a girl called Nell? A boy called Tod?"

Poster-size portraits of Fidel Castro, Malcolm X, Jesus, Ice-T,

Elvis, watched her from crumbling walls, unseparated by time or logic or ideology.

"Excuse me. Do you know Nell? Or Tod?"

FOURTEEN

"**W**ould you care for something to drink?" Lawrence Hitchcock's hands were poised over the Johnnie Walker bottle.

"If you have some kind of soda or diet drink," Cardozo said.

The light died from Hitchcock's smile. "Nothing stronger?"

He wants company, Cardozo realized. "Just soda, thanks."

Hitchcock went to work with highball glasses and ice cubes. With his high cheekbones and his hair receding into a severe widow's peak, his dark eyes seemed too large, like a panda's. "Annabelle, you'll have something."

Mrs. Hitchcock answered almost absently from her chintz-covered sofa. "A weak one." She was a short, stout woman with neatly styled gray hair. Her pearls matched the gray.

Hitchcock handed them each a tall glass with the etched shield of Yale University. He settled into the easy chair facing Cardozo. "To your health, Lieutenant. And how's the war in our streets?"

Cardozo raised his glass. "On schedule."

"Who'd have thought New York would turn into this?" Hitchcock shook his head. "When the hell do we finally hit bottom?"

"Now, Larry." Annabelle Hitchcock's tone was brightly chiding. "I doubt the lieutenant came all this way to discuss urban blight."

Hitchcock turned as though to say, *Well then, what did you want to discuss?*

"It's about your daughter," Cardozo said.

A silence fell on the softly lit, paneled living room. In the hallway of Mr. and Mrs. Lawrence Hitchcock's East Seventy-ninth Street apartment, a grandfather clock struck seven-fifteen.

Cardozo realized he was quite possibly bearing the worst news a parent can hear. He chose neutral words, feeling his way. "I understand she broke her ankle a year and a half ago?"

Hitchcock sat swirling his drink, staring at whirlpools. "Louisa was playing in an amateur theatrical down at St. Andrew's Church. They had her doing Rockette-like high kicks. They put her left foot in a device that was supposed to improve her balance. But instead it broke her ankle."

"Do you want to see the X rays?" Mrs. Hitchcock said. "We've still got them."

There was something in her tone that didn't fit the situation, something almost dotty, as if she were volunteering her child's graduation photos.

"Are you sure it's no trouble?" Cardozo said.

"None at all." Mrs. Hitchcock crossed to an inlaid cherry-wood secretary and opened one of the lower drawers. She brought Cardozo an enormous manila envelope stamped LENOX HILL HOSPITAL X-RAY DEPT.

Cardozo slid one of the X rays out. He held it up to the lamp on the table beside him. An astonishingly clean fracture showed.

"Could I borrow these? I'd like to compare them with . . ."

He broke off. Both Hitchcocks were staring at him.

"A body has been found. A young woman with the same type of fracture."

Mrs. Hitchcock's hand trembled as she set her glass down. Scotch slopped over onto a New York Yacht Club coaster.

In the hallway, a door slammed. A teenage girl came bouncing into the living room.

"Hello, all." She had a wild shock of red hair and she went straight to the bar.

"Our daughter, Louisa," Mrs. Hitchcock explained. "Home from Bennington for a few days."

"Who's that talking about me behind my back?" Louisa Hitchcock turned, holding a generous tumbler of what looked like a vodka tonic.

"Lieutenant Cardozo would like to borrow your X rays," Annabelle Hitchcock said. "Someone else has the same fracture."

"Really?" Louisa said. "Anyone I know?"

"A dead girl," Hitchcock said.

Cardozo reached inside his jacket and brought out the drawing of Ms. Basket Case.

Louisa Hitchcock took the drawing. She set down her drink and raised one hand and rubbed the back of her neck. It was as though she wanted to stretch her moment of being the center of attention. "You know who she reminds me of *exactly*? Betsy Frothingham. Except Betsy's alive."

"I'll say," Hitchcock said.

Louisa Hitchcock handed the drawing to her father.

Hitchcock sat frowning at it as though he were trying to work something out in his mind. "Never saw her. Annabelle?"

Mrs. Hitchcock drew in a breath, shaking her head. She handed the drawing back to Cardozo.

"Seems we're not much help," Hitchcock said. "Sorry."

"I've had a chance to compare those fractures." The voice on the phone was Dan Hippolito from the M.E.'s office. "There are similarities—Louisa Hitchcock had the same kind of spiral fracture as Ms. Basket Case—but it's nothing you could base a case on."

"Have you seen many of those spiral fractures?" Cardozo said.

"Professionally? Not too many in New York City. You usually see them in ski resorts."

"Why ski resorts?"

"The foot's restrained in the ski, and when the skier falls the ankle twists in a characteristic way."

"You think Basket Case was a skier?"

"I'll leave the educated guesses up to you."

A notion had been nagging at Cardozo, and now seemed to be the time to bring it up. "While we're on the subject of educated guesses . . . I've been wondering about that matzo residue in her mouth. . . ."

"What about it?"

"Any chance it might be communion wafer?"

Dan's voice hesitated. "You mean logically or chemically?"

"Either. Both."

"Logically, it's a stretch. Communion is usually wafer plus wine, and you take the wine after the wafer—chances are it would wash the wafer down and you wouldn't have so large a quantity of residue in your mouth. In fact, you might not have any."

Cardozo kept flipping the scenario through his mind. "And chemically?"

"There you're on more solid ground. In terms of the chemical breakdown, I don't see why the residue couldn't be communion wafer. But I wouldn't go out on a limb and say it was." The tone implied, *and I wouldn't recommend you go out on that limb either.*

"Thanks, Dan. That's what I wanted to know." Cardozo hung up the phone and pondered.

"Six detectives." Ellie Siegel was standing in the doorway of the cubicle. "For two days, six detectives have been scouring the runaway zones of the city with Nico's portrait." She was wearing a cotton blouse the color of pink dogwood blossoms. "So far nobody recognizes the girl. I guess memories tend to be short in runaway circles."

"Like the lives," Cardozo said.

"O'Reilly wants to cut us back to four detectives."

"Four's not enough."

"Talk to O'Reilly."

Cardozo turned a full circle in his swivel chair. "You talk to him."

"I have."

"Just once couldn't you have good news for me?"

"I was reading over yesterday's interviews with the doormen." She flexed an eyebrow. "You might want to look at this one."

She handed him the folder. He looked.

Juan Rodriguez, a midnight-to-eight doorman at 1012 Fifth Avenue, reported that twice in the last year, toward dawn, he had seen a man walking in the bushes at the edge of the garden. On both occasions the man had been carrying a cone-shaped newspaper-wrapped package.

As Cardozo read, a ripple of static electricity passed through the hairs on the back of his neck. His eyes flicked up. "Where's this doorman now?"

"Working the day shift. He's waiting for you."

*   *   *

On marble tables in the lobby of 1012 Fifth Avenue, candle-shaped lights glowed in designer hurricane glass.

"Can you describe him?" Cardozo was saying. "Age, height, build?"

"Medium." Beneath his green with gold brocade doorman's jacket, Juan Rodriguez shrugged heavy shoulders. "Everything was medium."

"Color hair?"

"Couldn't tell. The sun wasn't up. It was still dark."

"Any distinguishing marks?"

"Give me a break." Juan Rodriguez grinned. "He was on the other side of Fifth Avenue."

"But you saw what he had in his hand."

"That much I could see. Something wrapped in paper."

A woman stepped out of one of the elevators and stopped at the mirrored wall to check her lipstick. Cardozo had the impression of a blond, bored madonna wearing too much jewelry to be traveling the streets of New York without an armed guard.

"Juan," she said, "Tiffany's is sending a man to pick up a return. The maid has it."

Rodriguez held the door. "I'll see to it, Mrs. Oliphant."

Cardozo waited for the door to swing shut on Mrs. Oliphant and her shark-gray limousine. "You told the detective the man in the garden was carrying something wrapped in newspaper."

Rodriguez nodded. "It could have been newspaper."

"How could you tell?"

"It had a look. Pictures. Headlines. But at a distance I'm not going to swear."

"Could you see what was inside the paper?"

"Could have been a bottle."

"Did you actually see a bottle?"

A hesitant tilt came into Rodriguez's blue-shadowed jaw. "Just the shape. Like a cone. Like a . . . *bottle.*"

"Bottles aren't often cone-shaped."

"I'm not saying it couldn't have been something else."

"Did you see how this man was dressed? Jacket, overcoat?"

There was a flow of silence that Rodriguez finally broke with a tight shake of the head. "No overcoat. The first time I saw him was in spring and the second time was autumn."

"Shirtsleeves?"

"A shirt sounds right."

"And did you notice anything at all about this shirt?"

Sometimes, closing your eyes is another way of seeing. Rodriguez closed his eyes. "Come to think of it, there was one thing." He hesitated. "It looked like it could have had a kind of"—his thumb went up and made a pantomime of slicing his throat—"a priest's collar."

For an instant Cardozo could not feel his own heart beating. "A priest's collar."

"I'm not sure. This was a lot of months ago."

"Could it have been one of these men?" Cardozo handed Rodriguez the blown-up photos of Father Montgomery and Father Romero.

The doorman's dark eyes flicked from one to the other. "I couldn't say. Except I think I saw the same guy the day the garden opened."

"Which guy? The man with the newspaper or one of the men in those photos? Or were they the same?"

"I'm not sure." There was almost a persecuted note in Rodriguez's voice now. "I think he was with the first group that went in."

"So the man with the newspaper could have been one of these priests and he was at the opening ceremony."

"He could have been."

"Which one of these priests?"

"I'm not sure." Rodriguez's hands gestured helplessly. "There were a lot of celebrities. He was a nobody. Everyone was wearing raincoats. And he was wearing a cap."

"What kind of a cap?"

"Funny kind of cap."

"Funny how?"

"Floppy. Like a collapsed chef's hat."

"White? Cotton?"

"No. Brown tweed. Snap-brim. With too much overhang."

"A golf cap."

"Right. Like you see in old black-and-white movies."

FIFTEEN

The day was sunny and the air was bright. Cardozo crossed Fifth Avenue. The little stage in the Vanderbilt Garden had been taken away. The crime-scene team had completed their work, and the grounds were open to the public again.

He watched mothers pushing baby carriages, children playing, lovers holding hands. He watched solitary souls strolling or reading a paper or just sitting on a bench. The garden was like a beautiful daydream, a spot of perfection in a fallen city.

He walked to the lilac bushes on the south boundary and stepped through them into the woods. The three-foot hole where the body had been found had been repacked with earth, but it was not hard to spot.

He stood beside the dogwood tree. His gaze circled the grave, searching east-to-west, north-to-south, gradually spiraling out. There was fresh trash: a tossed-away diet Pepsi can that had not been there three days ago, a dried orange rind crawling with ants, a sheet of yesterday's *Times*.

As his eyes scanned, his thoughts took on a melancholy rhythm of their own.

He had known from the start that he was going to have a personal problem with the case. That he would be tempted to think with his memory, to see with his memory. Because, for all he knew, the runaway teenage girl in his own past had ended up just like the girl in the basket.

Sally Manfredo—if she was still alive—was the daughter of his widowed sister. Dark hair, dark serious eyes. He hadn't seen her since the night his sister had asked him to have a talk with the girl. He'd taken her out for a dinner of steak and silence.

"Sally, how are you getting along at home?"

"Okay."

He didn't believe her. All evening long he'd sensed some un-mentioned disquiet eating at her. "School?"

"Okay."

"Anything you'd like to talk about?" He reached across the tablecloth and touched her hand. "It doesn't have to get back to your mother."

"Uncle Vince, you're a cop."

"I'm not a cop now. I'm your uncle. Are you in any kind of trouble?"

He could see she was nervous, preoccupied. Her sixteen-year-old lips tightened.

"What's bothering you? Friends? Boys?"

She just sat there, silent. He noticed she was wearing makeup. Lipstick and a little eyeshadow. Otherwise her face was all her own, with that troubling perfection of youth.

"Is it drugs?"

"I'm not breaking any laws." She smiled. That was the first smile of the evening. "Wish I were."

"You know your mother's very worried."

"Of course I know. She's always worried. I wish she'd get off my case." Sally sat there poking a spoon at a frozen yogurt par-fait.

Cardozo had the same feeling he sometimes got questioning a suspect—she wanted to come clean about something, and if he just showed a little patience, she'd work up the courage to say it.

Minutes ticked by. The waiter refilled their coffee cups.

"You know what Mom does?"

Here it comes. "What does your mother do?"

"She searches my room."

In a way, Cardozo was surprised; in a way, he wasn't. "Know something? She used to search my room when we were kids. Our parents wouldn't let me read comic books till my grades were at least B-plus. So I hid my Batman comics. Your mom would search my room, find the comics, and turn them over to Mom and Dad." He sighed. "Who destroyed them."

"Uncle Vince, we've got to join forces and get her a second job. So she won't have time to worry about me. Do you know of any openings for a parole officer?"

"No." He grinned. "But there's a great opening in Binghamton for a prison matron."

Later, he very much regretted that joke. But at the time, he felt he was winning a little of Sally's trust. He even told her about the troubles he was having with his own daughter. He felt they were helping each other. It was almost eleven when he brought her home.

She kissed him good night on the lips. "Thanks, Uncle Vince. I'll never forget you."

The next day his sister Jill phoned, frantic. "What did you say to Sally?"

"Nothing—I just listened."

"What did she say?"

"Nothing."

"Then how come she's gone?"

"What do you mean, gone?"

"Her suitcase is gone."

Cardozo didn't trust his sister's view of other people's behavior. "Sally's testing. She'll be back."

But Sally didn't come home that night.

She didn't come home the next night.

After seventy-two hours she was officially a missing person. Cardozo got two detectives assigned to the case. Unheard of in New York City, where three kids disappeared every day and six were murdered.

In two weeks, the detectives turned up nothing to suggest kidnapping or foul play. They both reached the same conclusion. "That mother. That mouth. That temper."

"Jill's under a lot of strain," Cardozo said. But he knew what they were saying and he had a heartsick feeling they were right.

"The woman fights too much. Fur flies even where there's no cat."

Cardozo couldn't think of an excuse for his sister.

"A kid couldn't vanish like this unless she wanted to."

"Or unless she was murdered," Cardozo said.

"If she was murdered, something will turn up."

Since there was no justification for further police involvement, the detectives were transferred to more urgent cases. Cardozo reviewed their reports. They'd done solid, by-the-book jobs: they'd interviewed family, friends, neighbors, teachers. They'd canvassed bus terminals, car rentals, railways, airports. They'd checked charge cards and phone records.

There were only two remotely odd things that had turned up. One was a note tucked in Sally's high school yearbook. *Sally*, the writer had scrawled on letterhead of St. Andrew's Church, *you do that divinely—thank heaven for little girls with talent! Joe.*

The other oddity was a number on Jill's phone records that showed up three times the month before Sally vanished. It was the number of St. Andrew's Episcopal Church on the Upper East Side, and Jill didn't know anything about it.

Cardozo went up and asked the rector if Sally had been phoning him.

"Our resources are available to anyone in need." Father Joseph Montgomery wore a natty tweed jacket over his clerical shirtfront. He smoked a pipe and his eyes seemed to judge Cardozo. "Contrary to what some of us would like to believe, it's not only poor girls or black girls who get into trouble."

"Is that a yes or a no?"

"Did your niece ever mention this church or its activities to you or your sister?"

"No."

"Did it ever occur to either of you that possibly this young woman was in some kind of trouble?"

"Are you saying she discussed pregnancy with you? She's *sixteen*, for God's sake!"

"And possibly she was reaching out for help and you didn't hear her."

"And you did?" Cardozo showed the rector the note. "Is this your handwriting?"

Nothing in the rector's expression changed. "It resembles my handwriting."

"What does it mean? Sally does *what* divinely?"

"I couldn't say. I don't recall writing this."

"Did you send her someplace? Do you know where she is?"

"If you're asking whether or not I counseled your niece, I can't possibly comment. But it sounds to me as if you and the girl's mother might profit from a little honest reflecting."

Cardozo asked a friend in the D.A.'s office if the rector could be forced to open his records.

"Come on, Vince, he doesn't know anything. He's liberal, he's on record as anticop. He was being ambiguous on purpose—playing Solomon to get your goat."

"There's more to it. He wrote the note. He has that I-know-something-you-don't smugness."

"He has to be guilty of more than annoying you. You need proof of a crime and proof of his involvement."

But nothing turned up. Not that year. Not the next.

Jill went from frantic to subdued. She told Cardozo she was paying private detectives five hundred dollars a week to track her daughter down.

Cardozo told her not to.

She began crying. "I feel helpless. Things are happening to my child and I don't even know about them. I'm not even seeing her grow up—I won't have memories. I won't even have sound bites."

She began putting on weight. Drinking too much. Phoning in the middle of the night, drunk. "Vince, where is she?"

"I don't know."

"Is she alive?"

"I don't know."

"You're a cop—you must know."

"I don't."

Silence. Tinkling ice. "I think she's alive."

"I hope so. Get some sleep, Jill."

During the next two years she started hanging up a lot more photographs of Sally around the living room. Rotating the collection.

One evening, during one of their monthly unbearable dinners, she told him she was in touch with an L.A. psychic, a specialist in runaway kids.

Cardozo's heart collapsed painfully inward. "How much have you paid him?"

"Thirty thousand dollars."

Cardozo flew out to L.A. The guy was clearly a crook. Cardozo threatened prosecution. The psychic gave twenty-five thousand back.

When Cardozo put the money on the kitchen table, his sister withered.

"That man's reports were all I had to keep me going."

"They were lies. He's sending the same reports to eighty parents."

She raised her eyes. They were moist. "Frankly, Vince, I would rather have had the hope."

He would never forget that look on his sister's face. Hurting. Accusing. As if he'd driven a spike through her.

He tried to turn off the memory tapes. *That was six years ago. This is now. That was Sally. This is . . . someone else.*

He had been hunting through dead leaves for almost two hours when a butterfly caught his eye. He watched it gliding through a slanting cylinder of sunlight and then up across the shade to the branches of the dogwood.

It lit on a leaf and Cardozo saw that there was something oddly dimpled about that leaf and its neighbor. He moved the leaves aside.

A piece of thin red string had caught in one of the twigs. A cluster of dried stems dangled from one of its loops.

He counted. There were a dozen stems. Exactly.

A second bouquet. One could have been coincidence, but not two. Someone had tied flowers with string and wrapped them in newspaper and brought them here. Twice. Someone had known this place was the dead girl's grave.

And that someone had worn a priest's collar.

SIXTEEN

"Who were the first people to go into the garden?" Cardozo said.

"On opening day?" Father Montgomery was thoughtful. "The very first were the committee."

They were seated in Father Montgomery's study. Slanting sunlight sieved through the leaded panes of the window.

"And who's on that committee?"

"Myself—my assistant, Bonnie Ruskay, whom you've met—Tina Vanderbilt—Father Chuck Romero—Rabbi Green—Iman Zafr Mohadi."

"Were some of you wearing raincoats?"

"The day started out looking like rain—I imagine we all were."

"What about golf caps?"

"A golf cap in the rain?" Father Montgomery seemed sincerely bewildered.

"Do you own a golf cap?"

Father Montgomery rose and crossed to the closet and swung the door open. He took a tweed cap from one of the pegs and slapped it on his head and struck a golfing pose. "Voilà. It was a Christmas gift from Bonnie three years ago."

There was a knock and a brown-haired man in a summer-weight business suit stepped briskly into the room. "Good to see you, Lieutenant. Dave Lowndes." He extended a hand. "Counsel for St. Andrew's. We've met."

"I remember," Cardozo said.

"You've obviously become very fond of Father Joe's company." Lowndes's tone was chummy and joking. "Either that or you suspect him of something absolutely unspeakable."

"All kidding aside," Father Montgomery said, "Dave happened to be here on another matter. I asked him to sit in while you give me the third degree. Do you mind?"

Father Montgomery obviously knew his rights and Cardozo realized there was nothing to be done about it except play the scene his way—three civilized guys killing ten civilized minutes.

"Not at all."

Lowndes settled himself on the sofa. He pulled up his trouser knees just a little. He smiled. "And what is this little matter that couldn't wait?"

"Several small matters." Cardozo opened a St. Andrew's outreach newsletter and laid it on the desk top. "Did you ever drive the van in that picture?"

"It's our old van," Father Montgomery said. "I drove it now and then."

"Could I see?" David Lowndes said.

Father Montgomery handed him the newsletter.

"Did you ever drive that van in Central Park?" Cardozo said.

"Not that I recall."

"Do you know of anyone ever driving it in Central Park?"

"Not offhand."

"Tell me, Lieutenant," Lowndes said. "I take it this van figures in your investigation of the dead girl in the garden?"

"Possibly," Cardozo said.

"I frankly fail to see a connection."

"Just making sure." Cardozo reached into his jacket and handed Father Montgomery three photos of Jonquil. "Do you know this person?"

The rector stared blankly. "Should I?"

"Those prints were taken from the negatives you gave me."

"Just a moment." Lowndes's lean, angular body uncoiled from the sofa. He stood up and pulled himself to his full height. "Lieutenant Cardozo took negatives from you?"

"I gave him the negatives." Father Montgomery picked up one of the shots and tipped a critical eye at it. "I must have photographed her if she was on the roll. But it's hard to say if I know her."

"May I?" Lowndes reached for the other two photos.

"Apparently she's a transvestite prostitute," Cardozo said. "She works down in the meat-packing area."

"We've certainly done outreach in that part of town," Father Montgomery said. "But I meet so many people in my work—socialites, whores, politicians. My memory sometimes runneth over."

"And teenagers," Cardozo said.

"I beg your pardon?"

"You must meet teenagers in your work."

Father Montgomery nodded. "Oh, yes. Plenty of those too."

"There was an accident a year and a half ago—a teenager in your care broke her ankle?"

"In my care? Good God, any parent who'd entrust their offspring to me should be charged with criminal neglect."

"The parents sued."

"Sounds like the Hitchcocks," Lowndes said.

"Ah, yes—sing out, little Louisa." Father Montgomery nodded. "The poor kid had her heart set on being the next Julie Andrews. She slipped during rehearsal and strained an ankle, sprained it, something."

"Fractured it," Cardozo said.

"Beg your pardon?"

"She broke her ankle—a complete fracture."

Father Montgomery raised his fingers twelve inches in front of his face. Gold cuff links sparkled. Perfectly groomed fingertips danced. "I recall. Her mother brought charges—you'd have thought I had personally taken a sledgehammer to Pavlova's foot."

"Bear one thing in mind," Lowndes said. "The judge threw the case out of court."

"What caused the accident?"

"A device called a high-kicker. It moors the ankle. It's absolutely safe, all theatrical dancing schools use them." Father Montgomery added, a little sadly, "Of course, we don't use it anymore."

"I advised the church to play it very safe and conservative," Lowndes said. "Accidents do happen."

"Was this high-kicker involved in any other broken ankles?"

Father Montgomery drew back slightly in his chair, as though he needed more distance to see Cardozo clearly. "You mean at St. Andrew's?"

"It was never established that the high-kicker caused the accident," David Lowndes said. "As I understand the problem, the Hitchcock girl had only minimal talent and she couldn't keep up with the tempo. Incidentally, she was rehearsing alone with the musical director when she fell—it had nothing to do with Father Montgomery."

"That isn't quite what I was asking," Cardozo said. "Were other dancers in any of St. Andrew's' shows ever injured?"

Father Montgomery glanced at Lowndes.

"Father Joe can only answer from the best of his recollection. Unless you want to depose him and have him consult his records."

"The best of Father Montgomery's recollection will be fine."

Fine for now, Cardozo thought.

"There weren't any other injured dancers," Father Montgomery hesitated. "Not that I recall."

"And what's the name of your musical director?"

"Let's see . . . the director on that show was Wheelwright Vanderbrook—Baxter Vanderbrook's boy." Father Montgomery reached for the phone. "Bonnie, could you be a dear and dredge up the Vanderbrooks' phone number for the lieutenant?" He replaced the receiver. "Bonnie's a joy. I'd be lost without her."

A moment later Reverend Bonnie Ruskay, crisp and glowing in a slender-waisted dress, knocked on the door. "We don't have that phone number. The Vanderbrooks aren't with the church anymore."

Cardozo made a notation in his notebook. "One last request. Do you still keep your talent file in that drawer?" He nodded toward the desk. "The photos and biographies of your performers?"

"Updated yearly," Father Joe said. "Couldn't put on a show without it."

"Do you suppose I could borrow it for two or three days?"

Father Montgomery shot a look toward his lawyer.

David Lowndes sighed. "Could I trouble you to produce a warrant for the file? I know it means a delay, but it might be a good idea if we observed the legal niceties from this point on."

"It's no trouble." Cardozo smiled. "And it's no delay." He took the executed warrant from his pocket and handed it across the room.

Lowndes was clearly startled and just as clearly trying to show no reaction at all. His pale blue eyes examined the warrant. After a moment he nodded.

Father Montgomery opened the drawer, brought out the file, and placed it on the desk top. "Will that be all, Lieutenant?"

"Can't think of another thing." Cardozo tucked the shoe box under his left arm.

"Bonnie, be a dear and show the lieutenant out?"

Reverend Bonnie Ruskay led Cardozo into the hallway. The door closed softly behind them.

"David Lowndes told me I should be scolded," she said.

"What for?"

"For giving you the run of the rectory the other day. Apparently I should have known better."

"You're in the business of trusting people. He's in the business of not trusting them."

"And you're in the business of locking them up?"

"That's the court's business, not mine."

"That shoe box looks fragile. Do you want a shopping bag?"

"Thanks. A bag would help."

She took him through the kitchen into the garage. The air still smelled faintly of ammonia. There was a pile of empty bags on the backseat of the green sedan. "Hammacher Schlemmer or Zabar's?"

"Whatever."

She handed him a plastic shopping bag from Nobody beats the WIZ. "Are you looking for evidence against us? Because you won't find any. We're human beings, but we're not evil."

"I'm trying to find out why some kids grow up and some vanish." He slid the file into the bag. "Why some wind up adults and some wind up skeletons in a box."

There was a sad look in her eyes. "A lot of disturbing and ultimately unfathomable events happen in this life."

"Sorry. That's not good enough."

"What is it you want, Lieutenant?"

"I wouldn't mind getting out of here." He went to the garage door. "May I?"

She shrugged.

He bent down and gave the handle a twist and a yank. The door rolled noisily upward. He stepped into the courtyard. It was a walled space of cobblestones and ivy and flower beds. An orange fish was gliding in a dark green rock pool and a bird was singing in the branches of a pear tree.

He crossed to the rosebushes. Tight green embryos clung to thorny stalks. He reached out a hand and quickly snapped off a stalk of unborn roses. He dropped it into the shopping bag.

In his cubicle, Cardozo sat staring at the shoe box for five minutes before he lifted the lid.

The photographs had been arranged alphabetically—smiling

young people with a name, address, phone number, and brief bio paper-clipped to the back of each picture.

Every one of them somebody's kid.

He braced for the worst and walked his finger through to the *M*'s.

She was there—the very first *M*—Sally Manfredo.

He tugged the photo out and looked at her. It was like returning to the embrace of a familiar old song. Memories broke through the surface—that last dinner, coffee growing cold in two cups, the sixteen-year-old face across the table from him, the air faintly touched with the scent of her mother's jasmine perfume.

She was wearing makeup in the photo, the same makeup she'd worn that night. There was a kind of raw determination in her eyes, something unstated and dark.

Sally, he thought, *where did you go? Why did you go? Did you even mean to go?*

He turned the photo over and studied the typed sheet. The address and phone were her mother's. There was nothing more recent.

The bio stated: *The Boy Friend*—chorus. *Zip Your Pinafore*—Emily. Excellent comic timing. *The Pajama Game*—replaced. No contact since.

A handwritten notation followed: *present address unknown.*

There was a soft rap at the door. He looked up and saw Ellie standing there with a sort of unintentional grace.

"They say good news comes in small boxes."

He shook his head. "Not this box. We've got sixty kids to interview."

SEVENTEEN

Father Chuck Romero held the drawing of the girl's face at arm's length. He sat staring and frowning. "No, I can't say she's familiar. Not offhand. How long ago would this have been?"

"A year and a half," Cardozo said, "maybe two years."

"No." Father Romero shook his head. He had graying dark hair, beginning to thin at the top. His face was deeply lined and it seemed twenty years older than the hair. "I'm sorry."

"Maybe you recognize this young girl?" Cardozo handed Father Romero a photo of his niece.

The priest's eyes betrayed an instant's confusion, quickly covered over. "She's lovely. But I can't say I recognize her either."

"Her name's Sally Manfredo. She wanted to be an actress."

"So many do."

They were sitting in armchairs in St. Veronica's rectory in Queens. Bookshelves lined the walls. Leather-bound sets of Aquinas and Thackeray and Dickens had been pushed back to make room for Victorian pillboxes and small silver-framed photographs of young people.

"She did some amateur work," Cardozo said. "She played in two of Father Montgomery's shows six, seven years ago."

"That's it."

"That's what?"

"That's why she looks familiar."

"Then you *have* seen her before."

Cardozo could feel Father Romero give an infinitesimal recoil. "It must have been in one of Joe's shows."

"Is it possible she worked in one of yours?"

"No, that's not possible." Father Romero didn't look away, but at the same time he was definitely not looking back. "I'd remember."

"You must work with an awful lot of young people. Maybe she's in your files and you forgot."

"I don't keep records. Not of the theatricals."

"Really." Cardozo tried to gauge the nervousness that radiated from Father Romero. The hands trembled. The eyes blinked with the rapidity of a hummingbird batting its wings. There was a surprised, pained expression, as though everything in the universe was new to him and not necessarily friendly. Cardozo sensed something more was involved than mere state of mind. Some chemical agent.

"But I do have a memory for names and faces, and the name

Sally Manfredo isn't familiar." Father Romero handed back the photo. "I'm sorry. I wish I could help."

"What do you do for relaxation?"

"Relaxation?" Father Romero seemed startled. "Very little, actually. I pray . . . I meditate."

"No exercise?"

Father Romero patted his oversize tummy. "Not as much as my doctor would like, I'm afraid."

"Don't you play golf?"

Father Romero glanced over with a noncomprehending frown. "What gave you that idea?"

"Father Joe mentioned you were golf partners."

"Long ago."

"But you two still socialize."

"We see one another at ceremonial occasions—like the openings of one another's shows."

"And the Vanderbilt Garden ceremony?"

"Yes, that too."

"You were with the group that went in first."

"That's right. The four representatives of New York's major faiths. Joe seems to think Islam is a major faith locally. I believe there are fewer followers of the Prophet in the metropolitan area than practitioners of Santeria."

"Do you recall when this photograph was taken?" Cardozo handed Father Romero the shot of Sonya Barnett and the four clerics.

"I don't recall." Father Romero's face was perplexed.

"The odd thing is that you're all looking away from the stage at the same moment."

"There was a crew from TV right behind us. They may have asked us to turn around. Does it matter?"

"It just struck me as curious." Cardozo took back the photo. "Did you drive to the ceremony that day?"

"Driving's a nuisance in Manhattan. I prefer the subway."

"But you do drive?"

"I have a license."

"And a car?"

"I don't have a car, but the church has a van."

"I'd like to see it."

"Certainly." Father Romero led Cardozo across the lawn to the unattached two-car garage. He swung the door open and Cardozo realized he was a powerfully built little man.

It took Cardozo's eyes a moment to adjust to the dimness. Half the interior space served as a storehouse for dusty stacks of old furniture and cardboard cartons.

Father Romero thumped the front fender of the van. "She's a pretty beat-up old thing, I'm afraid."

Black paint was flaking off, and patches of blue peeked through. "This van is secondhand."

"Yes, indeed." Father Romero gave a laugh. "As a matter of fact, it was a gift from Father Joe."

"You've repainted it."

"We had to."

Cardozo studied the driver's door. Something had left an almost circular ridge under the paint. "Some kind of design was painted here?"

"A smiling sun."

"Why did you paint over it?"

"No particular reason." Father Romero stood shifting his weight. "The van needed repainting and it was too much trouble to restore the sun."

"Your name and badge number showed up in the report." Cardozo laid the flimsy copy of the three-month-old summons on the Formica-topped table.

Zondralee James glanced at the offenses: *driving through traffic signal, driving without corrective glasses, driving with expired insurance.*

"I made the report, all right." She bit off a mouthful of English muffin. "But I write two dozen of these a day."

"Was this the driver?" Cardozo placed the photo of Father Montgomery beside Officer James's coffee cup. "He may not have been wearing the clerical collar."

Officer James sat chewing. The diner was crowded. There was a lot of bustle around their table, but she didn't let it distract her. After a thoughtful moment she shook her head. "Sorry. I see a lot of faces in a workday."

Cardozo folded the St. Andrew's outreach newsletter open to page four and laid it on the table.

Zondralee James's eyes flicked from the shot of the van to the shot of Father Montgomery. They were golden eyes set deep in a narrow, fine-featured African face. "Okay, it's coming back. That rising-sun on the door. And there was some kind of writing. It doesn't show in this shot. 'God is love,' something like that."

"How did the accident happen?"

"It wasn't even a yellow light, it was *red*. This idiot drove right through—collapsed his hood into the side of a movers' truck."

Cardozo frowned. "I thought the truck hit him."

"Believe me, he hit the truck. Hard."

"Was there anything left of the van? Anything to salvage?"

She gave Cardozo a smile that said, you probably believe in the miracle of trickle-down economics too. "That van was beyond destroyed. Lucky he didn't kill himself."

She signaled the waitress for another cup of coffee.

"The license said he couldn't drive without glasses. So, of course, he was driving without them. He has time to put on his floppy tweed cap, but he can't take the time to find his glasses. I meet people like him every day. Think they're special—laws don't apply. They'd rather run down a pedestrian than admit they're blind."

The word hung in the space between them.

"Blind?"

She nodded. "I asked him, read the street sign over there. Broad daylight. He couldn't. He should be grounded, and I mean for good."

"According to the records, he's still driving."

"Then he must have friends at the department of motor vehicles. And they don't care if a killer's loose on Madison Avenue."

Cardozo fixed himself a cup of hot dregs from the squad room coffeemaker, closed the door of his cubicle, and put his feet up on his desk. He opened his notebook to a page headed *Wheelwright Vanderbrook* with the subheading *roses*. The facing page was headed *Father Romero* with the subheading *van*.

He lifted the phone and tapped in the number of St. Andrew's rectory. Bonnie Ruskay answered.

"Hi, it's Vince Cardozo. Sorry to keep bothering you."

"It's no bother." She said it so pleasantly that he almost believed her.

"Would you know if Father Montgomery gave a van to Father Romero at St. Veronica's?"

"Yes, he did."

"Why?"

After a long, considering pause, she finally spoke. "A parishioner gave us a new van, so we didn't need the old one anymore. Father Chuck needed a van."

"And was the new van the one that Father Joe totaled?"

"The driver of the other car totaled it. Father Joe wasn't at fault."

"All right, so we're talking about two vans."

"*You're* talking about two vans."

"How many vans has St. Andrew's owned?"

"I know of at least three since I've been here."

"That's counting the van you've got in the garage right now."

"That's right."

"How many of these vans had the beaming sun painted on them?"

"They're all supposed to—and when we get around to it, the new one will too."

Cardozo placed a check mark in his notebook beside the word *van*. "Thanks for your help, Reverend."

The moment he touched the receiver to the cradle the phone rang again.

"The roses in the two bouquets are the same." It was Lou Stein at the lab. "Americana Linda Porter."

Cardozo made a check mark beside *roses*. "What about the rose in that woman's hair in the photo?"

"Also Americana Linda Porter."

"And the stalk I gave you yesterday?"

"Also Americana Linda Porter."

"Can you tell if they come from the same bush?"

"I can if you want to pay twenty-four hundred dollars for a DNA analysis."

"How much for an educated guess?"

"Cheapskate. You'll owe me a beer. Ultimately, all Linda Porters are descended from the same bush—a hybrid developed by the American Rose Association in the early sixties. Cole Porter bought the patent and named it for his late wife."

"That bush must have had quite a few descendants by now."

"A lot fewer than you'd think. It never caught on with the commercial growers."

"Then the roses from the grave probably didn't come from a florist."

"No way. Florists don't handle them. Linda Porters don't freeze and they don't ship."

"Then they had to be grown locally."

"Very locally."

Cardozo thanked Lou and sat tapping his pen against the name *Vanderbrook*. He opened the bottom drawer of his desk and hauled out the telephone directory. A dozen pages had been ripped out, apparently at random, but not the page running from *Valjean* to *Vanderkolet*. He found a Wheelwright Vanderbrook listed, phone number but no address.

He tried the number and let it ring ten times.

He laid the receiver back in the cradle.

Just above Wheelwright Vanderbrook, a Baxter M. Vanderbrook was listed on Park Avenue. He dialed Baxter's number.

After three rings a man answered. "Hello?"

"I wonder if you could help me. I'm trying to get in touch with Wheelwright Vanderbrook."

"With reference to what?" The voice was cultivated and almost irritatingly nasal.

"He directed the music for a show at St. Andrew's Church a year and a half ago. I need some information on an accident involving one of the dancers."

"Is this some kind of joke?"

"Absolutely not. My name is Vincent Cardozo, I'm—"

The voice cut him short. "I find it absolutely appalling that you would phone me about a matter like this."

The connection broke, and a dial tone hummed in Cardozo's ear.

In her study, Bonnie Ruskay began to pace. Evening was a rose glaze coming over the wall of books. When she looked toward the window, shafts of violet light blinded her. When she closed her eyes she could see the police lieutenant's deep eyes and his knowing, worn-down frown.

Something about his question nagged at her. It was as though the question itself was whispering a message: *I know—I saw—I'm on to you.*

She lifted the telephone receiver. Her fingers were trembling. The first time she punched in the numbers she must have hit a wrong button. A voice answered that she didn't recognize.

"I'm sorry."

She broke the connection and dialed again, carefully this time. She braced herself for the machine but instead got a live human voice. "Hello?"

"Collie—you're home."

"Hello, Bonnie. You sound funny. Something the matter?"

"I hope not. Are you busy this evening?"

"Not especially." She could hear the thoughtful little frown in Collie's tone of voice.

"Could you meet me?" she said.

"All right."

"And Collie—don't use the van this time. I'll explain when I see you."

EIGHTEEN

High above the warehouse, a half moon glowed in a cradle of cirrus. On the dock, areas of darkness ribbed the spaces of pale light. Shadows danced across the boundaries.

Seated in the rear of the taxicab, Bonnie and Collie watched the shadows, the same dancing shapes she had watched for two nights. And the shadows watched back.

"Have you used the van lately?" she asked.

His eyebrows bunched together and his dark eyes focused nervous pinpricks of light on her. "You know I have."

"Besides the children. Have you used it for anything else in the last three months?"

"I don't recall." His voice was troubled. "I shouldn't think so."

From time to time headlights hunted through the darkness on the far side of the windshield. So far Bonnie had counted three police cars, one ambulance, five limousines.

"Try to remember," she urged, but gently, so as not to panic him.

"Why?" He turned, and she could feel fear radiating from him.

"The police have been asking." She kept her eyes fixed on the pier. The limousines worried her. Each time, the game was the same: the headlights searched the crowd for one special young girl or boy. When they caught sight of that person they dipped. That was the signal. The limo would stop and the young person would step over to the open door and accept a ride.

"What did the police ask?" he said. "Were they looking for me?"

"They asked who's been driving the van—where, why, when." She looked at him and sensed something choked off in his thin, almost emaciated body. "Maybe you used it running errands?"

He didn't answer immediately. "No. It's too much trouble getting it out of the garage. If I'd taken the van anywhere I'm pretty sure I'd remember. My memory's not that shot—not yet. I haven't used it. Except for the children."

"Then we're all right." Her hand closed around his. "But maybe you shouldn't use the van . . . not for a while."

They sat in stillness.

It was after midnight when a sixth limo peeled away from traffic and pulled up at the pier. The long black BMW dipped its headlights. A haggard figure in a tank top hurried smiling to the door.

"That's the girl." Bonnie sat forward on the seat and rapped the plastic partition. "Driver." The radio was playing and she had to raise her voice. "Do you see that BMW?"

"Yes, I do."

"Follow it."

"Can do." The cabdriver started his engine and flicked on his headlights.

* * *

In the narrow, dark lobby an old man in a caftan rocked in a squeaking rattan chair. "Yes, folks, how may I help you?" He had a high tenor voice and a smooth Jamaican accent.

"A man just brought a girl here," Bonnie said.

"Many, many men bring many, many girls to the Dionysius."

"This girl is underage."

The old man smiled. "We have no age requirement for our hotel guests."

"She's underage," Collie said, "and she's prostituting herself."

Eyes narrowed to slits. "And who the hell are you two—Father Bruce Ritter and Mother Teresa?"

The register lay open on the counter. Bonnie spun it around. A great many couples named Smith and Jones had registered.

The old man leapt up. "Get out of there."

Before he yanked the register away, she saw that the most recent Joneses had taken Room 202. She bounded up the stairs, and heard Collie clattering close behind her.

"You can't go up there," the desk clerk shouted. "You're trespassing. I'll call the police."

"And if you don't," Collie called over his shoulder, "we will."

The poorly lit corridor smelled of mildew and Lysol. Bonnie put her ear to the door of Room 202. Reggae pulsed through, capped with intermittent laughter.

She rapped.

The laughter stopped.

She rapped again.

"Who is it?" A man's voice, irritated.

"Is Nell there?"

The reggae stopped. There were whispers and skittering footsteps. "No Nell here. Go away."

"I have her stuff," Bonnie said.

Muffled voices conferred. "What stuff?"

"I'm not going to discuss it in the hallway."

The door opened a crack. An eye peeked out. The face was webbed with deep creases. Tightly curled white fuzz covered the head. The eye had to be seventy years old. It blinked, confused.

Collie gave the door a push. Wind chimes bonged.

The man stepped back, quickly closing his terry-cloth robe. "What the hell is this?" A fog of licorice mouthwash whooshed out of him. His gaze swung from Bonnie to Collie. Behind him, Nell sat bare-breasted on the edge of the bed.

"Who are these creeps?" he demanded, mustering righteousness. "Friends of yours?"

Nell leaned against the bedpost, pressing her cheek into the curve of the wood. She half smiled at Bonnie. "I know her." Something about Nell's voice seemed slow and heavily encumbered. "I never saw the guy before." She unhooked her tank top from the headboard and wriggled both arms into it.

"Hey," the man said. "We had a deal, kiddo. I gave you a hundred dollars."

"Did you?"

"You know I did. It's in your sneaker."

Nell just sat there, smoothing down her tank top, with her eyes on Bonnie.

The man picked up a Nike jogging shoe from the floor. He shook it, but nothing fell out. He shook the other shoe. "What did you do with my money? Don't think I'm letting you walk out of here." His eyes came back to Bonnie and Collie, appraising.

"Quit griping," Nell said. "You can afford it."

"I may have money—doesn't mean I have to stand still for this scam."

Bonnie opened her purse and gave him a hundred dollars.

"And the room's fifty," he said.

She gave him another fifty. "You were robbed."

Out on the sidewalk, Bonnie thanked Collie for the moral support and said good night. She climbed into a cab with Nell.

"It was you that got robbed," Nell said, "not the old geezer. He never gave me any money. He conned you and you went for it."

Bonnie looked at Nell. With the lights of Eighth Avenue jiggling past, the shadows under the girl's eyes were almost grooves.

"I guess that makes me pretty dumb," Bonnie said.

"So." The girl went hesitantly to Bonnie's bookshelves. She examined the leather bindings with their gold lettering in Hebrew. "I guess you've decided what to do with me."

"It's not my right to decide anything," Bonnie said.

"Does that mean no?" Nell seemed puzzled, thoughtful. Her

finger went slowly to the Greek bindings. "Then why've you been asking for me?"

"To talk with you."

"You've been watching me and following me so you could talk with me?" Nell looked over and quickly looked away. "That's a lot of trouble for a talk."

"It's a lot—but you've been on my mind."

"Now's your chance to get me off your mind." Nell's lip curled down petulantly. "Here I am. What do we talk about?"

"You."

"The history of me." Nell's face had a half-sneering look.

Bonnie realized the child was scared of people, uncomfortable with them unless she was putting on some kind of act. Tonight's act was the tough, shopworn angel.

"Would you like a Coke?"

"Coke's fine."

Bonnie brought two chilled cans from the little refrigerator and set them on the coffee table. She dropped into a chair and snapped one of the cans open. "Tell me about your home."

"What's to tell." Nell took the edge of the other easy chair. She had difficulty opening her Coke can, as if it had grown unexpected right angles. "I never had much of a home and I didn't like what I had."

"How long have you been pregnant?"

In the silence, Bonnie heard the labored sound of Nell's swallowing.

"The doctor says eighteen to nineteen weeks."

"That's pretty far advanced for an abortion."

"All right." The girl looked up suddenly. Her face was hard and didn't move. "I get the picture. Why don't you just hand me the pamphlets and I'll go somewhere else."

"I didn't bring you here to give you pamphlets. Or lectures. I happen to be pro-life, but that's not my agenda. I just wonder if you have any idea of the dangers of a late abortion."

"Look. I've been through this." Nell's eyes narrowed and her fists tightened. "I've wasted four weeks going through it. Tod said you were different. I don't know how you fooled him, but you don't fool me." Nell stood. "If all you're going to do is throw more pickled fetuses in my eyes, I'm leaving. Thanks for the Coke."

"Wait a minute. Please." Bonnie reached out a hand. "I'm not a zealot. We're talking about your choice."

"The hell it's my choice."

"It's up to you. You've got the power."

"No. It's up to you. You've got the money. And you use it to control people who don't." Nell was breathing heavily. Her face was flushed and she slapped at a drop of perspiration running down the side of her chin. "You don't know canary shit about me and I'm supposed to believe you care. What a friend I have in Jesus."

"I may not know you as well as I'd like to, but I want to help."

"You don't want to know me." Nell's eyebrows quivered upward. "Believe me. You don't."

"But I do, Nell. Can't you even listen?"

"I can hear. And you don't want to help. What you call helping is a picture you've got in your head. Reverend Bonnie's good deed. You see me, and bam—Nell's the one, Nell's going to be this week's good deed. The johns have a picture in their head and they see me, and bam—they make it come true this week too."

"I'm not trying to use you. I want you to have a choice and a chance."

"Set it to music and play it on a tambourine."

"I've been in touch with some people. Good, decent, warm-hearted people. I've told them about you."

"And they love me."

"They run a home in Maine. It's a clean, peaceful environment."

"And I can wash dishes and make beds and have my baby. You already offered, and I said no thanks, remember? Would you please just get your good intentions the hell out of my life?"

Bonnie was suddenly very tired. "I understand you've been hurt. You've every right to be suspicious and cynical. But my friends happen to be sincere. And so am I."

"Sincere and deaf, because you don't hear what I'm saying. I can't have this baby." Her voice had risen to a choked cry. "I can't have any baby."

"Maybe your doctor told you that, but it's only the opinion of one doctor."

"I'm HIV-positive. Do you know what that means?" Nell's face was white and sweat was pouring down her forehead. "The baby will be born dying."

"That's not true." Bonnie was thinking quickly now: *I didn't foresee this. It's getting out of control. I mustn't lose control.* She spoke calmly and calmingly. "With proper medical attention for you and the child—"

Nell cut her off, shouting now. "The father's black! Black babies don't get medical attention!"

"That doesn't have to be the case."

"And they don't get adopted! Especially not when they have AIDS!"

"How do you know the father's race?"

"He's the only one who wouldn't use a condom."

"Of course, condoms can fail—"

"All right, I'm ninety-nine percent sure."

Bonnie waited for the safe familiar silence to reenclose the study. "You've been through a lot of pain and a lot of betrayal. It's natural you'd see things in the worst possible light."

"I'm seeing this in the only light there is." The girl's breath was coming in sharp pants. She stared at Bonnie, blaming her for something, blaming her for everything.

Bonnie sighed.

"If it takes you this long to say yes," Nell said, "that means you're going to say no."

"You're so sure of how things are going to turn out." Bonnie was thinking that that certainty was the most treacherous gift God could bestow. "You're so sure of what you want." *But so am I,* she thought, and the realization shook her.

"That means no, right?"

Bonnie shook her head. "No, that doesn't mean no." She rose and crossed to the desk and opened the parish check ledger. "How much did you say that doctor wants?"

NINETEEN

"Oh, gosh, I've known Father Joe like forever." Johanna Lowndes waved her cigarette. "He's one of my all-time favorite people on earth. A truly simpatico mensch."

"How did you meet him?" Cardozo said.

"Through work." Lowndes was a little younger than Cardozo remembered, though she was trying to act older. In her blue jeans she was slender, and with a window backlighting her she was blond.

She affected a slightly goofy, actressy manner—he had a feeling she'd taken diction and breathlessness pointers from old Audrey Hepburn tapes.

"I've been in three of Father Joe's shows—as you can see." She flipped a nod toward the walls. Her walk-up Greenwich Village studio apartment was hung with posters strikingly framed in gold-brushed ebony—one each for *Anything Goes for Broke, Anything Goes Again,* and *Stingin' in the Rain.*

"How would you say Father Joe got along with his perform-ers?"

"I'd say he got along swimmingly. I mean, I wish I had the relationship with my own *father* that I have with Father Joe." She gave him that same look she'd given him in Vanderbilt Garden: *Why don't you come play with me, Daddy?*

"He never had arguments with any of them?"

"Come on, we're talking *theater.* Of course he argued. Some of his performers are assholes. But he never shouted."

"He never mistreated a performer?"

"Oh, maybe verbally—but only when they deserved it."

"Do you know of any performers who were ever injured during rehearsals or performances?"

"By Father Joe? No way. He never put a hand on anyone."

"Did any performers ever injure themselves?"

She was thoughtful. "There was a girl called Louisa—a couple of years ago. She twisted an ankle and sued."

"Anyone else? Any other ankles?"

She tilted her face toward the ceiling. A puff of cigarette smoke floated above her like a thought balloon in the funny papers. "Not that I recall. Not offhand."

"Was Father Joe especially close to any of his performers?"

She took a sip of her ginseng soda. "Close?"

"Did you ever see him make advances or hear of any advances?"

She flashed a drop-jawed stare. "You're kidding. You're not kidding? Father Joe wouldn't know *how*."

"So you're saying no."

"Yes." She nodded. "I mean no. Christ, why are words so *complicated*? You know what I mean. Father Joe is not of this earth. He certainly is not of this city."

"Did you ever see him drunk or drugged or disorderly?"

"You guys just don't want to get it, do you? Father Joe's a saint. A genius and a saint. Period."

"Have you ever seen this girl?" Cardozo showed her the artist's reconstruction of the face of Ms. Basket Case.

There was a beat of hesitation. "Oh, God—is she the one—the one I found?"

Cardozo nodded.

"I'm sorry . . . I don't recall seeing her. Alive, I mean."

"At St. Andrew's maybe? In rehearsal?"

"I honestly doubt it. I know it's only a drawing, but she doesn't look like a performer."

He handed her another picture. "What about this girl?"

"Now, *she's* a performer. Great eyes."

"Her name's Sally Manfredo."

Johanna Lowndes's face was a flawless, unwrinkled blank.

"She was in the chorus of *The Boy Friend*. She played Emily in *Zip Your Pinafore*. She was going to be in *The Pajama Game*, but they replaced her."

"Sorry." Johanna Lowndes gave back the photo. "I didn't play in those shows. I never met her."

* * *

"She looks familiar . . . very familiar." Tommy Lanner—teenage waiter/carpenter/check-out-clerk-but-I'm-really-an-actor/singer/dancer—studied the drawing of Ms. Basket Case's reconstructed face. He put a finger up to scratch the copper-blond curl behind his ear. "I get this little memory click that maybe we were in the same show."

"What show was that?" Ellie Siegel said.

"She could have been one of the dancers in *Anything Goes Again*. But something happened. She had to drop out."

"Why was that?"

"I'm trying to remember. These paint fumes must kill the memory cells in the brain." Tommy Lanner came down from the stepladder. He'd been repainting the kitchen in his East Village railroad flat, and the air was suffocatingly thick. "Maybe she broke her foot rehearsing. Maybe she and Father Joe argued."

"Which was it? A foot or an argument?"

Tommy Lanner went to the window and toyed with objects on the sill—a flowerpot, a toy fire truck, an empty beer can. In the window beyond his profile, TV antennas and bootleg cable hook-ups sprouted like aluminum weeds from the tar paper roofs of the East Village. "Maybe both."

"Did Father Joe argue with many of his performers?"

"It was part of his method for manipulating us. And the manipulation wasn't to get a performance out of us. It was to get power *over* us."

"What kind of power?"

"I could write a book." Tommy Lanner paused as though to mark off a space between himself and what he was about to say. "He asked me up to his apartment for a drink. I should have known he was drunk. But I guess I'm naive—a Texarkana farm boy."

Ellie Siegel wondered how many naive Texarkana farm boys bleached their hair.

"He put on a video of the Obie Awards—it showed him winning a prize—and I swear, he was feeling himself. Getting himself excited."

"So he was making a pass at you?"

"I never stayed around to find out what that old creep had in mind. He unzipped his pants and I was out of there."

* * *

Somehow, in the dark, it didn't seem to count.

Father Chuck felt along the bookshelf behind the leather-bound *Summa theologiae.* His fingers found the bottle. He uncapped it, one-handed, and brought it to his lips.

In a moment, when his nerves quieted down, he clicked the lamp on. It threw a bright splash of light across the broad desk top. The desk was bare except for a marble pen set and a small porcelain figurine of the pietà.

Father Chuck opened a drawer, rippled through documents, brought out a photo and a 3″ × 5″ file card. He placed them in the center of the blotter. He stared at them.

Sally Manfredo's dark eyes smiled back at him.

Why this girl? he wondered. *Why now, after all these years?*

A sound broke in on his thoughts. A coin was rapping at the window. He went and poked a finger through the slats of the blinds.

A teenager in an Ice-T tank top waved to him.

Father Chuck pushed the window up.

The boy—with that astonishing agility of the young—climbed in. He stood looking around the study. "How come you priests all like to live in the dark?"

He wore a New York Mets baseball cap and his blond hair was cut in a crew cut and ponytail. It was a very screw-you personal grooming statement.

Father Chuck gestured to the boy to sit. He crossed to his desk. "Have you given any thought to our last talk?" He turned the photo and the file card facedown.

The boy didn't sit. "I spoke to some friends of mine."

"Runaways like yourself?" Father Chuck wondered how on earth—in today's economy, in today's health crisis—any of these children managed. "Homeless? Starving?"

"We don't want handouts." A small crucifix earring dangling from the boy's left earlobe caught a wink of lamplight.

"I know." Father Chuck understood the defiant self-respect of those who had nothing left but their defiance.

"We're willing to work. We want to work." The boy handed Father Chuck a packet fastened with two pink rubber bands.

Father Chuck snapped the bands off. Photographs. He fitted a pair of half-moon spectacles to his nose.

Images leapt into focus: a young woman sunbathing on a dock, breasts exposed. A young man with tattooed biceps standing in torn Jockey shorts. In all, eight young people displaying their near-nakedness, smiling at the camera with faces that were small-eyed and just a little bit crafty.

Father Chuck felt himself wanting to blush, as though he had been caught peeking through a shower-room window.

"And these young people are the friends you've been speaking of?"

"I'm their agent. I make the deals."

"I see. They've appointed you their spokesman." Father Chuck's smile was neutral now, guarded. "I could offer part-time employment around the rectory for two or three youngsters. Are any of your friends experienced at lawn work?"

"For two hundred dollars you can have an hour with any of them you want."

Father Chuck felt himself pulling back without quite knowing why. "An *hour?*"

The boy nodded. "Do anything you want to them." His eyes said he knew secrets about Father Chuck that Father Chuck was only beginning to guess at. "Light bondage, heavy bondage, spanking, whipping, whatever gets you off. Feel free."

For Father Chuck this was a new frontier in audacity. If the boy was lying, he was absolutely at peace with his falsehood. If he was telling the truth, he was untroubled by anything remotely approaching guilt. "This is a joke."

"It's no joke."

Then it's some kind of entrapment, Father Chuck realized. *Someone has sent this child here to see if I'll take the bait.* "Who are you working for? The diocese?"

The boy's eyes said, *Cut the horseshit.* "You gotta be kidding."

"The police?"

"Oh, sure, I'm an underage cop."

"A politician? A newspaper? TV news?"

"I'm working for the best company on earth. Myself. Privacy and satisfaction guaranteed."

Father Chuck knew his limits, and situations like this were

among them. He gathered the photos into a neat little bundle. He rose from behind his desk and took six steps toward the boy. "You may take back your photographs."

The boy didn't answer. Father Chuck sensed something harden in him.

The boy took two steps toward Father Chuck and at the second step Father Chuck backed off.

"Keep them," the boy said. "Now that you've seen them, you're going to need them."

Father Chuck's hand shot out in denial, as if he'd been accused. "Now, wait just a minute—"

"Father—this is me you're talking to, Eff Huffington. I've been around, I know the score. You don't have to pretend. Unless you get off on pretending." The boy turned to go. "Think it over. You'll be hearing from me."

TWENTY

"Would either of you like coffee?" Cardozo's daughter Terri asked.

He glanced up at the seventeen-year-old girl. She had prepared the meal—paella, green salad, and homemade kiwi sherbert—and now, moving with slender, dark-haired grace, she was clearing the dishes.

"Sure," he said. "How about you, Ellie?"

They were sitting at the dining table in Cardozo's apartment.

"Half a cup for me," Ellie said.

Terri vanished into the kitchen and conversation drifted back to business.

"If Ms. Basket Case had worked in any of Father Joe's shows," Ellie said, "her photo would be in the file."

"Unless he took it out himself," Cardozo said.

"Let's stick with what we know for sure. We've interviewed the sixty-one names in Father Montgomery's talent file. They're all alive and well and accounted for. Except for Sally Manfredo."

"Which is a big exception."

"Except for one thing. Father Joe left your niece's photo in the file. Let's say something did happen to her—pray to God it didn't, but let's say it did. Let's say Father Joe was involved. Now, if he removed Ms. Basket Case's photo because he was involved with *her,* wouldn't he remove your niece's photo? You can't have it both ways."

"Maybe Father Joe isn't consistent."

She looked at him with genuine curiosity. "All right—your niece played in two or three of Father Joe's shows and she disappeared. It's painful. But it doesn't mean Montgomery had anything to do with Ms. Basket Case. You're a cop. Will you please think like one?"

Cardozo's gaze went to the files piled on the coffee table in the living room. There were three stacks—Ellie's, his, and Greg Monteleone's. Cardozo hadn't yet read Ellie's and she hadn't yet read his and neither of them had read Greg's.

"The bad news," Cardozo said, "is that the other priest on the videocassette puts on amateur musicals too. And he uses young people. Father Romero in Queens."

Ellie seemed to sag. "We have to go through more talent files? I can't take another unemployed actor. Not this month."

"Romero says he doesn't keep files. He says everything's in his head."

She tipped her plate to scoop up the last of her sherbert. "Do you believe him?"

"No."

"Then we need a warrant." Ellie licked her spoon. "Vince, did any of your actors recognize the drawing? Or your niece?"

Cardozo sighed. "No."

"Neither did any of mine."

"They all said Father Joe was a decent, sweet old guy. Never raised his voice, never raised a hand, never touched them."

Ellie and Cardozo were both silent, thoughtful. It was a moment before she spoke.

"One of mine said Father Joe tried to molest him."

Cardozo looked at her. She sat there in her blouse and button earrings, her hair pulled back from her face, and an odd stillness was flowing out of her.

"Come on, Ellie—what have you got?"

She took a hit of her wine, and it was definitely a hit, not a sip. "A kid by the name of Tommy Lanner. He thinks he may have seen Ms. Basket Case in the chorus of one of Father Joe's shows—and he thinks they argued—and he thinks she may have hurt her ankle."

"He said that without coaching?"

"I didn't coach him. But he could be mixing her up with the Hitchcock kid. That lawsuit was in the papers."

"And Father Joe groped him?"

"Not even. Lanner says he saw Father Joe fondling himself through his trousers."

"What were the circumstances?"

"According to Lanner, they were in Father Joe's apartment watching a video of the Obies."

"Do you believe this kid?"

"I haven't decided. He obviously resents Father Joe. Funny that Father Joe doesn't sense it."

"You told me to think like a cop. I'm going to suggest you stop reading minds. How do you know what Montgomery senses?"

"He kept Lanner's picture in the file. Anyone else would have thrown it out."

"Maybe he's in love with the kid. Maybe he's not expecting the cops to question every face in his files."

"My take on Father Montgomery is a little different from yours. I don't see him chopping up kids. I don't even see him smoking reefer or going to a porn theater."

"Why not?"

"What you're overlooking about Montgomery is, he's a genuine innocent."

"I don't buy it."

"Which is why he doesn't bother masking his attraction to prostitutes and transvestites."

"Bullshit."

"Which is why he leaves people in his files who are bad-mouthing him. He doesn't know enough not to be decent."

Terri came back to the table with the coffeepot. "I agree. At the worst he's a naughty little boy, not a dirty old man."

"What do you know about it?" Cardozo filled Ellie's cup and then his own.

"A little." Terri set a plate of Pepperidge Farm sugar cookies on the table. "I auditioned for one of his shows."

Cardozo's eyes came around. "When was this?"

"A year and a half ago."

"You never told me."

"Because I didn't get the role."

"You never told me you were interested in performing."

"I was interested for two minutes."

"And you think Father Joe is a naughty little boy?"

"Definitely. A naughty little boy and a sweet old poop."

It perplexed Cardozo that his own daughter's perceptions could be so far removed from his own. "And you don't think maybe there's just a touch of a pretentious phony about him?"

"That too."

"And you like him?"

"Why shouldn't I?"

"What kind of power does this guy have? Does every kid in this town love him?"

Ellie followed the exchange with a half-smiling look, as if to say, *I'm hip to this sitcom.* "Tommy Lanner sure doesn't love him."

Cardozo gave the cream in his coffee a ferocious stir. "Sounds like Lanner at least can spot a phony."

"Dad, all priests are phony. It's their job. They have to convince themselves they love people. Just like cops have to convince themselves they care whether people shoot one another."

"So what does that make Ellie and me, as phony as Father Joe?"

"It makes me tired." Ellie got up from the table. "And I've got a long drive back to Queens. So good night all."

"There's more dessert," Terri said.

Ellie kissed her. "I'm stuffed. It was a great dinner. Thanks. Next time we eat at my place, okay?" She collected her purse from the hall table. "I'll leave the files, Vince. So you can torture yourself."

She kissed him a chaste good night and was gone.

Terri began clearing the table. "You know, Dad, she's obviously interested."

Cardozo was looking through Ellie's files. They were an endless gray drizzle of detail. At this point she didn't know what was relevant and what wasn't, so she'd included everything. "Who's interested?"

"Ellie, obviously."

He found the Lanner file. "What's she interested in?"

"In you, obviously."

"Why obviously me?"

"You're so defensive. You don't see things." Terri stacked dessert plates and took them into the kitchen. "And you're overworked," she called. "You can't take care of the whole world. You're not in good shape."

That made him stop reading and look up. "On my last physical I scored as well as a thirty-two-year-old."

Terri came back with a rag and swept crumbs off the table into her palm. "But you're not thirty-two years old. You should marry Ellie. She wants you."

"Oh, sure, no woman can possibly resist my charm."

"You have charm, Dad. Use it while you've still got it."

It seemed to Cardozo that his relationship with his daughter became increasingly implausible. She had all the answers, even when he wasn't asking questions. "Ellie had a rotten marriage. She hates marriage. She hates men. She hates me. She thinks I'm flying on right-wing hunches and turning into a redneck."

"It doesn't mean you're not charming."

"Let's stop worrying about my life, which I can take care of. And let's worry a little about yours—which I'm not sure you can."

Terri didn't answer. He watched her fold up the leaves of the dining table.

"You don't tell me much about your life. I'm not complaining, I'm just mentioning."

"I don't want to worry you. You have enough on your mind."

"I'd have less on my mind if I knew what my daughter was up to."

"I'm not breaking any laws."

Sadness brushed him. "Don't be smart like that. Your cousin Sally said the same thing the night she disappeared. She said she wasn't breaking any laws and she wished she was."

"I'm sorry." Terri placed a hand against his cheek. "But stop worrying. I'm not Sally. I'm not going to disappear."

"Did she ever talk to you?"

"She didn't tell me much. Except she loved acting and she hated her home."

"She said that?"

"And I don't give a damn about acting and I love my home." Terri kissed him. "That's the difference."

TWENTY-ONE

"**D**oes anyone else have a question he wants to ask?"

Monsignor Flynn, the only priest in the room wearing clericals, gazed out at the space that had once been a living room. The walls were still covered in oyster silk and painted chinoiserie panels, but most of the eighteenth-century English furniture was gone. As leader and moderator of the group, the monsignor sat in the last remaining tapestry-upholstered wing chair. The twenty-seven others sat on folding wooden chairs.

"Does anyone have a problem he needs to share?"

No one answered.

"Nothing is too small to concern us. Nothing is so terrible it will shock us. The only terrible thing will be if any of you goes home tonight still carrying a burden he could have left here."

And still no one answered.

"Very well. Shall we stand and join hands and bow our heads to recite—"

Father Chuck Romero was sitting in the second row, and at that instant two things startled him: the first was seeing his own hand shoot up into the air; the second was hearing his own trembling voice. "I have a problem."

"Yes . . . Chuck. Won't you tell us about it?"

Father Chuck stood. "There's a boy who's been coming to me for counseling. A teenager. He's not a member of the parish. I'm not even sure he's Catholic, though he says he is."

"He must be very much in need."

Father Chuck tried to find words to wrap around what he'd been feeling lately. "The boy is grappling with devils no child should have to face."

"Why don't you tell us a little about these devils?"

"He deals drugs to other teenagers. He takes drugs himself. He's even offered me drugs. Once, to win his trust . . . I accepted."

"What drug was this?"

Father Chuck stood there silent, eyes down. "Crack. I only smoked a little of it. It was in a good cause. He's come to trust me."

The monsignor arched a sly but understanding eyebrow. "How has this trust shown itself?"

"More openness of spirit—more confiding of the details of his life. They're very painful." Father Chuck hesitated. Nervousness skittered inside him. These men were fellow priests, yet he didn't know how far he could trust their charity or their discretion. "It turns out that he's organized his friends into a prostitution ring. He's offered me a special rate—a house discount, he calls it—for any of the children I want."

Father Chuck smiled, trying to lighten the horror. The monsignor did not return the smile.

"The boy doesn't know what he's doing." Father Chuck's voice was shaking badly, and his throat was so in need of a drink that he could hardly force the words out. "He doesn't understand the harm that could come to these children or to himself. I don't know how to wake up his conscience without seeming to criticize him—or driving him away."

"Perhaps this boy needs to be criticized," the monsignor suggested. "Perhaps he needs to be driven away."

"No. Too many others have done just that. He needs help."

"Obviously. But must it be your help? Remember what brought all of us into this room: the recognition that we're limited, finite, fallible human beings. Has this boy committed crimes?"

Behind the monsignor, a grandfather clock bonged the quarter hour.

Father Chuck nodded. "Petty crimes."

"Perhaps you should talk with the diocesan liaison to juvenile justice services."

"I hate to throw him into the maws of a bureaucracy."

A hand went up. "I was in a situation exactly like this, and it pulled me under faster than quicksand."

There were murmurs of agreement.

"Chuck," another voice said, "watch your step."

And another voice said, "Chuck, watch your ass."

There was laughter and Father Chuck felt he was under assault. He had to fight to keep his knees from buckling. But he stood through the laughter. He even managed to join in, showing he was a good sport. And he stood through the concluding prayer. He'd never been so happy to reach an *amen* in his life.

Monsignor Flynn approached and touched his elbow. It was a touch so light it hardly seemed to impose its will, but it steered Father Chuck away from the group, toward one of the arched windows.

"Tell me, Chuck—has your behavior changed as a result of meeting this boy?"

"No."

"Do you find yourself thinking obsessively about him or his problems?"

Father Chuck concentrated on the view from the window, on the night where high rises made necklaces of light. "I wouldn't say so."

"Are you behaving compulsively? Neglecting your duties to others?"

Father Chuck turned. He had the uncomfortable feeling that he was being judged. "I don't believe so."

"Have you neglected prayer?"

"No." Father Chuck met the monsignor's challenge the only way it could be met: straight on, eye-to-eye. He noticed something that startled him: Monsignor Flynn's left eye was pale brown, but his right eye was pale blue.

Father Chuck wished he hadn't noticed. It broke his concentration. He heard himself stammer, "I p-p-pray . . . regularly."

"Are you drinking?"

Something in the space between him and the monsignor seemed to gather itself together and turn solid.

"Only moderately. There's been no increase. I have things under control."

"Control can be dangerous. You know, Chuck, as priests we often overlook the needs of a very special sinner in our lives—ourselves. I have the name of a good man if you'd care to discuss anything privately—and in depth."

"A psychiatrist?"

"A psychiatrist *and* devout. You don't find that too often nowadays."

"It's the boy that needs help, not me."

A ridge of pain formed across Monsignor's brow. "You're throwing water down a well, Chuck. Will you at least think about seeing this man?"

He thinks I'm crazy, Father Chuck realized with a jolt. He looked around the room, which was full of priests milling in civvies. *Half of them think I'm crazy and the other half think I'm dumb.* He felt a burn rise to his face.

Monsignor patted him on the shoulder. "I'll let you socialize. Good night, Chuck."

But the bantering good cheer of priests in recovery grated on Father Chuck's nerves. He hurried down the curved marble stairway of the old Cassandra Guggenheim mansion, now a school run by the Sisters of Mercy. Crystal chandeliers shone down on unicorn tapestries and steel-frame desks. He stepped through the carved Gothic doorway into the night.

Across Fifth Avenue, three boys were taking baseball bats to the windows of a Porsche. It seemed to Father Chuck that in this city even the breaking glass had a New York accent.

Poor boys, he thought. *No one cares. No one helps.* He felt a weariness that went to the marrow.

He had intended to take the subway, but the thought of changing trains at Queens Plaza depressed him. A taxi was approaching. For the second time that evening, he was surprised to see his hand, independent of his will, rise into the air.

* * *

At the sound of the whistle, Olga Quigley looked up from her article in *TV Guide*. Steam was shooting out the spout of the kettle.

She got up and filled the teapot, adding a couple of bags of Sleepytime herb tea to the pot. She arranged three chocolate macadamia chip cookies on a plate—they were Father Romero's favorite bedtime snack. Now the tray was neat and ready.

It took a moment to check her reflection in a hanging copper pan, to tuck a loose strand of dark hair back into place. Now Olga Quigley was neat and ready.

Her footsteps echoed on the bare floor of the empty corridor. She rapped on the study door. There was no answer. She nudged it open, clicked on the light with her elbow, set the tray down on the desk.

She noticed that Father had left several photos and a 3″ × 5″ card out. She glanced at the photos. They were pictures of young people sunbathing. The card had a name written on it in Father's big block printing: SALLY MANFREDO, followed by an address and phone number.

The front door slammed. She carefully replaced the card and the photos exactly as she had found them.

Father came into the study mumbling to himself. He seemed just a little bit startled to see her there.

"Must have been a long meeting tonight," she said.

"Yes, it was long."

She felt something close itself off in Father. He was in one of his moods. "I fixed your snack."

"Thank you, Mrs. Quigley." He stood still, polishing the right lens of his bifocals.

"I'll let you be. Just ring when you want me to take the tray." Mrs. Quigley closed the door quietly behind her.

She was in her bedroom watching the midnight movie—Debbie Reynolds tonight—when she realized Father hadn't rung or made so much as a peep in an hour and a half. She crept back to the study.

Father had set his reclining chair all the way back. His head was lolling to the side and his mouth was hanging wide open and he was snoring.

She sniffed the half-empty teacup and smelled alcohol. A bottle of 150-proof Jamaican rum sat uncapped on the desk. She shook her head. Father Romero was turning into a drinker. Father O'Malley before him had been a boozer and drink had killed her husband Jack, and she knew the signs.

As she placed the dishes on the tray, she noticed a pyramid of ash in the ashtray. She paused to examine it. Poking with the teaspoon, she discovered half a photograph and part of a card with the handwritten block letters ALLY MANFR.

TWENTY-TWO

With the edge of his hand, Collie flipped unruly waves of dark hair from his forehead. "Logically speaking," he said, "the highest test of love isn't whether you would die for another person."

"This is a dinner party." Anne stared across the table at him with hazel-eyed impatience. "Do we have to speak logically?"

"It's whether you would live for them," Bonnie said.

"No." Collie pushed a last knifeload of risotto onto a last forkful of osso buco. "It's whether you'd kill for them."

Bonnie clanked her fork down onto her plate. "That's not funny, and it's not even logical."

"It is logical, and I'll prove it. The soul is the most sacred part of the person. When you sin—and do we agree that killing is a sin?"

"Hear! Hear!" Bonnie's brother Ben rapped a butter knife on his wineglass full of mineral water. A high, clear note rang out.

"When you sin, you endanger your most sacred part. To risk losing what is most sacred, to actually lose it for the sake of another person—that has got to be life's highest sacrifice."

Bonnie couldn't help getting furious when men talked like that: put a penny in the logic machine, and out popped ethical sanction for murder. "But there's always another way. No one can avoid dying, but anyone can avoid killing."

"That's not the issue," Collie said.

"What is the issue?" Anne said.

"The issue is, what's the most you can give for love?"

"But giving the most when the most isn't required is wasteful." Bonnie felt her voice rising. "Nothing sanctions waste."

"That's well and good," Collie said, "if you see morals as a subdivision of ecology, but I could point to some relevant passages in St. Paul—"

Completely forgetting her responsibility as hostess, Bonnie shot to her feet. "Paul was an anti-Semitic, homophobic, epileptic cult groupie. He was not a saint, he was not Paul, I seriously doubt he was a he, and I know he was not rational."

Anne rose from the table and began clearing dishes. "Coffee, everyone?"

Heat climbed to Bonnie's cheeks. She felt rotten and embarrassed, as if she'd lost her temper at a child. "Please, Anne. You relax. I'll take care of it."

In the kitchen, she filled the espresso machine and scraped plates. Fiddling with her Hammacher Schlemmer gadgets and utensils, she had the sense of being safe in a space she could control. "I shouldn't start dinner this late," she said. "We always get into arguments."

"It was a delicious dinner." Anne worked a corkscrew into a chilled cabernet sauvignon and yanked the cork. "And it wasn't an argument. It was only a game. I enjoy these evenings of ours—I wish we could manage to get together more often."

"You're sure you don't feel outnumbered? We must come across as such church nuts, the three of us."

"You're like lawyers. I love it when conversation gets caught in a theological tangle."

"You couldn't mean that." Bonnie held out two wineglasses and Anne filled them.

"Admittedly, a little of this would help." Anne raised her glass. "But you can't have everything."

They clinked glasses.

Bonnie took a cool, tangy swallow. "Remembering how those two used to attack a bottle, a little of this would probably start a war."

At one time both Collie and Ben had had drinking problems.

Ben had licked his three years ago, when he had joined A.A. Collie had been an off-and-on binge drinker until the year before last, when he finally managed to sober up. Bonnie had not seen him touch a drop of alcohol since. She admired both men's sobriety. She sensed that it had taken enormous courage.

"It's odd." Anne swirled her wine. "You've wound up being the priest, and Collie and Ben are—well, they're Collie and Ben."

"If they were priests you might not have a boyfriend."

"If they were Catholic priests. But I don't know. You hear stories. A lot of priests play around. Even Catholics."

Bonnie held a pitcher of milk to the steam spout of the espresso machine. "Everybody likes cappuccino, right?"

She was sitting on the mossy velvet Victorian sofa, stirring the beige froth in her cup with a teaspoon, when she felt the faint pressure of Collie's weight settling on the cushion beside her.

"Didn't mean to get your goat," he said.

"Yes, you did."

"Angry?"

"No."

"Hurt?"

"Envious." She set her cup down on the coffee table neatly stacked with books and magazines. "I'll never have your debating skills."

"A priest doesn't need debating skills. They're the roundtable equivalent of an Uzi. Only troublemakers need them."

"You're not a troublemaker."

"I used to be. But no more. You've focused me."

"Have I?"

He nodded. "Now it's my job to look after you and the kids. I won't let anything happen to them—or to you."

They sat there, not talking. She felt herself wanting to pull back and wanting to reach out at the same time. There was a need in him that was suffering and solitary and confused.

Thirty seconds passed.

"You're sweet, Collie. I don't know what I'd do without you."

He sighed.

She kissed him lightly on the cheek. "I do love you. I hope you know that."

* * *

She was rinsing dishes and placing them in the dishwasher rack when her brother sauntered into the kitchen. "You're worried, Sis."

"No. It's nothing."

He took off his glasses. He slid a forefinger under her chin and tipped her face up till her eyes had no choice but to meet his. "You have that look."

"What look?"

"Enough priestly evasion. Spill."

She poured soap powder into the detergent dispenser and swung the dishwasher door shut. "The police are asking questions."

"That's one of the ways police earn a living."

"Sonya Barnett told them about the Hitchcock case."

"How do you know?"

"Because she called me up afterward. It's a safe bet the police went straight to the Hitchcocks. And the Hitchcocks don't like us."

"Aren't you being a tad paranoid?"

"They'd slant things. Look how they claimed Joe was abusing his performers."

"And they never convinced the judge. He threw that lawsuit out of court."

"But they may have convinced the police. A detective came back asking more questions. It's the third time."

She set the controls to *heavy load* and *hot dry* and twisted the dial to *start*. The dishwasher began making sounds like a Lebanese massacre.

"What kind of questions?" Ben said.

"He wanted to know about our old van that got wrecked." Just talking about it, she felt a dull, nervous something in the pit of her stomach. "I can't even remember the number of vans we've owned, so of course he wanted an exact number."

"Why does it bother you so much?"

"I get the feeling he's looking for ways to tie Joe into that dead girl's murder."

"How in the world does that van reflect on Joe or the dead girl?"

"I'm not sure." She dried her hands on a dish towel. "He wanted to know if Father Joe owned a golf hat."

Ben laughed. "A golf hat? You're making that up."

"No." She shook her head. "I gave Joe a golf hat three years ago for Christmas—he still wears it."

"You gave everyone golf hats. Joe's the only person silly enough to wear his."

"Don't you think it's an odd question?"

"Out of context, it certainly is. But this cop must know what he's doing. He wouldn't have made the grade to detective if he didn't."

TWENTY-THREE

A shadow fell across stacks of reports and interdepartmental memos that littered the desk, and Ellie Siegel stepped into the cubicle. "I've been on the phone to Judge Myers. She says any warrant she gives us to search a priest's possessions has to be very narrowly drawn."

"How narrowly?" Cardozo said.

"So a cockroach couldn't crawl through. We have to describe each item we're looking for."

"Father Romero's papers."

"I tried that. She says absolutely not. Too general."

"His papers relating to his theatricals."

"You talk to her, Vince—or ask another judge."

"None of my judges get to the office before eleven. But we might as well wait. Montgomery's going to keep us busy today."

Ellie's glance flicked around sharply. "What have you found?"

"Point one." Cardozo handed her the report on her Lanner interview. "The actor says Father Joe came on to him in a quasi-closety way. Forgive me, Ellie, I know Father Joe has won your heart, but that is not innocent, naive behavior. Point two." He handed her the DD5 on his interview with the Ninth Avenue hookers. "Father Joe has an interest in transvestite prostitutes, and this interest extends to photographing them, and possibly further."

"Possibly." Ellie's tone was dubious.

"Point three." Cardozo ignored the tone and handed her the medical examiner's report. "Dan Hippolito thinks the victim could have been involved in s/m sex. Connect the dots, and what have we got?"

"I'm not sure we even have dots." Ellie smoothed the wrinkles out of her skirt. "That s/m suggestion of Dan's is pretty iffy. The kid could have been wearing leather boots and no socks."

"Very tight leather boots to leave that much abrasion and residue."

"A kid who's picking her clothes off a garbage pile is not going to be too choosy about fit." Ellie threw the files back onto the desk. Her body language was almost in attack mode—arms on hips, head down as though she were ready to charge into him. "How about digging up some halfway credible evidence before we decide Father Montgomery is Joe the Ripper?"

"We've already got probable cause. Your actor. Eyewitness to misdemeanor."

"Come on, Vince. At worst Lanner's statement makes Father Joe borderline sleaze."

"Without the borderline."

"It's still a pretty mild accusation."

"The D.A. has gone to grand juries with milder accusations."

Ellie frowned at a fingernail. "And what if a grand jury won't buy Lanner's testimony? What if—for example—he has a rap sheet?"

"Give me a break. How many wannabe actors have rap sheets?"

"One way to find out."

They went into the squad room. Detective Monteleone was using the computer to track down a license plate from a hit-and-run.

"Are you going to be needing that thing for long?" Cardozo asked.

Monteleone shot him a dark-eyed look. "Forever."

Ellie arched an eyebrow and motioned Cardozo to come with her down to the second floor. Over in the corner of the squad room, the detention cage was filling up with the first haul of the day—four ratty, bummed-out–looking kids.

"What have you got over there?" Cardozo asked the duty lieutenant.

"Two pickpockets, public urinator, car break-in."

Cardozo thought of the aggravation and bullshit paperwork involved in even the simplest arrest and he couldn't see why a sane cop would bothering busting a street person for pissing. You couldn't fine them, they had no money; you couldn't give them a summons, they had no home; you couldn't lock them up, there was no room in the jails. "Urination's been upped to a priority misdemeanor?"

"The captain says we're making it a quality-of-life issue."

Which, translated, meant the commissioner was worried because an election was coming up and the mayor needed the swing votes in Manhattan's silk-stocking district.

"Can we use the computer?" Ellie asked. "It'll only take a second."

The lieutenant shrugged.

Ellie crossed to the computer. "Hi." She smiled at the sergeant whose desk space she was invading. "This'll only take a minute."

She called up criminal records and tapped Lanner's name into the keyboard. Print began rushing up the screen.

Cardozo frowned.

Lanner's misdemeanors covered two years and they came in chronological order. Shoplifting, Bloomingdale's; sentence suspended. Possession quarter gram cocaine, Limelight disco; sentence suspected. Petty larceny, theft videocassette recorder, complainant Joseph Montgomery; sentence suspended.

A silence oozed like squid ink.

"Forget him. He's a hustler." Ellie cleared the screen. "He has it in for Father Joe almost as badly as you do."

Cardozo followed Ellie back upstairs. "Okay, maybe I'm prejudiced against Montgomery. But it's not clouding my judgment. There's something wrong with the guy."

"Maybe."

"Don't give me that 'maybe,' like I'm an idiot."

"Yesterday you thought there was something wrong with Father Romero."

"There's something wrong with both of them."

As they came back into the squad room, Greg Monteleone was bent down closing the padlock on the steel cabinet where detectives stored their weapons.

"Thought you were using the computer," Ellie said.

"Just getting rid of my gun. Hot weather like this, it adds to the drain carrying the extra pounds all day."

"Greg, your day is barely two hours old. And you're carrying five extra pounds from yesterday's lunch."

Greg blew her a kiss. "And I love you, too, princess." He returned to his desk and handed Cardozo a special delivery letter. "Came in while you were downstairs."

"Thanks." Cardozo glanced at the sender's address, and he was aware of Ellie glancing too: the state prison at Dannemora.

She walked with him to his cubicle. "Who's your pen pal?"

Cardozo ripped open the envelope and pulled out a single sheet of prison letterhead. "His name is Martin Barth."

"Inmate?"

Cardozo skimmed the page of neat handwriting. "Says he's serving a life sentence."

"Know him?"

"Never heard of him."

Cardozo moved to the window. Noonday shadows were creeping up the brick wall across the alley. "He writes, quote, *I was deeply moved by the artist's reconstruction of the face of misery that was published last week on page one of the* New York Post. *I was acquainted with this unfortunate child and must talk with you immediately. I know how she died.*"

"I'm glad to see you." On the other side of the Plexiglas partition, Martin Barth fidgeted in a dark metal chair. "You have no idea how glad. Thank you for coming all this way."

"I wanted to come," Cardozo said.

To the right and left of them, the visitors' room stretched like a hundred-yard lunch counter. The space was dim and dirty, with a smell of ammonia layered over deeper strata of sweat and tobacco. Whatever that thirty-four thousand per prisoner per year in the state budget was going to, it wasn't sweeping and scrubbing or electric lighting around here.

"You must think it's strange I've asked to meet you."

There were dark circles under Barth's pale eyes, lines grooving the corners of his mouth. He stared out of horn-rimmed glasses that kept slipping down the bridge of his nose. Every time they slipped he made an irritated face and pushed them back up. He struck Cardozo as a mousy, obsessive, nearsighted man who probably had not yet accepted the reality of his situation.

"No, not especially strange," Cardozo said. "I get a few calls from prison."

"It's not as horrible a place as they say." Even though they were communicating through telephones, Barth leaned closer to the partition, confidingly. "It's here that I found my Higher Power. Do you know about the Higher Power?"

"It's like God, isn't it?"

"Very much like God. My Higher Power wants me to make a clean breast of all my wrongs."

Barth took a pack of Marlboro Lights from the pocket of his blue prison shirt. Sweat had plastered the cheap material to his narrow chest. He tapped a cigarette loose and lit it. He smoked like someone who was trying to learn how, who hoped it would make him look tougher.

Cardozo flashed that Martin Barth had waited till his forties to enter adolescence.

"Let me begin with some background. Before imprisonment, I was an agricultural futures analyst. I was employed by Salomon Brothers on Wall Street. I also did a little stock brokerage on my own, in violation of company rules."

A wry smile hinted that he and Cardozo were coconspirators, that they knew things about human frailty that no one else did. Cardozo smiled back, joining the conspiracy.

"I'm married to a lovely wife and I'm the father of two lovely children. I'm presently serving a life sentence for murdering one of my private clients."

Barth paused to exhale a shapeless cloud of smoke that slowly drifted up toward the ceiling vent.

"The dead girl whose picture the papers printed—I never learned her name. She was a runaway. I picked her up when I was jogging on the West Side docks about fifteen months ago. I took her back to a meat-packing plant in the vicinity. My firm traded in the stock of the company that owned the property, and I had keys. It was always empty during the day."

He ground out his cigarette.

"I once saw a pornographic film called *Lola and All the Trimmings*. I'm ashamed to say it made a lasting impression on me. It concerned a man who picked up a young girl and made her his prisoner. Ever since seeing it, I'd had a fantasy of picking up a runaway and taking her to the deserted plant, and doing whatever I wanted to her."

He broke off to light another cigarette.

"My fantasy came true. The girl was wild. She even had gold rings through her nipples. She was experienced in ways I'd only dreamed of—and completely willing. Her only qualm was the smell of the beef carcasses—even refrigerated they stank. So I lit incense."

"Where'd you get the incense?"

"I always kept some handy in my jogging pack—to set the mood in case I ever got lucky. She let me tie her hands and feet with leather belts. She was powerless. It was pure insanity. I kicked her, beat her, dripped candle wax on her." For that one smiling moment, Barth seemed lost in remembering. "I always had a fantasy about candle wax."

"Where did you get the candle?"

"My jogging knapsack."

Barth lit a third cigarette and now he had two going in the ashtray.

"The long and short was, I got carried away and accidentally killed her."

"How'd you do that?"

"I was fondling her neck—and it just happened. I suppose I choked off her air. When I realized what I'd done, I cut the body up."

"How?"

"With a meat saw. I loaded the body parts into a hamper."

"Where'd you get the hamper?"

"The company used reinforced Styrofoam hampers to ship meat to restaurants. I must have ripped her when I was making love—I found one of the nipple rings on the floor after I packed her. I kept it as a souvenir. That night I abandoned the hamper in the Vanderbilt Garden."

It seemed to Cardozo that Barth wore his guilt like a halo. His recital was frank and unflinching, and those were not always admirable qualities. There were times when people should flinch, and when they didn't, you knew the world was in trouble.

"How did you know how to carve up the body?"

"Years of experience with Christmas roasts."

"How did you get the body to the park?"

"I rented a van."

"Who from?"

"An outfit that specializes in fraudulently licensed vans and trucks—so you can park anywhere and not worry about getting ticketed. I said I needed the van for a moving job."

"Could you describe this van?"

"It was a blue Toyota. There was a smiling sun painted on the door."

"What was the name of the van-rental company?"

"I don't recall."

"What happened to the ring you found on the floor? Where is it now?"

"It's in my jogging knapsack in the closet at home. My wife will give it to you."

TWENTY-FOUR

Harvey Thoms looked at his watch. "You're sure this woman's home."

"My client's wife is getting herself ready." Pierre Strauss gave the buzzer another push.

"You mean she's putting on lipstick?" Thoms said.

"Possibly."

Cardozo did not relish standing in a small entrance hall with these two men. Strauss was a good quarter-century older and fifty pounds lighter than Thoms, but something murderous was edging into his body language and Cardozo had a feeling that in another two minutes they would be swinging at one another.

"Have you noticed," Thoms said, "a woman gets into a car and it takes her longer to drive away than a man. A woman has to put on lipstick. You can't drive safely without lipstick." Thoms laughed. "I may be prejudiced, but it happens to be a fact."

"For God's sake," Strauss said, "she's a human being."

"God bless the family of man."

"I don't often ask favors of the district attorney's office, but could you muster some kind of small-scale decency for the next half hour?"

The door opened and a pale, thin woman stood looking at them with tired eyes. Her gray dress had been bought when she weighed ten pounds more. "Hello, Pierre."

She had a quietly cultivated voice. Cardozo noticed that she was not wearing lipstick.

Strauss kissed her lightly on the cheek. He had an almost believable caring manner. It played all right in Eloise Barth's peppermint-striped vestibule, but Cardozo had seen it play a lot better on talk shows, where Strauss presented himself as the last performing civil libertarian in captivity. Even his wild, wispy, wise-old-man white hair played well on talk shows if they gave him a stylist.

"Eloise, this is Harvey Thoms from the D.A.'s office, and Lieutenant Vince Cardozo from the Twenty-second Precinct."

She acknowledged them uneasily. "Won't you come in."

"Now, as I explained on the phone, Lieutenant Cardozo is going to show you a warrant authorizing him to remove Martin's knapsack and any contents that may be in it."

Eloise Barth appeared to be listening, but barely. It was as if she would go crazy if she had to think anymore about cops and lawyers and warrants.

"Mr. Thoms is here to see that you comply with the warrant and I'm here to see that Lieutenant Cardozo does not exceed its mandate. Lieutenant, would you show Mrs. Barth the warrant?"

"I don't want to see it. The knapsack should be right here in the closet." She opened the hall closet. She pulled a chair over and stood on it and searched the shelf. She moved quickly, but her movements suggested exhaustion, as though this was something she wanted to get through fast so that she could lie down and die.

Pierre Strauss held the chair steady. "How are the children?"

"Doing their best."

Cardozo was able to see into the living room. It was a bright, clean space with a carved marble fireplace and a baby grand piano and comfortably child-proof furnishings. Almost too perfect. It looked like a gigantic doll's house.

"The knapsack's not here." There was a kind of blankness in her voice. "It must be in the bedroom closet."

Pierre Strauss helped her step down from the chair. She led the way down another corridor.

They passed the doorway of a darkened room. Two little boys were sitting on the floor in front of the television, flipping through channels. There was a flash of opera from Lincoln Center. A flash of yuppie lovers from the movie of the week. A flash of Barbara Walters interviewing a new Latin American dictator.

Cardozo realized the boys were watching the doorway, not the TV, sneaking a look at Mommy's visitors.

"How old are they?" Cardozo said.

"Timmy's four." Eloise Barth answered as if it were bad luck to talk to a cop about anyone she loved. "Allen's six."

She opened the bedroom door and turned on the light. Cardozo had the impression that the room had been stripped of luxuries— that the cotton spread on the enormous canopied bed had once been silk, that the tortoiseshell grooming implements on the dressing table had once been silver.

She opened the closet door. The inside was a jumble, as if she had packed all time-tumbled shards of her marriage into that space.

Pierre Strauss brought a chair and helped her step up.

After several minutes' silent searching, she handed down a blue nylon High Sierra backpack.

The zipper had not been closed. As Pierre Strauss passed the knapsack to Cardozo, a candle fell to the floor, and then a package of Bombay Girl incense, and a gold ring too small for even a child's pinkie.

* * *

"I have one question." Cardozo stood at the window, watching sheets of summer rain whip over First Avenue. "In your opinion, is Martin Barth the kind of man who would commit this kind of murder?"

Dr. Vergil Muller—the psychiatrist who had examined Martin Barth for the State of New York—drew in a deep breath and pushed himself up from the sofa. At six-foot-three he weighed a good three hundred pounds, and he left a permanent-looking dent in the leather cushion.

"A man abducts a runaway female, possibly underage." There was a suggestion of the southern Midwest in Dr. Muller's way of speaking—a kind of articulated drawl. "He has sex with her; he murders her; he dismembers her and abandons her body in a hamper in a public park."

Muller stepped around an exercise bicycle, went to his desk, rummaged through a clutter of papers, and slipped on a pair of low-grade magnifying glasses. He peered at a stack of books beneath the telephone, then crossed to the bookcase and searched two shelves. He pulled out a cobalt-blue–covered paperback the size of a telephone directory.

"You're asking me if Martin Barth is capable of committing statutory rape, homicide, and littering, in one repugnant deed?" Muller's gray gaze fixed Cardozo from above his glasses. "He sure is. He's a demented fuck. But you knew that. There's surprisingly little to be said about compulsive sociopaths, subcategory criminal, subcategory homicidal, though I could take five hours saying it. Let's see if the fortune-teller's manual can shed anything succinct in the way of light."

Dr. Muller returned to his dent in the sofa. He opened the book and ran his thumb down an index. "Tell me, Lieutenant, are you competent in psychobabble or do I have to translate?"

"I can follow the gist."

"Okay, I'm going to condense. The type of sociopath who left that girl's body parts in that basket would be male, in his late teens to early forties, from a broken home or dysfunctional family, one or both parents addicted to alcohol or drugs and/or abusive. He would have a history of poor relations with the opposite sex and with male authority figures. He would be unable to postpone gratification. He would see others as nonpersons; they would matter only insofar as they could gratify his ego needs. He would be deeply conflicted about sex and possibly about gender."

Muller turned a page. He crossed his right leg over his left, making an easier reading desk of his knee.

"He would see society as a collection of marks to be conned. He would have contempt for the morals, conventions, and rituals of society, which he would see as hollow theater. By age fifteen he would have done four of the following ten: One, run away from home; two, stolen repeatedly; three, lied repeatedly; four, set fires; five—" Muller broke off and looked over at Cardozo. "Can you believe I do this for a living?"

"What is that book?"

"The *Diagnostic and Statistical Manual of Mental Disorders,* published by the American Psychiatric Society. Essentially, it attempts to categorize a lot of random, raw anecdotal data."

"Is it accurate?"

"Well, as Lewis Carroll remarked, a stopped clock is accurate twice a day. I'd say the manual beats a stopped clock—I've known days when it was accurate four times. Of course, anything this general is bound to hit a few bull's-eyes."

"How well does that description fit Martin Barth?"

Dr. Muller slammed the book shut. "As well as a good off-the-rack suit. Needs one or two minor alterations. But it's a nice, workable general fit."

"What about the murder Barth's serving time for? Does it resemble the girl in the basket?"

"I hate talking on an empty stomach. Let's have a drink."

Dr. Muller took Cardozo to a neighborhood pub called Delilah's. "I have my one martini here every day at 6 P.M. They always save the same booth for me."

The place was crowded and noisy, layered with cigarette smoke and smelling thickly of grilled hamburger fat. The hostess led them to Dr. Muller's booth. She sent a waitress over with a martini for Muller, a diet Pepsi for Cardozo.

Muller stared into his drink. "How much do you know about Barth's history?"

"I read the file. He was running his own brokerage business

against company rules. One of his clients, a secretary in the accounting department, threatened to expose him. He went to her apartment and struck her with a cast-iron skillet till she was dead."

"Barth had sex with her before killing her." Muller took his first sip. He seemed to be feeling his way into the drink. "Afterward, he shaved her and had sex with her again."

"That wasn't in the file."

"The paraphilia didn't diminish culpability. And it didn't change the motive for the crime. He was covering his tracks."

"What's paraphilia?"

"Psychobabble for sexual perversion. In Barth's case, attraction toward juveniles. He'd probably been able to mask it until he killed the secretary. Once he had a female body in his power he couldn't resist the urge to infantilize the corpse and abuse it further. The experience blew the manhole cover off his repressions and he killed another young woman while he was on bail awaiting trial. His response on the Stanford-Binet showed marked sadistic pedophile inclinations."

"I take it Stanford-Binet is some kind of Rorschach?"

"Same principle, but they're photos, not inkblots. The patient makes up a story to supply the context. They're a simple projective test and a good fast way of finding out what sort of fantasies are bubbling in the unconscious." Muller took a mouthful of honey-roasted peanuts. "Barth's fantasies are quite bizarre. Disturbingly bizarre."

Muller sat sipping, tapping his finger in rhythm to an old Sarah Vaughan tune playing on the jukebox. Cardozo had a sense of something held back.

"Do those fantasies bother you?"

"Frankly, the amount of detail worries me."

"Why?"

"I don't think they're just fantasies. I get the feeling they could be memories. He may have killed other children."

"Has he confessed to other homicides?"

Muller shook his head. "No—not yet."

TWENTY-FIVE

"It's the same size," Lou Stein's voice on the phone said. "The same type as the ring found in the dead girl's nipple—of course, it's in much better shape; it's been safely indoors all this time."

"Made by the same jeweler?" Cardozo said.

"That I didn't say, and I didn't use the word jeweler. These rings are not one-of-a-kind or two-of-a-kind custom items—they come in from Taiwan by the hundred-gross. But the Barth ring does have trace blood on it—and it's the girl's blood type, not Barth's. I'd say it could easily be the ring from the other nipple."

"You tested the other stuff in the knapsack?"

"The incense and the candle are compatible with trace evidence on the clothing and torso."

"What the hell good is compatible? Do they match?"

"The traces are microscopic—there's no way of pulling an exact match. These are mass-produced items—the incense comes in from India by the ton."

"Okay, but we have the exact candle that Barth claims he used."

"The candle is meat by-product from Argentina, like one out of every three candles sold in U.S. supermarkets. There's nothing unique about the dye, there's no scent, there's no way of knowing if this is exactly the same candle. But there's nothing to say it isn't."

"Is that candle fifteen months old? It's in awfully good condition."

"Candles are relatively stable animal product—they don't wilt like flowers, they don't go bad like beef. Use and exposure is how they age. He used it once and put it away."

"Is that burn on the wick fifteen months old? It looks like he lit it last night."

"Under the circumstances, there's no reason it couldn't be fifteen months old. Or older. I seem to be telling you something you'd rather not hear."

"No, Lou, I appreciate it. Thanks for getting back to me so fast." Cardozo hung up the phone. He stared out the window. An idea had been growing in his brain. His life would be a lot easier if the idea would just roll over and die, but even Lou's lab results hadn't killed it.

"What's the verdict?" Ellie Siegel stood watching him from the doorway, her eyes clear and dark above high cheekbones. Somewhere in the squad room behind her a phone was ringing, but nobody was in any hurry to answer it. "Lou says it matches?"

Cardozo nodded. "Damn it, Ellie. Something feels off. The stuff in Barth's knapsack looks too new."

"Appearances aren't always the whole story. That's why we have labs."

"Barth says he rented the van from an outfit that used fraudulent out-of-state licenses to avoid ticketing and towing." Cardozo scooted back his chair. He rose. "But St. Andrew's owned a van of exactly the same description. And a guy in a clerical collar was leaving bouquets on the grave *after* Barth was in prison."

For a moment there was an appraising look in Ellie's eyes, almost a smile. "You're still dying for it to be Father Montgomery, aren't you?"

Cardozo looked over, surprised. "That's crazy."

"I agree."

When Cardozo returned to the precinct after lunch, he found a visitor waiting in his office. She was dark-skinned and slender and she was blond. At least the three-foot curly acrylic thing on her head was blond.

"Looking for me?" He closed the door behind him.

She slowly turned her eyes toward him. They were the inquisitive eyes of a small forest creature. "I heard a rumor down in the meat market. You're looking for *me*."

She rose, rippling with muscular curves, and he realized she was not a true female. She had dressed unisex—jeans that puddled around her jogging shoes and an oversize nylon jacket. She held out a hand. The gesture was ladylike in the dated way of a 1940s movie. He saw that she was holding his business card.

"You *are* Vincent Cardozo?"

"That's right. Who are you?"

"The name on my birth certificate is Lii Kaiiawaniwauii—there's no point spelling it for you, it's Hawaiian, like me." She saw him notice her ivory cameo ring. "Like it?" She showed him the peacock engraved on it. "I found it in a flea market. It's my good luck charm." She dropped fluidly back into the chair. "To keep things simple, I go by the *nom de street* of Jonquil—just like the fragrant yellow flower. Do you by any chance like fragrant yellow flowers?"

"I do. You know, you don't look at all like your photo."

"Which photo?"

"The ones Father Montgomery took." Cardozo opened his desk drawer and handed Jonquil the three photographs.

"Well, if it isn't guess who. But honey, that was then. I change my look three, four times a year. Have to keep the thrill fresh. What you're seeing is a new and even more thrilling me."

"Who gave you the rose you're wearing in those shots?"

"What makes you think it was a gift?"

"I'm asking."

"As a matter of fact, an admirer did give it to me. I have many admirers and many of them give me gifts. I'm not going to name names . . . unless"—Jonquil opened her purse and popped a cigarette into a holder and angled it toward Cardozo—"unless you tell my parole officer that I've been a good little girl. Is that a deal?"

He lit her cigarette. "What kind of dates did you have with Father Joe?"

She blew out a thin jet of smoke. "I date several gentlemen of the clergy—Episcopalian, Catholic, Jewish, Muslim. They tend to be very needy puppies."

"In what way?"

After a puckered silence, she seemed to decide that she could risk saying more. "A lot are working their way out of the s/m closet. They like to tie me up."

"Tie you up with what?"

"You're truly hungering for the sickening details, aren't you? They use whatever's handy. Ratty old leather belts will do."

"Leather belts around your feet?"

"And my hands too." She was flicking Cardozo with her glance. "Never forget the hands."

"And did Father Joe ever tie you up?"

"He wouldn't be the first Father who did, but could we save the specifics until my parole officer has gotten a glowing report from you?"

"Anything you like."

"No, honey." She touched his hand. Her touch was gentle, almost passive, without being in the least soft. Cardozo detected sinew in that wrist. "Anything *you* like."

"Would I be insulting you if I asked—"

"Please, insult me. I love it and I have a feeling you're good at it."

"Did you meet Father Joe through the St. Andrew's prostitute outreach program?"

"The dreaded P-word." She smiled. "No, darling, you would not be insulting me, and no, we did not, because St. Andrew's didn't have a prostitute outreach program when we met. As a matter of fact, it was I who gave Father Joe the idea for that program."

"Then how did you and Father Joe meet?"

"Through the *prisoners* outreach."

He stared at her. "Father Joe has an outreach program to prisoners?"

"Bet your ass."

"Which prison?"

"Dannemora. My old alma mater. That was my male period."

"I appreciate your giving me this time," Cardozo said. "I hope I'm not putting you to too much trouble."

Eloise Barth led him into the living room. It seemed to him that something had changed. The children's toys had been put away. There was less furniture than when he'd last seen the room: the piano was gone.

"It's no trouble—I want to see people." She walked just a little slowly, just a little bent over, like a very young old woman. "I want to talk about Martin—I want to understand."

She sat in an armchair, letting him take the sofa. A stillness flowed through the apartment.

"Your children are away?" Cardozo said.

"They're with their grandmother in Virginia." She exuded a melancholy stoicism. "They'll stay with her till things settle down."

"How are they doing?"

"They're just fine, thank you."

He thought of the years she and her husband had been together, all the energy and hope they had put into their family and home. He felt enormously sad for her.

"What is it you want to discuss with me?" she said.

"Father Joe Montgomery's name has surfaced in connection with your husband."

"Father Joe saved him." It was a flat statement of fact.

"Saved him how?"

She passed a hand across her face, pushing back a strand of hair. Her hair was dark but he could see that it had begun to turn a little at the temples.

"Martin was never especially religious. It took the shock of seeing the inside of a prison for him to realize he needed to get right with God. Luckily, Father Joe and the Barabbas Society were there."

"What's the Barabbas Society?"

"Priests and ministers and concerned lay people. Their political goal is to achieve racial justice in prison sentencing. Their pastoral goal is to help the wounded souls of the men and women in our prisons. To purge the hatred and the fear that drove them to crime in the first place."

"And how did Father Montgomery go about achieving this with your husband?"

Eloise Barth's wide brown eyes came around to rest on Cardozo. They had a bleary look, as if she hadn't slept in a long time. "Father Joe listened to Martin, encouraged him to tell what was in his heart, told him God loved him no matter what. That meant a lot to Martin. You see, all his life, he never felt that anyone really . . ." She broke off.

Cardozo let her take the time she needed. "If this is too painful a subject, please forgive me. And you may not know the answer. But did Father Joe suggest to your husband that he confess to the murder of the runaway girl?"

Eloise Barth exhaled, releasing tension. "I know he helped Martin come to that decision. I know he supported that decision."

"But would you say Father Montgomery persuaded your husband to confess?"

She looked surprised. "He didn't pressure him, if that's what you're asking."

"Is there any chance that Father Montgomery put the idea in your husband's head?"

"What idea?"

"Confessing to the killing."

She drew in a long breath. "Father Joe created a space where Martin felt safe admitting his guilt and discussing it."

"But do you know for a fact that your husband *was* guilty?"

"What are you saying? A jury found him guilty."

"Of the first crime. But not the second. Did he actually kill that girl?"

Eloise Barth did not answer. Cardozo could feel a cold current running just under the silence. She rose from the chair.

"It wasn't only Father Joe who counseled Martin to confess."

Cardozo watched her. "But he was the first?"

"No." An odd little glow came to her face, as if she'd set a trap in a game of chess and he'd fallen into it. "Father Chuck Romero of St. Veronica's in Queens also works for Barabbas. He was the first."

Her eyes were making such a show of hard-contact openness that Cardozo had to wonder what it was that she was not telling him.

"I'm sorry, Mrs. Barth, but that doesn't quite answer my question."

"Then I don't understand your question."

"Are you sure your husband killed the girl?"

"Aren't *you* sure? You have the proof. You took it from his closet."

"But you're his wife. What do you feel?"

"Feelings aren't facts, Lieutenant." She hesitated. "But if you want my feelings—I feel that for many years I didn't know the man I was married to. I feel that in the last year and a half I've come to know him. And to accept him. And yes, I'm sure he killed that girl. And I'm sure that without Father Joe and Father Chuck, Martin would still be carrying that crime in his heart."

TWENTY-SIX

"**D**oes it strike you there are some odd differences between the crimes?" Cardozo said.

Assistant District Attorney Harvey Thoms reached for the coffeemaker and refilled Cardozo's cup. "There are always differences."

"But these are the wrong kind. And too many for both killings to be the work of the same man." Cardozo sipped. The coffee was a mocha hazelnut vanilla blend, and it tasted borderline cloying. "The girl was a sadistic killing. Martin Barth didn't know her. He had no reason to kill her except he wanted the kick. The crime was carefully planned. She was bound and tortured and then dismembered and disposed of in a public park. Whereas . . ."

Thoms leaned back from his desk. His swivel chair creaked. He was watching Cardozo with subtly bored pale blue eyes.

"Whereas Barth knew the lady accountant. She was about to turn him in for breaking company rules. It was a straightforward utilitarian murder: shut the bitch's mouth. He struck her on the head and left her dead in her apartment. If there was any planning, it escapes me. More like pure impulse."

"Come on, Vince—a killer can't change his M.O.?"

"There's no law against it—but you don't often see it with sadistic murders."

Thoms's hand rested lightly on the Basket Case file, fingers drumming. "Dr. Vergil Muller says Barth didn't learn to be a sadist till he killed the accountant."

"Do you trust Muller's judgment?"

"He's done good work for the department. He's knocked down

insanity defenses, gotten convictions where we wouldn't have stood a chance without him."

"But we have dangling threads."

"Such as?"

"The van Barth says he rented exactly resembles trucks owned by Father Joe Montgomery and Father Chuck Romero."

Thoms sighed. "A van is not a one-of-a-kind product."

"Father Joe and Father Chuck were both involved with kids very much like the girl in the basket—and while Barth was in prison, they counseled him to confess to her murder."

Thoms frowned. "Am I hearing you right? It sounds like you're saying Barth took a fall for a priest."

"Or for *someone*. Look at the timetable and tell me it's coincidence. Monday the body is discovered; Tuesday we start questioning priests. Wednesday the priests are counseling Barth. A week later Barth confesses."

"How would Barth know so many details of the killing if he wasn't the murderer? The basket was held back from the newspapers. The dismemberment was held back. The nipple ring was held back. Barth not only knew about that ring, he had it in his possession. The ring links him to the victim and it validates the confession."

"One of the priests could have given Barth the ring. Barth could have slipped it to his wife on one of her visits."

"Why would Barth confess to someone else's murder?"

"He's in prison anyway, serving a life sentence—what's he got to lose? A second killing shows he's insane. An insanity defense could get him out earlier."

"No way we're going to allow a change of plea. So he's got nothing to gain by going that route."

"My gut still says we're making a mistake if we close the case."

Harvey Thoms's features locked into a mask. Agreeable. Interested. Let's-talk-it-over. "Have you got any proof against any other person?"

"One or two possible leads." It wasn't exactly a lie: more of an exaggeration.

"I've got files full of possible leads that never paid off." Thoms's left hand made a sort of breezy wave toward a stack of folders so tall it was almost toppling. "Next to dope, homicide is the fastest growth industry in this town. There's just not time to cross every *t* and dot ever *i*. Especially not for a Jane Doe that nobody even knew or cared about."

"Somebody knew her. Somebody cared."

The door to the inner office opened and a tall, heavyset man stepped through. His gray hair seemed to have a wave styled into it. "Harvey, have we got the documents in the Jennings case?"

Harvey Thoms turned. "Came in this morning. . . . Oh, Bill, I'd like you to meet Lieutenant Vince Cardozo. Vince, Bill Kodahl."

District Attorney Kodahl extended his hand. He was dressed in Armani's gentle look, a baggy but expensive suit in summerweight gray. He was wearing a spotless white shirt with monogrammed cuff links. His fingernails gleamed. "It's a pleasure to meet the cop who broke Ms. Basket Case."

"I'm not sure we've broken it quite yet, sir."

"Lieutenant, you did an A-plus job."

Cardozo could feel the D.A. reaching for charm—reaching hard.

"I've given a lot of study to Martin Barth's deposition," Kodahl said, "and believe me, it plays. I'm closing the case."

Cardozo returned to the Vanderbilt Garden that night. He sat on a stone bench just inside the unlocked gate. It was a desolate place after sunset. A lone light glowed above the lilac bushes. Trees were grooved lines in the darkness.

Above him, a solitary star popped out in a space between clouds. There was a footstep behind him. He turned. It was Ellie.

"How did I know when you didn't show up at the restaurant you'd be here?"

He remembered. "I forgot we had a date—I'm sorry."

"It wasn't a date. I just thought it might intimidate my ex a little if there was another cop at the table besides me."

"How did it go?"

"He says he can't find a buyer at the price I want, so why don't I accept the price he says he can get, or buy the house myself. He's cheating me. I know it. He knows I know it. And he knows I haven't got time to peddle a two-bedroom in Westchester." She sat down beside Cardozo on the bench. "Don't ever get divorced, Vince. Divorce is worse than marriage. It never ends."

Neither of them said anything. For a moment the dark was full of tiny night sounds. Crickets. Creatures rustling in the leaves. Birds. And then a rumbling wave of traffic gathered in the distance.

"What are you doing here, Vince?"

"I'm thinking of that girl."

"Don't."

"Those gold rings in her nipples. She was an exhibitionist. She wanted people to know she was alive. She want to be noticed and seen and heard and felt. And instead she wound up in that box— so far from all the other people in the world."

Ellie looked at him. "Vince. She wasn't your daughter. She wasn't your sister's daughter."

He knew Ellie and her impulse to comfort. "She was somebody's daughter."

"The case is closed."

"Something is very wrong." He patted his stomach. "I can feel it here."

"What you're feeling is, you haven't eaten since you had that hot dog and papaya juice at one o'clock." She stood up. "Come on. I'll watch you eat dinner. My treat."

"Guys who do this kind of stuff don't just do it once and stop." Cardozo stood. "Believe me, we're going to hear from this killer again."

TWENTY-SEVEN

The buzz in Pablo's head was getting stronger. The slash of light falling across the wall flickered unsteadily. Pablo squinted the framed Gothic-lettered mottoes into focus:

Suffer the little children to come unto me.
My kingdom is not of this world.
The kingdom of God is within you.

The place reeked dizzyingly of incense.

Pablo's head slammed against a half-open door. The unexpected pain jolted him momentarily out of his grogginess. "Christ, what the hell was in that pink pill?"

The shadow ahead of him turned. "The same as what's always in it."

"This one's hitting me different—I really need to sleep."

"You can sleep later. Come on."

Forcing his eyes to stay open, Pablo hobbled along behind the shadow. The hallway was dark and cold. Somewhere an air conditioner was roaring.

He shivered and started down a flight of stairs. His foot slipped. He skidded down three steps.

Now he was being helped up. He couldn't tell how many hands were holding him. Nausea swept him. "I need the bathroom."

"Why didn't you think of that upstairs?"

"I didn't need to go upstairs. Is there a bathroom in here?" Pablo pushed to his feet and reached toward a door handle.

"Just hold off a minute, will you?"

Something in that voice was wrong—something in the moment was off-center. There was barely time to register the fact, no time to understand it.

"I can't hold off." Pablo pulled the door open.

A hand seized him by the shoulder. A glint of metal sliced down through the air and then blackness fell.

"By any chance," Douglas Moseley said, "have you ever met Father Joe Montgomery over at St. Andrew's Church?"

"I had a little business with Father Montgomery," Cardozo said. "About fourteen months ago. How do you know him?"

Moseley headed the public relations firm of Moseley and Abrams. They were said to pocket twelve and a half percent of every contract let by the city of New York, and last year a tabloid had uncovered a declared taxable income in excess of five hundred million. Cardozo had to wonder how one of the most influential power brokers in city politics was linked to an elderly cleric best known for staging musical reviews.

"Father Joe and I are both on the board of Operation Second Chance."

"I'm not familiar with Operation Second Chance."

Moseley gave him a patrician blue stare above a beaked nose. "It's a psychiatric rehabilitation program for troubled youth."

"A city program?"

The stare chilled. "Cofinanced by matching city funds. Why do you ask?"

Behind his desk, Captain Tom O'Reilly cleared his throat, pushed a lock of graying hair off his forehead. "What Vince is trying to determine is, what sort of position Father Montgomery occupies in the unofficial heirarchy of the city. Vince naturally gives priority to city cases."

Moseley nodded. "Father Joe has a real commitment to New York City's youth and kids. He deserves every possible priority and consideration."

"Vince will see that he gets them."

They were sitting in O'Reilly's office. The captain had one of the three corner offices in the precinct, and the only one to get direct sun. Noon light bounced off a shelf of citations and awards, winked off the silver frames of family photos. On the shelf below, in shadow, photos showed O'Reilly clasping the hands of celebrities and politicians.

"I gather Father Montgomery is in some kind of trouble?" Cardozo said.

It was O'Reilly who answered. "Last night at eleven forty-three, a 911 call came in. A neighbor of St. Andrew's rectory heard breaking glass. A squad car went up. The cops had to pound on the door till the assistant rector came from across the street. Inside the rectory they found a young man unconscious on the floor. Father Joe was sitting in a chair."

"In shock," Moseley said. "There were signs of a break-in. The most probable explanation is that Father Joe struck the burglar in self-defense."

"We're sure the man was a burglar?" Cardozo said.

"It stands to reason," Moseley said.

"What was he struck with?" Cardozo said.

"Some kind of heavy object," O'Reilly said. "The reason we called you in—he died an hour ago."

Silence fell.

"Father Montgomery's been taken to the hospital," Moseley said. "He's still in shock."

"If there's nothing more to it than what you're telling me," Cardozo said, "the worst he's looking at is justifiable homicide."

"I'd hate to see him tarred with a charge like that," Moseley said. "He's given so much of himself to the community. And he's having health trouble. I wish there was some way we could spare him added difficulty."

O'Reilly was watching Cardozo. *Don't just sit there, you bastard,* his eyes screamed: *help me out of this.* "We'll do our best—won't we, Vince."

"Sure. Our very best."

TWENTY-EIGHT

Cardozo pushed the doorbell.

A young woman, small and Latin-looking, opened the door. She had her hair up in a dish-towel turban.

Cardozo and Ellie introduced themselves and showed their ID's.

The young woman stepped aside, wordlessly inviting them in.

"Would you mind telling us your name?" Cardozo said.

"Anna."

"And what's your last name?"

"Orgonza."

"And how are you connected with the rectory?"

"I clean it."

"How long have you worked for St. Andrew's?"

"Two hours."

Footsteps came bursting down the hallway. Cardozo recognized the blond assistant rector he had met here fourteen months ago.

"Hi, I'm Bonnie Ruskay—assistant rector of St. Andrew's. You're from the police?"

"Ellie Siegel."

"Vince Cardozo."

"We've met before," Bonnie Ruskay said. "Last year."

"That's right." Cardozo was surprised she remembered. Pleasantly surprised.

A man in an expensively cut business suit had followed her into the hallway. She turned to include him. "May I introduce David Lowndes, our attorney?"

"We've met," Cardozo said.

"Oh, yes." It was obvious from Lowndes's blandly handsome face that he didn't remember. "It's good to see you again."

"Is there any way I can be of help?" Bonnie Ruskay asked. "Or make your work easier?"

"It would be a help if you showed us around."

"I'll be glad to." Bonnie Ruskay watched Lou Stein and the six-person crime-scene crew carrying their paraphernalia into the rectory. There was dismay in her eyes.

"Do you contemplate a complaint against the church," Lowndes asked, "or against any of its staff?"

Cardozo shook his head. "Not at this point."

"All the same, Bonnie, play it safe." Lowndes's tone was joking. At the same time it wasn't joking at all.

"David and I feel the intruder broke in this way." Bonnie Ruskay led Cardozo and Ellie into Father Montgomery's study.

Cardozo examined the window. A small pane near the lock had been shattered. Most of the glass was missing. Only three jagged fragments remained clinging to the puttied sash bars.

Cardozo turned. His eye scanned the oriental rug where the splintered glass should have fallen. But it hadn't. Nothing flashed or twinkled. "Funny, there's no glass on the rug."

"The maid already vacuumed in here," Bonnie Ruskay said.

"That was before the young man died," David Lowndes said. "Before we knew we were dealing with homicide."

Cardozo told Lou Stein to mark the vacuum cleaner bag as evidence and take it to the lab.

On the wall, posters for Father Joe's musicals glowed in their gold-leafed frames. Cardozo's eye went to *Zip Your Pinafore*. Sally Manfredo's first featured role. "Didn't Father Montgomery keep a box full of photos of his performers?"

"Yes," Bonnie Ruskay said. "His talent pool."

"Is it still in his desk?"

"I don't know." She threw her lawyer a questioning glance.

"There seems to have been a break-in at that window," Lowndes said. "Which gives the police the right to examine anything in this room."

Bonnie Ruskay opened three drawers before she found the shoe box stuffed with photos. She placed it on top of the desk.

"Thanks," Cardozo said. "I'll take very good care of it."

"This is probably what killed the housebreaker." Lou Stein stood in the doorway. His plastic-gloved hand was holding an old-fashioned steam iron—a heavy, blackly corroded object actually made out of iron. "Apparently, it was being used as a doorstop." He pointed to several dark curving marks on the maple parquet floor. "And we have a nice set of fingerprints." He indicated a faint black-powdered pattern of concentric lines on the handle of the iron.

Cardozo swung the door through a 45-degree arc. It opened into the hallway. Something bothered him. His eye ran along the floor, stopping at the two dark curved marks. The iron could have been used as a doorstop; it could have scraped the parquet. That much he could accept. But there was a third mark.

"What's this mark?" His foot touched a straight-line dent just inside the door. "Think the iron made this one too?"

"Possibly. But far greater force was applied."

Cardozo swung the door open. He took a chair from the hallway and set it in front of the doorway. "Hold me steady, Lou."

He stood on the seat and examined the top of the door. There was a small dust-free area. He examined the half-inch protrusion of lintel at the top of the door frame. There was another area without dust, and the two areas lined up.

"Alternate scenario." He stepped down from the chair. "The door was left open three or four inches. The iron was placed up there, balanced between the top of the door and the door frame."

"A booby trap," Lou Stein said.

Cardozo nodded. "The intruder came through the door, and gravity did the rest."

"That's better, isn't it?" Bonnie Ruskay stood gazing at the door frame. "I mean, better for Father Joe. If he didn't strike the intruder himself?"

"Why don't you ask your lawyer?" Cardozo said.

Lowndes did not have a happy face. "Striking an intruder would be considered legitimate force. Rigging a lethal device would not be."

"Not even in his own home?" Bonnie Ruskay said.

"This part of the rectory is Father Joe's office," Lowndes said, "not his home. The public is admitted."

"Do you know of any reason," Cardozo said, "why Father Montgomery might have rigged a booby trap?"

"Yes, I do." Bonnie Ruskay pushed her hair back from her head. "He was mugged in the park three weeks ago. The experience left him feeling extremely vulnerable. He mentioned several times since then that he thought he'd heard someone trying to break into the rectory."

"Did he say anything was missing?"

"He didn't mention anything specifically."

"Do you know of anything missing?"

She looked toward her lawyer and then she shook her head. "Not offhand—but the windowsill's been rearranged."

Cardozo followed her to the window.

"The golf trophy's been moved to the table," she said.

Cardozo stared at the sterling silver cup with its engraving of two crossed golf clubs. His eye went to the window. In the courtyard outside, something sparkled on the cobblestones.

Lowndes was watching. "Did you find something, Lieutenant?"

"The intruder didn't break in this way," Cardozo said. "The pane was broken from inside. Which is why glass landed outside."

"Why would anyone do that?" Bonnie Ruskay said.

"You'd have to ask the person who did it." Cardozo snapped a finger, catching Lou Stein's attention. "Lou, would you get some of the glass from outside, see if it matches the broken pane? And we'd better have a look at the other windows in the rectory."

Father Montgomery's upstairs apartment was a far cry from the dapper photographer-ready manse that Cardozo recalled. The heavier furniture had been shoved into a sort of barricade by the window. Clothing had been thrown over chairs, ashtrays left unemptied, deli wrappings tossed on the floor.

"I don't understand this at all." Bonnie Ruskay was clearly startled at the state of the room. "Father Joe was usually much tidier than this."

Cardozo sniffed a half-full tumbler from the bedside table. He smelled rum. The drink had left a wet ring on the table. Cardozo wiped it with the side of his sleeve and set the glass back down next to a stack of paperbacks. He glanced at the titles: mysteries and thrillers and horror novels.

"Father Joe has insomnia," Bonnie Ruskay said. "He reads himself to sleep."

A bottle sat on the floor beside the bed. Cardozo picked it up. According to the label, it was 150-proof Jamaican rum. "Is Father Montgomery a solitary drinker?"

"Not that I know of," Bonnie Ruskay said.

"Was he having company in his bedroom?"

"I don't know. I don't live in the rectory."

Cardozo uncapped the bottle and passed it under his nose. The fumes almost made him gag. "Unusual stuff. Potent."

"I give him a bottle every year for his birthday."

"Then he must like it."

"I give that rum to several priests for their birthdays. None of them has ever complained."

Cardozo recapped the bottle. "Aside from the mugging, has anything unusual happened in Father Montgomery's life recently?"

"Unusual?" Bonnie Ruskay smiled. "Father Joe was planning to expand the church's condom outreach program. Does that count as unusual?"

"You'd have to tell me."

"A few parishioners were raising a fuss. But that was to be expected. Have you ever seen our newsletter?" She handed Cardozo a leaflet from a stack on the mantelpiece.

"You gave me several," he said, "last year."

"Oh, yes. I remember. Well, that's the latest. You'll see that we really haven't changed much."

"May I keep it?"

"Of course."

Cardozo folded the newsletter and slipped it into his pocket. His eye traveled to the king-sized bed. It looked as if a litter of unsupervised puppies had been calling it home for the last month. The bedsheets had been balled into ropelike coils. The exposed portions of the mattress were dotted with cigarette burns and stained with spilled drinks.

"Father Joe's been trying to cut down on cigarettes." Bonnie Ruskay sounded embarrassed. "He knows he has a problem."

"I take it the cleaning lady has been boycotting this part of the house?"

"Anna's new." The embarrassed tone became apologetic. "She hasn't had time to get to this part of the rectory."

"What about the one before? Is this the way she kept house?"

"Olga was a good worker."

"Then how did all this happen?"

"Is this relevant?" David Lowndes sounded edgy. He stooped to retrieve a Milky Way candy bar wrapper from the rug. He placed it delicately in the fireplace on top of birch logs already laid for a fire.

"Olga stopped showing up two weeks ago," Bonnie Ruskay said.

"Did she give any reason?"

"Excuse me," Lowndes said. "How is this discussion relevant to the break-in?"

"What difference does it make?" Bonnie Ruskay turned almost angrily to the lawyer. "So the world learns that Father Joe's gifts did not extend to housekeeping. Big deal."

Nor, Cardozo reflected, did Father Joe's gifts extend to interior design. The wall decorations were jarringly juxtaposed—an ebony crucifix had been mounted alongside polished spurs and saddle and a horsewhip.

"The bishop of Kenya gave that to Father Joe." Bonnie Ruskay nodded toward the crucifix. "The cowboy things are props."

"Props for what?"

"A musical set in the Old West. We put on an annual amateur theatrical."

Next to the whip, a photo framed in gold leaf showed a muscled samurai executioner holding a curved sword over a bound man's neck.

"That's from another of Father Joe's musicals. It was a rap update of the *Mikado*."

The executioner's arms were heavily tattooed. They reminded Cardozo of convicts' arms.

"Is Father Montgomery still working with convicted felons?"

"If you mean the Barabbas Society, yes—he was working harder than ever until he got mugged."

"And are you a member of the Barabbas Society too?"

She looked him directly in the eye, as though he had challenged her. "I am."

"No one broke in this way." Ellie had been examining the bedroom window. She squeezed her way back through the chairs and drop-leaf table that blocked it. "What about the bathroom?"

Cardozo flicked on the bathroom light. He crossed to the window. It was unbroken, locked from the inside.

There was a strong smell of mildew, strongest in the neighborhood of the bathtub. The plastic shower curtain had a film over the lower half, and it was dangling by three hooks, as though a falling person had grabbed it for support.

The tub had two gray rings dating from distinctly different epochs.

Soiled clothes were spilling out of the hamper. The toilet had been used as an ashtray. So had the sink.

Cardozo swung open the mirrored door of the medicine cabinet. The shelves were a jumble of toiletries, over-the-counter remedies, and prescription drugs. As he swung the door shut he caught Lowndes's reflection from the doorway.

"I thought you were looking for signs of a break-in. No one broke in through the medicine cabinet, did they?"

"No, and they didn't break in through that window either."

Bonnie Ruskay appeared in the doorway. "Would you like to see the guest room?" She led Cardozo and Ellie down the hall.

The guest room was sparsely furnished—there was a bed, a table, a lamp, a chest of drawers, and a chair. The only decorative touches were a gray shag rug on the floor and several Gothic-lettered mottoes simply framed on the walls:

Suffer the little children to come unto me.
The kingdom of God is within you.
You must become again as a child.

Cardozo tried the window. It was locked from the inside. He examined the panes and found them intact.

A smell of old incense mingled with all the other old smells in the room. On the bureau, a conical mound of ash had heaped in a small copper bowl. An ashtray beside it overflowed with cigarette butts. Ashes had spilled onto a packet that had once held two condoms and two servings of spermicidal lubricant but now held only one of each. Bright red lettering urged, *For God's Sake, Keep It Safe!*

"Those are ours," Bonnie Ruskay said.

Cardozo looked at her.

"The church has a safe-sex program. We distribute condoms, spermicide, and literature to young people—and to prostitutes."

"I remember," Cardozo said.

The same puppies who had worked over Father Joe's bed seemed to have done the same to the guest bed, only more so. The bedclothes were tangled with bath towels and underdrawers; the sheets were stained with what appeared to be spilled cola or coffee. Two bobby pins and an unrolled but unused condom lay in a valley on the pillow.

"Someone's been staying over," Cardozo said. "Any idea who?"

"I honestly couldn't say." Bonnie Ruskay seemed uneasy. "As I told you, I don't sleep in the rectory. My apartment is across the street. So I'm not always aware of the minutiae of Father Joe's social or working life."

A pile of Milky Way candy bar wrappers and Big Mac burger packing had been balled together on the table.

"Does Father Montgomery eat candy bars and Big Macs?"

"I don't know his private eating habits."

Copies of *Popular Mechanics, Soldier of Fortune, Guns & Ammo,* and *Trains* had been stacked on the chair. Cardozo leafed through them. They'd been thumbed over; ads and articles were ripped out. "And are these magazines his usual reading matter?"

"I don't know what he reads in private. They may not be his. Sometimes Father Joe takes in a runaway for a night or two."

Cardozo glanced at Bonnie Ruskay when she said that, and he saw Lowndes glancing at her at the same time. There was a warning in the lawyer's eyes and she couldn't have missed it.

"Have you ever met these runaways?" Cardozo said.

"Not all of them."

Lowndes cleared his throat. "How does that window look?"

"No one broke through it." Cardozo peered through a doorway. "Is this the bathroom?"

"It is." Ellie stood by the bathroom window, staring down at the roof of the garage. "Someone could have climbed up on the roof and got in this way."

The window was unlocked and open a crack.

"Did you find it that way?"

She nodded. "Haven't touched a thing."

A bath towel had been wadded into the space between the towel rack and the tile wall. Cardozo touched it.

The bath towel was dry. So was the soap. So was the bath mat.

He crossed to the sink. There was nothing in the medicine cabinet except an almost exhausted bottle of Advil and two more of the church's For God's Sake, Keep It Safe! packets, unopened.

A balding, limp-bristled toothbrush sat in a water glass on the sink rim next to a plastic hairbrush. A crack in the hairbrush handle had been patched with electrician's tape.

Cardozo tore a sheet from the toilet paper roll so as not to leave prints. He held the hairbrush up to the light. There were dark brown hairs in the bristles.

"So you think he broke in through that window," Lowndes said, "and brushed his hair before he went downstairs?"

"Your guess is a lot more colorful than mine, counselor." Cardozo set the brush back on the sink.

As he came back into the bedroom, he took his house keys out of his pocket, tossed them into the air, caught them. Showing the world the debonair side of Vince Cardozo. He tossed them again, didn't catch them, kicked them accidentally-on-purpose under the bed. Showing the world the klutzy side of Vince Cardozo.

He got down on his hands and knees. Dust balls had claimed

the space beneath the bed as their own ecological niche. He stifled a sneeze, yanked three generous strands from the gray shag rug, and slipped them into his fist with the keys.

TWENTY-NINE

A butler opened the door.

"Could I speak to Mrs. Schuyler, please?" Ellie showed her ID.

He seemed unimpressed. "Is she expecting you?"

"I doubt it."

"If you'd be so good as to wait here, I'll try to locate her."

He left Ellie standing in a small marble foyer. She could see through a long living room out French windows into a garden. The space bustled with big hair and jewels and couture. Voices chattered and a small orchestra was playing show tunes of the fifties. Uniformed servants circulated with trays of drinks and canapés. Gusts of laughter broke like whitecaps dotting the sea.

A small, very slender woman approached. She had gray-blond hair, puffed and ringleted, and too much suntan, and she was squinting. "Yes? I'm Samantha Schuyler."

Ellie introduced herself. "I need to ask one or two questions about the 911 call you made yesterday."

"I only have a moment."

"This will only take a moment."

"Would you mind the polo practice room? It's quieter." Mrs. Schuyler led the way up a flight of stairs into a room that housed a high wooden sawhorse with a saddle seat. There was no other place to sit.

"In your 911 call you said you heard a scream and breaking glass. Do you have anything to add to that?"

"Add to it?" Samantha Schuyler was thoughtful. "No."

"Or to change?"

"To change?" Mrs. Schuyler seemed surprised. "No. Someone screamed as if they were in shock—or pain. Frankly, it sounded as if they were screaming for their life . . . although I've never actually heard anyone scream for their life, so I couldn't swear."

Ellie was taking notes—not an easy thing to do standing. "Was the person who screamed male or female?"

"It could have been a very hysterical man—or a very hysterical woman." Mrs. Schuyler stood against the wall. Above her, somebody's dour ancestor, mounted on horseback and captured in oil paint, glared down unblinkingly. "Screams are screams—there's no particular gender to them. At least there wasn't to this one."

"You say somebody screamed, and glass broke. You're sure of that order. First the scream and then the breaking glass. Not the other way around."

Samantha Schuyler was silent a moment, running something carefully through her head. "I can hear it now. That person screams. Then the glass shatters. That's the order."

"How soon after the scream did the glass shatter?"

Samantha Schuyler walked to the window. As she moved, she flashed. She was wearing diamonds every place that a diamond could be attached to a body or dress. She stood gazing down at the party in her garden. "I wasn't standing here with a stopwatch."

"You were standing there?"

"Right here."

Ellie looked out. Across the garden, you could see the Gothic leaded windows of the rectory. One of the panes on the ground story was broken. "Could you estimate the time between the scream and the breaking glass?"

"It could have been two or three minutes. If it had been just the scream, I wouldn't have thought anything. After all, screams are par for the course over there. It could have been just the usual church wildness. But when glass broke, I knew something was going on. I've never heard them destroy property before."

"You used the words, *the usual church wildness.* What do you mean by that?"

"You know churches nowadays."

"I'm sorry to say I don't."

"It's only gossip. If you haven't heard it, I really don't know if I should repeat it. . . ."

"Mrs. Schuyler, a young man has died."

Samantha Schuyler's eyes swung around immediately, "Another one?" She caught herself. "I mean . . . who?"

"We don't know yet. But I hope you'll tell me anything you know that might shed light on it."

"I'm hardly a judge of what sheds light on what."

"You say you've often heard screams coming from the church."

"From the rectory. They don't scream in the church . . . yet."

"Do you have any idea who's screaming or why?"

"I certainly do. They give youth dances and wild parties. They're always keeping the neighbors awake. I've even heard rumors—" She broke off. "But you don't want rumors."

"What are the rumors?"

"Drug use and sex. That sounds like an exaggeration, I realize. But you have to know the background. The city wanted to put a methadone clinic in the neighborhood—naturally, we in the neighborhood objected."

"Naturally."

Samantha Schuyler glanced at Ellie. Her eyes said she detected irony and didn't like it. "The upshot was, St. Andrew's volunteered to lend space for a methadone clinic once a week. So now there are strange young men and women—and some not so young men and women—going in and out of that church all hours of the day and night. Rough-looking types—crazy, stoned, noisy. One step up from street people and criminals. You can imagine what that's done to the quality of life around here."

"Yes, I can." Ellie tried to sound sympathetic.

"*Then* the city wanted to put in a soup kitchen. Same story. We objected, St. Andrew's got around us and opened its own soup kitchen. Exactly the same people show up: Tuesdays, it's free methadone; Fridays, it's free lunch. And *now* the city wants to set up a homeless dorm. We're fighting it, but if we succeed in blocking it, no one doubts for a minute that St. Andrew's will open its garage to the homeless. Maybe it's a good thing this has happened. Maybe this man's death will focus attention on what St. Andrew's is doing."

"And just what is St. Andrew's doing?"

"Destabilizing the community. There's a lot more going on over there than soul-saving or counseling or consciousness-raising. It was inevitable that something ghastly was going to happen. And it's high time the police looked into it."

Cardozo placed the two case folders side by side on his desk top. The girl who had been discovered fourteen months ago in the Vanderbilt Garden; the housebreaker who had been discovered less than one day ago in the rectory of St. Andrew's Church.

It didn't seem likely there could be a connection. But still, the same church was involved in both cases, and it wouldn't hurt to check for similarities and rule out the possibility.

He opened the first folder. CASE UP61 #11214 OF THE 22ND PRECINCT . . . JANE DOE, CAUCASIAN, HOMICIDE BY MEANS UNKNOWN . . .

The skull-face of Ms. Basket Case gawked at him from the top page, eyeless yet staring. Two blue forms had been stapled to the folder. These were DD5 supplementary complaint reports, the progress update required at least twice yearly on all ongoing cases. Technically, any unsolved case was ongoing whether the detective had time to continue the investigation or not.

Since no court had passed on Martin Barth's confession, Ms. Basket Case was in a legal sense unsolved and therefore still open. Which was not at all the same as active.

Cardozo's updates—both identically worded—tersely summarized the situation: *There has been no progress on this case since last report.* These were the bottom carbons of triplicate sets, and his handwriting had come through faintly and unevenly.

After a moment, he opened the second folder.

CASE UP61 #12703 OF THE 22ND PRECINCT . . . JOE DOE, CAUCASIAN, HOMICIDE BY MEANS TO BE DETERMINED. A Polaroid flash shot showed the face of the housebreaker—sallow, shut-eyed, dead.

Cardozo's eye compared the numbers on the two cases.

He frowned, thinking for a moment that a computer must have goofed. The cumulative total of cases reported to the precinct couldn't have jumped fifteen hundred in a year and two months. Even counting all the lost credit cards and runaway dogs, all the stolen bikes and incidents of gender harassment, there was no way it could have climbed that fast.

He turned over a commissioner's directive and did a rough calculation on the back. Figure a 12 percent growth in real crime—a conservative estimate. Figure a 50 percent growth in nonsense crime, the borderline stuff that the mayor had mandated tracking and if necessary inflating, so that growth in paper crime would dwarf growth in real crime.

Cardozo realized the total was just about right. And—unless you happened to be the mayor or the mayor's minion—it was also meaningless.

"How was I supposed to know he had a pacemaker?" a voice from the squad room wailed. "He was a bum, he was stealing my garbage!"

A town house dweller on East Eighty-second Street had found a street person going through her trash bin. Having paid six hundred dollars in fines for unbagged trash, she'd lost her temper and kicked the man. He had dropped dead on the sidewalk. Detective Henahan was taking the woman's statement.

"How could he afford a pacemaker? I work for a living, and I can't afford a pacemaker!"

Cardozo got up and closed the door of his cubicle. He took his phone to the window and called Dan Hippolito at the medical examiner's office. "Dan, do you remember that autopsy you did last year, the Jane Doe we found in a Styrofoam basket?"

"I remember. Vanderbilt Garden. There wasn't a hell of a lot to work with."

"Could you do me a favor? You'll be getting an unidentified male housebreaker from St. Andrew's rectory."

"He's already here. Came in a half hour ago."

"Check for similarities between him and Jane Doe. Anything at all—no matter how small, or how dumb."

"I'll look." Dan's tone was doubtful.

"I appreciate it."

Cardozo replaced the receiver and dropped into his chair. He pulled the St. Andrew's newsletter from the housebreaker file. A zappy headline proclaimed, CONDOMS—THEY'RE NOT JUST FOR SATURDAY NIGHT.

Cardozo sighed and skimmed the article.

Beginning the first of next month, SAYOP—the St. Andrew's Youth Outreach Program—will be distributing condoms free of charge to any teenager who requests them. Condom recipients will be invited, but not required, to view the twelve-minute award-winning documentary film, "Sexuality and Responsibility in Today's Changing World: A Young Person's Perspective."

The phone jangled with completely unnecessary malice. His first impulse was to swat it. "Cardozo."

"Oh, yes, Lieutenant." The voice of a woman. Cultivated but with a broad edge of phoniness. A woman he knew he didn't know. "This is Mrs. Douglas Moseley's secretary. Would you be able to stop by the house at six-thirty tonight for a drink? We're at Sixty-ninth and Park."

Cardozo looked at the work piled up on his desk. Besides the housebreaker at Father Joe's, he had a stack of still-open homicides. You couldn't say *no* to a Douglas Moseley, but you could sure as hell be ornery about saying yes.

"How about seven?" he said.

"We'll make it seven." He could tell from the tone that she was miffed. "Mr. Moseley will be looking forward to seeing you again."

A butler admitted Cardozo to the Moseleys' Park Avenue penthouse duplex co-op. The voices and laughter and piano music in the living room sounded like a party, but the ashen-faced butler looked like a funeral. He led Cardozo to the library.

A woman was sitting at an antique mahogany desk signing checks. She turned. "Lieutenant Cardozo—I'm Paula Moseley, Douglas's wife." She raised the desk lid and locked it. She had narrow, almost squinting green eyes and her auburn hair had been expensively teased into a wild mane. She rose and gave him her hand. "Dougie is on the phone—could I offer you a drink?"

"I'll take a diet Pepsi if you have one."

She gave him a curious look. "Do you not drink alcohol at all or are you just not drinking tonight?"

"I'm just not drinking right now."

"Forgive me for asking. I deal with substance abuse in my work —mostly young people."

"What kind of work is that?"

She went to a small sideboard where a bar had been set up

against the wall of watered silk. Her hands made practiced, economical moves with glasses and bottles and an engraved silver ice bucket. "I'm in clinical psychology."

"Is that so."

She smiled as though she had been complimented. "I know, people are always telling me I don't look like a psychologist—as though I should wear spectacles and a beard and smoke cigars. Of course, you meet with a lot of drug abuse in your work too." She handed him his diet Pepsi in a highball glass. The glass had Harvard University's insignia etched into it.

"Drug abuse can play a part."

"Douglas has told me about you. Forgive me, but I'm fascinated." Her eyes flicked up. "Oh, there you are, Dougie."

Douglas Moseley glided into the room. He was in full evening dress and he was folding down the aerial of a cellular telephone. "Anyone need anything?" He thunked the phone down on the bar and poured himself a generous Stoli on ice. He clinked glasses with Cardozo. Light flashed from the emeralds in his cuff links.

"Thanks for stopping by, Vince. I know how busy you are. I understand you're acquainted with a good friend of mine—David Lowndes?"

"I've met him."

"David tells me that you headed the team that investigated that dead girl they found in the Vanderbilt Garden."

"That's right."

"David feels perhaps you shouldn't be on the rectory break-in case."

"Why does he feel that?"

Moseley's right forefinger was stroking the rim of his glass. "David senses some kind of bad blood between you and Father Joe Montgomery."

"He's nuts."

Moseley stood there nodding, not giving it much, just showing he was a man of goodwill, able to see all sides. "Nonetheless, it might save us all a lot of trouble if you were to remove yourself from this investigation."

"It's not up to me. I'm a grunt. I follow orders."

Moseley twisted his glass between both hands and studied the miniature whirlpool he had created. "Your captain says he'll be glad to remove you if you request it."

"He hasn't said it to me." Cardozo crossed the room and set his unfinished drink on the bar. "Is there anything else you wanted to discuss?"

Both Moseleys had shocked looks, as if they had gravely misjudged the man standing on their jade-and-beige oriental rug.

"In that case, thanks for your hospitality."

THIRTY

Ahalf hour later, Cardozo was sitting in a lawn chair in the yard behind a stucco home in Queens. Anger was still making his mind buzz. "Guys like Moseley think they own this city."

"And they're not far wrong." Tom O'Reilly reached for the sangria pitcher. He refilled Cardozo's glass and then his own. "Moseley is damned unhappy you're on the case."

"He said you'd take me off if I requested a transfer. Did you tell him that?"

"Of course not. But if you asked me to transfer you, I would."

Cardozo glanced at his captain. The red-jowled face maintained a careful neutrality. There were times when Cardozo distrusted neutrality. "So Moseley's bluffing."

"Be careful, Vince. He has power."

"Not enough to direct a police investigation."

"Don't be so sure. Father Montgomery's a well-connected man. His friends are going to see that he's spared any grief."

Cardozo stared up at the sky. The last light of day was flickering on the treetops. He could hear crickets in the bushes and a neighbor's dog barking, and somewhere farther off, a lone frog.

"You have to follow guidelines," O'Reilly was saying.

"Tell me once when I haven't followed guidelines."

"You can't comment to the press. No remarks about the investigation. Everything gets handled through the office of the deputy commissioner for press relations."

"That kindergarten. The department of cover-my-ass."

O'Reilly didn't deny it. "Those are the ground rules. If you can't accept them, save us all a headache and get off the case now."

"What are Montgomery's friends scared of?"

O'Reilly shrugged.

Cardozo frowned, sensing something off-center. "Don't tell me they've got you scared too."

"Don't make a conspiracy of it. It's normal consideration when the poor guy's blind."

"Blind?" Cardozo set his drink down with a soft clink on the glass-top table. "What are you talking about?"

"Father Montgomery can't see."

"Who says?"

"His doctor says."

"Since when?"

"Since they examined him this afternoon in Doctors Hospital."

A screen door slammed and Tom O'Reilly's wife came out of the house carrying a tray of hamburger patties and sliced sesame-seeded rolls.

"Are you staying for the cookout, Vince?" She was a slight woman with neat gray hair and cheerful blue eyes. "There's more than enough."

The idea of Betty O'Reilly's barbecued burgers was tempting, but Cardozo pushed up from his chair.

"Thanks, Betty, but can I take a rain check?"

The door to the hospital room was halfway ajar. Cardozo could see Father Montgomery sitting up in bed. He had a melancholy and beaten look.

Sonya Barnett, his actress friend, had pulled a chair to the bedside and was reading aloud from *The New Yorker*. "This magazine used to be so good," she said, "and now they've ruined it."

Cardozo knocked. "Am I interrupting?"

Father Montgomery turned his head and smiled. At least it was a brave try at a smile. "Not at all."

"We're just being cozy." Sonya Barnett tossed away her reading specs. Their fall was broken by a cord of pink gift-wrap ribbon tied around her neck.

Cardozo approached the bed. "Do you remember me, Father Montgomery—Vince Cardozo, your cop friend from a year and a half ago?"

"Why, yes." Father Montgomery's gaze seemed to float without finding anything to moor itself to. "You borrowed my talent file."

"And I've had to borrow it again."

"There haven't been many changes, I'm afraid. I haven't been as active theatrically lately as I'd like to be. Did you meet my good friend and neighbor, Sonya Barnett?"

"Yes, indeed." Ms. Barnett extended a hand. She was wearing a short-sleeved high-necked linen blouse, and her arm was almost completely freckled. She offered an enormous gift box of chocolates. "The round ones are champagne truffles. They're divine."

"Thanks. I already ate." It was a lie, but Cardozo intended to eat, and he hated to start a meal with dessert.

"Then I guess poor old Joe and I will have to eat them all ourselves." Which seemed to be Sonya Barnett's way of stating that she had no intention of leaving her friend alone with any member of the NYPD.

Cardozo drew up a second chair. "Tell me, Father—do you have any idea of the identity of the young man who was found in the rectory?"

"No, I don't—but I didn't really get a clear look at him. My vision . . . hasn't been good lately."

"Do you have any idea how he could have gotten in?"

"He must have broken in."

"There've been break-ins in the rectory lately," Sonya Barnett said.

"Did you report any of them?" Cardozo directed the question to Father Montgomery.

Father Montgomery hesitated. "No . . ."

"Well, you told me about them," Sonya Barnett said. "I can vouch for that."

"But you didn't report them to the authorities. Why not?"

"I did report a break-in. It was committed by a young man named Tom Lanner."

"Pew-ee." Sonya Barnett made a face. "Revolting young punk."

"But that wasn't a break-in," Cardozo said. "At least not according to the charge you filed."

Father Montgomery's jaw moved but only a stuttering sound came out. It was as if his brain had short-circuited and was seeking out new ways to connect old wires. "I didn't report the others because . . . I'd had an operation, and I was—I was recovering. . . . They'd given me a general anesthetic."

"The effects of that anesthesia linger," Sonya Barnett said. "Especially when you reach Joe's and my age. Remember how you were imagining things, Joe?"

"That's right. I couldn't be sure what was my imagination and what wasn't."

"Did thieves ever take anything from the church?"

Father Montgomery hesitated. "I'm not sure."

"Honestly, Joe." Sonya Barnett was shaking her head sternly. "Those scavengers cleaned you out—vestments, collection plates, books, candlesticks, chalices, the works!"

"I can't be sure," Father Montgomery said. "Aside from Tom Lanner . . . I had a feeling things had been rearranged . . . possibly mislaid."

"Or stolen. You've got to tell the truth, Joe. Stop protecting criminals."

"They're not criminals." Father Montgomery's voice was weary.

"What about the one who attacked you in the park?" Sonya Barnett arched an eyebrow at Cardozo. "What the dickens do you call that?"

Father Montgomery reached fumbling hands for a pipe on the bedside table. He packed it with sweet-smelling tobacco and struck three matches trying to light it. He was good at dawdling.

"Could you tell me a little about that attack?" Cardozo said.

Silence pressed down on the room. Father Montgomery exhaled wearily. Smoke spiraled through the air like a flattened galaxy. "I'd hardly call it an attack. It was a nuisance, really. A young man came up to me and demanded my wallet. Which, being a nonviolent man, I handed over."

"Damned pussycats like you are killing this town," Sonya Barnett said. "I'd have hooked that punk in the kisser."

"Did this young man have a weapon?"

Father Montgomery shook his head. "Nothing but his right
fist."

"Were you hurt?"

"You must have been talking to Bonnie." Father Montgomery
smiled faintly. "She's a dear, but a little overprotective of old
gents like me."

"Were you hurt?"

"He . . . hurt my eye."

"Can you describe him?"

"He looked angelic—"

"They all look angelic to you," Sonya Barnett scoffed.

"He was young."

"How young?"

"Oh, fourteen or so. I remember he was very frightened—it was
probably his first mugging. He wore a woolen watch cap pulled
down over his ears—khaki-colored."

"Height?"

"Maybe five-six, five-seven."

"Weight?"

"I'm terrible at estimating weight. It's probably part of my denial—I eat so much of Sonya's candy."

"That's what it's there for, you numbskull."

"Race?"

Father Montgomery's head tilted. "What does race have to do
with it?"

"Race is a useful part of the description."

"I don't see that it's relevant. In any case . . . I'm not sure I
can recall."

Give me a break, Cardozo thought. *You had your eyesight and
you didn't notice his race? The Supreme Court says laws should
be color-blind, not people.* "Did you report the mugging?"

"No."

"Why not?"

"What would have been the point?"

"Joe, you have no public spirit. We can't let these punks run
our lives."

"I know, I know." Father Joe raised a hand, silencing her. "I was tired—I suppose I was in shock. And I was scared. I've never been scared that way before. It seemed to paralyze my will."

"Why, Joe, you never said a word about it."

"I had a feeling I was being stalked."

"Stalked by who?" Cardozo said.

"I couldn't tell. Perhaps the mugger. Perhaps somebody else. Or perhaps I was imagining it. I thought I noticed robberies in the rectory and church, but I wasn't sure."

"Is that why you rigged a booby trap in the rectory?"

Father Montgomery nodded. "Yes, I put a steam iron on top of a door."

"Why, Joe," Sonya Barnett said, "you're a regular Thomas Alva Edison with your contraptions."

"I'm afraid that's how my poor housebreaker chap got stunned."

"Your poor housebreaker chap never recovered consciousness," Cardozo said.

Father Montgomery drew himself up a little higher in the bed. "He's still unconscious?"

"He died this afternoon."

"The hell you say!" Sonya Barnett cried.

Father Montgomery was making that stuttering sound again. "I truly didn't—oh, God—I didn't mean to—"

Sonya Barnett patted his hand. "Of course you didn't, darling."

Father Montgomery's fingers tore at the hem of his bedsheet. "I only meant to scare him off."

"Apparently," Sonya Barnett said, "you builded better than you knew."

Cardozo realized that Father Montgomery's defense rested upon proving his state of mind—intense fear—which in turn rested upon proving that the mugging in the park had actually taken place. He had a feeling that Father Montgomery realized it too.

Cardozo walked to the window. Beyond the double-glazing the colors of the day were finally dying. The darkening sky flowed with jet planes, blinking like a circuit board. "Tell me something, Father. Did anyone else see the attack?"

"There was a chatty woman with a dog—she was feeding the

birds—she tried to be helpful, but really there wasn't much to be done."

"Do you remember her name?"

"I'm not sure she ever told me. She had extraordinary red hair."

"Some women really should not resort to the dye pot," Sonya Barnett said, and Cardozo flashed that it was a point of honor with her to wear her hair gray, drawn back in a bun but otherwise unfussed-with.

"Father Montgomery." Cardozo turned and faced him. "Where were you when the intruder walked into the booby trap?"

"Well, when I heard the scream I was upstairs in my bedroom. I came downstairs and found the young man on the floor."

"But you didn't phone the police?"

Father Montgomery shook his head. "I suppose I wasn't thinking straight."

"Has anyone besides you been living in the rectory?"

Father Montgomery seemed startled. "My assistant, Bonnie Ruskay, works there and takes her meals there. But she has her own apartment across the street."

"Then who's been sleeping in the guest room?"

Father Montgomery's eyes blinked rapidly. "I've sometimes lent it to a young person in need of a bed for the night."

"Recently?"

Father Montgomery didn't answer.

"Do you have the names and addresses of any of these young people?"

Sonya Barnett laughed a low, mocking laugh—the trademark Barnett laugh. "Really, Lieutenant—do you think they would have needed to stay over if they'd had addresses?"

"There was no point taking their names," Father Montgomery said. "They were always giving false names."

"Why was that?"

"They were usually on the run from someone—their family, the police."

"You're a trusting man to take them in, Father."

"No more trusting than they were of Joe," Sonya Barnett said. "After all, what does a clerical collar mean? Joe could have been some kind of monster preying on young runaways, couldn't he?"

"Were you?" Cardozo said quietly. "Preying on runaways?"

Father Montgomery began laughing softly. "Very good, Lieutenant. Very good. But you'd have to ask them, wouldn't you?"

"Without their names and addresses, that might be difficult."

Sonya Barnett chuckled. "Joe's too clever for you, Lieutenant."

Cardozo nodded. "Obviously."

THIRTY-ONE

On the office wall above Dr. Barney Clayton's head, the large capital E of an eye chart glowed faintly, like a full moon riding the sky of a sunny afternoon.

"Father Montgomery had advanced cataracts on both eyes," Dr. Clayton was explaining. He was a thin, ruddy-faced man with a can-do smile that seemed to take hold of the space four feet around him. A polka-dot bow tie peeked from the collar of his white hospital jacket. "By the time Joe came to me, he had severe difficulty seeing. Early this year I removed the cataract from his left eye and inserted an I.O.D."

"An artificial lens?" Cardozo said.

Dr. Clayton nodded. "An intraocular device. It restored full vision in that eye. Unfortunately, a street kid mugged Joe three weeks ago, and that was the eye that got punched in the mugging. The globe of the eye ruptured along the suture. The lens was lost, along with most of the vitreous and a good deal of tissue. The result is that Father Montgomery can't see."

A high bell-like tone seemed to start ringing in Cardozo's ear. "Not even with the other eye?"

"Eventually, when the cataract on that eye is removed, he'll see. But at the moment the right eye can only distinguish light and dark and rudimentary shapes."

"Can he read with the right eye?"

"No."

"Recognize faces?"

"No. At the moment he recognizes voices, not faces."

"Can he walk down the street?"

"On a very bright day, perhaps—if it's a very familiar street with no traffic. But I wouldn't advise him to try it without a friend to guide him."

"Could he get around his home?"

"Certainly. As blind people do."

Something puzzled Cardozo. "If Father Montgomery was blinded three weeks ago, how is it no one knew till today?"

"Because he's a man of enormous determination. He kept it a secret. He pretended he could see. I discussed it with him. He's worried he might not recover his vision and could be forced to retire. It's not blindness he dreads, it's retirement."

"So for the last three weeks he's been operating by touch and sound?"

"And a rudimentary sense of light and dark."

"Would it have been physically possible for him to stand on a chair?"

Uncertainty flickered across Dr. Clayton's face. "Yes, if he'd wanted to."

"And could he have placed a—let's say a book—on top of a doorway?"

In the gray-walled stillness, Dr. Clayton stared at Cardozo. "He could have, but why on earth would he want to?"

It was getting close to eight P.M. when Cardozo let himself into his apartment. His nose detected a sour, fishy smell that got worse as he approached the kitchen. "If that's my dinner, I ate at the office."

Esther Epstein, the seventy-something widow from next door, was demonstrating something to Terri that involved a mixing bowl, an egg, and a can of 9 Lives tuna dinner.

"Hi, Dad," Terri said. "Esther's showing me how to feed Beverly."

"What's up, Esther?" Cardozo said. "Are we inheriting your cat?"

In cat years, Beverly was probably old enough to be Esther's mother. She was a standoffish Angora with a disagreeable whine, and Cardozo did not relish the idea of sharing a bathroom with her litter box.

"Relax," Mrs. Epstein said. "Bev's not moving. But the V.A. has me on a new shift at the hospital, so Terri's going to take care of the evening meal. You know how old animals need their routine."

"Boy, do I. Why don't you stay and have some dinner with us? We haven't had a meal together in six months."

"Thanks, but I can't." Mrs. Epstein shook her head and Cardozo realized she'd had her white hair bobbed and blued. "I'm working the eight-thirty P.M. to four-thirty A.M. shift."

"That's a strange shift."

"It's the twilight zone. They invented it special for me because they want to retire me. They think I'm lying about my age, which I am, but they can't prove it, because I run the computer and I've put a password on my file. They can't get into it."

Cardozo opened the refrigerator and saw that Terri had fixed him a plate of chicken-stuffed avocado. He brought it to the table along with a can of Lite beer.

"You're a clever lady, Esther. I hope you're clever enough to take a cab to work and a cab home."

"Nah, I hitchhike." Mrs. Epstein kissed Terri good night and then stood on tiptoes and planted a kiss on Cardozo's cheek. "Are you losing weight, Vince?"

"I wish."

"You'd better watch your nutrition. My Bev eats better than you do." She took the mixing bowl and waved good-bye. A moment later the front door closed.

Cardozo chewed thoughtfully on a forkful of chicken salad. Terri had seasoned it mysteriously and he couldn't recognize the taste. "What did you put in the curry?"

"A little ginger."

Sometimes little things about her amazed him. "Did you read that in a cookbook?"

"I made it up." She popped the top off his beer and poured it into a carefully angled glass. "Like it?"

"It's great."

She leaned across the table to give him a kiss.

He looked up, catching a vibration. "Going somewhere?"

"Out to a movie with my friend Alice."

"Hey," he called after her. "Don't stay out late. I worry about you."

Cardozo couldn't see her face.

Didn't matter.

His fingertips started inside her forearms. Slipped with light fleet play up and across her shoulders. Down over her breasts and stomach. Finally, lingeringly, deep between her legs. Here the movement slowed into a long, pleasuring caress.

From far, far away he heard her sigh.

He made the whole journey over again, this time with his lips. His hand slid beneath her, lifted her. He pressed himself gently against her. Then easily, slowly inside her.

A buzzing sound began chiseling through the thin shell of sleep. He pushed it away.

She cried out and whipped her head around and with one hand she flung her hair away from her face. He found himself gazing into the eyes of Reverend Bonnie Ruskay.

The buzzing wouldn't stop. He recognized the muted metallic bite of the phone bell. His soul grimaced and the dream leaked away. Eyes shut, he reached along the bedside table for the receiver. "Cardozo."

"Vince—it's Dan." The voice was clipped, urgent. "Sorry if I woke you."

"That's okay." It was not yet dawn. The corner streetlight still sent a yellow, mercury-vapor glow through the curtained window, dappling the bedroom wall.

"I just finished the autopsy on the kid from the rectory."

Cardozo could sense something hanging in the air. "And?"

"You'd better get over here."

"I'll be right up. Give me twenty minutes."

THIRTY-TWO

The latex squeaked as Dan Hippolito snapped his hand into the glove. He reached under the boy's head and raised it from the pillow. "Can you see that?"

Cardozo saw the shaved area on the top of the skull. He nodded.

"The signature of this blow matches the front tip of the steam iron." Dan's finger touched a black opening that looked like a bullet entry. The impact had pushed up a ridge of white bone and peeled-back skin around the hole. "If you were striking a blow with that iron, you'd normally grip it so the back or the bottom of the iron struck the head. But to strike a blow like this, you'd have to angle your wrist up and rotate ninety degrees. Not very likely."

"So what's the most probable scenario?"

"As far as this blow is concerned, I go with the booby trap. The iron was balanced on top of the door. The victim opened the door, the iron fell and hit him. The blow probably disoriented him, and he would certainly have been in severe pain, but it didn't kill him."

"What did kill him?"

Dan laid the head back on the pillow and rolled it gently sideways. Another area of hair had been shaved, leaving a section of naked scalp behind the left ear. Three deep lacerations crisscrossed the bald patch.

"The assailant gripped the iron in the normal way, as you would for ironing. He swung it down from a good three-foot height. He swung three times and each time was a direct hit. The victim was lying on the floor, his head positioned pretty much as you see it now. Which accounts for the contusions on the opposite side of the skull."

To Cardozo's eye, the blows looked vicious. "Could a blind man do that?"

"Sure, why not? Close range, aim doesn't have to be exact."

"How strong was the assailant?"

"He could pitch a hardball that would knock your eye out."
Dan rolled the head back to its original position. He pulled the
black nylon sheet over the boy's face and slid the body tray back
into the locker. "I can show you the rest in my office."

Dan led the way. At this hour of the morning, silence lay along
the deserted, fluorescent-lit corridor.

"The victim had sex an hour or so before dying."

"What do you mean, had sex?"

Dan unlocked his office door. "I mean he ejaculated. And I
think he had company."

Dan crossed to the desk. He handed Cardozo two color glossies
that looked like some weird landscape from *National Geographic*
that only an explorer could love. There was nothing on the shots
to indicate up or down.

"What are these?"

"Inflammation of the sphincter tissue. The dead man may have
had passive anal sex."

"I don't feel like looking at that guy's asshole before break-
fast."

Dan dealt more glossies across the desk top, like cards in a
faceup hand of poker. "In addition: an injection mark on inner
left forearm; the hands have been secured with leather belts; the
ribs on the left side show signs of beating or kicking; there was
burning of the skin around the nipple area such as might be
caused by contact with dripped candle wax."

Cardozo's eye alighted successively on the forearm, on the
wrists, on the ribs, and finally on the nipple.

The room was still, and the stillness knew something.

Dan picked up a plastic watering can and sprinkled the potted
corn plants that grew on a low table against one of the windowless walls. He had had the office barely two months: it had come
with his promotion to second chief assistant. The plants were a
statement: instant permanence. We're here for good—for the time
being.

"I compared him with Ms. Basket Case." Dan came back to the
desk and read from the year-and-a-half-old autopsy report. "*Feet*

may have been secured with leather belt; burning of skin possibly caused by dripped candle wax."

Cardozo sat musing. "So they both were into s/m sex."

"Surprising in people so young. Unless they were prostitutes satisfying older clients."

"Any other similarities?"

"Ms. Basket Case didn't leave us that much to compare. But the dead man had recreational levels of alcohol and cocaine in his blood, cocaine residue on the injection mark, and trace amounts of azidofluoramine in his liver."

Cardozo watched Dan polish his reading glasses. "What the hell is azidofluoramine?"

"Cutting-edge stuff. It's not prescribable yet. There's not even an analogue on the street. There are three ongoing protocols, but the data won't be published till next month."

"What's it used for?"

"Acute panic disorder."

"Any recreational use?"

"Sure—it zonks you out fast."

Something flickered in Cardozo's mind. "What drugs did you find in Ms. Basket Case?"

Dan flipped pages. "Her liver tissue was too far gone to pull any drug residue."

Cardozo listened a moment to the whisper of air in the over- head cooling vent. "Would a blind man want to have sex?"

Dan gazed at him with a noncomprehending frown. "What are you talking about? Blind men have sex all the time."

"What I mean is, if you'd just been blinded—would you feel like having sex?"

"If you'd just been blinded, maybe you'd feel there wasn't much left you could do *except* have sex."

"I checked the 911 tapes." Ellie didn't knock. She walked straight into Cardozo's cubicle. "Samantha Schuyler's call came in at 11:43 P.M. the night before last. She reported a scream and breaking glass. She's sticking to that order—the scream first, then the breaking glass. She's definite on that point."

Cardozo frowned. "He would have had to get hit before he broke in. Or at least before that window was broken."

"Accuracy may not be the lady's long suit. She says the church hosts a lot of disorderly activity—wild parties past midnight, loud music, drug use. She also implied that another young man may have been killed at the rectory."

"What do you mean, implied?"

"Sort of let it pop out and then acted as though it was a slip of the tongue. I checked the records. No other death has been reported there. None of St. Andrew's neighbors have phoned in a complaint—not even Mrs. Schuyler. Which makes me wonder if she isn't embroidering a little."

Cardozo nodded. St. Andrew's was in an area where residents picked up the phone to report the slightest quality-of-life violations—a noisy radio, a ripped garbage bag, a car alarm, a shout. For the kind of taxes that they paid, they were not about to have junkies puking into their trash cans, let alone orgies in the church. Mrs. Schuyler did not sound like a reliable source.

"The lab reports have started coming in. Prints on the iron match prints taken from Father Joe at the hospital."

"We expected that. Any prints beside his?"

"No one's."

"We didn't expect that."

"Seven full prints and three partials inside the rectory guest room window. No fingerprints outside the window."

"Doesn't prove a hell of a lot. The window could have been left open a crack. Someone could have climbed up on the roof and reached under and pushed it up—their prints would have wound up inside."

"Assuming they weren't wearing gloves."

"No one said anything about any gloves on the dead man."

"Not yet they haven't." Ellie stood with her hands in her skirt pockets, not moving, her arms tanned and bare to the shoulders of her blouse. "There was no window glass in the vacuum cleaner bag—which indicates none landed inside the study."

Cardozo nodded. "Which confirms the window wasn't broken from outside."

She handed Cardozo the report. "The glass that you found in the courtyard comes from the window."

"Which confirms the window was broken from inside." He sat thumbing the pages, jagged where bits of perforated printer-guide still clung to them. "Paint this break-in fake—and paint this death suspicious."

Ellie was staring. He could feel her radar running full tilt.

"Lou says he found incense residue and acrylic rug fiber on the dead man's clothes. The incense matches residue on the clothes in the Ms. Basket Case basket. How come you asked him to check that far back?"

"Just covering all the bases."

"And then a few." She smiled. It was a tolerant smile. It seemed to say, *I know you. I know your thoughts. I accept you as you are.* "The fiber matches fibers on the Ms. Basket Case clothes. It also matches the strands that you pulled from the rug in the rectory. How come you didn't tell me you'd done that, Vince?"

"Because you'd have told me it wasn't legal."

"Which it wasn't. But never mind, because Lou says it's no use to us. Ditto for the incense. They're both as common as hydrogen atoms."

Greg Monteleone knocked on the open door. Today he was wearing a peanut-butter–brown shirt with a strawberry-red button-down collar, and he looked as though a jokester had set the controls wrong on a color TV. "Letter for you, Vince. Looks like you've been invited to something ritzy."

He handed Cardozo a heavy cream vellum envelope. Cardozo's name and work address were neatly penned in ballpoint block letters across the front. A return address had been engraved on the back: 34½ East 69th Street. There was no sender's name.

Cardozo opened it. Holding the page by a corner, he drew out a sheet of St. Andrew's Episcopal Church letterhead.

He read it over quickly. An electric current rippled the hairs on his neck. The two lines of block letters had been printed by the same hand and pen as the address.

The murdered runaways are in the shoe box in the rector's desk.

There was no signature.

His eyes glided up to meet Ellie's. He handed her the note.

She read with a sort of understated frown, not giving it much voltage. She was silent for a moment. She walked to the window. Morning light slanted through.

She looked back at him. He could feel the weight of her skepticism.

"When was it postmarked?" she said.

He turned the envelope over. "Yesterday."

"That was the day after the 911 call. Do you recognize the handwriting?"

"Not offhand. I doubt the writer wanted me to." Cardozo opened the lower left-hand drawer of his desk. "It could be a malicious joke, but just to make life tough, let's assume it's not." He brought out Father Joe's shoe box of talent and dropped it to his desk top. A leaden thump resonated.

"Vince, your desk is a mess." Ellie pulled the straight-backed chair over. She sat down, legs primly crossed, and went to work moving piles of paper, stacking them into higher piles, clearing space.

"You want some coffee?" he said.

She nodded. "I'll need it."

Two minutes later, Cardozo brought two styrofoam cups from the squad room and handed one to Ellie. He nudged the door shut with his heel.

"Those are yours." She had arranged the talent photos in two piles. "M through Z."

Cardozo dropped into his swivel chair. M was Marie MacDonald, a freckled kid in time-warp pigtails who looked like an MGM child starlet. Her bio, phone number, and address were paper-clipped to the photo on a neatly word-processed page.

N was Tommy Nutter.

He had reached Q, Lily Anne Quinn, when he heard Ellie make a surprised sound. He couldn't tell if it was the photo in her right hand or the coffee in her left that had startled her.

His first taste told him it was the coffee. "Sorry. Glen said it was fresh."

"Sure it was, last week." She set down the cup. "This one's out of alphabetical order. And she doesn't have a bio."

Ellie showed him the photo: a female teenager, pigtails again, but nothing MGM about her: the two-piece bathing suit pose had a sleazy, provocative look, and the tongue-tip was flicked out over the lower lip in a let-me-entertain-you come-on. The name WANDA

GILMARTIN and the number 2 had been block-printed in ballpoint in the lower border.

"Gilmartin." Cardozo was thoughtful. "Rings no bells." After an instant he picked up the next photo in his stack. "What do you know. Richie Vegas is out of order too."

He laid the photo next to Wanda's. Richie stood shirtless, tattooed, street-tough and scrawny, scowling. Again, there was no bio; the name was block-printed in the lower border, this time with the number 1.

"Wally Wills—no bio." Ellie laid the photo on the desk top. The number 3 had been printed beside the name. Another shirtless teenager, standing in a wooden doorway, the sun in his eyes.

The clunking of the air conditioner suddenly seemed louder.

"Tod Lomax, number four." Cardozo placed the photo beside Wills's. Lomax's face had a drugged look. The doorway he was standing in looked the same as Wills's doorway.

"Would you call these pictures audition photos? More like rejects from a rent-a-chicken catalogue." Cardozo tapped a ballpoint pen against the edge of the desk. "We'd better run these names and photos through the National Register of Runaways."

Ellie didn't answer. Her mouth had narrowed into a troubled, tight line.

She handed Cardozo a photo of a young man with jet-black hair, brown eyes, and olive skin. He was sitting in an armchair, indoors. The photo had been taken with a flash that made little red pinpricks in the center of his eyes. He was wearing a dark blue shirt under a blue suit jacket, no necktie.

The name PABLO CESPEDES had been carefully block-printed beneath the photo; next to the name was the number 5.

Cardozo studied the wide, grinning face. His mouth was suddenly dry.

It was the face of the dead boy from the rectory.

"Let's see if this is his real name and if he has a record."

A minute and a half later Cardozo and Ellie were staring at the computer screen in the squad room. In theory, all police records—from 911 calls to fingerprints to rap sheets—were computerized for instant accessibility. In fact, the computers ate so many files and were down so much of the time—over a hundred days a year, in some precincts—that you never knew what you were going to get when you called up information.

Today the computer was cooperating, and fifteen seconds after Ellie tapped in the command, a face stared back from the screen.

"That's him," Cardozo said.

It was the same Pablo Cespedes as in the photograph, only the grin was more demented, the eyes more seriously goofy, as if he'd prepared for his mug shot by smoking a joint of Maui Wowie. There was no housebreaking on the sheet; only a single charge of theft. Pablo Cespedes was currently on probation and residing in a foster home.

Cardozo copied down the home phone on a sheet of scratch paper. He went back to his desk and dialed the number.

On the fourth ring a woman answered sweetly. "Hello?"

THIRTY-THREE

Dan Hippolito drew back the black nylon sheet. The dead boy's foster parents stared down into the body tray.

Freida Adler was a little woman with a lot of makeup. She grabbed her husband's arm. Jupiter Adler was a big man, built like a butcher.

"It's Pablo." Freida's whisper left mist like skywriting on the chilled subbasement air. "Oh, my God."

Jupiter squeezed her hand.

Cardozo felt a cold hollow in his stomach. "I'm sorry."

"Please." Freida sank down onto the slatted wood bench. "I need some water."

"Can she have some water?" Jupiter said.

Dan Hippolito brought a Dixie cup from the cooler in the hallway. Jupiter held the cup. Freida sipped.

"Are you feeling a little better?" Cardozo said.

Freida found a brave little smile. Her right eyetooth had a gray dead color. "Partially."

"I'll drive you home."

"How long did Pablo live with you?" Cardozo asked in the car.

"It would have been six months tomorrow," Jupiter said.

Freida spoke up from the backseat. "Pablo was very easy to get along with. Some aren't."

"Have you taken in other homeless kids?"

"We have room for four," Jupiter said. "Lately, with city cutbacks, we've had three."

"You do it full-time?"

"Now I do. I'm on workmen's compensation. Doesn't go far."

So it was a living for him, Cardozo realized. "What kind of work did you used to do?"

"Same as Freida. Case manager for the department of human resources."

"You come that close to the human misery in this city," Freida said, "you have to care."

The Adlers lived in a shabby eighteen-story high rise on Riverside Drive. A banner above the entrance announced luxury co-ops for sale. It looked as though it had been gathering soot for the last ten years.

A security officer watched the Adlers let themselves and Cardozo into the lobby. They rode up to the seventh floor in a small automated elevator that was smeared with graffiti.

The Adlers' apartment was dark and rambling and it smelled of cooking and Lysol.

A crime-scene crew arrived, and a print man and a photographer began going through Pablo's room. It was a small space behind the kitchen and Cardozo had a feeling it had been a maid's room long ago when the neighborhood had been upscale.

Posters of Julio Iglesias and Humphrey Bogart and Andrés Segovia had been taped to the wall. Cardozo tried to see the link. All three were performers, but Iglesias and Bogart were sex symbols. Segovia with his white hair and fishbowl cataract-correction glasses and his hand-powered classical acoustic guitar seemed an odd man out.

"Why Segovia?" Cardozo said.

"Pablo loved music," Freida said. "He played the guitar and he composed songs."

"The only trouble was, he played his guitar too late at night." Jupiter tossed a nod toward the window. "The neighbors complained."

Cardozo walked to the window. It looked out on an air shaft. Even in the middle of the day, the shaft was completely dark, as though the machinery that generated sunlight couldn't reach this far.

"When did you last see Pablo?"

"Two nights ago," Freida said. "He took his guitar with him. He said he was spending the night at his friend Andy's."

"How can I get hold of Andy?"

"Pablo didn't tell us much about Andy."

"Do you have his phone number, or his last name?"

Freida shook her head. "Pablo didn't want us calling his friends. He didn't want them knowing he was on probation."

"How many friends did he have?"

"Well, he had Andy." She glanced toward her husband.

"I can't think of anyone else," Jupiter said.

Cardozo noticed a gold-trimmed cloth on the dresser top. It reminded him of something a priest might wear. "Did Pablo ever play in the musical shows at St. Andrew's Church?"

Freida and Jupiter exchanged quizzical looks.

"Not that he ever told me," Freida said.

"Did he ever mention a Reverend Bonnie Ruskay or a Father Joe Montgomery?"

"Pablo wasn't going that amateur route," Jupiter said.

Cardozo examined the borders of the cloth for markings. "What route was he going?"

"He was looking for professional backing to put on a cabaret show."

"What kind of cabaret show?"

"One man—his own material—songs and stand-up comedy."

Freida noticed Cardozo fingering the cloth. "Pablo loved fancy things."

"Any idea where he got this?"

"A flea market somewhere."

Cardozo told the print man to bag the cloth.

"You should watch this." Jupiter handed Cardozo a videocassette from the bookshelf. "It's Pablo's audition tape. There's great stuff on it."

Sonya Barnett was sitting beside Father Montgomery's hospital bed, balancing a teacup on her lap. She looked up when Cardozo rapped on the open door.

"Mind if I join you?"

Father Montgomery turned. "Who is it?"

"Mr. Cardozo." Sonya Barnett's ringless, freckled hand shot out in greeting. "You and Father Montgomery are becoming serious chums."

Father Montgomery smiled from his nest of pillows. "I'm flattered that a busy lieutenant detective finds time to visit a boring old wreck like me. Could I offer you tea? Sonya brought some marvelous Darjeeling."

"None for me, thanks," Cardozo said.

"Or if you'd like something stronger," Sonya Barnett said, "one of Joe's parishioners sneaked in a bottle of Harveys Bristol Cream in that flower arrangement."

An enormous crystal vase of red roses sat on the chest of drawers.

"No sherry, thanks."

Father Montgomery laughed. "Well, if you haven't come for my hospitality, you must have come for my conversation. Sonya, you're going to have to help me scintillate."

"I'll bet Mr. Cardozo has come for information," Sonya Barnett said.

"From me?" Father Montgomery mugged astonishment.

Cardozo pulled up a third chair. "Does the name Wanda Gilmartin mean anything to you?"

"Wanda Gil—who?"

"Gilmartin."

"I don't think I've ever heard of anyone called Wanda Anything."

"Landowska," Sonya Barnett said. "The harpsichordist. Divine."

"Besides her. I certainly don't know this Gilmartin gal."

"Did you ever hear of a young man named Richie Vegas?"

"Never heard of him."

"Wally Wills?"

Father Montgomery shook his head.

"Tod Lomax?"

"The name's familiar. Where do I know that name from? Sonya, help me."

"Sorry, don't know him."

"How about Pablo Cespedes?"

Father Joe was thoughtful. "Cespedes, Cespedes . . . I used to know a Margarita Cespedes—her father was mayor of Havana in the Batista days. Margarita had two sons . . . terrific tango dancers . . ."

"Pablo Cespedes is the young man who was killed in the rectory. We found his photo in your talent file."

The smile dropped off Father Joe's face. "Then he must have played in one of our shows. I'm sorry, this old memory of mine is getting pretty lame. I just don't recall the name. Sonya, help me. You're good with names."

"Did you bring the photo?" Sonya Barnett said. "Let me see."

Cardozo handed her five photos.

Sonya Barnett put on her reading specs. "These were all in Joe's file?"

Cardozo nodded.

She gave each of the photos a quick, not-interested-but-not-quite-dismissing glance. "Joe, these don't look at *all* like your kind of talent."

"Now, Sonya, don't be such a snob. Talent isn't limited to one particular look."

"I very much doubt any of these people performed in a church musical."

"If they performed for us," Father Montgomery said, "their curricula vitae should have been attached to the photos."

"There was nothing attached to the photos."

"Well." Sonya Barnett handed back the photos. "Looks like we've got ourselves a little mystery."

THIRTY-FOUR

The cleaning lady let Cardozo into the rectory and led him to Bonnie Ruskay's study. The reverend was on the phone, but her eyes signaled Cardozo to come in.

He distracted himself by studying the titles in her library. Half the volumes were in Latin, Greek, or Hebrew. The books in English appeared to be works of weighty theological scholarship.

"Sorry." She hung up the phone and rose with a welcoming smile. "You must think I'm a terrible gab. That was my brother."

She tapped a finger against one of the framed photographs on her desk. It showed an intense-looking man in his twenties, with a dark beard, dark hair, dark eyes. He had his arm around an attractive young woman with curly hair.

"You and your brother seem to enjoy one another."

"We're great pals. My father's dead and my mother and I haven't been close since I became an Episcopalian, so I count on Ben to bring me news of the family." She nodded toward a small art deco Tiffany clock sitting on her desk. "Ben gave me that for the first anniversary of my ordination."

"It's beautiful. It's also seven minutes fast."

"I keep it set ahead so I won't be late." She saw him staring at a framed photo of a fair-haired man in a business suit. He had a crew cut and he was sitting in an easy chair with two fair-haired infants in his lap. "Those are my son and daughter."

"Wonderful-looking kids."

"Devils, but mine own."

"And the man?"

"Their father. My ex-husband Ernie."

"Who takes care of the children while you're working?"

"Their father has a housekeeper. He got custody."

Cardozo frowned. "Doesn't the mother usually get custody when the children are that young?"

"They're older now. In fact they're in school—St. Anne's. Doing very well. I'm allowed to see them between terms."

"I don't mean to pry, but that arrangement seems odd."

"My husband and children are Catholic. I was Catholic. When I converted to the Episcopal Church and became a priest, I destroyed a Catholic home. That was the basis for Ernie's getting an annulment."

"You said you were divorced."

"That too. Ernie asked for a divorce because only the court can grant custody. The judge was Catholic, and she gave Ernie everything he asked for."

Bonnie Ruskay smiled, but Cardozo sensed enormous pain behind the smile.

"That must hurt," he said.

"Mostly when family events come up—Christmas or Thanksgiving or Parents' Day at the kids' school. I'd love to be with them. St. Paul said the point of marriage was children—it's one of the very few issues that I think he may have been right about."

He detected a hint that she wanted very much to change the subject. "You don't sound like a fan of St. Paul's."

Her hand went up and grazed the bindings on a shelf of books. "I didn't write those because I agreed with him. Paul was a self-loathing closet case."

The books had fighting titles:

The Serpent and the Grail: Antifeminism and Homophobia in Hebrew Scripture and in St. Paul;

No Biological Resemblance to the Savior: Roman Catholic Doctrinal Opposition to the Ordination of Women;

The Son of God Was Also a Daughter: Reclaiming the Holy Anima as Spiritus;

St. Paul's Hostility to the Female: An Inquiry into the Religiously Sanctioned Marginalization of Sexual Identity and Sexual Choice;

Prophet of Fear and Loathing: What St. Paul Actually Preached.

Cardozo looked at her, impressed. "You wrote all those?"

"Guilty as charged." Her cheeks colored faintly.

"Which one's the easiest?"

"Easiest?"

"For someone like me to read."

She laughed. The sound had an edge of uneasiness. "They're technical homiletics—you wouldn't be interested."

"I would be. Seriously. Which do you recommend?"

She hesitated. *"The Son of God Was Also a Daughter* had some good reviews—but most bookstores don't carry theology. You'd have to go to a religious shop."

"Can you recommend any in the neighborhood?"

She jotted several addresses on a notepad. "These are good all-purpose shops." She handed him the sheet of scratch paper. "I hope my handwriting's legible."

"Very legible." He folded the paper and opened his billfold. He slid the list into one compartment and from another he took out the Xerox of the anonymous note. "Do you recognize this handwriting?"

She stared at the page. She probably wasn't aware that she was biting her lower lip. "Are you asking if it's mine? Since you just foxed me out of a sample, why bother to ask?"

"I'm asking if it's familiar."

She shook her head.

"Do you recognize the letterhead?"

"Naturally—it's church letterhead."

"Do you have this letterhead?"

"Of course I do."

"Could I see some?"

She stood absolutely still, and then she yanked open a drawer of the maplewood desk. "How much do you want?"

"Four or five sheets will be fine."

She handed him five sheets of church stationery. He slid them into a large departmental business envelope.

"Who else has that letterhead?"

"Father Joe has it, but anyone who comes to the church could get hold of it."

"Do you think a parishioner wrote the note?"

"I wasn't thinking of parishioners. But our last cleaning woman, Olga Quigley, left on bad terms. . . ."

"Did she quit or was she fired?"

"A little of both. She claimed she had to spend three nights a week with a sick mother. We discovered she was moonlighting at other jobs. If you decide to speak to her, you should realize that she doesn't like us."

"Do you have an address for her?"

"She used to live here in the maid's room. I don't know where she lives now."

"Can you give me her social security number?"

Bonnie Ruskay reflected a moment. She looked through several ledgers before copying down the number.

He took the piece of paper from her outstretched hand. He could feel she was irritated with him.

He broke the moment of awkward silence. "I noticed you don't have a Bible in your library."

"I've got a Bible." She pointed out a set of black bindings. "The New Testament in Greek and the Old in Hebrew. I don't believe in translations—they're pretty rotten. But let's not get into that."

He was staring at a curious implement mounted above the bookcase as a wall decoration. It looked like an ancient wooden back-scratcher with little pieces of piano wire mistakenly attached. "What's that odd-looking gizmo right above *Serpent and the Grail*?"

"That? It's something St. Paul himself might have invented. It's called a castigator."

"What does it do?"

"You flagellate yourself with it. Monks used it in the Middle Ages to quell sexual impulses."

"What are you doing with it?"

"As little as possible. I'm interested in the pathology of Christianity. Can you believe they were still using those things in the seventeenth century—eighty years before the Declaration of Independence?"

"Nothing people do surprises me." His eye traveled past the little whip to an ancient-looking framed etching. It showed a priest in a jungle clearing, serving communion to a group of bandaged Hawaiians.

"That's Father Damien," she said. "A very different sort of Christian from St. Paul—and unfortunately far less influential. He's a hero of mine."

"Why's that?"

"He went into a hostile environment and ministered to the lepers when no one else would."

Cardozo wondered if ministering to the socialites was her way of doing the same thing. "Father Damien caught leprosy himself, didn't he?"

"He regarded it as God's blessing."

Some blessing, Cardozo thought. He noticed a piggy bank on the shelf below the etching. "Saving your pennies?"

"That's an antique." She took it down and placed it on the desk. A red-and-white striped pig wearing a Panama hat and a blue-and-white starred apron stood in ready-to-waltz position on top of a cash register. "Do you have a penny?"

He handed her a penny. She dropped it into the coin slot. A music box inside the cash register tinkled a snatch of "Swanee River." With the concluding tinkle the drawer popped open.

"Sometimes with all the man-made grief around us, it's good to see human ingenuity spent on something harmless." She took out Cardozo's penny and handed it back to him. "Don't you agree?"

"Or on something beautiful."

She looked at him with interest. "Such as?"

He opened the departmental envelope and drew out the gold-trimmed cloth from Pablo Cespedes's bedroom. "What would you say this is—an altar cloth or a shawl?"

She unfolded it. "It's a priest's stole."

"Does it belong to St. Andrews'?"

She examined the border. "It's ours. This is our mark." She pointed to a letter *A* indelibly inked into the hem. "Thefts have been up in the neighborhood, so the police recommended we mark all our possessions."

"We found it in the dead boy's bedroom."

Her eyes had a questioning look. "Was he a professional thief, then?"

"He had a juvenile criminal record. We found his photograph in Father Joe's talent box."

The Tiffany clock made a muted ticking in the sudden silence.

"His name was Pablo Cespedes."

"I never heard the name."

Cardozo showed her the photo.

She shook her head. "No, I don't recognize him."

He handed her the four other photos.

She looked through them slowly. When she came to Lomax, her forehead wrinkled.

"They were all in the talent box."

A line of bafflement furrowed her brow. "I don't understand it. Are these people runaways?"

"We're looking into it."

"Are they . . ." She broke off.

"Are they dead? We're looking into that too. Is it possible they played in any of Father Montgomery's shows?"

"I don't recall his ever mentioning any of them. But the records are in his office if you want to check."

"Would you mind?"

The blinds were drawn in Father Montgomery's study. She turned on the desk lamp. While she searched the card files, he examined the framed posters for *The Boy Friend* and *Zip Your Pinafore*.

"My niece played in these shows."

Bonnie Ruskay glanced up. "Really? How was she?"

"I couldn't say. I never saw them."

"Me neither. They were before my time." She closed the Rolodex, frowning. "None of these people played in any of the shows; they didn't do tech work; there's no record at all of anyone by any of these names."

Cardozo watched her replace the files in their drawers. Her movements had a relaxed precision.

"Could I have some of Father Joe's letterhead?" he said. "Just for comparison."

"Five sheets?" She opened the middle desk drawer and counted them from the top of a neat stack.

Cardozo slid the sheets into his envelope, reversed so that he could tell whose was whose. "Tell me something, Ms. Ruskay. Was there a young man living with Father Joe?"

She glanced over at him. "From time to time Father Joe lent the guest room to needy youngsters."

"But was there one needy youngster in particular?"

"Lieutenant, what are you trying to get me to say?"

"Is Father Joe bisexual or gay?"

For that one instant her eyes seemed to hold flame. "Father Joe is one of the most Christian, kindly, concerned, loving, one-on-one ministers of the gospel that I have ever had the joy of knowing. In a social sense, perhaps that's perverse—he loves all human beings, and he goes the last mile for them; but in a moral sense, it's exactly what Christ preached." She closed the desk drawer and stood. "As for sex and sexuality, Father Joe is celibate. He's taken a vow. There's no secret about it. He even wrote an article on the subject for . . ." She broke off, as if the sound of her own voice had startled her. "I'm sorry. I didn't mean to lecture."

"I apologize for deserving the lecture." Instinct told Cardozo not to back off. "I understand Father Joe sometimes invited strange types into the rectory."

"Strange in what way?"

"Rough."

"Do you mean unpolished?"

"I mean dangerous."

"Who told you that?"

"A witness mentioned it."

"Father Joe is bearing Christian witness in an un-Christian time. He's a controversial figure. I'm sure you can dig up people who'll swear he practices animal sacrifice."

"I realize that. But all the same, isn't it possible he invited the dead man in, and the encounter turned sour, and Father Joe defended himself?"

"You're saying Father Joe brought an attack on himself—he deserved it?"

"I'm not talking about the attack in the park, I'm talking about what happened here in the rectory to Pablo Cespedes."

"The accident here wouldn't have happened if Father Joe had not been stupidly, senselessly mauled in the park."

"There's a problem. He didn't report that attack. There's no record of it."

Her gaze met his levelly. "Whether you can find a record or not, it happened. Father Joe isn't lying. He doesn't lie."

"I'm not saying he lied. But we need proof of that attack to justify the booby trap. Otherwise it's culpable homicide."

She sighed and shook her head. "This is so horribly unfair.

Father Joe has never intentionally harmed a human being in his life, not even in self-defense."

"Then would you object if I took hairs from the brush in the guest room?"

Her eyes narrowed on him. "What would be the point of that?"

"Pablo Cespedes claimed he spent nights at the home of a friend called Andy. We haven't been able to find Andy. Which makes me wonder if Andy was possibly a church."

"You think Pablo Cespedes was sleeping here?"

"I'd like to rule the possibility out."

Her eyes never left his. "Fine. You can take the hairs. In fact, I insist. They'll only prove Father Joe's innocent."

THIRTY-FIVE

Holding the note by the corner, Cardozo laid it on the steel-topped worktable. *The murdered runaways are in the shoe box in the rector's desk.*

To the right he placed a second note. The paper had curled and aged to yellow and the ink had faded to gray, but the words were still clear: *Sally, you do that divinely—thank heaven for little girls with talent! Joe.*

To the left he placed Bonnie Ruskay's handwritten list of religious bookshops.

"I have two questions. First: Did the person who wrote that list, or the person who signed himself Joe, write the unsigned note?"

Machines murmured in the buffered quiet of the lab. Lou Stein leaned forward without commenting and pushed his glasses down to the end of his nose.

Cardozo placed five sheets of St. Andrew's letterhead on the table and beside them another five sheets. The second group was marked with a small X at the bottom.

"Second question. Can you match the stationery of the unsigned note to either of these bundles?"

"Shouldn't take me long to match the letterhead—or to rule out a match. I don't do handwriting analysis myself, but I'll send these over to Marge Bonaventura. She's good and she's fast." Lou angled the tensor lamp lower. "They're all right-handed."

Something made a high-pitched squeaking sound.

Lou looked over. "You got a mouse in your pocket?"

Cardozo pushed the switch on his beeper. "Mind if I use your phone?"

Lou nodded toward the desk.

Cardozo called the precinct. Ellie's voice was excited. "I just got off the phone with the National Register of Runaways. Lomax and Gilmartin aren't listed."

"And?"

"Neither is Vegas or Wills."

He wondered if he'd heard her right. "*None* of them are listed?"

"Correct."

"Ellie, why are you beeping me about this?"

"It's amazing how far persistence will get you. I asked them to double-check, and it turned out Richie Vegas and Wally Wills were both *formerly* listed."

"Okay. That means they were taken off the list."

"Correct."

"Which means they must have showed up."

"Right here in New York."

"And?"

"They showed up dead. Homicides."

"Christ."

"Wills was investigated by a Detective Mort Kandelaft out in Queens."

Cardozo ran the name through his memory. "I don't know him."

"Vegas was investigated by a Detective Fred Huck here in Manhattan."

"Talk with Kandelaft," Cardozo said. "Talk with him now. I'll talk with Huck."

Cardozo replaced the receiver. When he turned, Lou was bent

over the worktable, squinting through a small square magnifying glass.

"Your list was written by a woman."

"No comment," Cardozo said.

"You don't need to comment. It's obvious from the depth of the verticals. A woman in a hurry." Lou moved the lamp to the right. "Your unsigned note was written by a man."

Cardozo took a small plastic evidence bag from his pocket. "One more favor."

Lou stretched out a hand. "Ask and it shall be given." He held the bag under the light. "Male Caucasian late teens."

"I need to know if that hair matches hair from the head of Pablo Cespedes."

Lou smiled. "And know you shall."

"Wanted to ask you about a homicide you handled three years ago," Cardozo said. "A runaway teenager."

"Glad to help." Detective Fred Huck thrust out a hand. He was a tall, friendly-looking man with a shock of graying blond hair. He gestured Cardozo into his office.

The small space showed signs of city revenue cutbacks—pea-soup–green paint curling off faintly grimy walls, shirt cardboard and duct tape replacing a broken pane in the window. Snowbanks of paper smothered the desk.

"The kid's name was Richie Vegas." Cardozo took a chair and handed Huck the boy's photo. "You found him over in Tompkins Square Park."

Fred Huck studied the picture. He had a cool look of blankness and then he snapped a finger. "Two weeks before Christmas. Sawed up in pieces in a basket."

Cardozo allowed his face to register no reaction.

"The worst of it was, a little girl found him. Ten years old, and she had to see a thing like that."

"Did you ever close the case?"

"I think so, but let me get the file."

Fred Huck came back six minutes later carrying a slim manila folder fastened with two rubber bands.

"Sorry to take so long. The files around here are a mess. Half are on the data base and the other half are lost." He sat at the desk and snapped the bands loose. "All the teenage males killing for the price of a pair of sneakers, it's not surprising one of them gets the tables turned."

Huck began turning pages.

"The body was found December tenth. Approximate date of death, first week in November. Identified from dental X rays the following February eighteenth. Returned to parents, February twenty-first."

"I don't remember reading about it," Cardozo said. "Was there anything in the newspapers?"

"The story made one of the local TV news shows. The D.A. wanted us to hold something back from the media, so we didn't publicize that the body had been chopped up. All we released was the basket."

"A large reinforced container?"

Huck nodded. "Trade name Styrobasket. Made in Kalamazoo."

"Do you have the crime-scene inventory there?"

"Sure do."

"Was a bouquet found near the gravesite?"

Huck gave Cardozo a bewildered look. "Bouquet?"

"Dead flowers—a dozen or so—fastened with a piece of thin red string."

Huck scanned the inventory. "Matter of fact, there was a scraggly bunch of dead flowers. No mention what kind of string."

"Did you by any chance keep them?"

Huck shook his head. "There's no property marker listed here. I guess we didn't."

"When did you finally close the case?"

"Struck it lucky May of last year. The killer confessed. Family man. A futures analyst from Salomon Brothers. A real Jekyll and Hyde by the name of Martin Barth."

"The pieces of Wally Wills's body were found March third, two years ago, in a Styrobasket on the old World's Fair grounds." Ellie sat in the straight-backed chair, summarizing in a quiet, unemotional voice from Detective Mort Kandelaft's file. "Traces of a matzolike substance were adhering to the roof of his mouth. Approximate date of death, the middle of the preceding January. No bouquets were found at the grave."

Cardozo rocked back in his swivel chair. "Which doesn't mean a bouquet couldn't have been left there."

Ellie nodded, conceding the point. "In order to hold information back from the public, the matzolike substance wasn't released to the media. Neither was the Styrofoam basket."

"They held back the basket in this case. They held back the dismemberment in the Vegas case." Cardozo steepled his fingers together. "Who decided that—Kandelaft or the D.A.'s office?"

"Kandelaft was following orders from the D.A.'s office. The case was closed that spring—May twelfth. The murderer confessed: he said he took Wills to a meat-packing plant and sodomized him and killed him."

Silence closed in and then a blast of PTP radio static pulsed through the squad room.

"And who was this murderer?"

Ellie handed Cardozo the file. "A Wall Street futures analyst by the name of Martin Barth."

Cardozo's fist slammed down on the desk top. The framed picture of Terri as a six-year-old jumped. "Barth confessed to killing Wills. He confessed to killing Vegas. He confessed to killing Ms. Basket Case. All young Caucasian runaways, all of them lured to a meat-packing plant and sawed up and left in a public park in a Styrofoam picnic basket. These are so obviously the same M.O. that a ten-year-old would see it. I can't believe nobody put them together. Why wasn't there at least some kind of press reaction?"

"Details were held back." Ellie shrugged. "It's standard operating procedure. In this case it meant the media didn't have enough to put the murders together. Wish I could explain it—but I don't understand how things work nowadays. Chiefly because they don't work."

Cardozo ripped through the files. "Clothes folded up with bodies—gray acrylic fiber sticking to clothes—incense residue sticking to clothes . . . None of this was given to the media."

"Vince, you can't know that."

"Did you read it in the papers? Did you hear it on TV? Because I sure as hell didn't. Candle wax on torso—leather fragments on wrists—leather fragments on shins—cocaine residue on injection mark—traces of azido-, azido-something-or-other in Vegas's and Wills's livers—"

"Azidofluoramine."

"Thank you. Why didn't the D.A.'s office see it? Why were three identical killings farmed out to three different detectives?"

"Okay, somebody screwed up. It happens."

"The only way this could have happened is because somebody screwed up on purpose."

Ellie's legs were crossed and she was languidly rotating one ankle. Body language for: *Watch yourself, Lieutenant. You're on the verge of losing it.* "This city is the murder capital of the world. Details get overlooked."

"These are not details." Cardozo felt anger like a dentist's drill going through his intestine. "And they're not going to get overlooked any longer."

Vince Cardozo and Pierre Strauss sat facing one another on upholstered chairs the color of driftwood. Cardozo had not come all this way to talk to Martin Barth's lawyer, but there Strauss sat, righteous and implacable, like a wall.

"When did you meet Wally Wills?" It was the seventh time Cardozo had asked a variant of the question.

"I forbid my client to answer."

The window in the VIP visitors' room at Dannemora faced west. Behind Strauss, Martin Barth stared at the setting sun touching down in the mountains.

"When did you meet Richie Vegas?"

"I forbid my client to answer."

"When did you meet Wally Wills?"

"I forbid my client to answer."

"How did you get them to go with you? Did you invite them for a drink, for a meal? Offer them money, drugs, what?"

"I forbid my client to answer."

"They were only kids, Marty. Hardly older than your own boys. Why did you kill them?"

"I forbid my client to answer."

Martin Barth began pacing. He wore loose-fitting prison blues, but Cardozo could see that a year and a half in Dannemora had put weight on his bones. Barth stopped at the table beside his attorney's chair. He picked up a pack of Marlboro Lights and tapped one loose.

"Marty, that's your third pack." Strauss gave him a light. "Cigarettes are going to kill you."

"Was it fun, Marty?"

Strauss sighed. "I forbid my client to answer."

Behind horn-rimmed glasses, Martin Barth's eyes kept flicking to the door. Outside, the guard's blue shoulder was leaning against the glass panel.

If I could only get this guy alone, Cardozo wished. "What do you do for fun now, Marty? Would you like me to send you a few cartons of Marlboro Lights?"

"My client does not need cigarettes. And he does not need you exceeding your authority."

"I'm within my authority."

"Bullshit. What's your authorization for this inquiry? These cases are closed. What the hell are you investigating?"

"That's my business."

Hair stood up on Strauss's head like wisps of meringue on a pie that needed more baking. "You're making it my business too."

"Martin Barth made statements to me and two other New York City homicide detectives. I have a right to clarify those statements."

"You have no right to ask about Vegas and Wills. My client has never been charged with those offenses."

"Come off it, he confessed."

"My client is under no obligation to incriminate himself."

"For chrissake. It was his admissions that closed the goddamned cases."

"Then anything my client has to say on the subject is already contained in the district attorney's files. And this interview is concluded." Pierre Strauss yanked Martin Barth around by the arm. "Come on, Marty. We're outta here."

THIRTY-SIX

"Since seven-thirty last night I've had eight phone calls from Pierre Strauss." Harvey Thoms's face was flushed and damp. Edginess rippled out of him. "Has he gone around the bend or what?"

"You can judge that better than me." Cardozo took a last delicious forkful of steak. "You've had more dealings with Counselor Strauss than I have."

In the mirrored, softly lit restaurant around them, businessmen's voices made a continuous murmur. Thoms leaned back to let the waiter take his plate. He'd eaten only half his shad roe.

"Strauss says you've been been nagging him, pestering his client."

"All I wanted was ten minutes with Martin Barth."

"Strauss says you've been trying to hang every murdered runaway in the last three years on Barth. You've been digging up unrelated cases."

"The murders of Richie Vegas and Wally Wills are very closely related. You might call them identical siblings."

"Related to what?"

"Ms. Basket Case."

For a moment Thoms wasn't saying anything. And then, "Ms. Basket Case was closed over a year ago."

"Just hear me out."

"Are you giving me a choice?" Thoms lit a Benson & Hedges filter king.

"Look at the points in common." Cardozo held up fingers, itemizing. "Three Caucasian teenage runaways. Dismembered. Abandoned in public areas in identical Styrobaskets. Identical acrylic gray shag rug fiber and incense were found on the victims' clothing."

Thoms exhaled one smoke ring and then a second. "You're

talking like a headline writer for the *Enquirer*. This is shit and you know it—coincidences, not links."

"Nine points are common to two out of three victims. First, alcohol and cocaine in the blood."

"Vince, this is fucking trivial!"

"But six points *aren't* trivial: A matzolike substance was found in the mouths of all three. The feet and wrists were tied with leather belts. The victims were beaten—"

The lines grooving Harvey Thoms's mouth deepened into angry furrows. "So help me, Vince, if your reason for going after Martin Barth after all these months is matzo balls and belts—"

"Their skin was burned with wax. Cocaine was injected, not snorted or smoked—*injected*. And one similarity is light-years beyond coincidence: traces of azidofluoramine in the liver."

"What the hell's azido—"

"Antipanic medication. The FDA has okayed it for testing, but it's not available to the public."

Harvey Thoms's bifocals began tapping on the white linen tablecloth. "Granting any or all of these points . . . it still doesn't add up to a case. Not in the sense the D.A. uses that word."

"I've saved the best for last." Cardozo waited for the waiter to bring their coffee. "Martin Barth confessed to all three killings."

There wasn't the slightest flicker of a reaction on Harvey Thoms's face. "Who says?"

"The detectives who handled the murders."

"I can't fucking believe this. Barth says he killed *three*? Give me those case numbers."

"You won't find the confessions. I checked the records. There's nothing in the computer."

Thoms threw down his napkin. "Okay. You've got nothing. You've got Strauss in an uproar and you're going to get my office in hot water for nothing."

"Barth's confession to Ms. Basket Case isn't in the computer either."

Thoms's stare was like an upraised fist warning Cardozo to stay back. "What the hell are you telling me? What's your point? Barth's been playing with the attorney general's computers?"

"I'm not sure Barth killed any of those kids."

"We went through this a year and a half ago." For that one

instant Thoms's eyes seemed to focus on a point far beyond the mirrored walls of the restaurant. "Why would he confess?"

"To close the cases."

"Why would he care?"

"Someone else cares."

"Who's this someone else? Who's Barth helping? Why's he helping?"

"I haven't got all the answers yet." Cardozo stirred his coffee. "But we found photographs of three dead kids in Father Montgomery's file—Vegas and Wills and the alleged housebreaker, Pablo Cespedes."

A sudden electricity charged the space between Cardozo and Thoms.

A thin smile bent the A.D.A.'s mouth. "Just like the anonymous note said." Thoms slid ramrod-straight to the edge of his chair. "Then you think Montgomery is behind the killings?"

"A year and a half ago you didn't want to hear this."

"A year and a half ago I could have been wrong. I could be wrong now. So could you."

"Right now a team of detectives is running down the other names in that file. There may be others missing or dead."

"It could be Montgomery." A glow came into Thoms's face. "A presentable case could be made. We don't know for a fact when he set that booby trap. We don't know for a fact he was mugged in the park three weeks before the break-in."

"There wasn't a break-in."

Their eyes connected.

"Hey." Thoms snapped a finger. "What if . . . Montgomery invited this Cespedes kid into the rectory. Made a pass at him, tried to get him to do drugs and s/m. The kid freaked. In the struggle Montgomery was blinded and the kid was killed." Thoms raised his coffee cup. "That kind of scenario I could take to a grand jury."

Cardozo told himself that this would be an excellent opportunity to keep his mouth shut. He lifted his cup.

Two cups clinked.

Thoms took a long, thoughtful swallow. "Who wrote the note?"

"We haven't got the handwriting analysis yet."

"You know what would be beautiful? If his assistant, the woman priest—if she wrote it, if she knows what he's done and she's ready to blow the whistle on him." It was a little less than a statement, but a lot more than a question. "What do you think?"

"It's going to be hard getting Bonnie Ruskay to testify against Father Montgomery. Maybe impossible."

"Why's that?"

"She worships him."

"Pablo was doing okay." Sy Jencks opened the manila file marked CESPEDES, P. He spread several of the sheets out on his desk. He stared at them, chest softly heaving. He had the squint lines of a Marine drill instructor and he wore his hair in a brush cut that was going gray. "Pablo was what the juvenile probation system considers a good bet. Never missed an appointment. Since release, never used drugs, so far as we knew. Had no bad associates, so far as we knew. Committed no infractions, so far as we knew."

Cardozo's ballpoint skittered across the sheets of his notepad. He flipped a sheet.

"He was in therapy at a city-funded project called Operation Second Chance, and so far as we knew he was doing well there too."

Cardozo glanced up. "Second Chance is the outfit that rehabilitates young offenders?"

"All of my probationees go there." There was a wry suggestion of a grin in Sy Jencks's pale brown eyes. "They have to. It's the law."

"And you say Pablo was keeping out of trouble—so far as you knew."

Sy Jencks pushed back his swivel chair. He gazed up at the ceiling. The cinderblock walls of his office had been painted industrial gray, but the overhead fluorescent lights tinted them a pale flickering green.

"Pablo was one of our stars. If you look at the stats, it seems very unlikely Pablo would turn housebreaker. He doesn't fit the profile. He wasn't an antisocial kid. He wasn't a violent kid."

"What kind of kid was he?"

"If anything, I'd say he was creative, solution-oriented; to coin the old cliché, a sensitive loner. Sure, he had a street veneer, but it didn't go deep. In his heart of hearts, Pablo was scared shitless of the streets."

"What was he on probation for?"

"He broke into a store and stole a guitar. Can you beat that? One stupid guitar. And he wasn't that good of a thief. Eight people heard the alarm, saw this skinny kid running with a guitar. Cops caught him in three minutes." Sy Jencks shrugged. His torso must have thickened since he'd bought his plaid cotton shirt, because the buttons were straining to stay shut. "First offense."

"What do you know about the friend he spent his last night with, this Andy fellow?"

The black telephone on the desk let out a series of piercing rings. Sy Jencks waited for it to stop and then he lifted the receiver and laid it on the desk top. "Pablo never mentioned any Andy to me."

"Then if he wasn't in his foster home, where would he spend the night?"

"Where do any of them spend the night? The streets." A lot of anger, a lot of sadness seemed to be tamped down in Sy Jencks's voice. "Or hustle a bed from some chicken hawk."

"Did Pablo ever mention Father Joe Montgomery at St. Andrew's Church? Or Reverend Bonnie Ruskay?"

"No, not to me."

"Father Montgomery served on the board of Operation Second Chance. There's a possibility Pablo could have met him there."

"Anything's possible, but Pablo never mentioned it to me."

"Did he ever mention any chicken hawks?"

Sy Jencks shook his head. "I was his probation officer; for me he had to be straight and narrow. If anything like that was going on, he might have told his therapist. Therapy talk is privileged."

"Who's his therapist?"

"Paula Moseley, at Operation Second Chance."

"*The* Paula Moseley—Douglas Moseley's wife?"

"I take it you've met the bitch?"

THIRTY-SEVEN

Cardozo propped his NYPD placard in the windshield and stepped out of the car.

Above the smoothly flowing traffic of East Eightieth Street, the headquarters of Operation Second Chance shimmered like a Renaissance mirage. A bronze plaque beside the entrance said the town house had been built by the Astors and once occupied by them. Inside, Cardozo saw that they'd left their chandeliers and marble statues behind.

A young man led him to a small elevator and took him upstairs to Paula Moseley's office.

She was all crisp hospitality. "How nice to see you again, Vince."

"Nice to see you again, Mrs. Moseley."

"Please. Call me Paula."

He looked around the tall-windowed room with its signed Jasper Johns lithos. "Beautiful office."

"Thanks. I believe the work environment should be like home. It relaxes the patients."

Cardozo tried to imagine street kids pouring out their gut aches in a three thousand dollar custom-built chair from the "Home" section of the *New York Times*. He wondered which city budget had furnished Paula Moseley's office. Which bureaucrat's brother-in-law had pocketed the 100 percent markup and the 20 percent kickback.

"I need to ask you some questions about Pablo Cespedes."

"Yes. Poor Pablo. Won't you sit?"

They sat in armchairs near the window. He had a sense that the meter was ticking, that this was a stall to eat up the minutes till her next patient came in.

"Pablo was killed breaking into St. Andrew's rectory."

Her big green eyes did surprise marvelously. "I had no idea of the circumstances. I'm astonished. Pablo wasn't a criminal."

Cardozo asked if Pablo had been involved in a sexual relationship.

"I'm sure he was sexually active, but he never mentioned any particular relationship to me."

"Did he ever prostitute himself with men?"

"He was pretty open with me, and he never mentioned anything like that. He did say something about three-way sex with a woman and a man. It sounded a little shady to me. The man had some connection with the entertainment industry. Pablo wrote songs and performed them. Supposedly the man was going to help him break into TV and music videos." Paula was silent. She did thoughtfulness very well too. "In fact, at our last session, Pablo said he was waiting for an audition with this person."

"Could this man possibly have been Father Joe Montgomery?"

"No way." Paula Moseley's eyes blazed. "Father Joe is a man of absolute personal integrity. I can personally vouch for that."

"Was Pablo acquainted with Father Montgomery?"

"I'd very much doubt it."

"Isn't it a possibility? Father Joe served on the board here, Pablo came here for counseling."

"Father Joe never came here. I frankly doubt that his path ever crossed with Pablo's."

"Did Pablo ever mention Reverend Bonnie Ruskay?"

"Never. I doubt he knew her."

"Apparently he told you a great deal about himself."

"Pablo was an extremely intelligent, funny, charming, and strange young man. He had enormous potential. He understood that the therapeutic process rests on trust, and yes, he told me practically everything about himself."

"Was he doing any drugs?"

"Absolutely not. He'd been clean and dry since his trial."

In the light of that reply and the drugs that had shown up in Pablo's autopsy, Cardozo had to wonder how well Paula Moseley knew her patients.

A buzzer sounded.

"You'll have to excuse me. My next patient is here. This has been delightful. Can we continue another time?"

"Sure." Cardozo rose. "Another time."

Cardozo sat at his desk in his shirtsleeves and winced. On the small TV screen, Pablo Cespedes whipped a guitar he had not bothered to tune. Grinning from sideburn to sideburn, he chanted, *I am God, I am God, God is in me.* . . .

"What *is* that racket?" Ellie asked from the doorway.

"Your tax dollars at work. Pablo Cespedes performing his own material. Apparently he thought he could get backers to put up the money for a cabaret act."

"Well, it's an alternative to holding up guitar shops."

"Barely. And if you think that's awful . . ." Cardozo stopped the tape and slipped another into the VCR.

An image came up on the screen: Father Joe Montgomery in drag—draped boa, slinking snakeskin, and a Marilyn wig—singing "Anything Goes." Cutaways showed a bespectacled Phil Donahue strolling with a mike and a tolerant-liberal smile through a largely female studio audience.

Ellie stared, small-eyed and for just an instant dumbstruck. "What the hell was he doing on *Donahue*?"

"Publicizing one of his shows, educating the public about transvestism—all the usual Christian good works."

Ellie seemed to succumb to a kind of fascination. She angled the straight-backed chair toward the screen and sat and watched. It was as though she was mentally dissecting every toss of the wig, each flipped wrist and wiggled hip. "You know, the scariest thing about that man is—he's not bad."

"You're absolutely right. *Bad* is not the word." Cardozo clicked the tape off. "How can an intelligent woman like Bonnie Ruskay be taken in by him?"

Ellie eyed Cardozo speculatively. A crystal of silence seemed to form in the air and then snap.

"Speaking of the reverend, I've been running down her ex-cleaning lady's social security records. The last current address they show for Olga Quigley is St. Andrew's rectory."

"Then she's working off the books."

Ellie picked up Pablo's cassette. She examined the label. It was covered in felt-tipped handwriting and one of the corners hadn't been completely glued down. She poked a fingernail at a ripple in the paper.

"Why do so many people swear by Father Joe?" Cardozo wondered. "What's his magic?"

"I guess cynical cops like you and me just can't tune in on his kind of charisma." There was something stuck behind the label. She carefully worked it loose and looked at it.

"Vince." She handed him a pawn ticket.

"A lot of people come through that door." In one thick grimy hand, the proprietor of Equity Loans held a pawn ticket; in the other, the photo of Pablo Cespedes. "This is not exactly a face to remember."

"What did he pawn?" Cardozo said.

"What do any of them hock? Junk." Beneath a sweat-stained undershirt, the proprietor shrugged a beefy shoulder toward the wall behind him.

Cardozo had never seen so many musical instruments hanging in one narrow, dimly lit storefront: trumpets, violins, concertinas, accordions, tambourines, guitars, saxophones in every size from midget to monster.

The proprietor turned and unhooked a guitar that had enough metal and enamel inlays to fill a dinosaur's mouth. He laid it on the counter. The strings sighed.

Cardozo examined the ticket tied to the neck of the instrument. "This isn't what he pawned. The numbers aren't even close."

"Somebody must have switched the tickets. It happens. I turn my back, some kid gets smart."

The proprietor didn't strike Cardozo as the type who'd turn his back on a blind man, much less the robbers, muggers, pickpockets, and crack addicts who made up the clientele of this and every other pawnshop on Ninth Avenue.

"We'd like to see the correct article," Ellie said.

"You're seeing it."

"How about that chalice in the window?" Cardozo said.

"*Chalice*? What do you think this is, King Arthur's attic?"

"The bronze chalice with semiprecious stones," Cardozo said. "Top shelf, left."

"It's a cup with cut glass."

"Garnets and carnelians," Ellie said.

A buzzer sounded. The proprietor peeked through the velvet curtain that backed the window display. He pressed a button behind the counter and the street door clicked open.

Bonnie Ruskay, blond and slender and lost-looking, stepped blinking into the shop. She saw Cardozo and smiled. "I wasn't sure this was the right place. You said *Exchange* on the phone, and the window says *Equity*."

Cardozo turned. "Ellie, you remember Reverend Bonnie Ruskay?"

Ellie nodded pleasantly. "Of course."

"Ms. Ruskay," Cardozo said, "did you happen to recognize anything in that window out there?"

"The collection plate and the chalice."

"When you bring the chalice," Ellie told the proprietor, "bring the pewter plate with the copper border—second shelf left."

Light flickered off the sweat on the proprietor's face. "The cup and the wok." His tone was angry, exhausted, but not yet resigned. He brought the chalice and the plate from the window.

Bonnie turned the chalice over. A mark had been scratched onto the base: *St. A.*

She nodded. "This is ours."

"Recognize anything else in the shop?" Cardozo said.

She examined the glass display case beneath the counter. It was crammed with timepieces, blenders, binoculars, like a cutaway view of a Dumpster. She pointed to the bottom shelf. "Could I see the base of these candlesticks?"

Twenty minutes later, fourteen items of church paraphernalia sat on the counter, all marked with the same little scratched *St. A.* "I'd like to take this chalice with me," Bonnie said.

The proprietor made objecting noises.

"This is stolen property," Cardozo said.

"You say it's stolen." The proprietor pushed a long, lone wisp of graying hair away from his forehead. "This lady walks in off the street and says it's stolen. You show me cop shields, she shows me a driver's license, but the one thing I haven't seen is proof—just show me the proof and you can walk out with the whole store."

"How much would it cost to redeem the chalice?" Bonnie said.

"Hold on," Cardozo said. "You're not going to pay for something that belongs to you."

The proprietor said nothing, did nothing, simply listened and watched, smiling a rueful old smile with rueful old eyes.

"This chalice was a gift to Father Joe from the Bishop of Lambeth." Bonnie opened her purse. "It means a great deal to him."

"A hundred dollars," the proprietor said.

Bonnie handed him the money.

"Now, wait a minute," Cardozo said.

Ellie shook her head as though she was staring at an old dog that just wouldn't let go of its favorite bone. She motioned him not to argue. "Tax included, of course."

"You want me to cheat the city?" The proprietor sighed. "Okay, I'll cheat the city."

THIRTY-EIGHT

Bonnie stood on the corner of Forty-ninth Street and Ninth Avenue, shading her eyes against the sun, looking for a cab.

Not promising.

Traffic moved past like freight on a stalled train: a bumper-to-bumper wall of Jersey license plates, trucks, vans, police cars, ambulances. Sirens howled. Horns exploded in raucous *up-yours* fanfares.

She didn't see a single cab, free or otherwise, so she decided to try her luck on Eighth Avenue.

As she hurried east she was struck by the pedestrian population, how different they looked in this part of town from the people you'd see in the neighborhood of St. Andrew's. There were no jackets here, no neckties either. The eyes were different here too—none of that polite looking-away you got on the Upper East Side. They sized you up, challenged you even, eyes of hunger and resentment and—disconcertingly—hate.

It occurred to her that she was the only white face on the block. She was ashamed of herself for thinking it; ashamed, too, of the impression she had that they were eyeing her.

Dear God, she prayed, *don't let me be a bigot.* She caught sight of herself reflected in a plate glass window. *They have every reason to stare,* she realized. *I'm carrying this crazy-looking chalice under my arm.* She wished she had asked the shopkeeper to put it in a bag for her.

She saw a cab free on Eighth, stopped in traffic. She hopped into it. "East Sixty-ninth and Madison Avenue, please." She placed the chalice on the backseat next to her.

The driver began a left turn toward the Hudson.

Bonnie sat forward in the seat. "I'm sorry, but I want *East* Sixty-ninth—you're going west."

The driver turned around and she saw dark-skinned incomprehension. She glanced at the license on the dashboard. The name was Arab and she wondered if he spoke any English.

"East!" Horns were blaring and she had to shout. She pointed. "Will you please take me east!"

The cab rammed another car. Brakes yelped and tires squealed and there was a crunching sound as the cab rammed again. The impact threw her forward into the partition.

The cab had stopped moving and she heard the driver of the other car screaming at the Arab. A one-eyed man with a squeegee came hobbling through the stalled traffic and began spreading filthy water on the windshield. The Arab leapt out of the cab to scream at the squeegee man.

She pulled herself back onto the seat. *I'd do better walking,* she realized. She looked at the meter to see what she owed. Three dollars. She wondered if the meter was fast. What would be a fair tip if she got out now?

She unsnapped her purse and looked for a five.

The door beside her suddenly flew open and a young boy jumped into the cab.

"I'm sorry," Bonnie said. "This cab is taken."

He sat smirking at her. His eyes were a flat gunmetal blue—the steel eyes of a robot. The sour smell of his sweat hit her like a slap. His tongue moistened his lip. "Nice cup."

She moved the chalice to the other side of her body. *This isn't happening,* she told herself. *This is New York. This is America. This is the First World. People don't jump into someone else's cab.*

The boy reached into his sock and pulled out a straight-edge razor, then flipped it open. "Don't make any noise and you won't get hurt. Give me the cup." He seized her little finger and held it against the razor.

He had the smooth-skinned faced of a seventeen-year-old. He wore a tiny steel crucifix in his left ear and his hair was a pure corn-silk blond dangling in a ponytail from under a New York Mets baseball cap.

A child, she thought. *Why is he doing this?*

"If you want to keep your finger, bitch, hand the cup over."

He began closing the razor on her pinkie. An electric white pain shot through her. She pushed the chalice at him. In a single bound he was out of the cab and running.

"Long blond hair," Bonnie said, "pulled back in a ponytail."

Her words felt fast and shrill and jerky, and she realized she was still keyed up. *Relax,* she told herself. *You're safe now. No one's holding a knife on you.*

"He was lightly built, but sinewy . . . compact . . . tanned. Like a surfer who had just climbed off a wave."

Lieutenant Cardozo was taking notes. "A pretty dirty wave."

They were sitting in her office. The window was closed and the low hum of the air conditioner made the walls of the room seem closer together.

"Did anyone else see this kid?"

"The cab driver."

"Did you get the driver's name or license number?"

Tiredness swept over her. She tried to hold it at bay, but little dots hovered in front of her eyes. "No, I was too confused."

Lieutenant Cardozo drummed his fingers on the edge of the armchair. He stopped. "Have you seen this kid around before?"

"Around where before?"

"Anywhere. Around the rectory."

"Why would he come around the rectory?"

"Father Montgomery has that woodworking shop downstairs for underprivileged kids."

"He wasn't one of Father Joe's."

"You're sure."

There was something openly exploratory in the way Cardozo was gazing at her.

"Of course I'm sure." But she wasn't sure. *Why do I feel I have to be definite with this man?* "I've never seen him before."

"He may have seen *you* before. He seemed to know you had that chalice."

"How could he not have known? I was carrying it unwrapped in the street."

"Pays to advertise, right?"

She held her annoyance in check. He was only doing his job, lightening the mood with a joke, trying to be friendly and easy to talk to. She nodded. "You're right. I was stupid."

"You weren't breaking any law. He was the law-breaker. And he sounds experienced. I don't think he just happened to see you and decided to jump you. He could have been staking out this church. Which means he's following you."

"I doubt that very much. I told you I've never seen him before today."

"You wouldn't see him till he wanted you to. These kids are experts. The last thing you need is some crack-wasted juvenile thinking he holds a first mortgage on your life."

"You seem to think that only semihuman filth on two legs could commit petty larceny."

"All kinds of people commit all kinds of crimes. The question is, why did this one commit this robbery and this assault?"

"It wasn't assault."

He flicked a glance in her direction. "You said he drew blood."

She looked at her finger. The cut was barely a dark line, like a piece of thread she might have tied there to remind herself of something. "A drop."

"That's one of the definitions of assault."

"He was a child."

"Half of them are nowadays. It could be he's staked out the pawnshop. He could even be doing business with them."

"What kind of business?"

"Thirteen valuable articles left this church and wound up in that pawnshop. He could be moving property from here to there. And it wasn't done in one haul, or you would have noticed."

"What are you saying?"

"It was done in small hauls. Someone was walking in and out of here."

"I still don't understand."

"It wouldn't be the first time Father Montgomery invited a criminal in here."

She shook her head in instant denial. "He's never invited a criminal here."

"Tommy Lanner. Actor-slash-thief. Stole a VCR."

"But that was years ago. And Lanner was smooth. He conned Father Joe. The boy that robbed me wouldn't be capable of a con."

"Whoever took that property felt free to come and go. And Father Montgomery wasn't stopping them at the door."

"There are other ways than being invited for thieves to get in. I believe it's customary for some of them to break in."

"Nobody broke into Father Montgomery's study. It was faked." Cardozo was watching her with his deep-set, dark brown eyes. "The window was knocked out from the inside. And it was broken *after* Cespedes screamed."

"That's not possible."

"A witness heard it."

Impatience crackled like static electricity along her skin. "And does this witness have a name?"

He didn't answer. There was weariness in the dark grooves of his forehead.

"Tell me, Lieutenant—do you believe that anonymous note too?"

He rose in pieces—first the square head, the square shoulders lifting from the chair, then the long legs heaving up the rest of him. "Ms. Ruskay, young people involved with St. Andrew's have died."

"Who besides that housebreaker? And he had nothing whatever to do with this church!"

"Father Montgomery had that housebreaker's picture in his file. And he had photos of two murdered runaways in that same file."

Bonnie stared at the lieutenant. She felt an icy swell of amazement. "Because he had their photos he killed them?"

He looked concerned for her and enormously sad. "Did it ever occur to you that Father Montgomery may have a dark side?"

"And did it ever occur to you that Father Joe is a humanistic liberal? He takes a hands-on approach to the social problems of this city. There are hundreds of people who'd love to discredit him and his policies and the social activism of this church."

Cardozo just stood, letting her shout.

"I hope you're not one of them."

"Why would you think I might be?" he said quietly.

"Because you're ready to believe anything—that Joe is a communist, a seducer of adolescents, a murderer."

"Did I say all that?"

"You don't have to." The sound of her own angry voice shocked her, but she couldn't stop herself. "Other people have said it. Frightened small men and women who can't face the fact that this society has got to change or go down the tubes. People who want to undermine everything this church has worked twenty years to build up, everything we stand for. That's the dark side, Lieutenant—the true dark side."

"I'm not denying it."

"Father Joe is responsible for one accidental death, and he's admitted it. He rigged that booby trap because there'd been break-ins and he was terrified after the attack in the park."

Cardozo shook his head. "There's no proof that he was ever actually attacked."

"You think he faked that too?" Disbelief took her. "And blinded himself?"

Cardozo sighed. "The pawnbroker surrendered your property —I'll see that it's returned to you. If you see this kid again, let me know immediately. And I mean *immediately*."

She watched him go to the door.

Bonnie, she chided herself, *what the hell is the matter with you? God made rednecks just as he made moral theologians. This man has no obligation to you except to be the person he is.*

"Lieutenant."

He turned.

"I realize you mean to helpful. I appreciate that."

"That's okay."

"And you're wrong. Joe was attacked. There's proof and I'll find it."

Bonnie closed the rectory door. Her guts were churning. She returned to her office and grabbed the phone and dialed David Lowndes.

"You sound strange," he said. "Is something the matter?"

"No. Well, yes. I'm concerned with the way the police are handling Father Joe. I have a feeling it could be the beginning of an orchestrated backlash against his policies."

"Now, isn't that a little paranoid?"

"The city's turning conservative and a lot of the police are openly right-wing."

"If you mean law and order, they've always been right-wing."

"They're saying Father Joe was never attacked in the park, that it's all a lie and a cover-up."

"What do they say is being covered up?"

"They think he killed the Cespedes boy intentionally."

For a moment David Lowndes didn't speak, and then he said, "That's asinine."

"Of course it's asinine—but we've got to find proof that the attack in the park actually happened. I'm going to offer a reward for eyewitness information. Is there any legal problem?"

THIRTY-NINE

At sunset, Barry Ignatius Cardinal Fitzwilliam crouched down beside the flower bed. He gave a sharp tug on the string. The wooden duck took a waddling lurch through the freshly mowed grass. Its painted bill opened and shut and a ratchet somewhere inside of it made a sort of quacking sound.

The infant—usually a quiet, dignified toddler—broke into golden laughter.

The cardinal offered his great-grandnephew the string. "Here, Barry, want to try?" He placed it in the little hand.

The little fingers closed into a fist.

"Pull. Go ahead."

The cardinal gave the duck a push from behind. The ratchet quacked and the child fell down and rolled on the ground in helpless giggles.

In the sky far above the garden, a waxen moon rode a pink-marbled tide of clouds.

The cardinal patted the little blond head.

If day has to pass into night, he reflected, *this is the perfect way.*

"Uncle Barry." His grandnephew's wife stepped from the house into the backyard. "Dinner will be ready in a half hour."

"You're spoiling me."

She stood dark-haired and lean in faded blue jeans, watching him. "And you have a visitor."

He saw that she was holding his briefcase. "Thank you, Nora." He took the briefcase and went through the door into a softly lit living room. He turned right and took the stairs down into the game room.

Bill Kodahl stood playing with one of the vintage pinball machines. Bells clanged. Lights raced like traffic speeding across a dozen highway clover leafs. In the score box, extra points and bonuses spun into the ten millions.

"Good evening, Bill," the cardinal said. "It's my turn to go first, isn't it?"

Bill Kodahl picked up his Scotch and soda from the edge of the machine. He turned. His smooth face had a hint of a new tan. "I hope you've got good news for me on Giuliano?"

"The sound quality's not very good." The cardinal handed the D.A. a tape from his briefcase. "There was a festival in the street outside and the choir was practicing. Giuliano's very, very troubled."

"And well he should be."

"He's willing to come clean."

"To his priest or to me?"

"The priest has persuaded him to come clean to you. But he wants the drug charges against his son dropped."

"You have to love human beings." Bill Kodahl smiled. "They never stop wanting the moon."

The cardinal sat with his briefcase open on his lap, tapping a finger on the combination lock. "Do you have something for me?"

"Afraid so. An undercover cop has photographed Father Mc-Coy dealing drugs in Canarsie."

"Lord."

"We've fixed it." Kodahl crossed to the sofa. He snapped open an attaché case and handed the cardinal a folder. "Regina Cosmato has charged Father Bozack with gross indecency. We probably can fix it." He handed the cardinal another folder.

"At least it's a woman."

"She accuses him of molesting her eight-year-old daughter."

"At least it's a female."

"Then there's Father Hoffman. He's been stealing art books from the gift shop at the Metropolitan Museum of Art."

"But he's done that for years."

"But this time the museum is being hard-assed." The D.A. handed the cardinal a third folder. "They want a variance to put up a new wing."

The cardinal sank deeper into the sofa. The prospect of involving himself in city real estate politics yet again gave him a headache the size of the living room upstairs. "What happened to the days when priests were content to sit in the rectory and drink themselves silly?"

"Just be happy they're not doing crack."

"In the inner-city parishes, some of them already are." The cardinal sighed. "What's happening to the world I used to know, Bill? I miss those days."

"I miss them, too, but it's no good looking back." The D.A.'s voice had that inflection: *There's more, and it's worse.* "I'm afraid there's one more thing we have to discuss."

He handed the cardinal a thick State of New York Department of Law manila envelope.

Suddenly the cardinal's breath was a block of ice in his stomach. He knew what was in the envelope. "Not another child. Not the same as before."

"Two weeks ago. In Queens." Bill Kodahl drained his drink. "A communion wafer in the kid's mouth."

The cardinal ripped open the envelope. He gazed at the photographs. They were the worst he'd seen. For the first time, the victim had not had time to decay. There was still flesh on the bones, still a face on the flesh, still an expression on the face. "But we were certain Father Romero was the murderer. And when he died, we were certain it was over."

"And going by the evidence in hand at the time, that was a logical conclusion."

"But Father Romero's dead—and the murderer's alive. He's taken another life." The cardinal stared at the district attorney. "We've made a terrible mistake. We completely misjudged poor Father Romero."

"We did what seemed best at the time."

The cardinal's eyes swung back to the photos. "Are we making another mistake to go on hiding these killings? It's been three years and they just get worse."

"Barry." The D.A.'s voice was a command. "It's not your worry. I'm handling it."

The sun had dropped below the skyline and East Fifty-third Street was in shadow. Halfway down the block, tucked between a dress boutique with a FOR RENT sign and an office building with a FLOOR TO LET sign, Cardozo found the first address from Reverend Bonnie Ruskay's list: gold Gothic lettering announced THE FISH AND THE LAMB: RELIGIOUS GOODS AND BOOKS.

He pushed open the glass door.

The shop was hushed and softly lit, with a smell of old books like the herbs in one of those after-dinner liqueurs for which only monks possess the secret recipe.

There was a wall of religious pictures and crosses and crucifixes in all sizes from mega to petite. The remaining walls were devoted to books.

Two women browsed the bookshelves. One was a nun, dressed in a short-skirted gray habit that marked some sort of compromise between cloister and Fifth Avenue, and she pinned Cardozo with a glance that seemed to say, *Are you sure you've come to the right place?*

He wasn't sure. He smiled at the nun. Her glance skittered away. He began searching the shelves. He found Bibles and gospels, prayer books and hymnals, works of scriptural interpretation alphabetized by author, but no Ruskay among the *R*'s.

"Do you need help, sir?" The clerk was in his early thirties, dark-haired and prematurely balding.

For just an instant Cardozo thought he knew the man, and then the sense of familiarity disintegrated, as though a kaleidoscope had been jiggled.

"I'm looking for some books on theology." Cardozo referred to the list he'd scribbled from memory. *"The Serpent and the Grail; Biological Resemblance to the Savior—"*

The clerk's dark eyes froze behind horn-rimmed glasses. Civility at that moment was clearly a stretch. "The title is *No Biological Resemblance to the Savior.* Those are books by Reverend Bonnie Ruskay. We don't carry her. We're a traditional Catholic bookstore."

"That's odd. She recommended this store to me."

Outside the shop window, traffic was a low and vaguely ominous hum. Somewhere in the street a car alarm began yodeling.

The clerk smiled. He had the squint lines of an accountant. "Reverend Bonnie Ruskay is more eclectic than we are."

Cardozo realized the nun was watching them. "Where would I find her books?"

"The Episcopal diocese has a store over on Third Avenue—they'd stock her."

After dinner, Cardozo sank into the comfortable embrace of an old armchair with Bonnie Ruskay's *The Son of God Was Also a Daughter: Reclaiming the Holy Anima as Spiritus.*

"Why are you reading that?" Terri asked.

Cardozo stared at the page, pretending he didn't feel the expectancy of his daughter's silence. "I want to get a feel for Reverend Bonnie's thinking."

Terri smiled and the smile showed beautifully young, white teeth. "And flatter her—and win her trust—and get information from her?" She lifted the book from his hands. She frowned at the author's photo. "Funny, she doesn't look like a reverend."

"What's a reverend supposed to look like?"

Terri's shoulders rose in a half-shrug. "I don't know. Dull. Earnest. Sincere."

Cardozo studied the photo. It showed a face of fine-boned intelligence with eyes that seemed to hold flame. "You don't think she looks sincere?"

"Not *boringly* sincere. You've met her. What do you think?"

What do I think? he wondered. "Too early to say." He tried to sound offhand about it. He didn't feel all that offhand, but he wasn't sure what it was he felt.

That night he dreamed he was making love with a strange woman. Her features were hidden: she wore dark glasses and dark blond hair covered half her face.

From far away came a wave that lifted them both and crested and then traveled past them, a shrug of eternity.

He angled his mouth and kissed a small pink birthmark on her left shoulder.

He lifted her glasses off and stared into Reverend Bonnie's smoky green eyes.

"Omigod," he heard himself say. "I didn't know, I didn't mean to . . ."

He was sitting up in bed. The familiar dappling of streetlight on wallpaper told him it was his own bed. The hands of the alarm clock, glowing in the dark, told him it was three thirty-five in the morning.

He lifted his feet out of the sargassolike tangle of bedsheets. He pulled his summer-weight bathrobe around him. His feet found his slippers and his slippers found the kitchen.

He was fixing himself a cup of hot milk when Terri came shuffling in, rubbing her eyes. "Are you all right, Dad?"

He shrugged, embarrassed. "Just had trouble sleeping."

"I heard you scream."

He stared at the saucepan as though staring was the most important part of getting the milk to boil. "I was just arguing with myself."

She lifted the saucepan off the flame just before it could boil over. She poured the steaming milk into a coffee mug and sprinkled a little cinnamon on top.

"What's bothering you?" She pulled out a chair and motioned him to sit down. She sat across the table from him. "Is it something at work?"

He sipped. The milk stung his lips. He set it down to cool. He exhaled heavily. "Sometimes it hits me how much I miss your mother."

Terri nodded. With each passing year, she seemed to take on more and more of her dead mother's features. The pale skin, the brown hair, the smile that smiled just a bit more on the right than the left, and now the same dark eyes that knew exactly how to look into him. "I miss her too."

"Sometimes I wish . . ." Cardozo gave the milk another try. This time it was his tongue that got stung. "I don't know what I wish. That's the trouble."

"I know what I wish. I wish you had someone in your life."

"I have enough in my life. I have you."

"Then how come you're lonely?"

"Who says?"

"That's why you're always working too hard."

"I'm not working too hard. I'm just getting done what has to get done and it isn't my fault this city has gone murder-crazy."

"You're always mixed up in other people's problems. You need some problems of your own."

"Problems like I see on the job, I don't need of my own, thank you."

"You need *something* of your own."

"I've got lots of my own—including a daughter who's a real pain in the ass when she starts with that amateur psychiatry."

Terri sighed a quiet, accepting sigh. She leaned across the table to give him a kiss. "I love you, too, Dad. Feel better. G'night."

He couldn't sleep.

He brought his briefcase from the hallway and began reviewing crime-scene inventories of the three runaway murders.

He cleared a space on the table and drew up a grid—the found items running down the left and the runaways' case numbers across the top. When he had filled the grid in, he took out the medical examiner's reports.

FORTY

Something looked different, brighter. At first Cardozo thought it was just the sun shining on the precinct facade, and then he realized someone had finally replaced the busted green globe beside the doorway. They'd even hung a brand-new flag from the pole over the steps: for a change, the New York City seal and the number 22 looked crisp and focused.

On the other hand, a worse-than-usual pandemonium was whirlpooling through the lobby. The eight-to-four tour was starting, and it took Cardozo almost two minutes to get through the gauntlet of backslaps and greetings, and reach the stairs. He found a message from Harvey Thoms on his desk: *Phone immediately.*

There was an area code, 516, and he realized it had to be Thoms's home number in the Long Island suburbs. It took him three tries to get through a busy signal.

"I spent all of yesterday afternoon searching records." Some kind of pressure had forced Thoms's voice into a higher register. "I couldn't locate any deposition by Martin Barth at all. Nothing in the Richie Vegas case; nothing in the Wally Wills case; nothing in Ms. Basket Case."

"I could see one file getting lost," Cardozo said, "but three?"

"About two hundred documents in unprosecuted cases have been misplaced. Justice is transferring records to a computerized data base. There are a few glitches in the program. At least that's the explanation I'm running into."

"Funny this glitch snagged all of Martin Barth's confessions."

"It doesn't mean Barth's records may not turn up."

"I'm not holding my breath."

"I'm still looking," Thoms said. "I'll keep you posted."

Cardozo stepped into the squad room. He poured two cups of

coffee and set the pot back into its perch in the coffeemaker. He stopped at Ellie's desk and handed her a cup.

"Either the department is very screwed up," he said, "or something very peculiar is going on."

She was wearing a blouse the color of smoked salmon and as he gave her the update from the D.A.'s office, she nodded as if it were an old, old story. "Maybe the D.A. should invest in a really high-tech storage medium—like paper." Her eyes had a look of thoughtful skepticism. "Did Captain O'Reilly get hold of you?"

"Not yet."

"He says it's important. He's in the muster room."

Cardozo chugalugged his coffee. "What now?"

Officers beginning the day tour had bottlenecked in the corridor. Lieutenant Carl Ross, the captain's right-hand man, was handing out tubes of black self-shining shoe polish. "Use it on your cap visor, too, and turn those radios off. Hey you, Fanelli, get your jacket!"

A weird light spilled through the doorway, as if a UFO had landed inside. Cardozo knew it couldn't be sun: all the windows on that side of the precinct had been painted over in pea-soup–green—grilles and panes and all—and the only thing that could get through that glass was a hurled brick.

"What's the fiesta?" Cardozo said.

Ross beamed. "NBC-TV."

Inside the muster room, a crew was trying to aim klieg lights so they missed the worst cracks in the walls and ceiling. For ten administrations mayors had been promising a new precinct. So far they'd only come through with Holiday Inn–style dropped ceilings, but after two years the leaks in the old ceilings were beginning to drip through the new ones.

Up on the dais, Captain Tom O'Reilly was barking out assignments like a seasoned TV actor: "Keep those street peddlers moving. Confiscate all goods except books or incense—books are freedom of the press, incense is freedom of religion."

As the cameras panned, the day-tour officers stood at attention, shoulders back and guts pulled in. Waists bulged with service revolvers, belt-loads of ammo, handcuffs and billy clubs.

At the watercooler a very fat man in a designer camouflage

outfit tossed down handfuls of pills with cupfuls of water. "Can we get a shot of a line of shined shoes?" he shouted.

A cameraman crouched.

"Any questions?" O'Reilly rasped.

A rookie patrolman raised his hand. "What about noisy radios?"

"Do not confiscate loud radios. The city council has directed that noise is environmental control, not a police issue. Ticket the radios and issue summonses, but do not seize."

O'Reilly turned off the mike and stepped down from the dais. He walked just a little off the vertical.

"You wanted to see me?" Cardozo said.

O'Reilly nodded. "Channel Four's getting some footage for their evening show." He looked oddly red-faced for this early in the day. "How about showing them around the neighborhood? Talk to some shopkeepers, show how we reassure the local businesses."

Cardozo realized he had been paid a compliment. "After my work's done, I'd be happy to. Unless you're reassigning me."

It wasn't what O'Reilly wanted to hear. "You've assigned an awful lot of men to the rectory thing."

"I sent six cops out to scour runaway camps and see if anyone recognizes some photos."

"What photos?"

"Wills, Gilmartin, Vegas."

O'Reilly tugged at his left ear. "Dead runaways from other precincts."

"Can we talk about this privately?"

They went to the captain's office. O'Reilly picked up a pile of vouchers from his desk. "You don't seem to realize we're living in a period of acute person-power shortage."

"And during this period of acute person-power shortage," Cardozo said, "the mayor has plainclothes cops picking up his laundry and escorting his daughters to discos."

"Let him. He's mayor. He can have plainclothes cops mow his lawn. You, on the other hand, are not mayor. Your job is the Cespedes case, which isn't even a homicide." O'Reilly flipped through the vouchers. "It certainly doesn't merit the man-hours and money you're running up. Are you skimming, Vince? Are you padding the account and keeping a dame on the side?"

"First of all, I'm not. Second of all, Ellie would never let me."

"Ellie thinks you're God. Not that she thinks that highly of God."

"And third of all, Cespedes *is* a homicide and it's connected to a series of homicides." Cardozo showed the captain his grid of the similarities among the four victims.

O'Reilly studied the grid, silent, absorbed. Cardozo could feel him lightening up. The captain was due to retire in sixteen months. Like any retiring brass, he wanted a fairy-tale ending. Breaking a front-page, top-of-the-evening-news multiple homicide case would not be a bad way to go.

"So far," Cardozo said, "these cases have been handled as separate killings by separate killers. Let me have those men and I can prove one person killed them all."

"Have you got a prime suspect?"

"Absolutely." A lie.

"Hard evidence?"

"Why take my word for it? Ask the lab." A bluff.

O'Reilly drew in a deep breath. "Okay, you can have the men for five days."

Cheapskate. "Thank you, sir."

Cardozo's heart was anything but grateful as he walked down the green fluorescent-lit corridor to the squad room. A message on his desk said to call Lou at the lab.

"What've you got, Lou?"

"Some interesting results. The anonymous note was written on letterhead from Reverend Bonnie Ruskay's supply. There's a slight packing crease running down the five blank sheets of her letterhead. The same crease shows up faintly on the anonymous note. The culprit was clever—used paper from the middle of the pile, not the top."

"Any prints?"

"Sorry. No clear prints."

"How are you coming on the handwriting?"

"I'm waiting to hear. But I've got one other result to pass on— Lifeways Labs ran DNA tests on the hairs you gave me."

Lifeways was a commercial state-of-the-art outfit up in West-chester. The NYPD used them for work beyond its technological capacity.

"And?"

"They don't match the hairs from Pablo Cespedes's head."

Cardozo felt a cold ball of shock inside his ribs. "Come on, Lou. Lifeways must have found a match."

"They found a match all right, it just doesn't happen to be Cespedes. The hairs are northern European and they match an-other homicide—a John Doe from the Seventy-seventh."

Cardozo picked up a ballpoint. "Would you give me that case number and the name of the detective in charge?"

"His name's Bob Reach and he's on his way over to you right now."

"Okay, Lou. I'll be here."

Cardozo replaced the receiver. His eyes came up to see a stranger standing in the doorway. He pushed back his chair and stood. "Detective Reach?"

FORTY-ONE

The stranger held out a hand. He was a tall redheaded man with tight, intense eyes in a narrow face. "We have to talk."

Cardozo gestured toward the straight-backed chair. "Have a seat." He closed the door.

Detective Reach handed Cardozo a folder labeled JOHN DOE. "A teenager turned up two weeks ago in Marine Park."

Cardozo flipped through the case file. He skipped the yellow sheets detailing Lifeways' electron microscopy results. He slowed at the medical examiner's report.

The autopsy photos showed that Mr. Doe had been dismem-bered. Death had occurred in early to mid-April of this year. *Probable cause: Asphyxiation due to central nervous system shut-*

down following massive ingestion of narcotizing agent, possibly azidofluoramine, an experimental antipanic medication.

Blood analysis showed alcohol and cocaine. Liver analysis showed toxic levels of azidofluoramine.

Phrases leapt up: *Hands and feet may have been secured with leather belts. . . . Signs of beating or kicking . . . burning of skin such as might be caused by contact with dripped candle wax.*

Lab analysis of T-shirt, jeans, tube socks, and sneakers found in the basket showed *incense residue* and *bits of acrylic gray shag carpet adhering to the fabric.*

The body had been found in a Styrobasket.

At the end of the file Cardozo found a sketch of a dead-eyed male. It could have been drawn by a robot of a robot. He held the drawing up. "I take it this is meant to be him?"

"Our artist sketched him like he would have looked in life. We searched the city. Couldn't find anyone who recognized him."

Cardozo opened his desk drawer. He took out the five photos from Father Joe's file that had been found without curricula vitae. He handed Reach the photo of Tod Lomax. "Maybe your artist should have tried for something a little more like that."

Bob Reach stiffened. His eyes went back and forth from the photo to the drawing. "Same jaw, same cheekbones, same eyebrow ridges—"

"Same guy. Seems to be something that's going around." Cardozo handed Reach the photos of Wills and Vegas. "These were the identical M.O. Plus one unidentified female."

Reach sat shaking his head. "I didn't hear about these."

"I didn't hear about yours."

"The D.A. wanted to hold information back. Not much got published. And what did, they screwed up."

Cardozo nodded. He turned a page of the John Doe file. "Your crime-scene inventory lists some flowers found near the grave. I take it these were stalks and dried leaves?"

Bob Reach's pale eyebrows arched. "I don't exactly recall."

"Could you do me a favor? Check the number of flowers—and were they tied with a red string—and was there a rose?"

After Detective Reach left, something incomplete nagged at Cardozo. He went to the filing cabinet and pulled out the folder on Ms. Basket Case. He didn't sit. He reread the file walking around his desk in tight circles. He reread Vegas and Wills and John Doe.

Four identical homicides spaced over three years. Four identical homicides investigated by four different detectives in four different precincts. Three of the four stamped *closed* when Martin Barth confessed. Even if Barth's confessions had somehow vanished from the data base, they were still recorded here in the original paperwork on Ms. Basket Case, Vegas, and Wills.

Which left John Doe—the odd man out.

Cardozo phoned Dan Hippolito at the medical examiner's office. "Dan, could you review three autopsies for me? Two are yours and one is Sileson's." He gave Dan the autopsy numbers.

"What are we looking for?"

"Any indication that these killings were the work of one person. Check out any similarities like this matzo stuff in their mouths. Give me your educated opinion."

"It may take a while. Spring is killing time in New York—we have corpses in holding patterns here."

"I appreciate it, Dan. And while you're at it, would you check if the records have been tampered with? Information lost or altered?"

"We're shifting everything to computer—a lot gets accidentally lost or altered."

"Let me know if there seems to be an intentional pattern of accident. Thanks, Dan."

As Cardozo swung around in his swivel chair, Ellie came into the cubicle.

"Bob Reach phoned." Tiny, almost invisible diamonds twinkled in her ears. "Your line was busy. Twelve dried stems were found in a bush forty-three inches from the grave. Assortment of mixed dead blooms fastened with red string."

"What about the rose?"

"Who says there was a rose?"

"What kind of rose was it?"

"What kind do you want it to be?"

"Don't do this to me, Ellie."

"It was an Americana Linda Porter. Are you happy? You don't look happy. What's the matter?"

"Meet John Doe from the Seventy-seventh." Cardozo shoved the file toward her across the desk top. "Identical sibling to Ms. Basket Case, Vegas, and Wills in every respect but one: the killer. Martin Barth was in prison when John Doe was murdered."

Ellie opened John Doe and flipped through the pages, frowning.

"One further detail. Martin Barth has vanished from the data base. Not a single confession on record."

The look that she gave him said, *You better stop eating that magic mushroom quiche for lunch.*

"Look at the flukes we're running into and tell me they're flukes. Four identical cases should have been investigated together. They weren't. There should have been a panic in the press. There wasn't."

"Vince, you're shouting."

"When one man confessed to three of the killings, he should have made page one, lead item in the evening news. He didn't. Any reference to the confessions was buried in three different precincts—"

"I can hear you." Ellie handed back the folder. "Please stop shouting."

"And the confessions themselves vanished from the central record. Gone. Wave an electronic wand. Never happened." Cardozo stacked the files on his desk. "I'd like to see the wand that makes John Doe vanish."

Ellie sat staring. Something flared up in her eyes. "Vince."

"What."

"Move John Doe from the top of the pile. Put it second from the bottom."

"What? Why?"

Ellie leaned forward and did it herself. Now she sat back in her chair and nodded. "The stain."

"What stain?"

"It looks like a coffee spill." The same nod, a little slower. "It runs right down the stack."

Cardozo rotated the files. He saw what Ellie meant: a dark stain went like a splayed-out plumb line through all four files.

"You're not paranoid," she said, "because I see it. And I'm not paranoid, because you see it."

An energy wave rippled through the cubicle like the snap of a flag in a breeze.

"Those files *were* together," Ellie said. "And someone spilled coffee on them."

They sat there not moving, not talking.

It was Ellie who finally broke the silence. "Vince, phone Lou."

Cardozo lifted the phone and dialed the lab. "Lou, I need you."

"Hey, if that isn't ESP. I was just about to call you. What's happening?"

"I'm going to send you four manila folders. They're stained. I want to know, is it the same stain on all four? At some point in their history, were they in the same place at the same time?"

"That sounds doable."

"I also need you to review three homicides for me." Cardozo read off the case numbers.

"What's the purpose?"

"Would you note any similarities to Ms. Basket Case. I think it's one killer."

"Okay, I'll get on it."

Cardozo lifted his coffee cup. "You said you had something for me."

"Just heard from my handwriting expert. You can rule out Father Montgomery—it's not his writing on the note. It resembles Ruskay's."

The coffee was bitter and Cardozo had no regrets setting it down. "You said it wasn't a woman's."

"That was me—this is my expert. Now, it could be someone imitating the way Ruskay's handwriting would look if she tried to disguise it. My expert raises an intriguing possibility: it could be Ruskay imitating her own handwriting badly so as not to appear to be the sender."

"I don't see it, Lou. That's awfully sneaky—almost childish."

"Just passing it along for what it's worth."

Ellie's eyes were waiting when Cardozo hung up.

"Disagreement over Bonnie Ruskay?"

"Who said Bonnie Ruskay?"

"Your face."

"You're a great comedian, Ellie, but don't give up your day

job." Cardozo leaned back in his swivel chair. "Lou's handwriting analyst thinks Bonnie may have sent the note."

"And you don't."

"Every time I'm with her she defends Father Joe. She's a tigress on the subject."

"Maybe she suspects or knows something about him but doesn't want to say it."

Cardozo shook his head. "Doesn't feel right."

"Maybe she's trying to incriminate him."

"And leave a handwritten trail to implicate herself?"

"She could be playing a game we don't understand yet."

"She's not the game-playing type. If she thought Father Joe was guilty, she'd come out and say so."

"Maybe you've figured her wrong. Vince, don't let her confuse you."

To Cardozo's ear, that word *confuse,* coming from Ellie, was like a silk hankie wrapped around a ticking hand grenade. He raised his head slowly to take a long look at her. "Don't try to control me, Ellie."

"Who'd want to control you? Who'd even try?"

Silence, he discovered, could be hard work. He put on his jacket.

Ellie gave a mischievous little wave. "Say hi to the reverend for me."

FORTY-TWO

When Bonnie Ruskay opened the door, she didn't seem at all surprised to see Cardozo standing on the sidewalk.

"I happened to be in the neighborhood. Is this a bad time?"

"Not at all. Come on in."

He followed her indoors. There was a lightness to her movements that gave him the feeling she was pleased to see him.

"I've been worrying about you. Have you been bothered by that kid anymore?"

"Not that I've noticed."

A door flew open and a giggling towheaded child came bounding into the hallway.

"Kyle!" Bonnie's voice was stern. "I've told you never to run through doors—you could hurt yourself or someone else."

The boy stood hanging his head.

"Come meet Lieutenant Cardozo."

The boy took two steps forward. His eyes stared down at the carpet.

"Hello, Kyle." Cardozo held out his hand.

"Kyle, Lieutenant Cardozo said hello and he's offering his hand. What do you say?"

The boy tipped a glance up. "Hello, sir." He took the hand. His pale blue eyes had a skittering shyness. "It's a pleasure to meet you."

"Likewise, Kyle. A great pleasure."

"Where's your sister?" Bonnie said.

"Hiding."

Bonnie smiled at Cardozo. "Children love the rectory—hiding is the one thing this place is good for."

"You let children have the run of the place?"

"Why not? I love them. Don't you?"

"There you are." A lanky dark-haired man came down the stairway grinning. "One rascal found, one rascal still missing."

Bonnie turned quickly. "Lieutenant, I'd like you to meet a great friend of mine. Collie, this is Vince."

They shook hands. Something about the man struck Cardozo as out-of-kilter: the lines in his face said he had to be at least thirty-five years old, yet he was dressed like a college undergrad—clean but torn blue jeans, a Fordham wrestling team maroon cotton T-shirt. The grin stayed on his face, like a word printed on a page, and it seemed to plead, *Please like me—I'm a good guy.*

"I'll get these imps out of your hair." Collie took Kyle by the hand. "Come on, kiddo, let's go look for Kelly."

Kyle's eyes glowed as if Collie was the perfect playmate and a favorite conspirator. "She's upstairs."

Cardozo watched them go.

"We're obviously not going to get much peace around here," Bonnie said. "It's a beautiful day for a stroll. How about it?"

They left through the courtyard.

"Father Joe usually does the gardening," she said. "I've been weeding lately, but it's looking kind of scraggly, isn't it?"

Cardozo paused beside the rose bush. "This is an unusual-looking plant. What kind of rose is it?"

"That's Father Joe's prize. It's called a Linda Porter—named for Cole Porter's wife. The Porter estate gave it to Father Joe as a thank-you after he staged *Anything Goes Again.*"

"Is it rare?"

"Not since Father Joe got hold of it. He's given cuttings to everyone on earth."

"Like who?"

"Oh . . . like me."

"And where did you plant yours?"

"I gave it to my mother for her birthday. She loves roses."

They walked to the gate. Cardozo's eye appraised the wrought-iron bars. They were fastened with a padlock. He recognized it as a junk item, made in Taiwan and overpriced for the American market and brand-named Eli to suggest it was a Yale.

"You should have a better lock than this," he said. "These things aren't secure."

He gave the cylinder an upward push against the shackle, then a sharp downward tug. He felt the shackle slip a notch inside the plug. The padlock snapped open.

"I'm embarrassed," Bonnie said. "You must think I'm an awful fool when it comes to security."

"No, you're like the majority of people." He swung the gate open. "You have a lot of trust. It's natural in a neighborhood like this."

They walked along a quiet block of town houses and shade trees and custom cars parked at clean curbs.

"Is Collie self-employed?" Cardozo said.

"Why do you ask?"

"It's an odd time of day to be free."

"Collie's writing two books on the buried elements of Eastern mysticism in Christianity."

"Does he live from his writing?"

"Barely." She laughed a good-natured laugh. "No one but Collie could live on the advances religious book publishers pay. Luckily, his needs are modest. He has a very undemanding job on Staten Island with very loose hours."

"I hope his books are easier to find than yours. I had to look all over town for one of them."

"I know. You tried at the Fish and the Lamb. You spoke to my brother."

"That was your brother?"

She nodded. "He told me all about it."

"How did he know who I was?"

"I tell him pretty much everything that's going on around here. He figured it out."

"He's a salesman?"

"He was pinch-hitting for a sick employee. He's vice-president of the company."

"Church suppliers?"

"And religious books. In fact, he's Collie's publisher."

"Interesting line of work."

"Somebody has to do it." She smiled. "It's not as dull as it sounds—especially if you love the church. Ben's a deacon."

"That's like a priest but not quite?"

"It's a lay position. Sort of a combination priest's helper and priest substitute. Ben says it's like having the keys to the bank but not to the vault."

The light-flecked pavement clicked under their heels. Cardozo felt they were strolling through the past. The violence that had made so much of New York uninhabitable had not reached here. This pretty street had not yet turned mean.

Or had it? he wondered.

His steps slowed. "As a matter of fact, now that I think of it—there is one thing I need to ask you."

"So this wasn't a social call." She turned. "It's all right. My feelings aren't hurt. I'll answer if I can."

In a pleasant way, she made him feel embarrassed. "Are you positive you've never heard the name Tod Lomax before?"

For just an instant, a sort of hesitation flickered in her eyes. "No. I'm not sure. I've been trying to remember."

"Would it help to have another look at his picture?" He handed her the photo of Tod Lomax.

She spent a good ten seconds studying it, and then her eyes came around to his. "I can't be certain. I may have seen him or someone like him."

"Where?"

"Around the rectory." She handed back the photo.

Their fingers brushed and he was struck by the softness of that accidental touch, by what it told him about the softness of her skin.

"When?"

"The first time was over a year ago. The second time was three or four months ago."

"What was he doing in the rectory?"

"The baseboards and the moldings in the dining room needed work. Father Joe hired a boy."

"Would he have kept any record of it?"

"We could look in the household accounts ledger."

They returned to the rectory. Cardozo followed her into the rector's office.

She opened one of the desk drawers and took out a family-Bible-sized ledger. As she looked through the check stubs her expression became perplexed. "Nothing for housepainting in the last four months."

"What about the first time—you said a year ago?"

"It was around the time the Vanderbilt Garden reopened." She rippled back through three fat inches of check stubs. "That's strange. I don't see anything."

"May I?" Cardozo lifted the ledger from her hands. He riffled slowly through the stubs for June. There were payments to Con Edison, to the phone company, to a plumber, a glazier, a roof tiler —and a stub for two thousand dollars to the order of *Cash*, in payment of *Miscellaneous*.

He made a mental note of the check stub number: 2727. "Could Lomax have been paid off the books?"

Bonnie shook her head not so much in denial as in doubt. "Anything's possible, but that wasn't Father Joe's usual way."

"Could we see if any work's been done in the dining room?"

Despite a row of leaded windows looking into the courtyard,

the dining room was a long, dark space made even more somber by walls painted moss-green.

"Father Joe wanted the trim brightened. He wanted a kind of oyster shell–gray."

Cardozo examined the baseboards and moldings. "He got his wish on three walls."

The trim on the fourth wall was a different color—butterscotch.

"That was the old color," Bonnie said. "Everyone hated it."

Cardozo counted the carved chairs placed around the lion-footed mahogany table. Ten. An enormous silver punch bowl sat in the center of the table, reflecting the gloom of the room but adding a fun-house distortion. Two silver candelabra flanked it. The candles had burned down unevenly.

"Do people eat in here often?"

"As infrequently as possible. I'm sure it was quite the place a hundred years ago, when rectories had full-time servants—but it's a little grand for nowadays."

"And gloomy."

"You noticed."

"Would it bother you very much," he said, "if it turned out that Father Joe was mixed up in something criminal?"

"Of course it would bother me. But he isn't." She straightened one of the tilted candles. "You know, Lieutenant, in my work I get to see people—just as you do in yours—and I learn to make judgments—just as you do—and I'm not a bad judge of character. I'm a lot better at people than it looks—and I'm certainly not as bad as you think I am."

"What do you know about what I think?"

"I know you feel sorry for me." She looked at him and there was a cool electricity in her gaze. "You see me as a do-gooding liberal who's never had an opinion tested in the crucible of the real world. You're hoping I'm strong enough to survive the disillusion when you show me that Father Joe is a rat."

"That's quite an exercise in mind reading. But the blade cuts two ways."

"Please. Read me. Cut me. I deserve it."

"You see cops as rednecks in city clothes. Right-wingers who trample on minorities and blindly support an unjust status quo."

"There's an element of that in every cop, isn't there?"

"Have you ever known a cop? Ever really talked with a cop? Ever sat down and had a meal with a cop?"

"Are you proving a point or asking me to have a meal with you?"

He was uneasily aware that they belonged to different tribes. "Tod Lomax was found dead two weeks ago."

"I'm very sorry to hear that."

"His hairs were in the hairbrush in Father Montgomery's guest room."

He felt an ice curtain drop between them.

"I've told you he worked here," she said. "He used the guest bathroom and he brushed his hair. Why is that such a surprise to you, Lieutenant? Why do you expect it to be a surprise to me?"

He sighed. "Do you have any idea where Father Montgomery could have met Tod Lomax?"

"I'd assume they met down near the West Side docks where the runaways congregate."

FORTY-THREE

The secret of getting information from a bureaucracy is confidence and swiftness. You must approach, intimidate, and seize in one brazen, continuous move.

Cardozo laid his shield and his ID on the bank manager's desk. "I need a photocopy of check 2727 drawn on the parish account of St. Andrew's Church."

The manager's eyes gave off sudden uncertainty. "I really should ask to see your court order. . . ."

"Fine. If it takes a court order to track down a piddling forged check, I'll get a court order." Cardozo snapped his shield case shut. "And maybe some reporter down at the courthouse will get a good story: the oldest bank in Manhattan isn't even reading the signatures on forged checks."

The manager's lips pressed into a thin line. She took off her oversize tortoiseshell glasses. "Would you please let me finish?"

"No, you let *me* finish. Next time you or your bank needs me or my men, I'll remember you made me go by the rules."

The manager's voice dropped to a whisper. "That won't be necessary. Seeing as you're with the precinct, we'll waive the formalities."

The photocopy was sitting on Cardozo's desk two hours later. The face of the check told him nothing new: it had been made out to *Cash* and signed by Bonnie Ruskay. What interested him was the stamp-endorsement on the back: the faint letters had been badly smudged, but he could make out enough to put together the words *Fidelity Mutual Corp. Inc.*

Fidelity turned out to be a storefront check-cashing operation on a low-rise stretch of Varick Street where the signs in the windows were mostly TRIPLE X ADULT FILMS and FOR RENT. The blinds were angled against the hot blaze of noon as Cardozo stepped through the doorway. A seven-foot zombie decked in shades, gold chains, and holster-hiding Hawaiian shirt stood eyeballing the clientele. He tracked Cardozo with the attentiveness of a heat-seeking missile.

Cardozo nodded hello and flashed his shield.

The zombie escorted him to the head of a shuffling line of surly suckling moms and nodding-out junkies.

Cardozo laid the photocopy on the countertop next to his shield. "Who'd you cash this check for?"

The employee didn't answer. His pockmarked heavy-jawed face stared at the endorsement. Eerie, high-pitched notes were spilling from his Walkman earphones, like crickets playing violin duets. "This check was cashed last year." It was a complaint.

"The law says you keep records."

Mr. No-Smile-for-You-Today gazed at Cardozo with drooping why-are-you-doing-this-to-me eyes. He reached under the counter and dug out a six-inch-thick ledger. He turned pages overgrown with paste-ons. A cloud of dust motes mushroomed up into the air. "That check was cashed by Nell Z. Dunbar."

A crummy Xerox of a picture ID had been taped to the paperwork. Cardozo studied the sunken cheeks, the crater eyes. "This is her?"

"One of those runaway teen hustlers. They hang out on the dock."

"When did you last see her?"

"This one? She was in here two days ago—trying to cash an S and A welfare check."

S and A stood for *stolen and altered*—the most profitable racket run through these check-cashing storefronts. The Human Resources Administration claimed it had tightened procedures and was annually losing "only a modest" hundred eighty million dollars through such scams. In fact, the department admitted off-the-record to an annual half billion siphoned off in fraud.

Cardozo peeled the Dunbar ID off the page.

"Hey." The employee's Queens Irish vowels shaded into a whine. "We need that."

Cardozo smiled. "So do I."

Cardozo's nostrils winced at the stench of unshowered bodies and fecal waste and decayed food. The dock on West Twelfth had once been an enormous warehouse. The interior was as desolate a scene as any Third World capital taken over by rebels and liberated by U.S. Marines.

With his clean shirt and tie, he was as invisible as a fire truck in Grand Central Station. The several dozen heads that were not stoned or unconscious turned. He could feel the low buzz spread: *Watch it—cops are here.*

He searched as he would have canvassed a neighborhood, door-to-door, only there were no doors, just the little unmarked squares of open floor that each of four hundred runaways had claimed as her or his own. The nearest square was occupied by a dark-skinned, one-legged boy playing with Walkman earphones.

"Have you seen this girl?" Cardozo held out the ID photo.

The gesture drew the boy's gaze. The eyes narrowed—exiled eyes, not caring, barely seeing.

The head shook. "Haven't seen her."

Each grave-sized plot of floor was furnished with junk pulled from the street—a discarded mattress, a wooden crate, maybe a lantern or a flashlight. Cardozo went to the next.

"Have you seen this girl?"

Callused fingers took the ID photo. "Never saw her."

At the northwest end of the warehouse, a wan-faced girl with pale blond hair sat barefoot on a mattress with burn holes. She was easily the hundredth person he'd spoken to. She was playing solitaire and she didn't look a day older than sixteen.

"Excuse me. Have you seen this girl?" Cardozo handed her the photo.

She looked at it, and a faint shimmer of revulsion came into her eyes. The eyes were cornflower-blue and the hair was feathery blond, hanging in braids down to her freckled shoulders.

With a jolt, he realized she was the girl in the photo. Deeper lines around the mouth, deader eyes, braids instead of bangs—but the face was hers. "You're Nell Dunbar."

She didn't deny it. She gave the picture back. "Lousy photo." She had a faintly regional accent. Cardozo would have said New England. "Fidelity cashed a check for you."

"They cash all my checks."

"Last year they cashed a check drawn on St. Andrew's Church. Two thousand dollars."

Resentment flared in the eyes. "And kept five hundred of it."

"What was that check for?"

"For me, what do you think?"

"In payment of what?"

Her breath came shallowly, quickly. "If they say I stole it, they're lying."

"I'm checking if your stories match."

"They gave it to me because they felt sorry."

"Two thousand dollars?"

"They felt very, very sorry."

He could see she wasn't about to explain her actions, least of all to a cop. "When you were at the church, did you happen to see this boy?" He showed her the photo of Tod Lomax.

Her eyes became somber. "Who says I was ever at the church?"

"You know you were there, Nell. Two thousand dollars didn't walk down here to you."

She shrugged. "I've seen Tod around—but not at the church."

"Where?"

"He hung out here a while ago."

"When did you last see him?"

"Two, three months ago. Three, I guess." She handed back the photo. "His family's looking for him?"

Cardozo nodded. It wasn't exactly a lie.

Her lips curled in a halfway smile. "He said they'd send someone. His mom, right?"

"Did you know him?"

She shrugged again and this time the shrug said she'd slept with a lot of people here and in the street and in rooms all over town, and there was nothing special in that regard about her relationship with Tod Lomax. As the braids swayed, something sparkled and Cardozo saw that she had a steel wristwatch strap woven into the left-hand braid.

"Why did Tod leave?"

"He met someone."

"A girl?"

"That would be strange." She smiled, fuller this time.

"What's so funny?"

"He met the priest from that church. The priest had an extra bed and he needed some work done."

"What kind of work?"

"Painting. Carpentry. Tod's good with his hands."

"Was this the priest?" He showed her a photo of Father Joe.

She shook her head. "Not the priest I met. It might be Tod's, but mine was a woman."

"May I?" Cardozo gestured toward a corner of the mattress. She moved over, and he sat down. "My name is Cardozo. Vince Cardozo."

He'd bought cigarettes and he offered her a Tareyton. She accepted. He gave her a light.

"Tell me, Nell, have you ever seen this boy?" He showed her Pablo Cespedes.

"Not that I can recall."

"This boy?"

She squinted at the photo of Wally Wills. "No, never saw him. But that picture was taken right over there." She pointed to a doorway on the river side of the warehouse.

"This girl?"

She took the photo of Wanda Gilmartin and frowned. "I never knew her—but she must have known Jeremiah."

"Who's Jeremiah?"

"He used to do hair. He knew how to weave things into the braid—like the wristwatch strap in mine." She handed back the photo. "And the chain in hers."

Cardozo studied Wanda Gilmartin's image. There was a streak of brightness in the hair—he had assumed it was a flaw in the print. But it could have been something else. "Where can I find Jeremiah?"

"You can't. He was killed in a fight last winter."

Nell walked with the detective out to the edge of the six-lane highway.

"If you need me for anything," he said, "don't be shy, don't be afraid—get in touch."

"Okay." *Fat chance,* she thought.

He gave her his card and she watched him go, sprinting through the traffic.

She had nowhere to put his card but inside her halter. It made the cut in her nipple uncomfortable, so she moved it to the other breast where the cut had had longer to heal.

She was walking back toward the warehouse when she realized that a white stretch Porsche limo had pulled out of the southbound traffic and was driving slowly alongside her. She looked over at the solid black one-way windows.

She'd seen the car before. It had followed her several times. Word on the dock was, *Don't get involved with the guy—he's a creep and an asshole and he's cheap—a hundred dollars to do things you have to get a tetanus shot for afterward.*

The limo stopped. The driver's window came down in a slow peeling motion.

"Hi." The driver leaned out. He was smiling and wide-shoul-dered with two gold chains showing in the unbuttoned V of his raspberry Izod shirt. "What's your name?"

"I don't think so," Nell said.

He stepped out and opened the rear door. A current of rose-scented air spiraled out of the dark, brushing her with coolness.

"Ever seen the inside of one of these? I bet you haven't, because this is a custom job."

"Thanks, but I really don't think so."

It was the coolness that held her. Coolness felt so good there in the sun.

"This baby has a queen-size water bed, a Jacuzzi, an entertainment center, and a fully stocked bar."

"What's the music?"

"You like the music?"

She moved closer to the coolness. A recorded male voice with big-band backup was crooning "Don't stop that line you're feedin' me / When you implant that need in me, / My heart gets up to speed in me. . . ."

Nell recognized one of the records her father used to play before he got put away for butchering her mother and sister.

A light came up in the backseat and an old guy in a toupee and a commodore's blazer was sitting there hungry-eyed, staring at her.

"So, can we say hello now? Call me Toe—Toe as in Knee as in Tony." He snapped a finger. He smiled. His mouth was too full of too many teeth and they were too white. "Hi, you beautiful doll. Dig the beat?"

She realized his voice was the same as the voice on the sound system. She couldn't remember the name, but she knew he'd been one of the big pop singers of the fifties, or the sixties, years before she'd been born.

"Whatever turns your crank, doll. Grab that high and come fly with me."

"Thanks." She shook her head. "But I don't think so."

He reached a hand. She stepped back before he could touch her.

"Might I be of service to you gentlemen?" A grinning white boy had joined the group. He stood with his hand outstretched. "Hi, I'm Eff, how can I help you?"

The driver turned. "What gives you the idea we need your fucking help?"

The kid was a foot shorter than the driver, and eighty pounds lighter. His T-shirt said *My family went to Baltimore and all I got was this lousy T-shirt* and it hung loose around his ribs. He wore a small crucifix earring in his left ear, and under his New York Mets baseball cap his blond hair was pulled back into a ponytail. "I represent this young lady. I handle all contractual arrangements for her services."

The man in the toupee snapped a finger at the driver. "Take care of this creep."

The driver took half a step backward.

The pupils of the kid's eyes became pinpricks.

The driver threw a punch, pitching his whole body weight into it.

The kid held out a razor. He let the big man step into the straight edge, and then he twisted.

The driver sank down to the tarmac, screaming.

"I got a lot of maybe's, a lot of 'gee, he looks kind of familiar,' " Ellie said, "but nobody knew where he went, who he went with."

"Nobody *admitted* they knew," Cardozo said. "These kids are not a forthcoming population. Except, one spaced-out kid gave me a possible lead." He laid the photo of Wanda Gilmartin on the table. "Do you think that could be a chain in her braid?"

They were sitting in a West Street bar called the Sea Shell. The place was dimly lit and Ellie had to angle the photo to the light. Through the window you could see the docks just across the traffic-choked West Side Highway.

"I thought it was just a bad print. But I suppose it could be something metallic."

"You don't happen to have a magnifying glass in that purse."

"Why would I have a magnifying glass in my purse?" Suddenly Ellie was practically snarling. "Do you carry a telescope in your wallet?"

"I'm sorry I asked. Excuse me."

The only other customer in the bar stood feeding dollar bills to the jukebox. Mamas and Papas golden oldies made an easy retro sound that went with the old movie posters on the walls.

"Come on, Ellie, what's bothering you?"

"I found it a very sad experience." She took the plastic straw from her ginger ale and snapped it into inch-long bits. "I saw a lot of AIDS out there. Runaways and druggies and prostitutes and petty thieves. Teenagers walking around looking like they're in Dachau. They need help."

"I don't know if help would help. It seems to me, to be alive in a place like that at a time like this is to be totally screwed up."

She gave him a wounded glance. "I was born in New York. I've spent my life here. I love this city. And I've seen it go further downhill than there's a hill to go down. Lately I've been trying to persuade myself it has the potential for one last rebound."

"You can stop brainwashing yourself. It doesn't."

She let out a long exhalation. "Sometimes the part of me that wants to be macho admires you for not getting upset about things. Sometimes I resent you for not getting upset at least a little."

"What do you want, Ellie? You think if I develop an ulcer it's going to help trace one single runaway on those docks?"

"You could at least care."

"Of course I care. What's got into you?"

"I don't know." She shrugged. "I guess those kids upset me."

"Then get angry at them, not me."

"I'm not angry. I'm depressed." She tapped a napkin to the corner of her eye.

"You've been working awfully hard, Ellie." He reached across the table and touched her hand. "Do you think maybe you should take the rest of the day off? Go home and get some rest?"

"Don't mother me, Vince."

"I didn't say a thing. I'm sorry."

The eyes that looked into his were moist and red. "Sometimes you can be so full of bullshit."

He pulled back his hand. "We're not communicating."

The West Street door flew open, and through the sudden dazzling trapezoid of sunlight, a man stumbled into the bar. At first Cardozo thought the man had been scalped, and then he realized it was a case of a toupee coming semidetached.

The man dropped a quarter into the pay phone and five seconds later he was brass knuckling the phone with the receiver.

The bartender, a big, bald old guy, put down the glass he had been polishing and went over. "Hey, buddy, what's wrong?"

The man in the toupee said he needed to get a call through to 911. It was hard to hear over "California Dreaming," but Cardozo caught something about a driver getting slashed by one of the lowlifes out there on the dock.

"Excuse me, Ellie." He crossed the room. He showed his shield. "Can I help?"

"Some shiv-packing crack-head out there sushi-sliced my driver." The man in the toupee had a blue contact lens riding way off center in his right eye. Blood trickled from his right nostril.

"How badly hurt is your driver?"

"His intestines are coming out on the pavement. What kind of animal could do that? What kind of animal does this city breed?"

Cardozo borrowed the bartender's phone and called the precinct. He told them to send an ambulance and a squad car down right away.

When he returned to the table, Ellie had risen from her funk. "Hey," she whispered, "that's Tony Franklyn—the singer. My mom's got all his records."

"He shouldn't be driving a limo in this neighborhood." Cardozo pocketed Wanda Gilmartin's photo. "Would you do me a favor, Ellie? Take care of his driver. I have to get uptown."

FORTY-FOUR

"All four victims were packed in reinforced hampers made by Styrobasket of Kalamazoo." Lou Stein was reading from scraps of paper clamped to his clipboard. "The clothing of all four showed traces of the same incense residue and the same carpet lint."

"The same?" Cardozo said. "Not similar? The same?"

Lou nodded. "The same. Wills and Lomax had wax on their skin in the nipple area."

"Same wax?"

Lou foraged through a tray of printouts on his desk. He pulled up a coil of paper and shook his head. "Not identical. Lomax had yellow dye." He flipped a sheet on the clipboard. "The rose in the Lomax bouquet matches the roses in the two Gilmartin bouquets —Linda Porter."

He handed Cardozo an eight-by-ten color glossy. It seemed to show a black rope woven of calamari tentacles, sprinkled with shining glops of calf's-foot gelatin.

"What's this?"

"I enlarged the lower third of Wanda Gilmartin's braid."

Cardozo felt a stab of disappointment. In enlargement, the curious glint in Wanda's braid looked a little more yellow than the other streaks in the photo, but it was still only a streak.

"Is this the best we can get?"

Lou gestured to Cardozo to come with him to a darkened corner of the lab where a computer monitor sat flickering. "The photo doesn't blow up well. The emulsion gives you terrible resolution—besides which, it's badly scratched. But this should interest you."

Lou punched up a file. The monitor flashed the message *processing,* and then the head and shoulders from the Wanda Gilmartin Polaroid scrolled up onto the screen.

Cardozo stared at the unmoving image of the young girl with her wide, dark eyes and her long black hair gathered into two braids. There was something in the face that he recognized—a beaten, pathetic look that he had seen in the eyes of cornered animals.

Lou's hands moved over the keyboard, calm, unhurried. Green light glinted off his bifocals.

The image on the screen flowed apart, changing to dots. The dots began melting like pieces of a jigsaw puzzle turned liquid.

"What's happening?"

"The program just enlarged and now it's enhancing—basically it's executing an iterative connect-the-dots algorithm."

"The machine's making guesses?"

"Highly educated guesses."

After several seconds of swirl, the colored streaks suddenly leapt into a new pattern.

Cardozo stared at the screen. There was a faint electronic pulsation to the image, as though it were made up of living microorganisms. Golden filament glinted through woven black hair—definitely metal, definitely twisted into interlocking links.

His mind was pumping, making connections. "It *is* a chain." He turned.

Lou nodded.

"That's it." A wave of certainty broadsided Cardozo. "That's the link."

"I need to check some evidence in an old homicide." Cardozo slid the request form under the grille and laid his ID beside it.

The clerk squinted. He glanced at Ellie Siegel. "Is the lady with you?"

"She is," Cardozo said.

"Is she a cop too?"

"She is," Ellie said. She flipped open her shield case.

The air-conditioning inside the property room seemed to have jammed at the coldest possible setting. There were goose bumps on her upper arms, but Ellie was smiling her lady-cops-are-cheerful-until-provoked smile.

The clerk grunted. He was dressed in jeans and flannel workshirt and regimental striped suspenders, and he twanged the right suspender. "They've been changing the storage system. It'll take me a minute."

He drifted back across the storage room, poking along shelves and into bins, peering behind shopping bags and brown paper parcels. Cardozo had the impression that, as a part of its cost-cutting, the city had decreed that any container that could possibly enclose anything would henceforth be used as an evidence bag.

The clerk returned with a bulging elastic-bound legal-size manila file. He blew dust off it, coughed, and slid it under the grille.

Cardozo signed and took the file to the steel-topped counter on the opposite side of the room. He snapped on a pair of disposable surgical gloves and opened the file. His nostrils took in the faint petroleum residue of the chemicals that had been used to soak trace material out of the evidence.

He carefully spread the contents of the package on the counter: One pair rotted blue jeans with pathetically child-size hips. One rotted camouflage T-shirt. One thick white candle, partially burned. Two small matching rings, the gold plate practically gone from one of them. One three-inch length of cheap gold chain.

He separated the chain from the other objects. Beside it he laid the laser printout of Lou Stein's computer-enhanced photo.

He adjusted the arm of the examining lamp and awaited Ellie's judgment.

She was silent. It was as though she were staring into motionless water. Her eyes flicked from the chain to the image of a chain. Back and forth. Finally they flicked to Cardozo. "They match. Wanda Gilmartin is Ms. Basket Case."

"I'm faxing you the drawing we published of Ms. Basket Case," Cardozo told Harvey Thoms. "And the photo of Wanda Gilmartin."

"Don't bother with the drawing." Thoms's voice on the line was clipped, unmistakably rushed. "I've got it."

"You'll see there's no resemblance between them. Yet Barth identified the girl from the drawing."

"You're telling me he was lying. You're telling me again."

"Only this time there's proof. He couldn't have recognized her from that drawing. Nobody could have."

"And the nipple ring?"

"If he didn't know her, he didn't kill her. If he didn't kill her, someone had to have given him the ring. Someone who was involved. Deeply involved."

"Okay, Vince. I know who you're talking about. I'll take this up with the D.A." Thoms's voice had a "good-bye right now" finality.

"Wait a minute. The D.A. had better look into the cover-up. It took some well-placed hands working overtime."

"The department appreciates your help, Vince. I'll see it's remembered."

The line went dead in Cardozo's hand. Rap music thumped somewhere, punctuated by the crackle of a dot-matrix printer in the squad room. Cardozo sat frowning.

He smelled Ellie's perfume—the faint but pungent sweetness of rose attar—before he heard her behind him.

"Look what the morning mail brought. My turn to get an anonymous note."

He turned in his swivel chair. Today Ellie was wearing a sleeveless teal dress that brought out the color of her eyes. She handed him a plain business envelope addressed to her in block printing. A sheet of folded Xerox paper was paper-clipped to it.

"I notice you don't get engraved stationery."

"Either my nameless friends aren't as fancy as yours, or they don't think I'm as fancy as you."

There was no return address. Cardozo studied the postmark. "Mailed yesterday from this zip code."

"The bad news always gets delivered faster."

"How bad?" He unclipped the paper.

"If your name's Vanderbrook, very bad."

He spread the sheet open. It was a copy of a cutting from the obit page of an eighteen-month-old *New York Times.*

Wheelwright Vanderbrook III, age 22, was found dead December 24 in a guest room at the Knickerbocker Club, apparently a suicide. Mr. Vanderbrook was the son of Baxter Vanderbrook, president of Consolidated Industrial Brands and chairman of the board of directors of the Metropolitan Museum of Art, and of the former Irene Morgan. He was a senior at Harvard University, where he was a member of the Porcellian Club. Known to his friends as Wright, he was also active in the musical association of St. Andrew's Episcopal Church, New York.

The words *musical association of St. Andrew's Episcopal Church* had been highlighted in yellow marker.

"Killed himself just in time for Christmas," Cardozo observed. "Thoughtful of him."

"Wasn't it."

"This was sent to you directly. Who knows you're on the case?"

Ellie's silence could have been meant as a reply. Or maybe it was just meant as silence. She sighed. "Reverend Bonnie Ruskay."

"Besides her?"

"Samantha Schuyler. Maybe a few others. I'll check my notes."

"Who did the autopsy?"

"Dan Hippolito."

"I'll have a talk with him."

"It started simple," Dan said. "Wright Vanderbrook was a clear case of suicide. Drug overdose, self-administered."

They were standing in Dan Hippolito's windowless, pale-green office two levels below First Avenue. Fluorescent light flickered down on potted corn plants and forty-year-old Danish modern furniture.

"Then it got tangled. The Vanderbrook family subpoenaed me to depose in the preliminary phase of the civil suit."

The silence seemed to reverberate.

"Who'd they sue?" Cardozo said.

"The family sued the pants off the Episcopal diocese."

"Why'd they do that?"

"I seem to recollect the charge was gross malfeasance of pastoral duty." Dan stared up at a whispering air vent in the ceiling. "A priest at St. Andrew's Church had been counseling Wright Vanderbrook. Vanderbrook senior claimed there was a homosexual relationship between them, and when the priest broke the relationship off, the son killed himself."

"So Vanderbrook senior claimed his son's suicide was the priest's fault?"

Dan nodded.

"What was your take on it? Any truth to the charge?"

"I honestly couldn't tell you. They didn't call me back to testify, and I didn't follow the trial."

"How was the suit resolved?"

"Dunno. After I deposed, after all the subpoenas and bullshit, I never heard another word about it."

Cardozo kept rolling it over in his mind.

"Want me to get the file out?" Dan offered.

One look at the stacks of files and slides and glossies on Dan's desk told Cardozo that the poor guy was up to his gazoo in deadlines. "I hate to put you to more trouble."

"Believe me, when it comes to trouble, you're bush league." Dan went to his files and searched through the *V*'s. He handed Cardozo a folder. "That's a relic. They tell me everything's going to computer."

"Lucky you."

"I'm going to have to take basic computer literacy. Can you believe it—a school kid again."

Cardozo sat in the armchair. His eyes moved quickly down columns of type. "Death resulted from a lethal injection of cocaine?"

Dan nodded. "Presumably self-administered."

"How presumably is that?"

"As in obviously. No way it was murder."

"Injecting cocaine isn't all that common, is it?"

"Injecting yourself to death with it isn't. But then, I only see the dead ones."

"Those four kids I asked you to look at—they had cocaine residue on injection marks."

"But they had a lot else, too—bruises, cuts, leather scrapings, alcohol in the bloodstream, azidofluoramine in the liver. If you're trying to fit Vanderbrook into the series, don't."

Cardozo closed the folder. "Then in your opinion the other four are a series?"

"With M.O. that close—I'd say there's very little question that all four homicides were committed by one killer."

For as long as Cardozo had known him, Dan had tended to conservatism in his guesstimates. Very-little-question was his way of saying absolutely 105 percent certain.

"The only problem I'm having is that matzo residue in the mouths." Dan smiled. "The computer seems to have eaten it. But I'll dig up the paperwork. Paper matzo would have a hard time disappearing."

David Lowndes scooped a brushful of glue out of the pail and slathered it across the wall. Bonnie peeled a poster off the roll and pressed it against the wet brick.

The light from the doorway of 4 Gracie Square caught the lettering: $10,000 REWARD FOR INFORMATION LEADING TO IDENTIFICATION OF ASSAILANT WHO MUGGED FATHER JOE MONTGOMERY IN CARL SCHURZ PARK 4 P.M. MAY 10. NO PROSECUTION.

"What's the penalty for posting bills?" Bonnie said.

David Lowndes gave her a chummy pat on the shoulder. "Not to worry. This is St. Andrew's work, and St. Andrew's can afford it, my sweet."

Sometimes David's easygoing, nothing-can-faze-a-lawyer manner put her off, but tonight Bonnie found a certain security in it.

They were getting back into his Porsche when she noticed the figure skulking in a phone booth on the corner of East End Avenue.

"That's him." Her eye recognized the silhouetted baseball cap and ponytail before her mind did. "The boy who robbed me in the cab."

"Are you sure?"

"Almost. What's he up to? Pretend to drive away."

David gunned the motor, ripped around the corner, braked, and backed up.

The boy was taking down the poster.

David floored the accelerator. The boy dodged through the headlight beams. David U-turned, wheels screaming up onto the sidewalk, and gave chase.

At East End their quarry ducked into the park.

David ran the red light. Behind them, a police siren howled.

David slammed on the brakes. "Sorry, Bonnie, but I'm not going to lose my license for this piece of white shit."

FORTY-FIVE

A butler admitted Cardozo to Mr. and Mrs. Baxter Vanderbrook's triplex apartment on East Seventy-first Street. "Would you wait here, please." It was not a question.

From the hallway, Cardozo could see two card tables set up in the walnut-paneled living room. Judging by the level of laughter and chitchat, he suspected there were a few more tables he couldn't see. Beneath gilt-framed Impressionists, men and women in evening clothes were playing bridge.

A tall, dour white-haired gentleman in a tuxedo approached. "I'm Baxter Vanderbrook. Don't you people believe in phoning ahead?" He took Cardozo into a study lined with leather-bound editions.

Cardozo apologized for the intrusion. "I wouldn't be bothering you, but I went to the courthouse to look up your lawsuit, and there's nothing on file."

"My lawsuit? What the hell are you talking about?"

"You and your wife brought suit against St. Andrew's Episcopal Church."

Vanderbrook's face was suddenly like a board with nails stabbing through. "I'm sorry, that's a matter I absolutely will not discuss."

"Baxter, what's going on?" A very erect, diet-slender woman in gray stood in the doorway.

"I'm speaking with a man from the police."

"I'm Irene Vanderbrook." Her eyes locked with Cardozo's—lonely green eyes the color of ivy in winter. She took four steps into the room. "Is it something to do with Wright?"

"The discussion has been concluded," Vanderbrook said. "You can get back to your hand."

"I'm dummy."

"Then bid my hand. Three hearts."

Mrs. Vanderbrook's fingers went to her gold necklace. "Three hearts?"

"Three, goddammit, *three*."

"All right." She turned and was gone.

"My wife is not well," Vanderbrook said. "She's had one breakdown because of this business, and if you people cause her to have another, I warn you: I'll sue." He drew in a long breath. Diamond studs twinkled on his boiled shirt. "The butler will show you out."

Cardozo did not bother waiting for the butler. A dark-haired young woman in emeralds and violet silk stopped him in the front hallway.

"I take it you're from the police and Daddy was not hospitable?" Her voice had a sort of desperate laughing music. She held out a hand armored in gemstones. "I'm Pierrette Vanderbrook."

"Vince Cardozo. You're Wright's sister?"

"I had that pleasure."

"Your brother's name has surfaced in an investigation."

"Daddy hates discussing Wright's death." A white line ran along her left jawbone, not an ugly line, but just noticeably lighter than the pale olive of her face. "Maybe I could help you."

Cardozo took an envelope from his pocket. "Do you recognize any of the people in those photos? Did you ever see any of them with your brother?"

Pierrette Vanderbrook opened the envelope. She studied the faces of Gilmartin and Wills. Earrings glistened on either side of her wondering stare. She shuffled Vegas and Lomax and Cespedes. Cardozo could make out other, fainter lines on her forehead and nose. He felt he was looking at a well-restored photograph of an extremely handsome young woman.

"I'm afraid I've never seen any of these people. They don't look like Wright's sort at all."

The perpetual smile did not go with what she was saying. It occurred to Cardozo that it might be the result of plastic surgery.

"Never drive drunk." She handed back the envelope. "I did, and I went through a windshield. I saw you noticing. The surgeons patched me up well, wouldn't you say?"

"You're a very attractive young woman."

She smiled wryly. "Now, let's not exaggerate, but thank you."

"What can you tell me about your parents' lawsuit?"

"Which one?"

"Against the Episcopal Church."

"It didn't get anywhere."

After a late dinner, Cardozo and Terri were sitting in the living room. A Dvořák symphony was playing so softly on the CD player that it was almost a halo on the silence.

Terri glanced over. "What are you reading?"

He had his feet up on the footstool and a stack of files on the floor. "An old case. Wanda Gilmartin."

One eyebrow came down in a frown. "You never mentioned a Wanda Gilmartin."

"We used to call her Ms. Basket Case till we learned her right name."

"You closed that case."

"The lid popped up again."

The phone rang. Terri answered. She made a face and whispered, "Aunt Jill."

Cardozo took the receiver. "Hello, Jill."

"I got worried when I didn't hear from you." The voice was slurred yet manic. He could tell she'd been drinking.

"I'm sorry, were you supposed to hear from me?"

"You know what day it is today. It's Sally's birthday."

His body went rigid as if she had thrown a punch. "My God, I forgot. I'm sorry."

"Nobody wants to remember but me. Everyone else treats her like a dead person."

"Sally's not dead."

"Then why haven't you found her? You're a cop."

"We're doing everything we can."

"Then everything's not enough." Jill began crying. "I saw her today."

Cardozo felt wearier than he had since Sally's last birthday. It seemed that every birthday there was a new Sally sighting. "Where was this?"

"On television. A commercial. I swear it was her. I tried to get a tape in the VCR to record it, but by the time I got it to work they were back to *Donahue.*"

"What was this commercial?"

"It was . . . I don't remember, it was a product."

"Sally was modeling a product."

"You know how she always wanted to be a model."

"What's happening to you, Jill?" He felt he was talking a plane down in a storm. "How do you get this way? You've got to stop saying *yes* to every idea that crosses your mind on a fourth vodka."

"Three. I've only had three."

"You're burning yourself out. What's more, you're burning *me* out."

"All right. I can tell I'm a nuisance. You don't want to listen to me."

"I'm listening."

"Your kind of listening just isn't enough, Vince. It's just not enough. It's a lucky thing your wife's dead, because if she were alive, she'd divorce you."

The receiver clattered sloppily to the cradle and a dial tone cut in.

She didn't mean that, Cardozo told himself. *She's just drunk and upset.*

He went back to his files. He kept hearing his sister's voice and it ripped at him like a hacksaw. He closed Gilmartin and opened Vanderbrook. He couldn't concentrate.

"Hey, Terri, when you were trying out for that musical, did you ever run into a young guy called Wright Vanderbrook?"

"Sure. I met him at the audition."

He sensed she knew something, and she was wearing her knowledge just a bit slyly.

"And?"

She shrugged. "And I dated him for a while."

Cardozo was shocked. It shocked him how shocked he was. "You *dated* him?"

"I do have dates, Dad."

Cardozo's brain was sending him a warning signal: *pull out of this conversation now.* But he couldn't help himself. "But Wright Vanderbrook was older."

"Seven years older. That was the attractive thing about him."

"I can't believe you actually dated this guy."

"We spent our time playing four-hand piano duets." She smiled, remembering. "We were going pretty strong through Mozart."

Easy now, he told himself. *She's my daughter, but she's seventeen years old. I don't own her. . . .*

But there was something trapped inside him, some feeling that she was still a little girl, that she was still *his* little girl, and it pushed him beyond the point where he should have quit. "What do you mean, going pretty strong?"

"We played a lot of Mozart four-hand sonatas. In fact, we played all of them. Which is going *very* strong."

Cardozo liked to think he knew what to get worked up about and what not to and yet here he was letting doubt edge in, dark and razor-thin. "I don't understand what you're saying."

She flicked him a look of amused impatience. "I'm saying it's a lot of music, even for a Mozart freak. Which I'm not, but he was. And then the Schubert sonatas broke us up."

"What was there to break up? What were you to each other?"

"Four hands on a keyboard."

"What does that mean?"

She got up and went into her bedroom.

Cardozo followed her. "Hey . . . I'm talking to you."

She had pulled a cardboard carton out of the closet and was sitting on the rug, sifting through letters and magazines and sheet music. She handed him a dog-eared folio album. "Here's what broke us up."

He looked at the cover: *Franz Schubert, Compositions for Piano Four Hands, edited by I. J. Paderewski*. A printed sticker had been carefully centered at the bottom: *Property of W. Vanderbrook*.

"Page fifty-nine," she said.

He had a feeling she was trying to be patient with him, and he felt like an old idiot. He turned to page fifty-nine. Dozens of alternate fingerings had been penciled in over the notes.

"We always had trouble keeping together in that passage. He said it was my fault; I said it was his fault. He said I had no sense of the Schubert style; I said he was a twit with no sense, period. He told me to get lost; I stormed out. He was too stubborn to phone and apologize; I was too stubborn to phone and apologize. So we never spoke to one another again, and a few months later he killed himself."

"Why did he kill himself?"

"It had nothing to do with me, Dad."

"How do you know?"

"Because we weren't lovers. The story going around was, he met someone else and they *were* lovers. I mean a real love affair. Sex, passion, obsession. It went sour and he never pulled out of the depression."

"Who was he in love with?"

"It was only a rumor."

"What was the rumor?"

She sighed. "The rumor was, Wright's parents found a lot of love letters from the rector at St. Andrew's. The church had to buy them back."

"I understand," Cardozo said, "that Mr. and Mrs. Baxter Vanderbrook sued the Episcopal Church a year and a half ago?"

Bishop Griswold Hancock's keen blue eyes fixed on him over the gold rims of half-moon reading spectacles. "They brought suit against the New York diocese."

"I can't find any record of the suit."

"Because it was never tried."

"And why was that?"

"Because it was utterly without merit."

They were sitting in the bishop's office in the parish house of the Cathedral of St. John the Divine. The bishop's desk stood between them, a grand piano–size island of paperwork, reference books, and blinking telephone buttons.

"From what I've been able to piece together," Cardozo said, "the Vanderbrooks sued on the grounds that their son received counseling from St. Andrew's and then committed suicide."

"Those are the bare bones of fact in the matter." The bishop removed his glasses and began tapping them against the blotter. "No one disputed them. What we did dispute was the way the Vanderbrooks dressed those bones up. They claimed that the counseling caused the suicide."

"And did they produce any evidence?"

"Purported evidence. Love letters supposedly exchanged by their son and a minister of the church."

"You say *supposedly*."

"Examination showed that the letters were a fiction."

"Forgeries?"

"The court never went into the question of forgery."

"Then how were the letters a fiction?"

Shafts of light slanted through the barred window, dappling the oriental rug.

"They were a fiction in the sense of something that never occurred in actual life." The bishop turned in his brass-studded leather swivel chair. Now he was speaking to the grandfather clock. "Furthermore, these letters were offered by a parishioner of St. Andrew's—a former parishioner—who was suing the church on another matter."

"Who was the ex-parishioner?"

"The settlement of the Vanderbrooks' suit forbids me to discuss the matter."

"What was the unrelated suit?"

"It wouldn't be ethical to tell you. The important point is that the Vanderbrooks withdrew their suit. Which is proof presumptive of the falsity of their claims."

"You don't seem to want to come out and say the Vanderbrooks' claims were false."

"There was no trial. Nothing was proved. Nothing was disproved."

There you go again. Saying it without exactly saying it. "Why do I get the impression you're picking your words very, very carefully?"

"Because we're discussing a court matter and I'm using the court's words. If you'd prefer me to answer in plain words, then put your question plainly."

Ouch, Cardozo realized: *I've just been dressed down by my elementary school principal.*

"If . . ." the bishop said, *"if* you're asking me about the character of the rector of St. Andrew's and of his assistant—and it's obvious to me you are—then I can only tell you that I have the highest personal and professional regard for Joe Montgomery. As I do for Bonnie Ruskay. She's a world-class scholar in Aramaic and ancient Hebrew. She's done fantastic work on the Dead Sea scrolls. He lectures at Columbia on social work and social justice in the light of the Gospels. Their ministry is Christian in the core sense of the word and ethically impeccable. In the entire city of New York, you couldn't find two more dedicated or decent individuals."

FORTY-SIX

It was Parents' Day at St. Anne's school, and Cardozo and Ellie and Terri were careful to arrive after the speeches. Students and parents and faculty swarmed the school auditorium. It looked as though it was also the gym, and possibly the cafeteria too. A student band was providing soft rock from the stage.

"Smile," Cardozo said. "We're in deep cover."

"As what," Ellie said, "a family?"

"Something like that."

"I feel like such a fraud," Terri said. "I *never* went to these things at my school."

"Just keep smiling. No one's going to arrest us. No one's even going to spot us." In the entire crowd, Cardozo counted three nuns' habits. Secularization had clearly hit the Catholic school system.

"I see him." Cardozo nodded unobtrusively toward the small refreshment bar that had been set up on the free-throw line of the basketball court. A heavyset man with brush-cut blond hair was ladling himself a cup of punch. Cardozo recognized the face from the photo on Bonnie Ruskay's desk. "Excuse me, guys. I have to go be a part of the community."

Cardozo crossed to the bar and took a plastic cup from the top of the stack.

"I'll fill you," Bonnie's ex said.

"Thanks." Cardozo held out the cup.

Bonnie's ex tipped a ladleful of green something into it. "Mad-house."

"This is the first year I've been here."

"This year it's the worst I've ever seen." Bonnie's ex had hair so fair that his eyebrows looked like skin grafts. "Your kid's in first form?"

"I'm ashamed to say she's a lot older than that. But I've never been able to make it to one of these before. I'm a cop."

"Is that so?" As if by agreement, they fell into step and strolled under the backstop, over to the sideline.

"I'm in construction and roofing." Bonnie's ex offered his hand. "The name's Ernie Stevens."

"Vince Cardozo. Good to meet you. Have you built any inter-esting roofs lately?"

Ernie pointed to the ceiling. "That roof's mine. And I'm reroof-ing a shopping center over in Astoria. What about you? Any inter-esting cases lately?"

There was an unoccupied table between the parallel bars and the punching bag. They sat on folding chairs.

"You might have read about one of mine," Cardozo said. "A homicide up at St. Andrew's rectory?"

Ernie's forehead wrinkled. "You . . . me . . . meeting like this—it's not an accident."

Cardozo shook his head. "Not exactly."

"She didn't send you to me, did she?"

"No, but she showed me your picture."

"She's got my picture?"

"On her desk—with the kids."

"Right." Ernie nodded. "With the kids." He turned in his chair to look around the gym. "They're here somewhere. I'll introduce you." He drained his plastic cup. "They'd love to meet a cop."

"A housebreaker was killed," Cardozo said. "Father Joe rigged a booby trap."

"So Father Joe finally got a dose of the real world—and turned out to be as much of a redneck as the rest of us."

"Why do you say that?"

"My wife left me to become an Episcopal priest. I guess I view Father Joe as the other man."

"Your ex-wife doesn't seem to think he could kill."

Ernie toyed with a tiny American flag on a toothpick that someone had left on the table.

"Bonnie couldn't see evil in Jack the Ripper even if you showed her the six dead hookers. Seriously, I've known Bonnie since we were kids. Nothing's changed. Even then she was the neighborhood saint. And her playmates." He smiled, remembering. "Words can't really describe her brother Ben and their friend Collie. You'd have to meet them."

"I've met them."

"You get around."

"They seemed decent guys."

"Which nobody can deny. I guess you'd have to have known them when they were kids. They were religious groupies. Bonnie and Ben and Collie played church the way other children played house. When they were six years old they were putting on bathrobes and giving communion and last rites. I was the neighborhood roughneck—I'd lead gangs and break up their Masses. Bonnie and Ben and Collie loved it. Martyrdom. It was all make-believe."

"I understand."

"Except one thing wasn't make-believe. They all three wanted to be Catholic priests. Ben applied to the seminary. They told him to go into the world for three years and test his vocation. He went to work for the biggest church provisions company in the state—

and in three years he was running it. Never reapplied to semi-nary." Ernie stopped. "Why am I telling you all this?"

"Because I asked and you're a good citizen."

Ernie shrugged. "Which brings us to Collie. He was a different story. Collie was accepted at the seminary—and then he decided he wasn't a priest."

"Why'd he decide that?"

"He was in Panama with the U.S. forces during the invasion. Something changed his mind. He's never told me what." Ernie twisted in his seat. "My kids better show up soon, or you're going to know the life story of everyone I know. I must be boring you to death."

"Not at all."

"Okay. Which brings us to Bonnie. Say when. Bonnie had great hopes the church would open up to women. She applied to the seminary and they laughed at her—said no woman could ever be a priest. So she did the next best thing—married me. I should have realized it was a rebound." Ernie chuckled with sad self-mockery. "Around that time, the Episcopal Church very quietly began or-daining women. One day she told me she wanted to take classes at the Episcopal seminary. I should have seen the handwriting on the wall—but no, not me. Next thing I knew, she converted. Which I couldn't square with my conscience. I'm what you might call an obedient Catholic. Endangered species, right? I expected my kids to have a Catholic home. So we annulled the marriage."

"But doesn't an annulment leave them kind of . . ." Cardozo didn't want to say the word *illegitimate*.

"If the curia had decreed an annulment *de principio,* the mar-riage would never have existed, and the kids would be out-of-wedlock. I'd never have done that to my own flesh and blood. We asked for an annulment *per causa.* That leaves the kids in the clear. The marriage only ceased to exist when Bonnie ceased being a Catholic. The way canon law sees it, she died."

Curious doctrine, Cardozo thought. "And what does canon law say now that she's ordained?"

"Probably says she went to hell."

"Do you agree?"

"She's a decent person. She's doing what she thinks is right. I can't see God punishing you for that."

"Her family's reaction must have been . . . mixed."

"Hard to say. They're troubled people. Her father died of alcoholism. Ben used to have the same problem. He used to go on benders. Almost killed himself."

"Has your ex-wife ever had any alcohol or substance abuse problem?"

Ernie shook his head. "Definitely not her style. She'd never do anything to disgrace the kids."

"Even though the church says the kids are motherless."

"The church and the children don't agree on that. Frankly, neither do I."

"But you're free to remarry."

Ernie looked pained at the suggestion. He lifted a hand to massage around his eyes. He was still wearing a wedding ring. Cardozo had to wonder if the ring was a masquerade for Parents' Day, or if he wore it all the time as a widower might, as a sign of remembrance and loss.

"I hate to interrupt when you two have got a good dialogue going." Ellie Siegel approached, beaming a friendly smile. "But I'm dead. Are all these seats taken?"

Cardozo got to his feet. "Ellie, meet Ernie. He's telling me about roofing and construction in the big city."

Ernie rose with careful gallantry and pulled out a chair for her. "I don't know if that's the kind of subject you're interested in." He gave her a long glance.

Ellie sat down. She returned the long glance. "I'm very interested."

"Ernie did the roof we're sitting under."

"Really." Ellie looked up. "How'd you do that, Ernie?"

"It was a challenge—a composite roof truss without queen posts."

"Really."

"You don't want to hear this."

Ellie shook her head. "I do, I do."

"No queen posts, you can't run struts. No struts, how do you hold the weight of the glass?"

"Well, hello there." A dark-haired woman approached the table, leading two very young, very blond children.

Ernie cleared his throat. "My friend Laura Lupecano. And my

kids, Kelly and Kyle. Fellas, I want you to say hi to Ellie and Vince Cardozo."

"Siegel," Ellie corrected. "Ellie Siegel. I'm just a family friend."

"Like me." Laura had pretty, heavily made-up eyes, and she was holding an almost-empty plastic cup with lipstick prints on the rim. "Tell you one thing, we're pretty good friends to come to Parents' Day, right?"

"Vince and I work for the same company," Ellie said. "I figured he needed a little moral support."

Cardozo got up and pulled out a chair for Laura.

She smiled. "Thank you." She sat. "What company is that?"

"The police," Ernie said. "They work for the police. So watch what you say." He laughed. "Just kidding."

"Really?" Laura's pencil-line eyebrows went up. "You hear that, kids? These guys are cops."

"Can I have your autograph?" the little girl said. She wore pink bows in her pigtails and she had the irresistible smile of a four-year-old flirt.

"May I," Laura corrected.

"Sure thing." Cardozo ripped a sheet from his notebook, signed it, and passed it to Ellie. She added her signature and handed it to the girl.

The freckled face broke into a delighted grin.

The boy was hanging back, looking away from Cardozo. He appeared to be six years old or so, with eyeglasses that gave him the precocious scowl of a very young Einstein. Cardozo had recognized the boy instantly: he had been playing hide-and-seek with Collie in the St. Andrew's rectory.

The next move's up to you, kid, Cardozo thought. *You can tell your dad we've already met and blow your secret meetings with your mom—or you can keep it under your hat. Whatever makes you comfortable.*

The boy held out his hand. "Hello, sir."

Cardozo took the hand. "Hello, young man."

The boy looked him in the eye. "It's a pleasure meeting you, sir."

"Likewise."

FORTY-SEVEN

"**E**veryone was there—Dinah and Bianca and Betsy and Jackie and Bruce and Bob and Oscar. Lord only knows how Samantha is able to corral the cream of the A-list, but time after time after time she pulls it off." Whitney Carls stopped short. "But if you wanted to hear about a silly old party you'd have gone to it yourself."

"I want to hear about anything that concerns you," Bonnie said. "Why don't you tell me how you're doing? You personally?"

They were sitting in her office, in the easy chairs by the window. The herbal tea they were drinking had grown cold. She could remember when Whitney had been a heavy drinker, a towering presence at dinner parties, a large man and one of the most sought-after in New York society. She could remember when ten minutes alone with Whitney had been a treat, a tonic, when women had fought one another for a piece of his time.

A lot had changed.

"I'm doing *rotten*." He looked at her. His eyes bulged through thick glasses, not wise-owlish, but sad-owlish. "This damned wig looks stupid and all evening long the guests were staring at me."

She had to admit, the wig looked clownish. Yet she understood the impulse behind it. He'd had thick, beautiful hair until chemo had robbed him of it. With everything slipping away from him, he needed to hold on to some echo of the past. But she wasn't sure this was the right echo.

He was waiting for a comment. She couldn't think of one to offer.

"Everyone saw I'd lost weight. I could feel them wondering, Why the hell did Samantha have to invite this old corpse? I hate dying, I hate being a drag on the party, I just *hate* it!"

"You're not dying."

"Well, I sure as hell am not *living*."

"But you *are*, Whitney."

"Oh, I suppose, if you mean literally."

"Don't overlook the literal truth. And don't believe you can know what other people are thinking."

Any more than I can know what Vince Cardozo is thinking, she reflected. *He seems urban redneck, right-wing, no more in sympathy with my beliefs than I am with his.*

"I hate hospitals," Whitney was saying. "I hate sickness. Why does this have to happen to me?"

"It's normal to feel that way. And you're doing fine."

"If this is fine, I'm sick of it! Three weeks of these chemicals, and then three months' waiting, and then six weeks of chemicals. When will it all end? Christ, don't answer that."

Bonnie wondered what a man like Vince Cardozo would do in Whitney's situation. Would he feel sorry for himself and crumble?

No. He's built that cop facade to survive earthquakes and hurricanes.

She tried to analyze Cardozo's strength. She sensed defiance, estrangement from God and love. Negative strength.

Could I bring Vince Cardozo around? Could I help him see good in all people, God in all people?

She smiled at the presumptuousness of her ideas—St. Bonnie saves the world. Today, it was a daunting enough task to see God in Whitney Carls.

"While you're waiting for the next round of treatment," she told him, "maybe you should focus your thoughts on something else."

He sighed. "Could I tell you the awful truth, Bonnie? I'm broke. All I have is the monthly check from Mama's trust, and what with the bond market, it's next to nothing."

When all else fails, try giving them some pastoral theology. "Have you considered prayer?"

"I feel like such a fraud praying. I don't believe in it."

"What about just talking to God?"

"What have I got to say that God would be interested in hearing?"

It seemed strange to Bonnie how few people realized that the purpose of prayer was to transform the person who prayed, not to persuade God.

"You could discuss something you've thought, something you've seen that gives you joy."

"Like the platinum cuff links in Tiffany's Fifth Avenue window?"

"Why not, if you think God would like them."

"God's got better taste than that."

"Whitney, listen to me. Nothing in this world is beneath God. No thought, no deed, no fear."

"You sound like some sort of spiritual Marxist."

"You could offer your feelings to God. . . . You could say, 'Lord, I make you a gift of my sorrows that they may fall back upon me in joy.'"

"It isn't very me, Bonnie." He pulled back his starched cuff to look at his watch. "Goodness, I've got to be going. Tina Vee wants me to take her dog to the vet. Can you believe it, I've gone from being that woman's walker to becoming her dog's errand boy."

Bonnie walked Whitney to the front door. "I'm sure she's very grateful to you for all your help."

"No, she's not. She's an astonishingly selfish old woman. Well, thanks for listening." He gave Bonnie a good-bye peck on the cheek.

She watched him go. The sky had darkened and it felt like rain was coming. Halfway down the block he turned, a brave childish smile on his frightened old-man face, and waved to her.

She waved back.

When she returned to her office, the phone was ringing. It was Imogene, Tina Vanderbilt's social secretary. "Mrs. Vee has been waiting a half hour for Whitney Carls. Is he there by any chance?"

"He just left."

"I hope he's coming here. Mrs. Vee's counting on him to take Lulu to the vet."

"I'm sorry, but he didn't tell me his plans."

Bonnie replaced the receiver. She sat there. Silence poured in like a tide and she realized that at that moment she was alone in the rectory.

It baffled her how uncentered she felt with Father Joe away in the hospital. She wondered how he had managed to run the parish and give the sort of caring and counseling that these people needed. She thought of them as the affluent poor—choked with riches and still starving.

Her thoughts drifted to her own riches: her children. She picked up their photo from the desk. She gazed at their faces and felt a skip in her heart.

Behind her, a pigeon cooed. She saw that the window had been left open a good four inches.

That's odd, I should have closed that window when I turned on the air conditioner. . . .

She got up and closed the window and stood looking out into the courtyard. A breeze stirred the leaves of the pear tree. Shadows and light dappled the brick wall. The iron gate that led out to the street was ajar.

There should be a padlock on that gate.

She held herself without moving for a moment, focusing her thoughts.

Maybe the sexton took the padlock off. Anyway, it's still afternoon; it's too early for ghosts to be lurking. . . .

She turned back to the desk to check the time. The little Tiffany clock wasn't there.

Everything else—the pen holder, the letter opener, the stacked correspondence—was exactly in place. Beside the phone, her coffee trembled in its cup.

She crouched down and looked along the carpet. There was no fallen clock—but the closet door had swung partway open.

She felt the first whisper of alarm.

Five minutes ago that closet door was shut.

She had the sensation of falling over a precipice.

Oh, God, someone took the clock; they're hiding in that closet, watching me right now.

The phone gave two rings. The answering machine clicked on; a dowager voice came on the line. "Bonnie, are you there? My secretary told me you just spoke. It's Tina—are you there, darling?"

Bonnie seized the phone. "Hello, Tina."

"Bonnie, darling, where on earth is Whitney? Isn't he feeling well?" Tina was obviously trying to sound concerned—no easy task for her. "He's been so strange lately."

Bonnie's eyes swung back to the closet. It seemed to exhale darkness.

"I'm sorry, Tina, could you hold on one moment?"

Braver now with Tina on the line, Bonnie laid the receiver down on the desk. She crossed to the closet and yanked the door all the way open.

Nothing moved.

She pushed raincoats aside.

There were no feet hiding among the galoshes and track shoes, no crouching intruder.

Nothing seemed out of place.

She should have felt relief. Instead she felt an inexplicable sense of wrongness.

She returned to the phone. "I'm sorry to keep you waiting. If you have questions about Whitney's state of mind, I'm sure he'd be happy to answer them. I know he'd be touched by your concern."

"My dear, one doesn't simply ask a friend—why are you being so idiotic and moody?"

"Why not?" Bonnie turned to the window. She was surprised to see the courtyard gate shut now, the padlock back in place. "It's more direct than asking me to tattle, isn't it?"

Tina Vee's sigh came across the line. "Bonnie, dear, are you feeling all right?"

Bonnie focused her stare beyond the gate. In the shadow of a doorway across the street a figure stood slender, motionless. There was a cockiness in the stance that spelled young, male.

I'm imagining it.

She blinked. The figure was still there.

"I think you've picked up some bug from Whitney."

Bonnie took a deep, shaky breath and blew it out slowly. "I'm fine, thanks."

"Talk to you soon then."

She couldn't see the figure's face, but he seemed to be watching her. He patted the pockets of his jeans. His hand took out a pack of cigarettes and shook one loose. He brought a lighter up to his mouth.

She saw the New York Mets cap, the blond ponytail. Her stomach turned to jelly.

The receiver in her hand was making check-your-extension-there-seems-to-be-a-receiver-off-the-hook sounds. She pressed the cradle and got a dial tone and dialed Vince Cardozo's number.

Thunder burst outside. A shock passed through the floor. In the street, a car alarm went off.

A voice on the phone said, "Cardozo."

"It's Bonnie Ruskay—I'm sorry to bother you."

"You're not bothering me."

She felt flustered. "I think I just saw him—that teenager—he's standing across the street."

"What's he doing?"

"I think he's watching the rectory."

"Has the rectory got a burglar alarm?"

"No. Father Joe doesn't believe the church should hold private property."

"You mean, he doesn't believe the church should *keep* its private property."

She sensed that this police lieutenant knew some things about the world that she did not—and that he was making fun of it and of her.

"It wouldn't make any difference. I think he's already broken in."

"I'll be right up."

FORTY-EIGHT

"**I** appreciate your arranging for the alarm." Bonnie Ruskay had to shout over the sounds of the workmen. "You certainly got them here fast."

"No trouble," Cardozo said. "I called in a marker."

A workman had pushed four straight-backed chairs into the middle of the hallway. The seats were upholstered in the green that's found on very old dollar bills. The workman was standing on a stepladder, drilling into the paneled ceiling. The electric lights had begun flickering.

Cardozo could see that the wiring in the rectory needed checking. He could also see that now was not the time to mention it. Bonnie Ruskay had an overloaded expression: too much was going wrong at once. "How do you suppose your intruder broke in?"

"He could have gotten in through my office." Her tone was embarrassed, almost apologetic. "I was letting a parishioner out the front door."

She led Cardozo to her office.

"That window?" Cardozo said.

She nodded. In her eyes he saw confusion flecked with fear. He felt sad for her. Something good and decent in her life had ended. This rectory had once been a haven where nothing bad could ever happen; now it had turned into a very different place.

Cardozo crossed the study. He took an atomizer from his briefcase. It was designed for perfume, but he had filled it with gray print powder. It had been an April Fool's gift from Ellie three years ago, but he found it worked as well as a spray gun and was far less bulky.

"Did the kid threaten you?" he said.

"No."

"Speak to you?"

"No. We were never close enough."

He passed the beam of a penlight over the window ledge. A small grease stain glimmered faintly. He sprayed the area, then bent to blow off the excess powder.

"Did he take anything?"

"I'm not sure. A clock is missing—that little desk-top model from Tiffany. It's not valuable, except sentimentally."

Three concentric ridges of a partial print showed.

"He was standing in a doorway over there." She pointed out the window to the row of storefronts across the street.

"You're sure it's the same kid who held you up in the cab." Cardozo fitted a 90-mm lens to his 35-mm camera, focused, and flashed.

"No, not a hundred percent sure. All I could really see was a blond ponytail and a blue baseball cap."

In a generic way, the description reminded Cardozo of the kid who slashed the limo driver on the West Side docks. Not the kind of person you needed breaking into your office.

He shot four exposures, just to be safe.

His eye went to the iron gates shutting off the courtyard. "Did you remember to change that padlock?"

"I'm sorry . . ." She gave him an apologetic look, as though she had let him down. "I forgot."

He wasn't certain what to make of Reverend Bonnie or her apologetic looks. "I'm not asking you to do me favors. Safety is in your own interest. I don't mean to frighten you, but . . ."

Instinct whispered, *Go ahead. Frighten her. It may be the only thing that will wake her up.*

"If this is the same kid, he's stalking you."

She gave him a look. He could see he had startled her and she was doing her best not to react. It was as though she needed very much to prove she could be a calm, unflustered hostess.

"Doesn't it seem odd," she said, "that anyone would risk breaking in just to steal one little clock?"

"It's a fact of life that weirdos are odd. The kid might be on crack, which means he could do anything no matter how stupid or risky. Or, if he's been here before, he may not see breaking in as a risk. He may regard this place as an open house."

"If that's another dig at Father Joe, it's not very subtle."

"It's not meant to be subtle. I'm not running for election."

She colored faintly and he concentrated on not noticing the milky texture of her skin.

"At least you're frank," she said.

"You don't know for sure who Father Montgomery was bringing in here. You don't know what he was doing with them."

She seemed very tired. He felt guilty pushing her to the edge, but he needed to get past her defenses.

"And you *do* know?" she said.

"I know a few things. And I'm finding out a few more." He opened his briefcase. "Are you absolutely sure you don't recognize Wanda Gilmartin?"

He could feel her humoring him as she took the photo from his hand.

"I honestly don't recognize her. Is there some reason you keep thinking I should?"

"She was the girl we found in the basket in Vanderbilt Garden."

Bonnie Ruskay's glance came up to his, startled.

"That's the fifth dead kid in Father Montgomery's file."

"Have you told her parents?" Bonnie said.

"We haven't been able to find her parents. She may have been using a false name."

"I'm sure there's an explanation."

"There's always an explanation. I'll bet there's even an explanation for Wright Vanderbrook."

Anger flared in her eyes and then she covered it. "Wright has nothing to do with any of this."

"I disagree. I think he could have a lot to do with it. The Vanderbrook family brought suit because of the way Father Montgomery counseled their son."

Now she was back in control of her eyes. They challenged him. "That lawsuit never reached court."

"The Vanderbrooks still thought they had grounds."

"Why do you have to unearth these discredited old lies?"

"It's not a lie that Wright Vanderbrook is dead and his parents thought the church had a hand in it."

"He's dead because he was a tragically confused young man."

"That's all there was to it? Confusion?"

"No. That's not all."

She got up from her chair and went to the bookcase. She moved with a grace that under the circumstances he found almost flabbergasting. This was a lady who never fell apart.

She brought back a leather-bound photo album. She laid it open on the desk. The pictures showed a young man with curly light brown hair and fine, almost feminine features. In one he was playing the piano, dressed in evening clothes. In another he was standing at a kitchen sink, in a bathing suit, washing potatoes.

"He was young," she said. "He was beautiful; he was gifted."

Cardozo wondered who had taken all these photos of Wright Vanderbrook and why. In shot after shot, on the beach, on horseback, at a banquet table, the boy's pale green eyes seemed sleepy, almost narcoleptic. "Was he involved with drugs?"

"I never saw it."

"Was he close to Father Joe?"

She hesitated. She must have suddenly seen where the question was leading. "Father Joe was close to all his young people. And closer to Wright than to most because Wright was needier."

"Was it a sexual relationship?"

Her jaw fell. The album slid from her lap.

At last, he thought. *Thank you for a direct answer.* He bent to retrieve the album and handed it back to her.

"I told you that Father Joe took a vow of chastity. He made God a promise."

"A lot of people make promises," Cardozo said. "They even make them to God."

"But Joe keeps his."

"I wouldn't know."

"I do know."

He didn't answer. He could feel her curiosity like a faint exploring pressure on his skin. *Is this what they mean by faith?* he wondered. *This lady is not only a believer in the sanctity of Joe Montgomery, she won't rest till she has me believing too.*

"Lieutenant, don't you ever take a person's word?"

"In life? Sometimes. In work? It's safer not to."

"Not even a priest's word?"

"Priests can be just as secretive as anyone else."

"Secretive?" She looked at him, eyes pale and troubled. "Are you talking about anything in particular?"

"You asked me to return a photo of two kids in the Vanderbilt Garden. What was the real reason?"

She drew in a breath. "They're my children. The court only allows me to see them between school terms. They shouldn't have been there."

"Then why were they?"

"Because it was an event—and I love them—and I don't think it's dishonest to disobey an unjust custody decree."

"But you do mind leaving proof lying about. In law that would be called cognizance of guilt."

"I'm not trying to protect myself—I don't give a damn about myself. But I can't let Collie be hurt."

"How could Collie be hurt?"

"He stayed neutral in the divorce, and my ex-husband trusts him. Kelly and Kyle go out for excursions with Collie two or three times a month—and the excursions just happen to end up here."

"You must have a great deal of confidence in Collie to let him ferry your children around."

"My brother and Collie and I have been best friends since we were children. As long as I've known Collie he's been absolutely trustworthy."

Something about the explanation nagged at Cardozo. It seemed to fit, but still he wondered about it. His mind was telling him one thing about Bonnie Ruskay and his instinct was telling him another and he couldn't get the two messages to agree.

"I hope I've cleared myself of all crimes?"

"Almost all," he said. "There's one other question. A check you wrote to *cash*—number 2727."

"You seem to know my account better than I do. Offhand I don't recall it. I probably ran short of cash and dashed to the bank."

"It was drawn on the parish account. Two thousand dollars. A check-cashing service cashed it for a girl by the name of Nell Dunbar."

He could feel her very carefully not reacting.

"Is that a question?" she said.

"No. The question is—what was that check paying for?"

For just an instant, her mouth quivered. "I can't answer that."

"How were you involved with Nell Dunbar?"

"It was a pastoral matter. I'm sorry, there's no way I can discuss it."

"Then I'm sorry too."

He stood, and she rose with him.

"I'm not hiding anything that concerns you or your work." Her eyes were almost pleading. "I wish you'd just believe that."

"I don't have your capacity for faith." He smiled. "I must strike you as an obnoxious, doubting kind of guy."

"No, but you're thorough to a fault."

"You've had a dose of me and my thoroughness."

She didn't deny it. She walked with him into the hallway.

"Be sure you reset the alarm every time you open the door," he reminded her. "It has to become second nature—or it's useless."

"I'm a klutz with electronic gizmos and you're kind to care."

She walked with him to the sidewalk. She touched his elbow. It was the first time she had ever reached out and just touched him. "Thank you."

"Look," he said, "wouldn't you feel better if you had a guard?"

"The police have enough trouble on their hands without worrying about me."

"Guess you've had enough complications with the law for one lifetime."

She looked perplexed. "I don't follow."

"This investigation on top of the lawsuits. First you walk the civil gauntlet, now the criminal. Frying pan to fire."

"We haven't had that many lawsuits. Only two. The Vanderbrooks and the Schuylers. And they were both nuisance suits."

"What were the Schuylers trying to prove?"

"Samantha sued to get half our garden. The court turned her down."

"All the same, it's tiring. You beat back the lawyers, you beat back the cops. But I'm not kidding—if this punk keeps hanging around, you're going to get a guard."

"We'll see."

Cardozo admired spunk, but spunk alone wasn't always the answer. "There's no 'we'll see' about it."

Cardozo phoned ahead, and Mrs. Schuyler's social secretary said to pop by anytime between five and seven, no trouble at all. When he arrived at the Schuyler town house, champagne corks were popping in the living room and uniformed servants were circulating with silver trays of hors d'oeuvres. A butler handed Cardozo over to a young woman wearing prim glasses and no jewelry.

"Hi," she said. "We spoke on the phone." She led Cardozo through a babbling sea of coutured dresses and tailored Italian suits.

"Mrs. Schuyler, Lieutenant Cardozo is here to see you."

A blond hairdo was chattering with a red hairdo. Both hairdos turned, but it was the blond hair that spoke.

"How do you do." A jeweled hand went out. "I'm Samantha

Schuyler and this is my dear friend Allison Fitzregis. Maggie, get the lieutenant something to drink."

"No, thanks," Cardozo said.

"We'll never be able to talk in this madhouse." Mrs. Schuyler had not bothered to let go of Cardozo's hand. "Let's go find ourselves a little nook."

She pulled him on a figure-eight through the room, introducing him to two dozen friends, and Cardozo realized that Samantha Schuyler was delighted to have a real live police lieutenant to show off to her chums.

"A pipe burst in the polo practice room. So if we want any privacy I'm afraid we have to talk in the humidor. Do you mind tobacco?"

When she opened the door he understood why she asked: The floor-to-ceiling maplewood drawers that took up three walls must have been stuffed with cigars: the small room had the sweet, over-poweringly dank smell of cured leaf.

Mrs. Schuyler sniffed. Raisin-sized diamonds at her ears and throat sent out blips of blue light. "Is the air all right?"

"The air's fine."

"I won't let Houghton smoke anywhere else in the house."

She settled herself into a stuffed leather armchair. Cardozo took the matching chair. He saw that she had brought her champagne glass with her.

"It's about Wright Vanderbrook. I need a little filling-in."

Samantha Schuyler's smile took on a mean edge of satisfaction. "So it took a man to find out about that saga. How much of the story do you know?"

Cardozo outlined what he'd been able to put together from the medical examiner's report. "And this." He handed her a Xerox of the *New York Times* obituary.

Her expression took on a pearly glaze. "He was a wonderful boy and it's a wonderful write-up. Pity he had to be dead to get it." She gave the obit back. She sat sipping champagne. "After Wright killed himself, notes were found. Do you know about those?"

"Only rumors."

"They were babyish, scrawled outpourings. The wording left

no doubt—all the time that Wright had supposedly been in counseling he'd actually been having an affair with his counselor."

"How did you happen to get possession of these letters?"

"The cleaning woman discovered the originals." Mrs. Schuyler drained her champagne glass. "She made copies on the parish Xerox—for security—and as I was then chairperson of the vestry she brought them to me. They indicated an extremely sick relationship. Naturally, we petitioned the bishop to reorganize St. Andrew's."

"You asked him to fire Father Montgomery?"

"Fire them both." Mrs. Schuyler was looking at Cardozo with half-mast eyes. "Ruskay and Montgomery are like the two faces of a counterfeit coin. There's a very sick relationship between them—what do psychiatrists call it, folie à deux? Alone, each of them is quite harmless. But together . . ." Her gaze dropped modestly. "We explained the whole thing to the bishop. The old fool said, flat out, Montgomery and Ruskay stay. Couldn't budge him. God knows what those two had on him. But I can imagine the sort of thing."

FORTY-NINE

Bishop Griswold Hancock presided that Sunday at the eleven o'clock service at St. Andrew's. Bonnie assisted. It was a full house, as it always was when the bishop gave the sermon.

The congregation took communion in shifts. As many as could fit knelt at the altar railing while the others waited in the aisles. The bishop served the wafer and Bonnie followed, serving the wine.

"The body of Christ." The bishop made a sign of the cross with the wafer and placed it in Tina Vanderbilt's cupped hands.

"The body of Christ." And in Whitney Carls's cupped hands.

"The blood of Christ." Bonnie raised the chalice to Tina's lips. Tina's eyelids fluttered as she swallowed.

"The blood of Christ."

Eyes open but averted, Whitney Carls took a tiny sip. As he rose he tugged at his wig.

Bonnie heard Tina whisper. "Would you just leave that damned wig alone! It's not a toy!"

Shadows moved single-file back to the pews. A new batch took their places.

An angelic-looking blond child caught Bonnie's eye at the far end of the railing.

As she worked her way down, something about him kept tugging her eye. He was dressed in high ghetto style: Hawaiian shirt, bright red floppy cotton trousers, a blue baseball cap worn backward over his ponytail.

Even before she saw the crucifix earring, a wind of recognition chilled her.

"The body of Christ." The bishop placed the wafer in the boy's hands.

Now Bonnie took the bishop's place.

Holding the chalice in both hands, she raised it to the boy's lips.

She began to pronounce the formula: "The blood of—"

She broke off, realizing that he had two hands free, she had none free. At this instant he could do anything to her he wanted.

"The blood of Christ." Her voice shook.

He did not sip the offered wine: it was as though he had not heard her. Above the rim of the chalice, his gaze met hers. His eyes were a steely, dead blue. Ice went through her.

She moved on to the next communicant, a gray-haired lady wearing a diamond pendant on her jacket.

"The blood of Christ."

Her hand trembled lifting the chalice.

When she looked back, the boy had left the railing.

In the vesting room, Bonnie had one arm out of her surplice when she heard a sound behind her. She turned and her heart jumped backward in her breast.

"Hi." The boy was standing there.

She hadn't even heard the door.

His hand was extended, lazy and menacing at the same time. "I'm Eff."

The organ was booming out a postlude, the Widor toccata, and she doubted a scream would be heard.

The extended hand was empty, but she couldn't see the other one. Panic rose in her throat. She swallowed, forcing it back. "You've been following me."

"I've had my eye on you."

"Why?"

"Come on. Let's be friends." The hand stayed there, unwavering, demanding that she shake it.

Instinct told her to chance it. A step forward brought her within switchblade range.

"I'm Bonnie." Her hand closed lightly around his.

Right away it felt like a mistake. His hand gripped hers. And held on. And very slowly pulled her toward him.

"Nice to meet you, Bonnie. Real nice. And I mean it."

She could feel his body pumping out heat. Suddenly he let her go. She stepped back.

He was reaching into the rear pocket of his trousers. He pulled out a flattened cylinder of something. As he unfolded it she recognized one of her flyers.

"Is this thing serious? Ten thousand dollars' reward for information leading to identification of"—he had trouble with the next word—"assailant who mugged Father Joe Montgomery?"

The silence seemed to dangle. She pulled in a deep breath.

"It couldn't be more serious."

"And you mean this?" He pointed to two words at the bottom of the flyer: NO PROSECUTION.

"Absolutely."

"Then you got yourself a deal." Three strutting steps brought him to the mirror. "I was there when Father Joe got mugged." He unbuttoned his shirt to the navel and winked at his reflection. "I can identify the guy that did it." He turned, grinning. His eyes locked in on hers. "It was me."

A glassy stillness rippled across the room. She knew he was lying: Father Joe had said his assailant was black.

"Are you willing to repeat that statement in front of the police?"

"I'm not afraid of cops."

"The bank's closed today. I won't be able to get the money till tomorrow."

"I can wait a day."

Now came the hard part. "I need your name and address."

"What for?"

"For the check."

"No checks."

"The parish would never let me withdraw that much cash. I'll give you a banker's check. Certified. It's exactly the same as cash."

He looked at her a long, evaluating moment. "Francis Huffington. Two F's. Care of Snyder." He spelled out the name. "Five seventy-three West Sixty-ninth Street. Apartment four F."

There was a knock on the open door. "Am I interrupting?" Ellie Siegel was holding a sheaf of Xeroxes.

"Not at all," Cardozo said. "Ellie, you remember Reverend Bonnie Ruskay from St. Andrew's."

Ellie's eyebrows arched up. Her eyes seemed to take a moment deciding whether to be cordial or not. "Of course I remember the reverend."

"It's good to see you, Detective." Bonnie rose from the straight-backed chair. "Have you been well?"

"Always. I'm always well. And you? Don't get up, please." Ellie smiled coolly. "I did some microfilm searching at the newspapers, but it can wait."

"We're not doing anything but waiting ourselves," Cardozo said.

"Really." Ellie's tone was absolutely flat.

"It's my fault," Bonnie Ruskay said. "I asked someone to meet us here and he's late."

"What have you got?" Cardozo said.

"Pretty much what we expected." Ellie perched the copies on the desk on top of a teetering pile of departmental paper. "The white press never linked Vegas and Wills or Gilmartin. The stories got buried in the back pages and they suggested that the victims were black or Hispanic. What it reminds me of is the black hooker murdered at the Soldiers and Sailors Monument the night the white lady jogger was wilded in Central Park."

"What about the *Amsterdam News*?"

"They carried all three stories, but basically they published the NYPD handout. They did run one editorial saying the police should investigate links, but there was no follow-up."

"*El Diario*?"

"*Nada*. It's all there. Enjoy." Ellie waved and was gone.

"What did she mean," Bonnie Ruskay said, " 'the white press'?"

"The major media." Cardozo glanced through Ellie's Xeroxes. After ten minutes of shuffling paper and counting dust motes in the air, he looked again at his watch. "Francis Huffington either forgot he had a date or he never intended to show in the first place."

"He could be held up in traffic," Bonnie Ruskay said. "Or on a subway."

"Believe me, if a kid like this wants to get somewhere, nothing holds him up. It's obvious what's happened."

"It's not obvious to me."

"He tried to work a scam on you, you tried to outscam him, and he couldn't think of a bigger scam to get around yours."

She sat with a stunned look, as though he'd taken out a .45 Magnum and blown a hole through her lace blouse.

"This kid has mugged you, he's broken into your office, he's stalked you, he's robbed you. You didn't seriously expect him to walk in here and give himself up."

She stared at him a moment before picking up her handbag. "Sorry to have wasted your time."

Cardozo felt a trickle of impatience. "I didn't say it was a waste. It's the smartest way of handling him. You called his bluff and you scared him off. He'll think twice before he pesters you again."

"I'm sure you're right."

The phone rang. "Cardozo."

"The printing on the obituary envelope doesn't match the anonymous note." It was Lou Stein. "My handwriting expert says we're dealing with someone else."

Bonnie Ruskay mouthed a good-bye and headed for the door.

"Hey." Cardozo covered the mouthpiece. "Remember to reset the alarm."

"I'll remember."

"We've found three partials on the obit," Lou was saying. "Two we can't identify. We don't have any matches on file, so they're not anyone we've comparison-printed. We compared the third partial with the prints on the duplicate obit." Lou sighed. "Of which there are many—mostly yours."

"I'm sorry, Lou. I couldn't exactly snap on a pair of plastic gloves in front of Mrs. Schuyler."

"Assuming the only other prints on the dupe are hers . . ."

"Which they are."

"Then we have a match. Mrs. Schuyler mailed the obit."

"Hallelujah." Cardozo took a long swallow of room-temperature coffee. He stared out the window at the brick wall across the alley. So the rouged, fluffed-up old puppet had more than just a mean tongue. "She's got a mean pair of hands to go with it."

"Beg pardon?"

"Sorry. Just thinking out loud."

"Okay. Moving along to those manila file folders. You're right on the money. At some point in their history, they were stacked together—the same cup of mocha coffee with nondairy creamer spilled on them all."

"Can you date that coffee spill?"

"It's hard to date coffee, but assuming the rancid butter on the Vegas file was spilled at approximately the same time, judging by the bacteria I'd put it in the vicinity of two to four weeks back."

Cardozo ran a quick calculation through his mind. "That fits our time frame."

"Glad to shed light."

As Cardozo replaced the receiver, Ellie came gliding back into the cubicle. Her face had a mysterious kind of smirk.

"Okay, Ellie—how can I help you?"

"If that's a serious offer, you could fix the New York State lottery for me. Or pay my Con Ed bill. Or shoot my ex-husband."

"Not now. Please."

"I love to watch you get angry. I love the way you scrunch up your face when you're on the verge of losing it."

"Not funny." He leaned back in his chair, palms upraised. "Give it a rest . . . please?"

"I was only trying to lighten the mood a little."

"Sure."

"Vince, you have to keep a little perspective on yourself—and on her too."

"I can handle it."

"By letting her use your office to make dates?"

"She thought she was helping."

"Watch out." There was fatigue in Ellie's eyes, but there was caring too. "Look what that woman's done to her ex. . . . You want to wind up like Ernie?"

"How's he wound up?"

"Fixated. Addicted to a memory. He'll never find satisfaction with another woman. Let alone peace of mind or self-respect. There are women who do that to men."

"What's with all the insight? Did I ask for a guru? Did I send for a shrink?"

"I was only trying to be a friend, okay?"

"Fine. Be a friend. But keep one thing straight. You don't own me."

She stared levelly across the desk, stretching the moment of sudden silence. "Who'd want to?"

"Okay." Cardozo brought his swivel chair upright. "Truce."

"Did I miss something? Was there a war?"

"There was about to be. Do us both a favor. Get off her case. Keep an open mind."

"An open mind about Reverend Bonnie?" Ellie mustered a smile. "For you, Vince, anything. Even the impossible."

FIFTY

"When are you and Anne going to get married?" Bonnie asked.

"We're thinking of early autumn." Ben lifted his glass of mineral water as though to toast her. "But we haven't picked the date."

"Every year you say you're thinking of early autumn. Tell me the truth. Is it ever going to happen?"

"Why the rush?"

They had finished their meal and were lingering over *café filtre*. Tonight had been her brother's turn to pick the restaurant. He had chosen a new place, The Cottage, a brownstone in Turtle Bay. The restaurant was one of a new wave—throwbacks to the French eateries of the fifties.

"You're still a Catholic," Bonnie said, "and a conservative one. You make very brave noises about living with a woman, but it doesn't suit you."

"Maybe it suits Anne."

"Maybe Anne's wrong and the Church is right."

He gave her a look of quiet amazement.

"Not about everything," she said. "But maybe they're right about the sacraments."

"Okay . . . something's on your mind. I've felt it all evening. Tell me what the problem is."

"This was supposed to be our fun dinner."

"Out with it, little sister."

Music was playing softly on the sound system. It sounded like an accordion, a guitar, and Yves Montand. The walls around them were brightly splashed with the blues and whites and earth-reds of Provençal pottery.

"I've just been wondering . . . What if the Catholic Church is right about ordaining women?"

"Now you wonder." He sighed, shaking his head. She could feel his good humor, completely lacking in mockery.

"Lately I've felt I don't have the kind of strength a priest needs. And I keep feeling it's because I'm a woman." She picked up an unused butter knife that the waiter had forgotten to remove. She carefully aligned it with the edge of the table. "I'm sorry. Am I being insensitive to discuss this with you?"

"Hell, no. Why would you think that?"

"You wanted to be a priest and they turned you down."

"They turned you down too."

"But you abided by their decision. I didn't. Maybe I'm getting what I asked for."

"What's really bothering you? Specifics, please."

"It keeps coming up in counseling. Some of my parishioners' problems are idiotic. One woman's been dropped from the party A-list. One man is losing his hair. But they're really suffering. I feel their pain and it's like a wall I can't get past."

"That's the way it should be."

"Father Joe never brooded about A-lists or falling hair."

"You're not Father Joe."

"But I'm trying to fill his shoes. And I don't know if I can."

"The trouble isn't that you're a woman—the trouble is, you're human."

"You'd say anything to make me feel better. You're my little brother and you've always been like a big brother to me. I should be taking care of you and instead I'm crying on your shoulder."

"What's a brother's shoulder for?"

"I'm worried, Ben. What will I do if Father Joe doesn't come back?"

"Of course he'll come back."

"You don't know what's been going on. You don't know all of it."

He looked across the table at her, serious now. "Then tell me all of it."

She didn't answer. She moved her wineglass in a tight circle.

"Is it his eyes?" Ben said.

"His eyes will be fine. At least the right eye will be. It's something else. The police are trying to hurt Joe."

"Explain, please."

"They found pictures in his talent file. Young people who never played in Joe's shows. One was the dead girl in the hamper in Vanderbilt Garden."

Ben stirred a tiny teaspoon of sugar crystals into his coffee. "And the others?"

"Young people found over the last three years the same way."

"In hampers?"

She nodded.

"How did the pictures get into his file?"

"I don't know. Joe doesn't know."

"Do the police know?"

"They think they know. They think they know a lot of things.

They think Joe wasn't mugged. They think he hurt his eye fighting with the housebreaker."

"What difference does it make?"

"They think he killed the housebreaker."

"That's crazy."

"But it's what they believe; I'm sure of it." Her hand shook and half her coffee went into her saucer. "I was in the precinct today."

He studied her face. "Why were you in the precinct?"

"I offered a reward to anyone who witnessed the mugging. A boy came forward and confessed."

"Good. Then you have proof."

"He was lying. He's white. Father Joe's mugger was black. But I thought if the boy made a statement, it would help Joe."

"Sis, that's awfully close to perjury."

"Don't worry—he didn't show up."

"Did the police actually *say* they suspect Joe?"

"Not in so many words. But there's circumstantial evidence. He hired one of the dead teenagers to work around the rectory. They even asked me about Wright Vanderbrook and Joe. They keep coming back to Joe's sex habits."

"Does he have sex habits?"

"Of course not." She watched her brother drain the last of his coffee. "They got an anonymous note."

"That doesn't mean anything."

"It was on church stationery."

"Maybe they think you sent it. Did you?"

"Of course I didn't."

"They're testing you. They haven't got a case, so they're seeing if they can break you down till you tell them what you know."

"I've told them the truth."

"Know something, Sis? You haven't got a thing to worry about. And neither does Father Joe, with you in his corner."

She sighed. "Thanks for dinner. And for listening. Next time's on me."

They said good-bye on the sidewalk. It was a mildly humid night.

Ben laughed and hugged her. "And don't you dare worry."

He hailed a cab for her and she kissed him good night.

*   *   *

Fifteen minutes later, Bonnie stepped out of a cab and stood on the rectory doorstep, looking through her purse for the key.

Something made a scraping sound on the pavement behind her.

She angled her head around, tracking the sound, and peered into the smoky night. Parked cars lined the empty sidewalk. Shadows spilled from darkened doorways.

Only my imagination. Too much wine, too much coffee.

She let herself into the rectory and felt along the wall for the light switch. Overhead, a light bulb flickered and flashed like a gunshot and went out.

She stood a moment in the darkness, trying to connect with her own breathing. A short, shrill warbling sound startled her. The burglar alarm was flashing its tiny green lights, demanding that she punch in her code.

She tapped four buttons. The alarm fell silent. She waited to see if it really meant it or was just pretending.

It seemed to mean it.

She gave the street door a shove shut and reached to slide the bolt. The alarm began yelping again and the door flew back against her hand.

A shadow pushed through the wedge of light.

Her body gave a jump inside her clothes.

The shadow had weight. And speed. And a voice. A boy's voice. "I have to talk to you."

She froze.

In light slanting through the fan window, she could see the outline of a turned-around baseball cap. She had the impression the shadow was smiling.

"It's me. Eff."

She stepped back. "What do you want?"

"Punch in your code. Otherwise they send someone."

"Tell me what you want."

"I'm sorry I didn't get to the precinct. My mom had an accident. She's—" His voice broke. "I need to talk to someone." He struck a match. "Can you see the buttons?"

She gazed at this young man with his desperate eyes and the sad bravado of his blond ponytail. *What do I feel for Eff Huffington?* she asked herself. She searched her heart and was ashamed to find a complete blank.

"I wouldn't blame you if you told me to drop dead, but the doctors say she's not"—he began sobbing—"she's not going to make it."

Her counselor's instinct told her she was standing three feet from real pain. Maybe not the pain he claimed—maybe a different, darker, unnamed pain—but pain nonetheless.

She hesitated only an instant. She tapped her code into the box. The electronic yodeling stopped. "Come with me. We can talk down here."

She led him to her office. The air conditioner pulsed like a weary heart. She drew the curtains.

"Make yourself comfortable. Have a seat."

He didn't sit. She watched him examine the photos on her desk. *If I can't figure him out,* she told herself, *at least I can put a human face on him.*

"Are you thirsty? Would you like something to drink? A snack?"

She brought things from the little refrigerator beneath the bookcase: a bowl of fruit, a plate of cold cuts, jars of mayonnaise and mustard and relish, two pop-top cans of ginger ale. She arranged them on the desk top, giving herself time to find the words she wanted to say.

"How did your mother's accident happen?"

The silence in the room seemed to stick like gelatin. He studied the objects on the desk. She felt him sizing her up through her possessions.

Finally he went to the refrigerator and reached behind the orange juice. He brought out a bottle of beer.

She looked at him, surprised. "That's Carlsberg. It's Danish—you may not like it."

An odd smile curled up one corner of his mouth. "Beer's beer." He felt around the side of the refrigerator for the magnetized bottle opener. It was as though he'd known it was there. He popped the top off the beer bottle. It rolled across the rug. He made no move to pick it up.

She set a coaster on the edge of the desk near him. "What hospital is your mother in?"

He didn't answer.

She waited him out.

He lifted the bottle and toasted her. *"Salud."* He took a long swallow. His T-shirt was wet through at the armpits and plastered to his chest. A stream of Carlsberg ran over his lower lip and trickled down his chin.

He set the bottle down on the desk beside the coaster. He wasn't exactly testing a limit, but she could feel him nudging it.

"That's bad for the wood." She moved the bottle onto the coaster.

He was tapping something against the knuckle of his left thumb. He opened his fist and she saw it was a switchblade knife.

Her stomach went into free-fall.

"You are one dumb bitch. I've been following you. I know everywhere you go. I can get you anytime."

He flicked the blade open. The walls of the office seemed to close in and the loudest sound was the beating of her own heart.

"I want my money."

Bonnie drew in a long breath and slowly exhaled. "I haven't got money here."

"I want my ten thousand."

"You've searched this place, you know there's no cash here."

With a sudden force that was completely crazy, he rammed her backward against the desk. The sour, almost rancid smell of his body engulfed her. "Yo, bitch. You pay—or I play."

Holding her down with one arm, he touched the tip of the blade to her throat. Heat radiated from the steel, stinging through her.

He kissed her on the mouth, hard, his tongue a sour jab of beer.

He pulled back, grinning. "Better start saying your prayers, bitch. 'Cause playtime do be commencing."

FIFTY-ONE

I t was just after four in the morning when the phone beside Cardozo's bed jangled. He was still half asleep as he lifted the receiver. "Cardozo."

"Vince . . . it's Bonnie."

Something jagged and breathless in her voice alerted him. He pushed himself up to sitting and clicked on the light. "What's the matter?"

"That boy was here. Eff Huffington."

Cardozo felt his heart muscles contract.

"He had a knife. He—" She began stuttering.

"Take it easy. What did he do?"

There was an awful silence and even before she said it, he knew exactly what Eff Huffington had done to Reverend Bonnie Ruskay.

"He raped me. For six hours. He said he'll be back for more unless I give him his money."

"Have you washed?"

"Have I . . . no, I haven't washed."

"Don't. Don't throw anything out, don't clean up, don't touch anything. I'm coming up right now."

Terri stood in the hallway in her bathrobe, staring at her father with shocked eyes. "What's happened?"

"The son of a bitch attacked her."

When she opened the door of the rectory, her eyes were swollen and dead. There was nothing in them, not hate, not fear. Her raincoat was trembling and Cardozo saw that the collar of the dress beneath it was torn.

"Come on. My car's over here."

She let him take her hand. Her touch was cold. "Where are we going?"

"I'm taking you to the hospital."

In the car as they were heading down Lexington, she began tearing at her face, forcing her eyelids and lips apart. A wordless sound pushed out of her throat. He reached with his right forearm and eased her hands down.

"Don't. Please don't."

He placed her hands on the dashboard. She stared at them as if they had preceded her into death.

"You're safe," he said. "It's over."

The emergency room was a Third World bazaar under rocket attack, faces screaming in a dozen languages, telephones jangling, stretcher wheels screeching, nurses' heels clattering. A fire alarm clanged every ninety seconds and no one reacted.

He used his ID to get her into an examining room. A young woman doctor helped her out of her raincoat.

A hammer dropped in Cardozo's heart when he saw that the dress underneath was a checkerboard of bloodstains.

"He didn't use a condom." Bonnie Ruskay had the voice of an automaton, without inflection or color. The expression on her face was not just pained but completely baffled. "Please test me for HIV."

"The antibody doesn't show immediately. We'll test you later. For the moment, this will calm you." The doctor slid a needle into her patient's arm.

Cardozo watched Bonnie melt slowly down and down into a space of drugged and grateful nonbeing. He felt sick for her, sick for the city. This was what it was coming to.

The hospital kept her overnight.

He stayed in her room, guarding her. During the night she reached for his hand.

Cardozo stood staring at Ellie Siegel's desk with its neat arrangement of paperwork *in,* paperwork *out;* its single perfect white carnation sitting in a blue glazed vase the size of a pill bottle. A determined effort had been made to separate that desk top from the confusion of the squad room around it.

Ellie's fingers slowed on the typewriter keyboard. She looked over at him.

"Bonnie Ruskay was raped last night," he said.

"Oh, my God." Ellie's face turned pale. She moved a stack of files from a chair to her desk top. "Sit. Talk."

He sat. Didn't talk. Just sat.

"How's she doing?" Ellie said quietly.

"She's coming apart."

Ellie handed him a full coffee mug. "Here. I haven't touched it."

"It was that kid that's been stalking her. Eff Huffington. I hate that kid. I hate what he's done and what he is. This used to be a town where decent people could live. I'll be damned before I let this city roll over dead because of a bunch of punk savages."

"Sometimes you sound just like me."

"I'm assigning her a round-the-clock guard." He raised the mug and allowed a thin dark trickle to pass through his lips. The coffee tasted sludgy and bitter, as if it had been thickening in the bottom of the coffeemaker for the better part of a week. "Greg Monteleone and Tom O'Bannon will work twelve-hour shifts."

Ellie was watching him, her eyes big and pained beneath sunken lids. "I'm sorry, Vince. I really am." She reached out with the tip of a tissue. "Hold still. You've got a piece of apple Danish on your chin."

He gazed at Ellie, feeling the soft mothering touch of her finger. "Thanks." He pushed up from the chair and headed toward his cubicle.

"What's your rush?"

"Huffington gave Bonnie an address. I wrote it somewhere in my notebook."

"Probably phony," Ellie warned.

"Doesn't hurt to make sure."

The *Oprah Winfrey Show* was blasting through the door. Cardozo pushed the buzzer. There was no spring to the button and he had a feeling the wiring was dead. He knocked.

When no one answered, he pounded.

A tall man with acne and a graying red beard opened the door. Finally.

"I'm looking for Eff Huffington."

The man pushed out a dazed silence.

"Francis Huffington. I want to talk to him."

A woman in jeans crossed the room and turned down the TV. "Huffington. He lives here. Which one of you is Snyder?"

"We're both Snyder." The woman eased the man aside. She had a helmet of chemically blond hair and lips the color of spit on pink bathroom tile. "Who are you?"

Cardozo showed her his shield. "I'm looking for Francis Huffington, also known as Eff. In case the name's not familiar, he's the kid you're boarding for the city's foster care service."

"You don't have to get smart-ass. What do you want with him?"

"I'm a cop—figure it out." Cardozo did a body swerve around her and pushed past the door into the apartment.

The furniture looked like a team of black belts had been using it for karate practice. An eight-year-old Hispanic girl was moving the nozzle of a vacuum cleaner along the edges of carpet that had been wall-to-wall somewhere else.

"It's not our job to keep him out of trouble." The woman was shouting. "We haven't got eighteen hands. We're not responsible for that kid's behavior."

"Where is he?"

"How do I know?"

"You and Mr. Snyder are drawing seven hundred a month untaxed to know where he is, that's how you know."

"He's at therapy."

"When does he get back from therapy?"

Mrs. Snyder turned. "Isn't today his drug counseling day, Alvin?" She pitched her voice like a cue in a rehearsal.

"Right."

"He goes to drug counseling after therapy. Then he's got an hour before vocational training and he usually doesn't bother to come home till afterward."

Cardozo wondered exactly how many bureaucrats and civic freeloaders were making bucks off this kid. "How often do you see this foster child of yours?"

"Every day." Something in her eyes backed off. "Every other day."

"Where's his room? The city pays you to give him a room; where is it?"

"Hey, come on now." The man's voice was low and he

sounded terminally exhausted. "Let's just sit down and break out some Rolling Rock and talk about this."

"Screw talking about it." Cardozo strode down the hallway, pushing doors open.

The room with the waterbed and the barbell set and the pink vanity was obviously the master bedroom.

Behind him the sound of *Oprah* came up again, loud.

The room with the toilet was a no-man's-land of dripping pipes and sweating walls.

The kitchen was a holding cage for flies.

That left one last door, a room with the shade down. He snapped it up and momentum took it whipping around the rod. Sunlight washed across an unmade bunk bed.

Mrs. Snyder came speeding, spinning after him. "Hey—I didn't see your warrant."

He flung open the closet door. He estimated two dozen pairs of women's shoes in the rack—all of them scuffed, most of them open-toed. "I don't need a warrant. You need a lawyer."

Her face pumped with goggle-eyed rage. "I happen to be a paralegal with a top Wall Street law firm. My husband's a certified public accountant. Bonded."

"Then listen up. Eff Huffington is not just another recession-scarred trick-or-treater getting back in touch with his inner ape. He's a one-man crime wave and if you protect him you're both accomplices—and unlike Eff you're not juveniles, at least not legally, got it?"

Her shoulders writhed inside her Mostly Mozart T-shirt. He braced, not sure what was coming. Her hands yanked the shirt up.

"See?" she screamed. "See what that crazy little shit did to me?" A breast exploded free. She lifted it to show him a colorless three-inch track crosshatched with pink stitching. "He's a maniac —a monster—I could tell you things about that kid—"

"No, you couldn't. Put it away."

She pulled Mozart back down. "He threatened to kill us. Alvin's a wreck. I'm a wreck."

"Why's he going to kill you? Even Eff has a reason."

"If we ever tell . . ." She sank onto the bunk.

"Tell what?"

"He doesn't live here. We haven't seen him in four months. He said if we ever tell anyone . . ." She sat wiping her eyes with the back of her hand. "You don't know the things he's done. He cut a girl's ear off, that little girl Juanita out in our living room."

"Where is he now?"

"All he said was"—her words fought through what seemed to be an asthma attack—"in case there was an emergency—"

"Believe me, this is an emergency."

She pulled a piece of newspaper from a wallet in her hip pocket. Seven barely legible digits had been scrawled in the margin. "He said call this number."

A woman answered on the second ring. "Pierre Strauss's office. May I help you?"

What do you know. "Is he in?"

"Who may I say is calling?"

"Vince Cardozo, Twenty-second Precinct."

A moment later Strauss came on the line, all phony jocularity. "Yes, Vince."

"So you take messages for Eff Huffington."

"I represent Francis Huffington, yes."

"Why would you want to handle a reptile like that?"

"Every accused person is entitled to a defense."

"I appreciate the constitutional lecture. I'd appreciate it even more if you'd tell me where your client is. I need to talk to him."

"Any communication you have for Mr. Huffington can be sent right here, care of my office."

"He raped a woman."

"Just give me the time and place of the arraignment, and rest assured my client and I will be there."

"The lady hasn't brought charges. She hopes she won't have to."

"Fine. Then my client doesn't have to appear."

Cardozo slammed down the phone. Rage was running so hard in him that his toes burned from wanting to kick.

He closed his eyes and turned a full circle in his swivel chair. He ran it through his mind and it didn't make sense.

Pierre Strauss was a high-powered high-ticket civil liberties lawyer. He defended left-wing causes and billionaire gonefs. Eff Huffington wasn't in either category.

Cardozo went to the computer in the squad room. The amber logo of the resident software glowed out of the blue-green monitor screen.

Greg Monteleone sat dunking a cheese Danish into a paper cup of Pepsi. Cardozo had never understood Greg's taste in flavor combinations.

"Hey, Greg, mind if I use the computer?"

"Be my guest."

Cardozo jabbed a finger at the keyboard. A menu appeared on the monitor. He selected the *criminal records* option. He typed the name *Francis Huffington* and pushed *enter*.

Eff's record scrolled up the screen. He had pleaded guilty to two felony charges. In February three years ago there'd been a breaking and entering. In March the year before last there'd been possession of a deadly weapon.

Juvenile Court had suspended both sentences and Eff was currently on probation. The file listed Sy Jencks as the probation officer.

"How about that," Cardozo said. "Jencks."

"Who's Jencks?" Greg spoke through a mouthful of compost.

"He was Pablo Cespedes's probation officer too."

Sy Jencks opened the manila folder that contained the probation file on Eff Huffington. "Doesn't make sense." He leafed slowly through the sheets. "I can't believe Eff would mug a priest —and say so. Of all the admissions the kid could possibly make, this one is suicide. Did you actually hear him say this?"

"Not personally," Cardozo said. "He confessed to a friend of mine."

"Could I ask what makes you believe your friend?"

"My friend's a priest."

"So we're talking what now—two priests?" Jencks looked up. His pale wry eyes seemed to weigh and then dismiss the possibility that Cardozo was putting him on. "That's even weirder. The terms of probation are, Eff can't go near a priest."

"Why's that?"

"Clergy used to be his target of choice." Jencks's blunt-tipped fingers played with the edges of the file. "Since age twelve he's been shaking down pedophile priests—and priests who weren't pedophiles but who were scared of that kind of accusation."

"This priest was a woman."

Jencks's face registered confusion.

"An Episcopal priest. He raped her."

Jencks sat shaking his head in low-key wonder. "Christ, he barely got acquitted of murdering the last priest he tangled with."

"Run that by me again?"

Jencks slid the folder across the desk top. "Father Charles Romero."

"Chuck Romero—over at St. Veronica's in Queens?"

"You knew him?"

"I spoke with him once."

"Very popular man with his parishioners . . . did a lot of work with troubled teens . . . a real loss to the community."

Cardozo scanned pages dense with dot-matrix print. "I heard Romero was killed, but I didn't know there was a sex accusation."

"It was given very little publicity. The D.A. persuaded the judge to keep the media out of pretrial. The D.A. looks out for the diocese. So do a few of our judges."

Cardozo turned a page. "I see Eff pleaded self-defense."

"He was always pleading self-defense. The priest could be ninety years old and in a wheelchair—Eff would still have to fight for his honor. He claimed Father Romero made advances and when he refused, Romero threatened his life."

"And the jury bought it?"

"The jury never got a chance to buy it. The state dropped charges after three days of pretrial. Eff pleaded guilty to possessing a deadly weapon."

FIFTY-TWO

Cardozo found the number in the D.A.'s roster and punched it into his phone. A woman answered. "Yes?"

"Counselor Fairchild?"

"I seemed to be, the last time I walked past a mirror. Who are you?"

"Lieutenant Vince Cardozo, Twenty-second Precinct. I'm running a homicide investigation. Eff Huffington's name has come up."

"Only his name? Lucky you."

"According to the records, you prosecuted Eff for the murder of Father Chuck Romero."

"I tried to."

"After three days of pretrial, you moved for acquittal. Why?"

"It's hard to give a short answer to that."

"I've got time for the long answer."

"I haven't. Besides which, I'm not at liberty to discuss details of the Huffington-Romero case."

"Someone had better discuss the case—because Eff Huffington seems to think it's open season on anything in a clerical collar."

"I'm afraid Mr. Huffington had that notion long before he murdered Father Romero."

"Let me update you. Since you dropped that murder charge and let Eff go, he's blinded one Episcopal priest and just this week he raped another."

Silence pulsed across the line.

"This is a joke," she said.

"Wish it were."

"We'd better meet. There's a restaurant bar on Franklin called the Donegal. Think you can find it?"

*   *   *

"It looked open and shut: vicious juvenile victimizes kindly priest, and kills him. I was certain the state was going to get a conviction. But two days into pretrial, Eff changed his testimony."

Assistant District Attorney Deborah Fairchild had pale blue-green eyes, pale blond hair, pale taut skin. She also had a habit of speaking a little too rapidly. "Have you heard any rumors about the so-called communion killer?"

"Not yet," Cardozo said.

"I'm not surprised—no one wants the story getting out."

She looked at the table across the aisle and then behind her. The Donegal was a bright art deco blare of etched mirrors and black-and-white wall and floor tile. A fifties jukebox lent a glowing dash of amber. Someone was playing mid-century rock 'n' roll. "Sh-boom, sh-boom" sounded loopy and optimistic, riding the even roar of all the voices around them.

"There's a rumor going around about a series of murders—dismembered bodies found in public places with communion wafers in their mouths." She was wearing a jacket of crushed linen and she kept pushing the sleeves up. "This is exactly the kind of case that the department wants to keep under wraps."

"Why?"

"The D.A.'s office has a gentleman's agreement with the Church. Whenever anything heinously criminal pops up in confession, the priest passes it on." She flicked him an arched glance. "That's how the D.A. built a case against John Gotti. Whenever a priest gets into trouble that could embarrass the Church, the D.A. hushes it up. And if it can't be hushed up, the D.A. still won't prosecute."

"How does this connect to Eff's case?"

She hesitated. "A patrolman heard screams in the Pennsylvania Railroad yard. They were coming from a Toyota van parked under an overpass. He shined his light in. Father Chuck was dying in the front seat and Eff was halfway out the passenger door. He had the murder weapon tucked in his belt—a straight-edged razor. *Murder weapon*'s the wrong word. Eff claimed self-defense."

"Naturally."

"He said Father Chuck had invited him into the van—heard his confession—gave him communion."

"In the van? What was this priest supposed to be doing, riding around with wafers and wine in the glove compartment?"

"Hear me out. According to Eff, Father Chuck then made sexual advances. Eff refused."

"Oh, sure. A kid like Eff would fight for his honor."

"Father Chuck threatened him, said he'd had sex with two dozen children and young people—and killed three of them, a girl and two boys. Eff went into what the defense called homosexual panic. He shoved a razor into Father Chuck's stomach and killed him. None of the forensics backed up Eff's story, but the D.A. instructed me to move for acquittal."

"What grounds?"

"That Eff acted believing his life and bodily integrity were endangered."

"Did you believe Eff's story?"

"The department believed portions of it and I'm a member of the department."

"That's a crock. Eff routinely accused priests of making passes. That was his M.O. You people bought it and let him get away with murder."

"Come off it, Lieutenant. You say you're a cop, but you sound like an outraged TV sleaze-show host."

"Just for the record." Cardozo flipped open his shield case. "I know why I'm drawing my salary, Ms. Fairchild—why are you drawing yours?"

"Look, Lieutenant. I'm willing to believe you're a decent person. I know I am. Which means you and I are on the same side. So please hold your fire. I've had a lousy week and I've got a rotten headache."

She cooled her coffee with a little more milk from the metal pitcher. Her hand trembled as she lifted the cup. "Let's say for the sake of argument there really *is* a communion killer and the D.A.'s been trying to keep it out of the press and off the talk shows. Let's say the D.A. heard Eff's change of testimony, which by the way was in chambers and off the record. The D.A. would have realized there was no way Eff could have that information unless Father Chuck actually *was* responsible for the killings. It boiled down to the perfect disposition of the case: the killer was identified and disposed of, and there was no need for the public ever to know. Which would be reason enough to give Eff a deal and shut him up."

"You're telling me this is what happened?"

"I'm only conjecturing."

"Do you personally have any knowledge of a communion killer case?"

"Like everyone else in the prosecutor's office, I've heard rumors. They're not especially credible." She glanced at her watch. "Coffee's on you. I have to run. I've got a date with the D.A. five minutes ago."

"Take my advice and be ten minutes late. This concerns your boss's ass."

She opened her mouth to say something, but the look on his face dropped her back into her seat.

For the next five minutes or so Cardozo told her about the basket killings and Martin Barth's three lost confessions. By the time he finished, the ashtray in front of Deborah Fairchild held a small array of half-smoked lipstick-stained filter tips.

"The system is losing records all the time," she said, "but this is a little *too* bizarre."

"Officially, the killings were investigated as unrelated crimes. But there was a unified investigation."

"How do you know?"

"You're going to laugh. Someone spilled coffee on the files."

She didn't laugh. Her eyes were a troubled green.

"I had the lab check it out. It was the same coffee, the same spill on all four files. Two weeks ago those files were stacked on the same desk in the same office."

"Christ." Her voice sagged.

"I know this poses a dilemma for you—and no one's asking you to be a whistle-blower."

They sat in silence. He could feel her apprehensiveness floating between them like the smoke.

"Then what are you asking me?"

"I want to nail Eff. I need to know what that unified investigation uncovered."

"It's not going to help you get Eff. He's not the communion killer. If he were, we'd never have made a deal. Believe me, *that* cynical we're not. The only way you're going to nail him now is if that priest he raped is willing to press charges."

Eff's eyes stared into Bonnie's. The razor flicked teasingly across her nose. The rancid fog of his body stench closed in on her. Strength drained out of her legs and she felt the stinging sensation of her sphincter threatening to loosen in fear.

"My suggestion is this," Tina Vanderbilt was saying. "Of course, I'll make a formal proposal to the vestry at our next meeting, but I thought it would be best to line up your support as early as possible. We need a flower code."

"A flower code?" Bonnie said. They had been sitting in her office for the last half hour, and she was having trouble concentrating on the discussion.

"Exactly. Flowers in the church should be only white, or the shade of the walls."

"Which at the moment are ivory." Whitney's fingers made wig-arranging motions.

Tina slapped his hand. "Do stop tugging at that wretched thing —you only make it look worse."

After an instant of silence, Whitney stood. Pulling himself stiffly upright, he walked quickly and quietly from the room.

"For God's sake," Tina said, but she was chiding a shut door.

"You do know he's dying," Bonnie said, "don't you?"

"Of course I know he's dying—who couldn't know it with that awful wig he's wearing?"

"And yet you treat him like that?"

"We all die—what's so special about it? Why should I treat him any differently from usual?"

Bonnie wondered if Tina had ever felt the tactile nearness of death. "I don't think you mean that."

"I do indeed mean it. All our lives we are governed by taste— and when we lose sight of that, we lose the one thing that distinguishes us from the animals."

Bonnie was amazed. "*Taste* is all that distinguishes us from animals?"

"God gave us taste and it's up to us to make the most of it."

The moment felt skewed and surreal. Bonnie couldn't shake the conviction that Eff was standing right behind her—that Tina saw him, but wouldn't dream of being so ill-mannered as to mention it.

"Which brings us," Tina was saying, "to the question of the flowers for funerals."

I'm not going to look behind me, Bonnie told herself. *He's not there. I don't need to look behind me.*

"Here's where I have a real bone to pick with the vestry. There's no earthly way that variegated flowers could ever be appro—" Tina broke off. "Bonnie, is something the matter?"

Bonnie switched filters on her attention, focused hard and tight on here and now, on Tina's mother-of-pearl–colored cloche turning slowly through the silvered light. "I'm all right."

"No, you're not."

She felt his presence hanging in the air behind her like a tapestry. But she refused to turn in her chair. She stared beyond Tina through the windows to a breeze licking a branch of the pear tree.

"Have you heard a word I'm saying?" Tina was grumpy now.

"Of course I have." Bonnie breathed in through her mouth. She was afraid if she breathed through her nose she would smell him. "Every word."

When Cardozo arrived at St. Andrew's rectory, Bonnie greeted him with a smile that was too quick, too bright. He handed her a manila envelope marked NEW YORK POLICE DEPARTMENT—OFFICIAL BUSINESS ONLY—PENALTY FOR PRIVATE USE.

"What's this?"

"The paperwork to charge Eff."

The smile dropped off her face.

"All I need is your signature."

They went to her study. Right away he noticed something missing from the bookshelf. "What happened to that antique piggy bank?"

"I gave it away." Her voice was flat, almost without affect.

"Too bad—I liked it."

"Then I'll have to get another one." She sat down in an armchair and stared at three sheets of boilerplate with particulars laboriously typed in by Vince Cardozo, typos laboriously corrected in ballpoint by same.

"I'm sorry to have to put you through this, but Eff has a very slick lawyer—Pierre Strauss. I need a major felony charge to get him off the streets." He offered his ballpoint. "You sign where your name's typed in at the end."

She stared at the pages and then at him. "I keep hoping it's a dream. I close my eyes and tell myself to wake up and when I open them again nothing's changed."

He was standing close enough to smell the sweet chamomile of her hair. "I'm told that often happens."

"Would you mind if I didn't sign just yet?" She looked away. "I need time. I can't . . . do anything important. Not for a few days."

"I'll leave these. Sign them and phone me."

"Thank you."

"Bonnie," he said. "It's okay. Believe me. It's okay."

"I'm sorry. You've been wonderful to me. And I need to be alone."

He tried not to show how much that hurt him. "Of course. I understand."

FIFTY-THREE

Cardozo sat on a scuffed leather chair in St. Veronica's rectory, listening to the new rector speak in his quiet, resigned voice.

"The prosecutor's office never told us why the state dropped the murder charges—except that new evidence had come to light." Father Gus Monahan shook his head. He was a small, burly man with sad, preoccupied eyes. "No one would say what this new evidence was. No one would answer questions. Too busy asking them, I guess."

"What were they asking about?" Cardozo said. "Did there seem to be any particular focus to the questions?"

"Mostly about Father Chuck's private life."

"Did Father Chuck have problems in his private life?"

"Without a doubt he had problems. Every priest does. One of Chuck's greatest problems was that he didn't have a private life. He was a workaholic. As his date books showed."

Cardozo felt the prickling of a doubt. There was a defended quality about Father Gus that suggested he might be protecting his predecessor's memory. "Would it be possible for me to see his date books?"

"The diocese had us turn Father Chuck's papers over to the district attorney. Those that he hadn't already destroyed himself."

"What papers did Father Chuck destroy?"

"His personal correspondence—his diary—his counseling records."

"Do you have any idea why he destroyed them?"

"The obvious one—sanctity of the confessional."

"He told you this?"

"He didn't have to. It went without saying."

"There was no other reason?"

"If there was, he never discussed it with me."

"Who did he counsel?"

"Anyone who asked. He had a special empathy with young people—runaways, teenagers who'd gotten mixed up with prostitution and drugs."

"Is there any record of who his counselees were?"

Father Gus thought for a moment. "All I can think of is his date books, but we never got any of them back."

"You were working here at the time?"

"I was Chuck's assistant. I look back on it as the happiest time of my professional life. Except for the end."

"Maybe you can recall the names of some of the counselees."

"I might have seen one or two passing through the rectory. But Father Chuck was a popular man. People were always dropping by."

"Do you know if he ever counseled the boy who murdered him?"

"Eff Huffington? He may have thought he was counseling Huffington."

For a long moment Father Gus didn't speak. A vibration was coming off him and Cardozo tried to catch it.

"Chuck took people at their word." Father Gus let out a long, rolling sigh. "He believed the best of them. He thought it was a contradiction in terms to say that a child could be evil."

"You didn't share that opinion."

"Huffington made a profession accusing priests, shaking them down. I always suspected he was setting Chuck up for some kind of scam."

"Did Father Chuck say anything to give you that idea?"

"Chuck spoke evil of no person. Not ever. Just as he refused to believe it. It was Huffington's reputation that worried me. The boy had a history, and here he was seeking out Father Chuck at all hours of the day and night—spending time with him, sometimes alone with him."

"And you know for a fact that Father Chuck kept records of their meetings?"

"He kept records of his meetings with everyone. Noted everything except what was discussed. He had to protect himself."

"Against what?"

"In the old days an unbalanced female parishioner might claim a priest molested her. Nowadays kids do it."

"Were there ever accusations of that nature against Father Chuck?"

"Maybe one or two parishioners tried to stir up trouble—but Chuck's records were beyond reproach."

"Yet he destroyed them."

"You know lawyers. They can make anything look questionable."

"Was Father Chuck under investigation?"

"We all are, potentially. My guess is, Chuck looked over the records and saw the sheer quantity of time he spent with Huffington. He didn't want to chance what a lawyer would make of it."

"What did you make of it?"

"That in some ways Chuck was a good-hearted fool. Well, what can you expect of a man who believes in unicorns?"

"I beg your pardon?"

Cardozo stared at Father Gus and Father Gus stared right back.

"Chuck kept a unicorn on his wall."

Cardozo closed his notebook. "Would you mind showing it to me?"

"I don't see how it could do any harm."

Father Gus led Cardozo into a dark hallway and up a narrow flight of stairs. He opened a door. A smell of disinfectant and old clothes came whooshing out of the dimness. Father Gus turned on the light.

A poster of a unicorn hung over the four-poster bed. The walls were crowded with posters advertising Father Chuck's amateur musical shows. A photograph of a samurai executioner was hanging over the fireplace. It was the same as the photo in Father Joe Montgomery's bedroom.

"Did Father Chuck see a lot of Father Joe Montgomery?"

Father Gus nodded. "They were great buddies. Worked together on musical shows. Worked together in the Barabbas Society."

Cardozo stepped around a rocker and crossed to the window. A small forest of houseplants was growing on the sill.

"Chuck loved plants," Father Gus said. "Those were his. He thought every living thing was holy."

Cardozo tried to hear what the silence of the room was telling him. The room of a priest whose best friends were plants and a unicorn. The scent of loneliness, of giving up was heavy in the air.

One of the panes had been broken and patched with plywood. "When was this broken?"

"Before Chuck died. Haven't gotten around to calling the glazier."

"How did it happen?"

"There was a break-in. Church paraphernalia was stolen."

Cardozo pushed the window up and leaned out. The room faced the street across a small leafy lot. A vine trellis built against the brick wall looked as though it would afford access if you were light enough and limber enough.

As he brought his head back inside, he noticed black powder flecking one of the sash bars. He recognized print powder.

"Have the police been here recently?"

"Three people from the district attorney's office were here a while back."

What did they think they would find here, Cardozo wondered, *and why were they still looking for it so long after the murder charge had been dropped?* "How long ago was that?"

"Couldn't have been more than two or three weeks. But you'd have to ask Mrs. Quigley—my housekeeper."

Cardozo turned. "Your housekeeper's name is Quigley?" The name of Father Joe's former housekeeper had been Quigley. It seemed an odd coincidence.

"Olga Quigley. Darling woman. I couldn't have a life without her."

"I'd like to talk with her."

Olga Quigley was relaxing in the kitchen with a mid-afternoon cup of tea.

"You kept house for Father Romero?" Cardozo asked.

"I did indeed." She spoke with a trace of a brogue. "I've been at this rectory twelve years."

"And you also kept house for Father Montgomery over at St. Andrew's?"

This time she hesitated, stirring nonsugar and nonmilk powder into a mug decorated with scenes of Cypress Gardens, Florida. "What if I did?"

"Seems odd—keeping house for two different priests."

"When I was younger and stronger, I kept house for three priests. I've had to cut back since my hip trouble."

"How'd you happen to work for Father Montgomery?"

"He told Father Romero he needed a housekeeper part-time. The work here kept me busy only three days a week, so Father Romero recommended me. I'm a good housekeeper." Her tone was aggrieved, as if she were defending herself against an accusation. "I understand what priests need. They're not like ordinary bachelors."

"Why did you stop working for Father Montgomery?"

Olga Quigley's wide, dark eyes stared at Cardozo out of a long, oval face. There were plenty of gray streaks in the black hair that she pushed away from her forehead. "When you're a servant, you're not supposed to notice. Or say anything. Certainly not to the cops."

"No one's going to know we spoke."

Father Gus had left them alone. Light from the window dappled the spotless porcelain sink, the copper pots hanging beside the old-fashioned hooded six-burner stove, the table with its neat cloth and bowl of fresh fruit.

"I'm not going to give testimony in court," she said.

"I'm not asking you to."

"I worked for Father Joe ten years. I did good work for him. He was happy with me. Never an argument. Never a problem. Then that woman came."

"Bonnie Ruskay?"

Olga Quigley nodded. It was clear she was not in the habit of allowing the name to pass her lips.

"The world is falling apart. Law-abiding citizens are afraid to walk down the street. Senior citizens are getting raped. A Greek bishop was shot last week in a holdup. Children are murdered every day in this city. And now we have to put up with woman priests. *Divorced* women priests."

"Aside from being a woman priest and divorced, was there any particular reason you disliked her?"

"I didn't dislike her—I distrusted her. And I had grounds."

"I'd like to hear them."

"She changed Father Joe."

Olga Quigley's motivation was beginning to be about as inscrutable as a billboard: she was a lonesome, sad, no longer young woman who had invested ten years in dusting off two priests' lives. And then another woman had breezed into the picture and usurped half her world. Possibly the better half.

Cardozo realized he would have to question Olga Quigley gently, leave room for face-saving, for evasion, even for lying if she felt she had to lie.

"Tell me how she changed Father Montgomery."

"She involved him in things no priest should be involved in." Olga Quigley's eyes began flicking restlessly around the kitchen, alighting everywhere but on Cardozo. "All day long there were prostitutes in and out of that rectory—and kids on dope—and things going on. It makes me feel dirty just to remember them."

Her hands twisted in her lap and the skin tightened across the bridge of her nose.

"One morning after a dance, I was cleaning the young people's game room. I found condoms in the punch bowl, and packets of

I-don't-know-what—some kind of jelly to kill the sperm. She was encouraging children to use these things. And there were videos."

Cardozo said nothing to interrupt the flow. Olga Quigley slowly turned eyes to him that were grave and melancholy.

"I wondered what kind of videos she was showing the children, so I put one on the VCR. It was so horrible I quit my job. No way could I work there anymore after I saw that."

Cardozo wondered if Olga Quigley was overreacting to a safe-sex video. "Can we talk a little about this tape? What was it—pornography?"

"Worse."

She was having trouble with this, and he didn't push. A moment went by.

"Children tied up," she said. "Gagged, injected, burned."

"Burned how?"

"I've been trying to forget."

"Try to remember. How were they burned?"

"Candles."

Cardozo was suddenly aware of another sound in the kitchen besides the hum of the refrigerator. It was rain snapping softly against the window.

"Was Father Chuck involved in any youth activities?"

"None like that."

"Of course not. But did he ever work with Father Joe or Reverend Bonnie?"

"He had his own youth activities—no time for the likes of theirs."

"Did he keep records?"

"Of what—softball games? Saturday night dances? Musical shows? He was too busy doing things for people to write it down."

"And he counseled young people."

"Old people, young people—anyone who asked. He always had a half hour and an open heart for anyone in need."

"What kind of social life did he have?"

"He had no time for that sort of foolishness. Neither had Father Joe till that woman moved in."

"But Father Chuck was friends with Father Joe?"

"They played golf together."

"Nothing else?"

"Not that I ever saw."

"And was he friends with Reverend Bonnie?"

"She was always trying to buy his friendship—but he saw through her."

"Buy his friendship how?"

"Giving him presents. Every Christmas there was a bottle of imported 150-proof rum. You couldn't put the stuff in your system; you'd explode. He never touched it. Poured it down the sink. Once she gave him a golf cap for his birthday. A silly thing. He never wore it."

"A tweed cap with a snap brim?"

She looked at him with surprised eyes.

"He never wore it—or you never saw him wear it?"

"I know the clothes he liked and the clothes he didn't."

"I'm sure you do—and a great deal more." Cardozo closed his notebook and slid it into his pocket. "I'm sure you made Father Chuck very comfortable."

He opened his wallet and laid a business card on the tablecloth.

"If you remember anything unusual Father Chuck ever said about his counselees or the young people he worked with—or if you come across anything he left in writing—would you call me at this number?"

After the police lieutenant had gone, an anxious electricity seemed to hover over the kitchen table. Mrs. Quigley saw that he had not touched his tea. She emptied the cup down the sink. She took the card he had left and went to her bedroom.

She opened the bottom drawer of the bureau, moved aside stockings and wool socks, and carefully lifted out a manila folder. She sat in the easy chair and spread the folder on her lap.

For a long reflective moment she gazed at the scraps of half-burned paper. On one of them the letters ALLY MAFRE had been printed in Father Chuck's thick block capitals, and beneath them, in the same hand, an area code and a phone number.

Mrs. Quigley added the business card to the collection. She closed the file, picked up the remote, and aimed it at the TV.

FIFTY-FOUR

Cardozo handed Greg Monteleone a cup of coffee fresh from the squad room coffeemaker. It was 4:05 P.M.

"Greg, when you were working vice, did you run into much s/m?"

"If you mean personally," Greg answered through a mouthful of doughnut, "I'm taking the fifth."

"Could you step into my office for a minute? I'd like you to take a look at something."

Greg sauntered into the cubicle. Today he was wearing a cotton polo shirt the color of lime jelly beans. A gold chain twinkled in a V of store-bought tan.

Cardozo handed him four autopsy photos—one each of Gilmartin, Vegas, Wills, and Lomax.

Greg stared at the photos. "You realize you just ruined my coffee break." He held them under the desk light and then he went to the window and looked at them in sunlight.

"Do you see the marks where wax has preserved the skin?"

Greg slowly shook his head from side to side. "I see."

"Do you think that stuff is s/m?"

"It sure looks s/m to me. Explain it to me, Vince. The country's falling apart and people have still got time for homicidal bullshit."

"Don't ask me to explain people. What scene do you think those kids were into?"

"Earning enough money for their next pipe of crack."

"Think it could have been the same practitioner all four times?"

"I'm not a coroner, Vince. And my s/m days are pretty well behind me. But I know an s/m madam who might be able to help."

*　　*　　*

Sybil Stoller placed the five Polaroids side by side on the mahogany-and-rosewood inlaid coffee table. Her heavily made-up brown eyes took a moment to gaze at each of them. "These look like street kids to me—underage and stoned on downs. No, I don't recognize any of them."

Cardozo handed her three autopsy photos of Pablo Cespedes, taken just before the medical examiner had cut into him. "Can you tell me anything about the markings on this young man?"

A deep-crimson fingernail pointed without hesitation to the faint rows of parallel welts on Pablo's back. "Those are made by a castigator."

They were sitting on metal and leather in the high-ceilinged living room of Sybil's Sutton Place South apartment. The air smelled of fresh-cut hothouse lilac. Signed Rauschenberg lithos dotted the walls. A hidden sound system piped unobtrusive Mozart.

Cardozo played dumb. "What's a castigator?"

"It's a self-flagellation device monks used in the Middle Ages—updated for modern times."

"Are they common?"

"I haven't seen them mass-produced in sex shops, but they're fairly common custom items."

"Do you have any?"

She gave him a slow glance over high, chiseled cheekbones. She viewed talking to cops, he sensed, as part of the rent she paid for her space on earth.

"I don't use castigators and I don't allow my clients to use them. They cut the skin. No scarring, no scaring—that's the rule around here."

Cardozo pointed to abrasions on Pablo's chest and under his armpits. "What causes these—the castigator again?"

"No. Those are a signature."

"You're going to have to educate me. I don't know what a signature is."

"What do you know about Kentucky fried?"

"It's bad for your arteries."

"That's funny, Lieutenant." Her eyes said, *Your meter may not be ticking, but mine is, so may we forgo the comedy please and get the hell on with this.* "But we're talking s/m, not diet. Kentucky fried is your basic chicken in a basket. You put a kid in a restraining basket and do light to medium s/m. The usual rules apply—no cutting, no burning."

She explained that once a wicker basket was outfitted with restraints, it had a signature—it left a recognizable pattern of pressure marks and abrasions on the skin.

"Actually, there's more than a signature here. He's been burned." She put on a pair of severely styled gold-framed reading glasses and studied the photo of Pablo's chest. "With candle wax."

"You've got sharp eyes."

"Thank my optometrist for that. Okay. Here's what I think. There's a thing that's been going on for about four years—it's called Colonel Sanders. It's a variation on Kentucky fried. In traditional s/m the *m* is willing, but in Colonel Sanders the *s* tries to scare the shit out of the kid. Which involves crossing the borderline—you get into burning and cutting. The whole game is the kid's terror—so there's a lot of demand for kids who have never done it before. I personally won't handle it. First of all, I don't handle kids. Secondly, I don't get into terror and mind-fucks."

"But you think, because of the burns, this is Colonel Sanders."

"Not exactly." She gave him a long look and drew in a deep breath. "There's a version of Colonel Sanders—it's called Omaha, don't ask me why. I think that's what you've got here."

"Educate me about Omaha."

"The *m* dupes the *s*. The kids pretend to be fresh, but in fact they know the score. To keep from freaking, they're completely downed out."

"On what?"

"Whatever they can get hold of. Antipanic medication's the best, but it isn't easy to get hold of."

"You seem to know the scene."

Beneath her hi-tech halo of dark auburn hair, her face was as untroubled and unlined as cheesecake. "I don't know *that* scene, Lieutenant, but I do know the street. There are five dozen kids cruising Fifty-eighth every night, two blocks from here. For two hundred bucks, you can do anything to them you want. They're lucky to have the life span of a mayfly." Her finger tapped the Polaroid Pablo. "This kid is blitzed—you could hit him with a falling safe and his reaction would be, 'Oh, wow.' " She tapped the autopsy photo of the chest and face. "These marks and the burns—my instinct says it's Omaha."

"Are kids ever killed playing Omaha?"

"Not that I've heard of. No *s* could go that far and still be accepted in the s/m community."

"What about accidentally killed?"

"That's the risk you take in s/m, but it's rare."

"Who handles Omaha?"

"There you've got a problem: it's not even semilegit. Any form of chicken is child prostitution—and most of it's run by pimps who are kids themselves, so they can't be prosecuted. As I said, I steer clear." Sybil angled her wrist. A platinum, wafer-thin Pathek-Philippe glowed against the deep tan of her forearm. She made a show of noting the time. A hint to her visitor. "I wish I could be more help." She rose from the brass-studded leather love seat.

Cardozo collected his photos and stood. "Perhaps you could be. Have you ever run into a man by the name of Joe Montgomery?"

"Father Joe Montgomery?" She gave him a good-natured who's-fooling-who look. "Come on, Lieutenant, do I look like the kind of nice Jewish girl who runs off to confession every Wednesday?"

"Maybe he comes to you."

She walked Cardozo into a hallway hung with Parisian gallery posters advertising exhibits of Miró, Chagall, Picasso.

"First of all, I'm a physiotherapist licensed by the State of New York and I regard my clients' records as medically privileged. Secondly, any clergyman using our services would be smart enough to use a false name. Thirdly—yes, I do have priests and ministers and rabbis as clients; no, I won't tell you who they are; and no, Father Joe Montgomery is not one of them—though I've met him socially and frankly he needs his ashes hauled—badly."

She eyed Cardozo appraisingly.

"And you look a little needy yourself. Please feel free to drop by if you're interested in any specialties of the house."

"Thanks, it's not my scene."

"Maybe you don't know yourself. A lot of cops have trouble coming out as s/m-ers."

"If I ever get the urge, I'll let you know."

They reached the door.

"By the way, how's Greg?"

"He's great."

"Greg and I are old friends. We go back a long way."

"He told me."

Sybil smiled. "Say hi for me."

"Did Father Joe ever try to convert you?" Cardozo said.

"Sure," Jonquil said, "to rum punch."

"Did Father Chuck?"

"Who said Father Chuck was even a customer?"

"You haven't said he wasn't."

"I don't discuss Father Chuck." Jonquil was painting her toenails, one bare brown foot up on the bed, concentrating on each toe like a medieval monk illuminating a manuscript. "It's unlucky to speak ill of the dead."

They were sitting in Jonquil's tiny room at the George Washington Hotel on Lexington and Thirtieth. The hotel was a flophouse for whores, pimps, junkies, muggers, and small-time criminals who had made the streets just mean enough that they didn't care to sleep in them anymore; but Jonquil's room was a little girl's dream, a space of ruffles and dolls and with a silk square dangled over the lampshade. It exuded an atmosphere of sweetness and scrubbing and things exactly in their place.

"Did Father Joe or Father Chuck ever ask you to give up hooking, or not to use condoms?"

Jonquil threw back her head and let out a throaty laugh. The laugh said, *I am Jonquil the Magnificent, completely at ease with who I am and what I am.* "As I've told you three times, we're not discussing Father Chuck. So are we talking about Father Joe sober or Father Joe after he's had a few? Because they're two different people. Father Joe sober gives me condoms by the dozens—asks me to hand them out to the other girls."

"And Father Joe drunk?"

"I don't believe in violating client-hooker confidentiality."

"The other hookers talked about a priest who drove around in a van and told them not to hook, not to use condoms."

"Right. Drives a van with tear-drop windows, and *God Loves You* painted on the side. He likes to be called Damien—he's a nut."

There was no air conditioner. The room was warm, borderline uncomfortable, but an electric fan on the bureau sent ripples of jasmine through the damp air.

"You've met Damien?"

"Honey, I've met everyone."

"Is Damien his real name?"

Her contact-lens-blue gaze glided silkily toward him. "No one uses a real name down in the Market."

"How often is this Damien person down in the meat market?"

"No more often than Father Joe. There's no pattern to it." She stared at her toenails, sucked her breath in slowly, then leaned all the way forward and blew on them. "One week he's there two, three times—then four months go by and you don't see him."

"How recently have you seen him?"

She screwed the top back on the nail polish bottle and stood. "Not lately."

"Has Father Joe ever tried to involve you in s/m sex?"

"Some priests like it, some don't."

"Does Damien like it?"

"Damien's a child. If it doesn't kill him, he likes it."

"And if it kills someone else?"

"He might still like it. Want me to ask him?"

"You're playing games with me, aren't you?"

"A few."

"I need to know what Damien's real name is."

Jonquil adjusted her curly blond wig. Light blinked from an oversize emerald set into what looked like a high school class ring. She looked in the mirror, and then she looked at him. "How are you doing on that effort to get my parole shortened?"

Cardozo forced back his shoulders, stretching wide in the straight-backed chair, and got to his feet. "It's in the works."

Her eyes were suddenly crafty as a purebred cat's. "You just make sure it stays in the works, honey, and you'll be hearing from me."

"I hope that will be soon."

"As soon as you care to make it."

Jonquil closed the door behind the police lieutenant and quickly locked it. The smile dropped off her face.

"It's in the works," she muttered. "Bull*shit*!"

A siren screamed down Lexington Avenue. She slammed the window. Below, in the alley, gunfire rattled.

I am not interested, Jonquil said. *I am not even going to look.*

She yanked down the window shade and switched on the bureau light. She studied herself in the mirror.

She frowned. The mirror frowned back.

She liked mirrors.

She knew what to expect from them, whereas windows could shock—especially the windows of the George Washington Hotel.

She angled the silk lampshade, tipping a bit more glow onto her face. She smiled at her reflection, showing teeth.

She winced. The recession of those gums was as bad as anything the economy had gone through in the last ten years.

Time's a-wasting, Jonq, she reminded herself. *You are fast approaching the less-than-lovely age when no one in this world is going to do you any favors—you got one thing going for you, girl, and it's not your pretty face or your robo-tits—or your dick . . .*

In the eighties she had seen a future for herself in New York. She'd thought if she sacrificed for the right number of years, saved the right amount of money, she'd have it made. But the city had changed. The future was decaying. The cannibals had taken over, and they were breeding more cannibals. Now, if she had a chance to get out, she knew she'd have to grab it.

She reached underneath the panties in the middle bureau drawer. She took out her account book. She sat on the edge of the bed and totaled up the money she had saved for the second stage of the operation. She calculated thirty-three hundred more would pay for the plane ticket and the hospital in Tangier—and then she could marry that New Jersey construction company owner who thought she was a woman. . . .

As she turned the pages of the book, she was aware of loud, pulsing rap music pushing down from the room upstairs. She grimaced.

Girl, she told herself, *there is only one way you are going to get your ass out of this roach motel alive.*

She fluffed her wig, recentered it, tied a turquoise bandanna across her forehead. With a glide, a stride, a saunter, she stepped into the hallway and took the stairway down to the lobby.

She moved like a countess walking in her garden, like a woman entitled to anything in the world. She asked the desk clerk for change for the telephone. She went to the pay phone and punched in seven magic digits.

Three rings.

A man's voice, recorded. "I welcome your call, but I am not available at present to come to the phone. At the signal, please leave your name, your number, and any brief message. I shall get back to you as soon as possible."

"Hi, Father Damien?"

A babble of cracked-up voices floated over from the other side of the lobby. She pressed a finger over one ear.

"It's your sinful little girl Jonquil—how ya doin'? Well, Father, I just been entertaining a big, hunky cop. He's *very* interested in learning about s/m and I need to confess something *awful*."

FIFTY-FIVE

"I seemed to remember," Dan Hippolito said, "that when I did the postmortems on Vegas and Ms. Basket Case, there was a film—a kind of residue of a matzolike substance in their mouths.

But no such thing shows up in the autopsy reports in our computer."

The blunt end of his ballpoint tapped two of the three reports. Cardozo, sitting with his hand against his cheek, leaned a little forward to get a clearer look the documents on Dan's desk. Fluorescent bulbs cast a jittery, nervous light.

"I do over four hundred postmortems a year," Dan went on. "It's been fourteen months since my last vacation—I figured maybe I was inventing memories. So I went back and reviewed my original notes." He turned tattered sheets in an old spiral-bound notebook. "And there it was: residue of matzolike substance."

He tapped his finger halfway down a page, turning the notebook around so Cardozo could see the notation.

"So I contacted Howie Sileson, who did the postmortem on Wills. Exactly the same story." Dan sounded excited now, in a cautious way. His ballpoint tapped the third report. "According to the autopsy in the computer, there was nothing in Wills's mouth but some sadly decayed teeth—but Sileson's work notes showed a foreign substance, possibly matzo."

In the corridor outside Dan's office, voices passed. A moment later gurney wheels squealed.

"The matzo disappeared from three autopsy reports." Cardozo stared at the reports and the reports seemed to stare back. "Seems a little coincidental."

"I don't think it's a coincidence. I don't even think it's an accident. Someone deleted that information from the files."

"How would they get access?"

"The how is easy. If you're smart enough to push the power switch, nothing on that computer is secure. What baffles me is the why. Why would anyone *want* to go through old reports and remove every mention of matzo? If the kids had died of *tainted* matzo," Dan said, "I could see the manufacturer might not want his product named. But as nearly as I can piece together from these reports, Gilmartin and Vegas and Wills were knocked out with drugs and then they were sawed open and bled to death. Matzo had nothing to do with it."

"Maybe not in the way you're thinking. . . ." Cardozo's eyes snapped up. "I remember you telling me you thought these matzo residues could have been communion wafers."

Dan sighed. "Given the state of these corpses and the amount and condition of the residue, that would be tough to prove or disprove. Matzo and communion wafer are both yeastless bread. They break down the same chemically. The only difference is, some matzo is salted."

"But not the matzo residue in these kids' mouths."

"No, not that Sileson or I found."

"So it could have been communion wafer."

"Vince, how many times do you want to go around this circle? All I'm going to answer is, it's possible."

"Was there wine in their stomachs?"

"The bodies were too decomposed to analyze the stomach contents." Dan ran his forefinger along the edge of the Vegas printout. "You're wondering if they had communion before they were killed."

"Yes, I am."

"That's a sickening notion. How'd you come up with that one?"

Cardozo didn't answer and Dan didn't seem to expect him to.

"Communion works the other way around. Wafer first, then wine. There wouldn't be wine in the stomach if there was still a wafer in the mouth."

"Okay." Cardozo reflected a moment. "Didn't some churches used to have communion with just the wafer?"

Dan nodded. "The Catholics did. Communion in one kind. The priest got to have bread and wine, while the poor slobs in the congregation had to make do with plain unleavened salt-free bread."

"So the residue still could fit the communion theory."

"You really like that theory, don't you? I'll tell you why I don't. A communion wafer's a damned small quantity of food. Not enough to chew. Not enough to mix with your saliva. You swallow it clean. It's highly unlikely there'd be residue, let alone this quantity of residue."

Cardozo sat wondering. Suddenly it came to him. "Unless the killer was giving communion to a dead person."

"You win, I surrender." Dan raised both palms in the air as though they could fend off bullets. "Give communion in one kind to a dead person and you'd have residue. But you'd also have a pretty demented priest."

Cardozo stepped from the street into the Fish and the Lamb. As the door shut behind him, the roar of the world sheared off and the smell of old bindings and herbs rushed up like a half-forgotten memory.

"And how did you make out in your search for Reverend Bonnie Ruskay's works?" It was the same prematurely balding, bespectacled man who had waited on Cardozo before, but the we're-old-friends smile was brand-new.

"I found one. *The Son of God Was Also a Daughter.*"

"That's probably her best. Once you get past her questioning of tradition, she's a wonderfully original thinker."

"She's also a friend we have in common." Cardozo took out his shield case.

"She told me. I'm Ben Ruskay, her brother."

"She told me," Cardozo said.

Ben offered a hand. "How may I help you today?"

"I need some information. Where do Catholic churches get communion wafers?"

"Most in the East order them wholesale from a Carmelite convent in Wisconsin. That's where we get ours."

"And the Episcopal churches?"

"They could use the same source—though there's an order of Episcopalian sisters that also makes them."

"If you're not a priest, where would you buy them?"

"Communion wafers?" There was a look of open startlement on Ben's face. "If you're not a priest, why would you want them?"

"Just assuming you did."

"I suppose you'd have to go to a retail shop like us—we stock them in case a local church runs short."

"Have you ever sold communion wafers to a nonpriest?"

"That we knew wasn't a priest?" Ben's forefinger stroked his receding hairline. "The assumption is, anyone buying wafers is a priest or a nun. In fact, most people buying from us are old regulars. On the other hand, we're not a gun shop. We don't require an ID."

"Then you'd sell to anyone wearing a clerical collar."

"And to any nun or any layperson claiming to be buying on behalf of a church."

"Have any new customers bought wafers in the last three years?"

For an instant Ben's dark eyes were two nests of frown lines. "I'm not always in the shop. I wouldn't necessarily know a new customer. But I could look it up."

"If it's not too much trouble."

"Not at all." Ben stepped toward his desk in the rear of the shop. "And perhaps you need the names of other shops in the metropolitan area that sell communion wafers?"

"Thanks. That would be a help."

"I'd like to keep the originals of those runaway photographs," Lou Stein said. "Did you notice they have scratches on them?"

"I noticed they were pretty beat-up. What kind of scratches?"

"Patterned scratches. Could be handwriting. I'd like to play around with them."

"Play with them, Lou. Have a ball."

"The Pablo Cespedes photo too."

"He's all yours."

"By the way, Eff's a secretor. We recovered blood cells from the Ruskay semen. Type A-positive."

Cardozo felt the muscles of his stomach knot.

"The good news for Bonnie Ruskay is, the blood tests HIV-negative."

Cardozo wanted to believe it, but he had to wonder. "How can a hustling lowlife like Eff be antibody negative?"

"Freaky things happen with HIV. Maybe he's been lucky. Maybe he's been careful."

"He wasn't careful with her."

"Just in case he's raped anyone else, I've sent samples up to Lifeways for DNA matching."

"How long will that take?"

"I told them to rush it. A day or two."

"Thanks, Lou." Cardozo hung up the phone. He slowly became aware of an almost palpable prickling of the skin on the back of his neck. He turned in his chair.

Ellie stood in the doorway. "Your line was busy." She was watching him like an animal tuning in with its sixth sense. "You had a call."

"Oh?"

"Not her, Vince. Another woman. Deborah Fairchild at the D.A.'s office. Would you call her."

Cardozo tapped Fairchild's extension into the phone.

"You're right." There was a revved-up note in Fairchild's voice. Not enough sleep and too much coffee. Or maybe she had a source of legal prescription speed. "A special D.A.'s task force was working on the Vegas, Wills, and Ms. Basket Case homicides. But the files are long gone—deleted."

"Then what do you have?"

"City and state accounting rules require financial records to be kept for seven years. I found the one thing they couldn't delete— the expense vouchers."

FIFTY-SIX

Moon Song Café was a restored fifties diner north of Canal, decorated with posters of Cary Grant and Barbara Stanwyck and other great faces of the black-and-white screen. A bouncy hostess escorted Cardozo to a back table where Deborah Fairchild sat nursing an iced cappuccino. Cardozo ordered the same and sat.

Deborah Fairchild pushed a two-inch-thick wad of Xeroxes across the Formica-topped table. Beneath carefully styled blond hair, her face was drawn and grim. "They called it Task Force Babar."

"Like the elephant in the children's books?"

"God knows how they pick the nicknames. They probably pay someone's brother-in-law's public relations firm a quarter million."

Cardozo glanced at the expense vouchers. $32.50 for a cab

ride; $42 for a camera; $98.60 for lunch with "lawyer"; $57.60 for flowers; $104.72 for miscellaneous. And those were only the first five. Cardozo smelled scam like a streak of fat running through pork.

"Funds were transferred to the task force from the D.A.'s discretionary budget." Deborah showed him a Xerox of a bank transfer order. The white numbers were just barely legible against the streaked black background. "They rented an office just after the second body was discovered. They shut it down after Eff changed his testimony. Four thousand thirty-six dollars rent per month. They were putting aside an additional nine percent of that for commercial rent tax. Of course, they didn't owe rent tax. It went straight into someone's pocket. If an outside accountant went over these figures, he'd find indictable fraud."

A waitress brought Cardozo's iced cappuccino. Deborah Fairchild waited till she was gone before continuing.

"Babar exercised fiscal restraint in only one area that I can see. Task force members already on salary with the D.A.'s office drew their regular pay. They weren't accounted to Babar. They could have double-dipped, and with an arrangement this crooked I'd have expected them to. I've been wondering about it, and I think they needed deniability. They wanted as few names as possible on Task Force Babar records."

She laid another bank transfer on the pile.

"But here's the giveaway. One of the top forensic psychiatric consultants in the city was being paid from Babar funds—Vergil Muller."

A tremor of bemused recognition went through Cardozo. "I know him."

"Then you know he's a specialist in pedophiliac priests."

Cardozo's eyes met Deborah Fairchild's. Her courtroom training showed. She was like a mirror, giving him exactly what he gave her, taking nothing, adding nothing.

"I hadn't realized that," Cardozo said.

"He was hired after Eff changed his testimony."

Cardozo considered the implications of the time frame. "The D.A. set up Babar after the discovery of the second communion killing. Babar got first look at forensics and the M.E.'s reports. They altered them just enough to hide the similarities, then passed them on. So the police never put together a single, coordinated investigation. Babar ran their own. What they discovered, we don't know. But when Eff accused Father Chuck, Babar brought Muller in to evaluate Eff's information. Muller felt it was authentic. So Babar put together a deal."

Weariness seemed to silt down on Deborah Fairchild. "Frankly, I don't see any other explanation for the timing." She laid down Xeroxes of bank drafts. "This check for a quarter million dollars was issued to Pierre Strauss for 'legal fees.' " Her voice put quotes around the words. "These three checks totaling $475,000 were issued to 'confidential informant' on May twelfth, May fifteenth, and May nineteenth."

"And if those were the dates that Barth made his three confessions, we know who the informant is."

"I tried to check that out." Deborah Fairchild lit another cigarette. "Since the cases were closed unsolved, there are no confessions or depositions on record."

"A New York State first." Cardozo lined up the three confidential informant checks side by side. They had been drawn payable to account 21-47-531-2468 and there was no endorsement—only a rubber bank stamp. "What have you found out about this account?"

"Twenty-one is Chase Manhattan; forty-seven is money market. The rest is a personal account that was opened just long enough to cash those checks."

"Who opened it?"

"A woman by the name of Eloise Forbes. I can't locate the name anywhere. It could be an alias."

Cardozo's eyes followed the paper trail of canceled checks. "A thirty-foot billboard couldn't spell it out more clearly: The D.A. doesn't want to indict a priest for murder, not even a dead one. He goes to Strauss with a deal: Persuade one of your convicted clients to confess to murdering three runaways. I won't prosecute; I'll lose the confessions; I'll lighten whatever sentence he's serving."

Deborah Fairchild's hand shook as she flipped hair out of her eyes. "The finagling on this is clever. You have to admire the way they exploited the built-in incompetencies of the criminal justice bureaucracy."

"But it's blown up in their faces with the Lomax killing. Father Chuck can't be the killer."

Deborah nodded. "They've got a problem."

"And if Eff's information came from the real killer, then he's still out there and Eff knows who he is."

"Under the circumstances, that knowledge is worth bucks."

"And Eff's life isn't worth a nickel."

"Was it ever?"

"I thought you people believed in redeeming young sinners."

"That was fine when the city had money. This is the nineties, Lieutenant."

Cardozo was thoughtful. "I wonder who's getting those bucks. I have a feeling it's not Eff."

There were antiques in Vergil Muller's office that Cardozo had not seen there a year and a half ago—inlaid tables and seventeenth-century maps—and the place had a new-car smell.

"Eff Huffington's trial for murder centered on one question." Vergil Muller was peddling his exercise bicycle. He was dressed in gray sweat clothes. "Was Father Romero a pedophile or not? The D.A. called me in to evaluate Eff's testimony and to look over the evidence."

"I'd have thought that would be a job for the defense," Cardozo said.

"Forewarned is forearmed. The D.A. had to know how solid the defense's case was. Even with a weak case, Strauss can be a formidable opponent. When he has a strong case—a prosecutor's best strategy might be to slit his own throat."

"But you didn't tell the D.A. to slit his throat."

"Oh, didn't I? I told him to fold the case."

"Why?"

"Off the record, there was evidence that Romero was a practicing pedophile. A presumptive case could be made that Eff killed him in self-defense."

"What kind of evidence?"

"Overwhelming. Father Romero's diaries and date books and personal letters were a treasure trove. I'd love to have quoted them in my own work, but the D.A. refused. I had to give them all back."

"You found admissions of wrongdoing in those diaries?"

"Not in your sense. But they were a stream of obsessive paraphiliac mentation—" Muller broke off. "I really shouldn't be discussing this with you."

"I appreciate your giving me this time." Cardozo flipped back through his notebook, dissatisfied. "While you were on the case, did you ever run into a woman by the name of Eloise Forbes?"

"Not in connection with the Huffington case. Eloise Forbes figured in the homicide that brought you and me together." Vergil Muller grinned as though he and Cardozo were in on the same joke. "The girl in the meat-packing basket. How time flies. Remember her?"

Cardozo looked up. "I do indeed."

Vergil Muller passed a hand across his forehead, sweeping sandy hair back over his bald spot. "Forbes was the maiden name of Martin Barth's wife. She gave me invaluable background on her husband."

"April before last," Cardozo said, "your husband confessed to murdering three runaway teenagers. The following May you received close to a half million dollars from the district attorney's task force investigating those murders."

Eloise Barth opened her mouth, but before she could make any denial, he handed her copies of the bank records of her money-market account.

The weight of the documents seemed to crush her. She sank back into the sofa. She looked them over slowly. Finally her eyes went to Cardozo, defeated. "It's not the way it seems."

"Nothing ever is."

"I didn't know what they were paying me for."

"I'm sorry, Mrs. Barth, but if you cashed those checks, you knew."

"Not everything. Not the details."

"If Pierre Strauss was representing your husband, he made sure you knew the details."

An impatient hand pushed dark hair away from her face. "What was the harm? Martin was serving a life sentence anyway, and the real killer—" She broke off.

The only sound was the deep, reassuring ticktock of the grandfather clock. They were sitting in her living room. The baby grand piano had come back, and the curtains looked new.

"The real killer?" Cardozo prodded.

Eloise Barth sighed. "He was dead."

"And who was he?"

"He was a black man. After years of injustice and humiliation, he gave into his rage and went on a rampage. It could have happened to anyone in his position."

"What was his name?"

"I never knew his name."

"Who gave you this information?"

"He'd been a client of Pierre Strauss's. He died in a police shoot-out."

Cardozo played with pieces in his mind, trying different ways of fitting them together. "When did Pierre Strauss take your husband's case?"

Eloise Barth hesitated. "He came into the case six months after Martin's conviction."

"And he offered a deal with the D.A.? Three confessions in exchange for . . . various considerations?"

She was silent. Finally she said, "I have two children to raise and no husband to help support me or them. I barely make thirty-five thousand as a paralegal; that hardly covers our maintenance and mortgage and the boys' school. Pierre was offering money."

"I'm not criticizing you," Cardozo said. "I'm just trying to get at some truth."

"I wouldn't have gone along with it, except . . . ." She rose and paced to the window. She stood staring down at Park Avenue. "It could have started a race riot if the truth had gotten out—a black man killing those white runaways. The blacks have been through enough in this country."

"How did Strauss explain the communion wafers?"

She threw him a startled glance. "I beg your pardon?"

"Communion wafers were found in the victims' mouths. Was this black man a priest?"

"He was an unemployed laborer."

"Pierre Strauss gave you a line. He wasn't asking your husband to cover for a black man. The man he was protecting was a white priest."

She stared at him, stunned. "That's impossible."

Cardozo had kept the original autopsy on Ms. Basket Case in his own files. Unlike the autopsy in the data base, it had not been doctored by omission. He rose and handed her a copy of it.

She sat down in an armchair. At first she didn't seem to understand what she was seeing. Then, as she silently read, her face became a grave mask. Cardozo sensed that her capacity for rationalization was about to snap.

"It wasn't a race riot you were helping avert, Mrs. Barth. It was a church scandal."

For a long moment Eloise Barth sat there with her eyes closed. She finally opened them. "I have something for you."

She left the room and returned with a large gray envelope. She handed it to Cardozo. "Those are the receipts for the things in Martin's knapsack."

Cardozo opened the envelope and took out two receipts, one for Bombay Girl incense and one for a Happy Hostess number three dinner candle. Each was unambiguously itemized and dated. He looked over at her, surprised. "You bought those things?"

She nodded. "Pierre told me to. He told me to keep the receipts, just in case. He says you never know."

"There's no receipt for the nipple ring."

"I didn't buy that. Pierre gave it to me."

"May I keep these?"

"I want you to keep them—and use them."

Cardozo rose. "Mrs. Barth, I'm sorry."

"Don't be. In the long run, truth is the best disinfectant."

FIFTY-SEVEN

Beyond the window of Bonnie Ruskay's office, an early summer shower was falling. Raindrops struck the air conditioner with light pinging sounds. Ribbons of wetness gleamed on the brick walls of the courtyard.

Sitting safe and dry in the soft light of the office, Cardozo took a gamble. For twenty minutes he told Bonnie Ruskay all he had been able to piece together about the murdered teenaged runaways.

As she listened, her forehead became lined and her eyes narrowed in disbelief. "That's impossible. I knew Father Chuck. He could never have done such a thing."

"How well did you know him?"

"We weren't close friends, but we adored one another. It was a case of instant sympathy. He traded musical sets and props with Father Joe and we celebrated Christmases together. He was a kind, sweet man—absolutely dedicated to giving joy to others."

"And you gave him a golf cap for Christmas."

"The same golf cap I gave a lot of people." She had a remembering smile. "I gave one to Father Joe. They were golf partners. Joe was heartbroken when Chuck died."

"Father Chuck was murdered."

"I know. A boy he'd tried to help turned on him."

"Eff Huffington killed Father Chuck."

She stared at him. The color bled from her face.

"The papers never gave his name," Cardozo said. "He was too young to be named, but not too young to name others." He explained Eff's accusations against Father Romero. He explained the D.A.'s cover-up. "Barth's confessions were supposed to be the end of the story. But there's been another killing since—Tod Lomax. The Lomax killing throws the other three into question again. The D.A. realizes he's made a mistake. He needs someone to take the blame for Lomax and if possible for all four. Obviously, it can't be Father Chuck, and it obviously can't be Barth."

There was something fiercely concentrated in the quality of Bonnie's attention. "And then a housebreaker is accidentally killed in St. Andrew's rectory, and the district attorney realizes he has just the man for the job—Father Joe. That's what you're telling me?"

"The D.A. doesn't discuss his strategies with me—but something is obviously going on."

"Does this mean you're changing your opinion of Joe?"

"Just because a person gets framed doesn't mean they're innocent. The rightly accused can get the same short shrift as the wrongly accused."

She looked at him as though she was trying very hard to get a reading on him. "So you think the D.A. is going at the right man the wrong way."

"I didn't say that."

"Then I need a hearing aid."

"I'm saying Father Joe had better be ready to defend himself."

"Thanks for the advice, but how?"

"If he was in on the original cover-up, now's the time for him to say so."

"Joe wasn't involved in any cover-up."

"He counseled Barth to confess."

"Joe sincerely believed Martin Barth was guilty."

"Barth confessed to three identical killings. How many of those did he admit to Father Joe?"

"I don't know."

"How can we find out?"

"We can't. Confession is privileged."

"Even if it's a lie?"

She didn't say anything.

"If Father Joe can produce records that show discussion of a cover-up, the D.A. won't risk going against him."

"No priest keeps records of confessions."

"This was counseling, not confession. Under state law he'd have to keep records."

A kind of wariness edged into her eyes, as if she knew exactly what he was going to ask next.

"Can you search Father Joe's papers?"

"Without his permission? Absolutely not."

"You can get his permission. You can at least ask him what Barth admitted."

"I have no right to ask that."

"Look, we're both on the same side."

"Are we? You think Father Joe could have killed those runaways."

"I've never said that."

"You don't need to—it's been clear in every question you asked from the very beginning. But I know Father Joe's innocent."

A silence passed.

"I have to ask you something," he said quietly.

"As long as it's not to betray someone else."

"Olga Quigley found a videotape here."

There was a change in Bonnie's expression. She looked puzzled and hurt, as if he'd criticized her unjustly. "Olga didn't find that tape—she broke into my desk and stole it."

"She says it showed—"

"I know what it showed."

"Why did you have that tape?"

"A child brought it to us. A child who performed in it."

Cardozo watched her, motionless in her armchair by the window. One of her earrings caught a wink of light.

"We were trying to get the city to pass a mayoral ordinance against child pornography—we needed proof." She raised her eyes. There was a melancholy distance to her gaze. "You're not thinking that Joe had anything to do with—" She broke off.

He felt a darkness between them, and a deep-down unknowability in her.

"I can prove Joe's innocent," she said suddenly. "I can even prove it to you. If Barth's confessions are false, and Eff Huffington knew enough to implicate Father Chuck . . . then Eff knows who killed those children. Eff can tell us."

"Unfortunately, Strauss and the D.A. have built a protective wall around Eff."

"I know how to break through that wall."

"I wish you'd tell me."

"Use me for bait."

"No way."

She shot him a defiant look. "Eff thinks I've cheated him out of what's rightfully his. He wants the reward money and he'll risk arrest to get it."

"I want Eff to get justice, too, but not like that."

"You're a fool not to play the cards you've been dealt."

He sat staring at her, wondering about her, not understanding a thing about her. "Then I'm a fool."

"They told me to knock and walk right in."

Cardozo looked up. It took him a moment to recognize the

dark-eyed man in his doorway as Ben Ruskay from the Fish and the Lamb.

"Hi, Ben." Cardozo offered the straight-backed chair. "Have a seat."

Ben sat. "I ran off the list of wafer charges over the last three years. Most of the charges are to churches. Three are to convents."

He took an envelope from the inside pocket of his gold-buttoned blue blazer. Cardozo had the impression that he had put on his best clothes to come to the precinct. Some people did.

He handed Cardozo the list. Cardozo studied it. Arrows had been inked in beside the names of eleven individuals.

"I've cross-checked the other purchasers against the national registry of Catholic priests. Only one name doesn't match up with the registry."

Cardozo saw two arrows beside one of the names. "J. C. Wheeler?"

Ben nodded. "The diocese has asked us not to sell Wheeler any more liturgical items."

"I've been to three other church suppliers in the area. Wheeler has made one-time wafer buys at all of them, and their computers have the same memo—*Don't sell.* What do you know about him?"

Ben took a moment to reflect. Voices and ringing phones floated in from the squad room.

"She's a zealot," he said. "And a Catholic-basher."

"Wheeler's a she?"

Ben shot a glance that was so world-weary it was almost comic. "She runs an anti-Catholic magazine. She prints some pretty irresponsible things."

"Such as?"

"She accuses clergy and church personnel of hypocrisy. Immoral behavior. If you talk to her, I'm sure she'll be glad to give you back issues."

"I intend to talk to her."

Ben's eyebrows went up, dark circumflex accents over his eyes. "One request. Please don't mention the shop or my name. She's capable of sending her minions to blow us up."

FIFTY-EIGHT

"**M**s. Wheeler—" Cardozo began.

She raised a finger. "Ah-ah. The term *Ms.* is sexist and classist. At *OutMag* we use first names. Mine is Jaycee. Yours is . . . ?"

"Vince."

"Okay, Vince, now that we've got that straight, how can I help you?"

Jaycee Wheeler was sitting cross-legged on an ancient sofa in a fifth-floor loft on West Twenty-second Street.

Cardozo had the rocking chair, and he was doing his best to keep it from rocking. "Are you an ordained priest of any Christian denomination?"

"Fuck it, no." Her big pale blue eyes, glowing over sculpted cheekbones, seemed to laugh at him. "I sure as hell am not."

"Did you buy five hundred communion wafers from the Calgary Shop?"

"That's right."

"Did you buy five hundred communion wafers from Hofbauer and Swayze?"

Her hand went up to push blond bangs back from a young, unlined forehead. A ring glinted on the fourth finger. It was made out of interlocked flip-tops from aluminum soda cans. "Right again."

"And five hundred from the Fish and the Lamb?"

"Yes, I did. And I've bought wafers from a dozen other church supply houses and I can give you the list if you want." She uncrossed long legs, stood, gave her blue jeans a shake, and went to a rolltop desk with two hundred paper-stuffed pigeonholes. She began searching through a sheaf of bills.

"Would you mind telling me why you've stocked up on communion wafers?"

"Believe me, we're not stocking up. We use them as fast as we can get our hands on them."

"How do you use them?"

She tipped an armload of paper into his lap. "Do you know anything about *OutMag*?"

He smiled. "Only that you're troublemakers."

"Right. We're also a gay-interest monthly magazine. We see ourselves as gadflies on the body politic. One of our projects is to shake up the Catholic hierarchy. We've found we get the biggest bang for our buck throwing wafers on the cathedral floor during Mass. By the way, contrary to what the diocese tells the press, the wafers are not consecrated."

Cardozo carefully transferred the lapful of paper to the bare wood floor. "Consecrated or not, why such resentment against the Church?"

"Oh, God, we have seminars on this and I have to give it to you in thirty seconds?"

"Sixty seconds."

"I resent the Church because it oppresses me. It oppresses you, too, though as a cop you're probably not aware of it."

"You look pretty unoppressed to me."

"Thank you. That's because there's never been any choice for me. I'm a dyke. In America, that makes me a gender-deficient Barbie doll. Which means I have to fight for the rights you take for granted."

"What rights?"

"Come on, Vince. Mobs can roam American cities at will, they can overturn cars and trash stores. They can torch and murder to their hearts' content. But my people can't even hold hands, let alone peacefully protest. I've been whipped on by the police—treated like a dog—snatched out of a picket line, laid on the street and truncheoned. When I go to the corner deli for milk, I never know whether or not some heterosexist is going to throw a brick at me. Or rape me."

She struck him as too sassy and far too savvy to buy in to such a limp, standard-bleat victim rap.

"Have you ever been raped?" he said.

Her face went tight around the eyes. "Have you?"

"No."

"Well, I have been. Three years ago. He raped me because I'm a lesbian and the cardinal says lesbians are unnatural and evil. Raping an unnatural woman doesn't count as rape because rape is what she deserves."

"The cardinal never said that."

"Not in so many words, but his Eminence is creating a climate of violence with that mouth of his. But why should he worry—he whips around the city in a bulletproof car with a police escort."

Her hands balled into fists. Beneath the loose-hanging denim work shirt, her body had a hardened compactness that suggested she worked out at women's self-defense classes.

"Do you call that Christianity, Vince? I call it democracy on hold."

"I didn't say a word."

"You don't need to. You've got a gun."

"It's less help than you'd think."

"It may not help, but it evens the score. Which is more than the laws of this land do."

"Was your rapist ever caught?"

"The cops were able to trace him—I ID'd him."

"Was he sentenced?"

"There was no trial. My lawyer worked out a deal: I agreed never to discuss the rape; the record was expunged. In exchange, my attacker made a large cash contribution to the magazine. Which I hope to hell is still ticking the bastard off."

"Your attacker is a rich man?"

"It may not have been his money. The Church may have helped him out. They have that hush-money fund for child-molesting priests."

"Is he a priest?"

"Am I a child? I've said too much."

"Who's your lawyer?"

"His name is Pierre Strauss."

Cardozo made a face.

"I like Pierre," she said. "He goes for that pound of flesh and he gets it. You know what he got the judge to do? Sentence my rapist to eight weeks in a reorientation program for juveniles."

"So you got revenge on your rapist by humiliating him. And

you want revenge on the Church because you think they sanctioned the rape."

"Not just the rape. Not just me. They contribute to a public
mind-set that no one who disagrees with them has rights. No right
to dignity. No right to safety. No right to life. Unless you're not
born yet." She dropped back onto the sofa. She sighed. "Or are
you one of those cops who thinks God is a Catholic and the
Church can do no wrong?"

"No comment."

"Because the Church does plenty of wrongs. Priests preach
against consenting gays, and then they molest altar boys. And the
Church covers it up. Or didn't you know?"

"No comment."

"Maybe you feel the Church is justified. In that case you probably feel the Church has a right to cover up the communion killings
too."

She gave him a quiet, steady look. She had lobbed her bomb-
shell and she was watching him now to see whether she'd scored a
hit.

He didn't speak, didn't react.

"You're not going to sit there and pretend you don't know
about the communion killings."

"I've heard rumors. Nothing credible."

"Believe me, there's more to it than rumor." She drew her legs
up beneath her. "I'm in touch with a small-time hustler. He works
the lower West Side docks—deals dope, pimps the runaways to
chicken hawks. He knows pretty much everything that's going
down. He's heard about a priest who's cruising the docks. The
priest claims to be a vigilante taking action against the Church's
enemies. He's confessing teenage male and female prostitutes and
giving them communion."

"Why is that vigilante action?"

"The runaways are disappearing."

On the other side of an unpainted composition-board partition,
a phone was ringing. A man's voice answered.

"What's the priest's name?" Cardozo said.

"He calls himself Damien."

The first association that sprang up in Cardozo's mind was
Jonquil's friend Damien, the anticondom, prochastity, prostitute-

proselytizing priest. The second association was the etching on Bonnie Ruskay's wall—Father Damien giving communion to the lepers. "Is that his real name?"

"My information's sketchy. My guess is, he's a closeted bisexual priest getting his rocks off and using a false name. He's also high up enough in the Church to get away with this shit."

A dark-haired young man came into the office with a lightly lumbering step. He handed Jaycee a set of cover proofs. He had a soft cast on his right forearm and hand.

"See if the printer can bleed the yellow." Jaycee handed the proofs back. "Vince, meet the other half of *OutMag*, Scott Rivera. Scott, meet Vince Cardozo. Vince is with the police."

"I heard. I was in the other room." Scott sat on the window ledge. He took out a patterned blue handkerchief and polished his rimless spectacles.

"Don't you have something better to do?" Jaycee said.

"I'm doing it."

"How did you hurt yourself?" Cardozo said.

Scott's dark eyes came around coolly. "I didn't hurt myself. Some guys from New Jersey did it for me."

"Scott got bashed," Jaycee said.

"Sorry to hear that."

Scott put his glasses back on. "So tell me, Vince, are you part of the Damien cover-up?"

"You're a real son of a bishop of Kerry," Jaycee said. "You know that? Damien is my story. I've done the legwork, I've done the spadework. Vince came to me, not you. If he has information, it's mine."

Scott looked again at Cardozo. "Do you have information, Vince?"

"Wish I did. Do you?"

"Jaycee does."

"You bastard."

"It's coming out in the next issue."

"Fuck you," Jaycee said.

Cardozo had the impression that these two were suffering a severe case of cabin fever. Either that or a dangerously high overdose of one another. He hoped the magazine was worth it.

"What's your information?" he said.

Jaycee snapped a pencil in two. "There isn't any. My contact hasn't been able to set up a meeting."

"With Damien?" Cardozo said.

She nodded.

"Watch out. Damien sounds dangerous."

"No one said he's a lamb," Jaycee said. "He's killing kids, after all."

"How do you know?"

"She doesn't know," Scott said. "Damien claims the sacraments save these teenagers and that's the reason they vanish from the streets."

"Don't give me that," Jaycee said. "He's killing them."

"All we need is the proof. Vince, you got any proof? Care to help us win our first Pulitzer?"

"If I were you two," Cardozo said, "I'd be very careful."

"*OutMag* doesn't scare," Jaycee said.

"In fact," Scott said, "if you'd like to catch *OutMag* do a profile in courage, come to St. Pat's this Sunday."

"Scott, you dumb shithead!"

"Take it easy," Scott said. "Vince isn't going to tell—are you, Vince?"

Cardozo shook his head. "Why should I? It's not my department." *Besides,* he thought, *the cops probably already know.*

FIFTY-NINE

Barry Ignatius Cardinal Fitzwilliam climbed the eight winding steps to the pulpit. Silence fell, like the hush before a curtain rises in the theater. The pews of the cathedral were a sea of expectant faces.

He unfolded the notes for his sermon and laid them on the lectern. They were a blur. He reached beneath his chasuble and alb. He took his bifocal glasses from the pocket of his cassock and fitted them to his nose. The sheet of neat, tiny handwriting leapt into focus.

Today, taking a text from II Corinthians as his jumping-off point, the cardinal preached on "our duty and our privilege, as Catholics, to avail ourselves of the supernatural and healing power of the sacraments."

He raised his eyes to his congregation. The distance prescription of his lenses was off. Faces and clothing lost their boundaries and softly overflowed into one another.

"It is our duty, also, to promote the public morality of our entire civil society on the basis of fundamental moral values. Above all, we must support the government in its efforts to promote the traditional family."

Somewhere in the rear vaulted space of the cathedral, there was a stir, a surge of sound. The pews seemed to tremble in glassy ripples.

The cardinal nudged his spectacles low enough to peek over the rims. A disturbance was sweeping the congregation. Heads whipped around.

"We must not be afraid to speak out against those who oppose traditional family values." The cardinal leaned nearer to the microphone, enunciating sharply. "We must support legislation curbing the activities of those who would defy God's ordained social order."

Murmurs and cries swelled. Brightly colored sails dotted the sea. The cardinal pushed his glasses still lower.

Protesters in the pews had silently raised placards. The messages flew at him:

STOP CHURCH HOMOPHOBIA.

DON'T JUST PREACH LOVE—PRACTICE IT.

CATHOLIC MEANS UNIVERSAL. OPEN THE CHURCH TO WOMEN AND MINORITIES OR CHANGE THE LABEL.

The lettering on one placard assaulted him like a fist in the eye:

CATHOLIC CHURCH—STOP HUSHING UP THE COMMUNION KILLINGS!

The protesters began tossing wafers into the air. Forty plainclothes cops rushed down the aisles to arrest them.

The cardinal covered the mike with his hand. He leaned to shout to an assistant: "That young woman with the communion killer placard . . . Tell the police I want to speak to her."

In the vesting room, a priest lifted the miter from the cardinal's head.

The cardinal shuddered. "Terrible scene out there. The worst yet."

"Yes, your Eminence." The priest helped the cardinal out of his chasuble. "You're very tense, your Eminence."

A knot had formed in the cardinal's shoulders and he couldn't shrug it loose. His hands trembled as he undid his cincture.

The priest lifted off the alb. "Very tense, your Eminence."

A knock sounded at the door. The priest's eyes asked the cardinal's permission.

The cardinal nodded. He practiced his face. He was about to need it.

The priest opened the door. Two plainclothes cops pushed a young woman into the room. Her hands were cuffed in front of her. The cardinal looked at her, and his stomach became a sick wad of pain. Her hair was cut spiky, like a boy's, and she wore jeans and work boots.

"Young lady," he said, "I couldn't help but notice your placard."

"I'm glad I accomplished something." She had an educated voice, but defiance crackled off her like electricity.

"Where did you get your information on the so-called communion killer?"

"As a reporter, I'm protected by the First Amendment. I'm not going to reveal my sources."

"You could be of great service to the people of this city and instead you're making a grave mistake."

"Making mistakes is a civil right in a democracy."

"But not a moral right."

"Your Eminence, I was raped by one of your followers."

"I have no followers."

"Then you haven't looked in your rearview mirror lately. He raped me because I'm a lesbian."

A shiver went to the roots of the cardinal's hair. The incredible thought came to him that this person was of the same sex as Our Blessed Savior's mother.

"He believed the experience would set me straight." Her lips pulled back in a rictus of hate. "He didn't use a rubber, because you say condoms are immoral. Which is how I was exposed to the AIDS virus. Which is why I'm HIV-positive. Thank you for sharing your morals with the people of this city, your Eminence."

"My child, I understand your bitterness, but I pray to God you won't let it harden your heart."

A scream came out of her. "Then don't send your minions out to maul my people!"

One of the plainclothesmen seized her by the collar of her sweatshirt. "Show a little respect there."

"Let her go." The cardinal sighed.

"She'll go all right," the plainclothesman said. "Straight to women's detention."

She whirled on him. Her face was a mask of unbelievable malice. "Aren't you afraid I'll enjoy myself there a little too much?"

The cardinal turned away in shock and sorrow.

From his office, he phoned the district attorney. "Bill, word has gotten out—there were placards about the communion killer this morning in church."

"Those are just rumors spread by that nutty *OutMag* outfit." Bill Kodahl's voice, as always, brimmed with a kind of watch-out-world-get-off-my-runway confidence. "Those people are bluffing; they don't know a thing."

"He says Martin Barth confessed to three killings. Not just the girl in Vanderbilt Garden. Two others—very much the same. Runaways packed in reinforced baskets."

Bonnie was sitting in a chair drawn close to the hospital bed. She brought her eyes around to Father Joe.

"He asked if you knew."

It took her a moment to realize that Joe wasn't going to answer. She felt a darkness in her stomach.

"He says Martin Barth's confessions were phony—a trick to close the cases. He wonders if you knew."

Father Joe stared at her. The eyes seemed to see her, to judge her even, yet she knew they saw nothing beyond the raw contrast of light and dark.

"There's been a fourth dead runaway. He says they can't blame Barth this time. He says you may be charged with the killings."

"All of them?"

"That's what he says."

"Really." Father Joe seemed quietly amazed, but not the least troubled. It was as if he'd been awarded an unimportant honor.

"He asked if you kept any records of your discussions with Martin Barth."

Father Joe pushed a button to crank himself higher in the hospital bed. Gears hummed softly. "Why does he want to know?"

"Barth's confessions have been lost. He says they've been lost on purpose."

She glanced toward the half-open door. A nurse passed in the corridor. She lowered her voice.

"But if you have records, and they show there was an attempt to redirect blame, the D.A. won't dare prosecute you. At least that's what Cardozo thinks."

She couldn't be sure how much Father Joe had understood of what she'd been telling him. He seemed lethargic, sedated.

Father Joe reached for her hand. "And what do you make of all this?"

On the other side of the window with its spotless view of the East River, a tugboat hooted.

"I'm not sure."

"Poor, dear Bonnie. It's a lot for you to face alone. Are you holding up?"

She didn't believe in lying, and not lying required a kind of wary compromise with the truth.

"I'm fine." She smiled, as though a smile would be proof.

Damn it, she thought, *why am I smiling? Why am I even pretending to smile? He can't see me.*

"You don't have to smile," he said. "Not for me."

"Joe." She turned. "Are you starting to see again?"

"I know when you're smiling." He patted her hand. "And I know when you're not. You're very, very tense. I can feel it in your fingers."

Hospital noises flowing from the rest of the floor seemed suddenly quieter.

"Would you do me a favor?" she said. "Just hold me for a minute?"

He pulled her toward him, put his arms lightly around her.

SIXTY

"Interesting thing about the photos of the dead kids," Lou Stein said. "There's a light leak."

At the far end of the darkened room, Wally Wills smiled out of the screen. Cardozo hunkered forward in his chair. Squinting, he could see an odd, faint gap in the coloration of the wall behind the boy.

"You can see it with a magnifying glass, but it's really obvious in enlargement."

There was a click as Lou pressed the control. The carousel projector rotated to the next slide. The upper right quadrant of the Wills photo, softened by enlargement, now filled the screen: Wills's brush-cut brown hair, his squinting right eye, a corner of his ear.

A lightning zigzag of pure white snaked down from the upper right-hand corner, crossed the wall, and touched his ear.

Another click, and Wanda Gilmartin popped up on the screen.

Click again. Enlargement of the upper right quadrant. Same lightning, sparking through the wall behind her.

"Hairline fracture in the lens casing."

Lou continued through the photos of Cespedes, Lomax, and Vegas. Always the same zigzag in the upper right.

"Now, the interesting point about the other photos in Father Joe's box is, they don't have the light leak."

Click. Harlequin and Columbine tap-dancing with top hats balanced on cane tips.

Another click. Enlargement. No zigzag.

Click again. Harlequin lindy-tossing Columbine over his shoulder.

And again. No zigzag.

"The dead kids weren't photographed with the same camera as the tap dancers. It's the same model Minolta, but it hasn't got the lens fracture. Since there's no reason a photographer would have duplicate low-tech Minoltas, two different cameras probably means two different photographers. Now I'll show you another interesting point about the runaway photos. There are scratches on all of them except for Pablo's."

Lou flashed the runaway series again. Cardozo could see marks on Vegas and Wills that might have been faint indentations in the glossy surface of the print.

"The scratches are hard to discern, but some of them show benzene-derivative traces—like you'd get if a sheet of paper was placed over the photo and someone wrote in ballpoint on the paper. I tested two working hypotheses. One: each of the four scratched photos was put into an envelope. The envelope was then addressed to be sent through the mail. Since there are no scratches on the Cespedes photo, that one probably wasn't mailed. The benzene in ballpoint dye penetrates paper—but it's colorless, so it doesn't bother people who use ballpoints. However, provided there's a sufficient density, the derivative shows up green under ultraviolet."

Lou projected another series, the same photographs reshot under ultraviolet radiation. Now the runaways glowed with spearmint-colored hen tracks.

"The pattern appears to be random, and it's different on each face. So here comes working hypothesis number two: all four photos were sent to the same addressee. In that case, at least some of the scratches should reinforce one another."

The next series showed successive superimpositions of the four photographs, again under ultraviolet. Lou had rotated the photos with respect to one another, producing a maelstrom of detailed confusion.

"There are four photos, four ways to orient each photo inside an envelope. In addition, the photo can face the front or the flap of the envelope. I won't bore you with how many thousand combinations that makes possible. Matter of fact, I didn't bore myself

—a computer searched. But one combination is very, very interesting."

Click. The four faces, superimposed, rotated, tracked with green, looked like a nightmare deconstruction of a human face generated by a man-hating cyclotron. But in almost the exact center of the image, the green tracks closely paralleled one another.

A nervous hoping fluttered from Cardozo's stomach up to his chest.

Lou reached a hand to the projector to sharpen the image.

A ghostly number 2 leapt into glowing focus, followed by a series of curves that was almost the handwritten word *High*.

Cardozo sat back in the steel chair, feeling hot certainty in his gut.

"You like?" Lou said.

"I like."

Lou clicked off the projector and stretched to flick the wall switch. Overhead fluorescent light blinked on in the narrow, windowless room.

"Did I mention? We finally got those results from Lifeways." Lou stood and yawned. "The semen that we recovered from the reverend."

"No. You didn't mention."

"They pulled a DNA match."

"Who else has Huffington raped?"

"It may not have been rape, but it matches the semen we recovered from Pablo Cespedes's anus."

A hard stab of shock went through Cardozo. His ballpoint pen made a clinkety-clank sound as it fell to the uncarpeted linoleum floor.

"Vince. What's the matter? What's happening to you?"

"Nothing. Just lost my balance for a second." Cardozo straightened up and inhaled slowly. "So Huffington and Cespedes were acquainted."

"To say the least." Lou took a long swallow from his coffee mug, wiped his lips with the edge of his hand. "Make sure the reverend has an antibody test."

It was like turning a corner very quickly and coming upon a three-car collision. Cardozo stood there in Lou Stein's office, blinking, trying to convince himself that this was real. "She's had an antibody test."

"If it comes back negative, make sure she has another in six weeks."

The first thing Cardozo did when he got back to the precinct was to order more copies of the photos. The second was to reassign eight detectives, effective immediately. Their job was to hit every street and avenue and alley in the city whose name started with High—bang on every door in every building on those streets whose number ended in 2—and see if anyone recognized Pablo or any of the runaways.

It was a little after four when Tom O'Reilly called Cardozo into his office. "From what I can see, Vince, this Eff is small-fry."

O'Reilly had loosened his tie and he had one foot up on his desk and Cardozo didn't think that tumbler of Coca-Cola in his hand was just Coca-Cola.

"You're using a lot of men."

"I know that, sir."

The dangerous moment dangled.

"I've gone out on a limb with you," O'Reilly said. "You'd better know what you're doing."

"I know exactly what I'm doing, sir."

"Have you ever seen any of these kids?" Detective Sam Richards asked.

The man who lived in the first floor rear was wired up to an IV tree with four plastic bags. It jerked forward as he reached for the snapshots. His eyes were enormous in his skeletal face, and they went from the photos to Sam Richards to Ellie Siegel. He was obviously curious about this Oreo cop team—the black man and the white woman—with their pictures of half-naked white kids, but he wasn't about to involve himself.

He shook his head. "Can't help you." He handed the photos back.

Ellie and Sam thanked him. He closed the door, and they could hear the wheels of his IV tree squeaking.

Sam sighed. "Scratch another off the list."

Three twenty-two Highland Road, the Bronx, had fallen to Ellie and Sam as part of the 2-High search. The residents were black, elderly, and scared. It was a terrifying building—and not just because a sixteen-year-old girl had been caught two nights ago making phony 911 calls and then throwing rocks off the roof at responding officers. There were bullet holes in every door. Garbage had been set afire in the hallways. Laths poked, pulped and broken, through cracked plaster. Water dribbled from busted pipes.

"Imagine being a senior citizen," Ellie said, "and having to live here."

Sam grimaced. "I'd feel safer in the bear cage in the Bronx Zoo."

As they were leaving, a rat scuttled in the walls. Sam checked the mailboxes one last time. "We missed one. There's a cellar apartment."

Beneath the stairwell, a flight of wooden steps led to a door covered in steel plate. Eight bullets had left pockmarks in the steel. Sam knocked.

"Who is it?" a woman's voice called.

"Police, ma'am." Sam held his ID up to the peephole.

Bolts slid. The door groaned inward. A fresh smell of lemon-scented furniture polish floated out.

A small, gray-haired, neatly dressed woman stood looking up at them. Light sparked off her glasses.

"Sorry to trouble you, ma'am," Sam said.

A friendly little smile lit the old woman's eyes. She projected patience as if she had invented it. "You're not troubling me."

Sam showed her the photos. "We'd just like to ask if you recognize any of these kids?"

She took a long time studying each photo in turn. Finally she handed them back. "No, I'm sorry, I've never seen any of them."

"Thank you for your time, ma'am."

"You're very welcome."

The old lady watched the policeman and the policewoman climb the flight of stairs. Their shadows followed them along the sweating cellar wall.

In the little apartment behind her, a phone rang. She closed the door and bolted it and hurried to answer. "Hello?"

"Hi, Grammaw."

She smiled as she always did when she heard his voice.

"Why, Eff, honey, you got some mail. It just came."

"Thanks, Grammaw. You gonna be home this afternoon?"

Grammaw opened the door at the very first knock.

Eff stood there smiling a smile that was part mystery, part prank. "Hi, Grammaw. Looking beautiful."

He kissed her and a light came into her eyes.

He meandered into the apartment. He was wearing a clean blue denim work shirt rolled up at the cuffs and blue jeans and brand-new–looking brown calfskin Wellington boots. Out of respect, he was holding his New York Mets cap in his hand.

"I got some cakes and cookies," Grammaw said. "I can make some coffee."

Visiting Grammaw was like walking into a party where he was guest of honor. "Haven't got time today, Grammaw. Maybe next time."

"You got holes in your jeans."

"That's the style."

"Just because it's style doesn't mean it's good or you gotta do it." Her eyes narrowed. "What's wrong? You walk like you got something tucked in the back of your belt."

"I got something tucked in the back of my belt."

A worried knuckle flew to Grammaw's mouth. "Eff—you're not carrying a gun!"

Life had kicked some bad shit to Grammaw very hard and Eff made it a point to kick some good shit to her nice and easy. Today it was roses, a dozen red ones that he'd ripped off from a Korean deli.

"Happy birthday to my favorite girl." He held the bouquet out to her.

Grammaw stared at him, not speaking, not moving. A tear rolled down one of her cheeks. It was as though she was asking God, *Where did I get this angel?*

He pushed the flowers into her hands. "Where's my mail, Grammaw?"

She was shaking her head, blinking away tears. The unhurried, unhurrying notes of a siren passed in the street, weaving into the stillness. "On the table."

He went to the table and picked up the envelope and looked at the handwriting. "Okay if I use the bathroom?"

"Course it's okay."

Eff went into the bathroom and turned the lock so carefully that there was no click at all. He opened the envelope.

It contained a piece of lined paper and a photo. A time, a date, and an address had been written on the paper. Nothing else. The photo showed a young man standing on a dock in Jockey shorts, flexing his muscles. The name *Sandy* had been block-lettered on the bottom border, followed by a number sign and the number 6.

Eff slipped the photo and the piece of paper into his pocket.

He lowered the toilet seat cover and quietly stepped up onto it. He reached his finger into the opening where the window chain ran into the sash. He found the loop of the wire he had hidden there. It took a moment to work his fingertip into it.

He pulled up the zippable plastic sandwich bag. From the stash of grass, coke, and pills he took a pink pill and enough grass to roll four joints.

When he came back into the other room, Grammaw had set out a plate of Pepperidge Farm oatmeal cookies.

"Coffee's almost ready."

"Sorry, Grammaw—gotta hurry."

Eff went to the refrigerator and took out a bottle of wine cooler.

"There's alcohol in that," she warned him.

"I'm a big boy, Grammaw." He kissed her good-bye. "Take care of yourself now and stay pretty. I'll be phoning."

SIXTY-ONE

Assistant District Attorney Harvey Thoms lowered his head, swung right along the pale green corridor, and strode through a gaggle of nurses guiding a patient tethered to an IV tree.

He had reached the even-numbered rooms now, the semiprivates with river views, and his steps took on a more rapid rhythm as he came to 1612.

The door was half ajar and he pushed it all the way. He could see the hospital bed cranked up to sitting and he could see there was no one in it. His gaze swung to the chair where a loose-limbed orderly sat thumbing through a movie magazine.

"Where's Montgomery?"

The orderly looked up. Spots on his once-white hospital smock said he'd had creamed spinach for lunch.

"Montgomery. The man who's supposed to be in that bed. What have you done with him?"

The blank Third World face had no answer.

Thoms knocked on the bathroom door and shoved. He flicked on the light. Montgomery's toiletries were still there, jumbled on the glass shelf. The bath towel was damp to Thoms's touch.

He turned. "Who the hell speaks English around here?"

There was no knock. Just a sound of feet banging into a chair, and when Cardozo glanced up, there was Harvey Thoms, faintly purple in the face and breathing hard.

"Where's Father Montgomery?"

Cardozo slowly brought his chair upright, slowly rested an elbow on the desk top. "Last time I saw him, he was in Doctors Hospital."

"Not now he isn't."

"So?"

"We need him for questioning."

Cardozo's eye went to the burly, bored cop in shirtsleeves standing by the cubicle door. He wondered if that was the other half of this *we*. "In connection with?"

"The deaths of Pablo Cespedes and Tod Lomax."

Cardozo turned it over in his mind and didn't like it. "Why today? Why all of a sudden?"

"New evidence has come to light."

"I sure as hell haven't seen any. And I'm in charge, remember?"

Thoms didn't answer. He gave off an air of hyperactive energy beginning to slip off the leash.

"What have you got—your own forensics team going over the

crime scenes? Or maybe a private task force? I'd consider it a professional courtesy if you'd share."

"The D.A. has reconsidered the available evidence." Thoms handed him a two-sheet boilerplate authorization.

Cardozo's eyes scanned. Someone with a bad ballpoint and a worse tremor had misspelled Montgomery's name four times. "This is a warrant for arrest."

Thoms nodded. "Technically, there's enough to hold Montgomery on suspicion."

"Come on, Harvey. This isn't new evidence, this is a change in policy. What's the reason?"

"Latino pressure groups are making noise. They want to see some progress on the Cespedes killing."

"So it's a public relations move. You think the city is going to burn down if Father Joe is allowed the free exercise of a few of his rights."

"Whose side are you on, Cardozo?"

"Same side as you and the D.A. Just trying to clear up a few questions and see that the bad guys get caught."

"Any information you turn up regarding Father Montgomery's whereabouts, you be sure to let us know."

"Immediately." Sarcasm sounded in Cardozo's voice before he could hold it back. "Count on it."

Something flickered in Thoms's eyes. "Don't play games, Vince."

"Never on office time."

Thoms walked to the window and stood staring out. "You didn't warn him, did you?"

Cardozo had to laugh. "How the hell could I warn him? How do I know what you guys are going to be cooking up?"

"That's a *no*?"

"You bet that's a *no*."

After Thoms had gone, Cardozo phoned Bonnie at the rectory. "The D.A.'s men went up to the hospital to arrest Father Joe. They couldn't find him. Seems he's vanished."

"That's not possible." The surprise sounded genuine.

"You haven't heard from him?"

"He can't *see*."

"Will you let me know if you do?"

*   *   *

The door of the Sea Shell bar swung open. Eff looked up from his drink. A figure stood silhouetted against the spill of late-afternoon sunlight. Eff waved.

Sandy McCoy saw the wave. He approached the table, not exactly weaving but not exactly walking a straight line either. "Nell says you wanted to see me."

"Got a job for you, bro." Eff extended a welcoming hand and pulled Sandy into a chair.

Sandy was wearing a tank top and he had a bandanna tied around his forehead. It was very street, very don't-fuck-with-me, a look that black boys and Hispanics could pull off and white boys like Sandy McCoy couldn't.

"Thirsty?" Eff offered.

Sandy's startlingly pale eyes were all iris, barely a pinpoint of pupil in them. They probed the dimness and found the bar with its mirrored shelves of liquor.

The bartender was polishing the cash register. Except for him and Sandy and Eff, the Sea Shell was deserted.

Eff signaled the bartender for another diet soda. "And a tequila sunrise for my friend."

"Tell me about this job." Beneath his floppy dark bangs, Sandy was sweating bullets and birdshit.

Eff could see he'd taken some of that killer Ecstasy that had been hitting the streets lately. "It's an acting job."

"I can't. Something's wrong with my dick. It hurts when I come."

"Not that kind of acting." Eff smiled. "This guy's a priest. You pretend to be a repentant sinner getting confession and communion."

The bartender brought their drinks and took Eff's empty. Eff and Sandy clinked.

"I haven't been to church in a long time." Sandy radiated a nervousness that was almost electric. "I don't remember all that getting up and getting down and crossing stuff."

"Tell him you used to know but you're too stoned to remember." Eff handed him a neatly rolled joint. "Smoke it in the men's room."

When Sandy came back there was a goofy smile on his face and an easy float to his walk.

"Let's see your tongue," Eff said.

Sandy opened his mouth.

Eff dropped a pink pill onto his tongue and handed him a fresh tequila sunrise.

Sandy swallowed. "What was that?"

The guy did not possess the smarts of a flea.

"Just to be sure you stay mellow." Eff pushed up from his chair. "Come on, time to move. It's getting late."

"Fuck it!" Eff screamed. "You've gone past it!"

The driver stamped on the brakes. The taxi veered to the right and slammed to a stop. A shuddering vibration slid through Sandy and made him feel sick and dizzy. He tried to hold images and sounds in focus.

Eff thrust a fistful of singles at the driver. "Learn English, asshole!"

Sandy stood on a quiet tree-lined sidewalk. Above the slanting roofs, a nearby steeple made a thread of fire in the setting sun.

Eff steered him up the block and into a service alley.

Trash cans were lined up with collars of black plastic bags neatly visible under the lids.

Eff pushed Sandy up three wooden steps to a porch. Their footsteps echoed clumsily on the hollow planking.

Eff pushed a doorbell.

In the distance, an ambulance siren howled.

It was two minutes before the door opened. A priest stood in the doorway, dressed to celebrate Mass.

"Come on in, Sandy." The priest smiled, and his whole face glowed. "Eff has told me a lot about you."

The gold-embroidered vestments formed a sort of whispering waterfall. There was no fixed point for Sandy to focus on.

"This is my body, which I gave for you." The priest made a sign of the cross.

Sandy's vision held the image like a series of time-frozen overlapping stills, and the cross looped into a cloverleaf.

A wafer levitated from a napkin placed across a silver plate.

Sandy opened his mouth to receive it.

The priest placed it instead in his hands.

"Whoops." Sandy heard himself, and it was like another person giggling. "My mistake." He knew he was screwing up, too eager to do it right and too goofy when he did it wrong.

What the hell was that pink pill? he wondered. *I've never been like this before.*

Instinct told him to get up off his knees. He used the altar railing to push himself to standing. Wobbling, he turned from the altar.

Above a sea of empty pews, the church was a dark cavern. The door at the end of the aisle seemed a million uncrossable light-years away, like a star glimpsed through the wrong end of a telescope.

Hands held him. He floated forward through the wash of darkness. Beyond the door, moonlight fell on a rising sun. The sun had a face, and the face was smiling. Beneath it, white lettering on the side of a blue van spelled GOD LOVES YOU—SO DO I.

He floated up, and now they were driving along a street dotted with trees.

"Tell me, my son, how long have you been a runaway?"

"A few years," Sandy heard himself answer. No giggle this time. He was doing better, getting a grip on it.

"How long have you been taking dope?"

"A few years."

"When you let drugs take you to the bottom level of society, you break your parents' hearts. You steal from them, betray them." The head of the man on the seat beside him was not so much turned as aimed. The voice could have been talking for a moment or an hour. "You take your girlfriend into shooting galleries and trade her body for dope and you know it's not right."

"Right," Sandy said.

The van passed through gates and into a garage.

"Tell me, my son, how long have you been prostituting yourself?"

"Fuck, I don't know. . . ." *Tell the sucker what he wants to hear.* "Years."

Hands helped Sandy float out of the van and up a flight of stairs. Here there was a wall of lettering to focus on:

Bring me young sinners.
Suffer the little children to come unto me.
He who dies with forgiveness of sins . . . wins!

A wave of nausea took him. "I need the bathroom."

"Right in there."

He knelt at the toilet and tried to vomit. Empty retchings racked him till his ribs ached. Nothing came up. *It's that pill, I know it's that pink pill.* He staggered back into the other room.

On a bureau, incense burned in a small copper bowl. The place reeked.

A voice suddenly coaxed behind his left ear: "The peace of God?" It was like a drug dealer's whisper in the street, offering something forbidden but delicious.

Sandy turned. "Sure, why the hell not?"

In that last instant his vision had an ice-water clarity. The arm of a white robe flew through space, blazing with gold trim.

SIXTY-TWO

Bonnie sat bolt upright, suddenly wide awake.

The blackness of the bedroom flowed around her, full of tiny silences. A slit of light peeked through the blinds. It seemed to be pulsating.

A sound brushed the air—a kind of squealing—muffled, distant.

She recognized what had awakened her: the cry of brakes. Or was it a human cry?

She held her breath, listening.

Outside the closed window, faint above the hum of the air conditioner, glass broke. A numbness climbed the back of her neck.

She pushed up from the bed. Sluggish legs carried her around the ridged, straight-backed Victorian armchair. She pushed up a slat of the blinds and stared out.

Across the way, one of the rectory windows winked.

That's just a streetlight, she told herself. *There's nobody in the rectory—if anyone had broken in the burglar alarm would have gone off.*

She waited. The rectory windows stared back at her like eyes with nothing alive behind them. There was only the deserted street, the shimmering gray vault of the New York night.

The light winked again, on the ground story, in the rector's window.

Down in the street, brakes yelped. A metallic blue Toyota van lurched to a stop, wheels shrieking against the pavement. A man in a security guard's uniform jumped out and crossed to the rectory door.

She let the blind fall back. She yanked a raincoat from the closet and buttoned it on the way down to the street.

The guard was shining his flashlight through one of the windows. A walkie-talkie was sputtering on his hip.

"It's my fault." Bonnie caught her breath. "I forgot to reset the alarm."

Smoky eyes studied her from beneath slitted lids. "When was that?" He had a deep southern accent, like a white sheriff.

"Just a little while ago."

"This *is* New York City. These *are* the nineties." A bright finger of light moved across brownstone and bay windows and up to gables and dormers. "Let's make sure these windows haven't been forced."

She unlocked the door. Something cool and faintly stale drifted out. Tiny red lights were dancing on the alarm box. She punched in the code.

"Want me to take a look around?" He stood on the doorstep, smiling at her strangely.

"No. Thank you. It was my fault. I'm sorry."

She could feel him wondering about her.

"Sign here." He held out a metal clipboard.

She signed.

He touched a hand to his cap.

She closed the door, and she could hear him outside, speaking into his walkie-talkie. A moment later the van drove away.

Her eye scanned the dimness. She breathed through half-parted lips.

Deep inside the house, something made a scratching sound. Halfway down the corridor, the door to Father Joe's study was ajar.

She moved toward it. The lamp threw a soft splash of light across the desk top. The file cabinet was open and Father Joe stood feeling through the files.

He'd lost a terrible amount of weight in the hospital.

He was an orderly file keeper, and she could see what he was doing: his left thumb was in the *B* section of the top drawer, and his right forefinger was counting off the letters of the alphabet. He carefully tugged out the *M* folder.

Now he turned toward the desk. He seemed to orient himself by the light. It broke her heart to see how he moved with an old man's caution. He tested every step with a slow, sweeping outstretched hand before committing himself.

The plane of his hand was an inch higher than the back of the chair. He bumped into it and muttered and shoved it impatiently out of the way.

He found the desk and opened the folder. He held a page under the lamp. First he bent down and brought his eyes close to the page, and then he stood up and brought the page close to his eyes. He tried different focal lengths—far, medium—and finally he sighed in frustration.

She'd never in her life heard him sigh like that. Exasperated. Almost giving in to rage.

Almost, but not quite.

"Dear Lord, help your foul-tempered servant."

He stood there silently. She could feel him calming himself, centering himself.

He turned once more, orienting himself this time by the desk at his back. He walked in a slow, straight line to the wall. His hand struck the paneling. He felt to the right, as far as the mantelpiece.

He crouched down at the fireplace. He felt for the andiron and the brass cup of long decorator matches. He struck a match and moved it back and forth in front of his eyes.

He opened the folder and held the first sheet to the flame. When it had caught, he groped under the log and found a piece of kindling.

He held the paper to the thin strip of wood until the wood was lit. He laid the kindling under the log. He balled the next sheet and fed it to the fire.

"Joe," she said.

He went on with his work, unsurprised. "Hello, Bonnie."

"You should be in the hospital."

"I have to burn these."

"What are they?"

"Records of my discussions with Martin Barth and anyone else whose initials are *M.B.* I wish I could be more exact in my blitzkrieg, but I can't."

Her head suddenly ached so heavily that it seemed filled with lead.

"By the way, I'm really much better at getting around than I seem. I've just been in bed so long my legs are weak."

"I can't let you burn those papers."

He turned. Despite the weight loss and the hospital pallor, he had a look of sinewy determination. "Anything a parishioner tells me in confidence remains confidential. I don't care what the law says."

"Is there something you're hiding?"

"Absolutely not."

"Then what's the point?"

"The point is, I'm not an agent of the state. These papers could be shopping lists and the police still would have no right to see them. I won't ask you to agree with me; I won't even ask you to help me destroy them. But please, my dear, don't try to stop me."

"Have you heard anything from Father Joe?" Cardozo asked.

"He hasn't called." There was something hesitant, almost jittery in Bonnie's voice. It could have been a bad connection.

"Let me know if he does." Cardozo hung up and sat drumming his fingers on the edge of his desk.

"Bad news?" Ellie stepped into the cubicle carrying a stack of fresh-looking files. Today she was wearing a dress with bold, splashy orange-on-gray patterns like graffiti on a wall.

"No news."

"Sometimes that can be just as bad."

"Worse. What are those?"

"Results of the 2-High canvass."

"Anything turn up?"

"Zilch." She looked at the desk, then at him. Without a word, she cleared a space in the paper chaos and thunked the DD5s down. "Beirut couldn't be any worse than Highland Road. I don't see how those old people survive."

Cardozo leafed through the stack. Something flagged his attention, some subliminal shadow of a missed possibility. He leafed back through the stack and stopped at a list of tenants in one of the buildings. "You and Sam interviewed a woman called Delphillea Huttington?"

Ellie nodded. "She was an old sweetie."

"I wonder if that could be a typo." He lifted the phone and dialed the number. A woman answered. "Hello, Mrs. Huttington —or is it Mrs. Huffington?"

"The name is Huffington."

"I'm looking for a young man who goes by the name of Eff Huffington?"

"Well, my grandson Francis sometimes uses the nickname Eff."

"I sent your grandson a letter at your house. Did he ever get it?"

At the word *grandson,* Ellie turned around.

"Oh, yes, Father." The woman's voice became friendly. "It's so nice to visit with you at last, even if it's only on the phone."

"Nice to visit with you, Mrs. Huffington."

"Eff got your letter yesterday. He said he was going to take care of it right away. I'll tell him you called. I'm sure you'll be hearing from him."

"How can I get in touch with Eff? It's urgent."

"Lord, I wish I knew. He never has an address. The only time I see him is when he gets in touch with me."

"I appreciate your help, Mrs. Huffington."

"Don't mention it."

Cardozo hung up.

Ellie was staring at him. "I didn't think of it. Delphillea Huffington is black, Eff's white."

"She adopted him."

"But she's a decent human being. He's a monster."

"She got him too late. He was already formed. All he learned from Delphillea Huffington was how to sucker sweet old ladies."

Cardozo tapped the tip of a ballpoint pen against the desk top. "When I said I'd sent Eff a letter, right away Mrs. Huffington called me Father."

"Then Father someone has been sending Eff letters there." Ellie was staring out the window. "And photos of the communion killer's victims were sent to the same address."

"Father's sending the photos." Cardozo was on his feet. Suddenly he had no ability to sit still. "They're order forms. He's telling Eff, *I want this one, I want that one. Bring them to me.* Eff's leading those kids to the slaughter."

The basement apartment was tidy but dark. Delphillea Huffington had brightened the space with Caribbean paintings. A small art deco Tiffany clock gleamed on the coffee table, and across the room, on top of a spinet piano, a stone-studded chalice caught the glow of the music lamp.

"I hope Eff's not in any kind of trouble," Mrs. Huffington said.

"Not at all." Cardozo had shown a fake ID. He had claimed to be from the review board of the city foster care department. "If anyone's in trouble it's going to be one of our caseworkers."

Delphillea Huffington tilted her gray head back against the needlepoint cushion of her rocking chair. She stared at the ceiling.

"We're reviewing the way Eff's case was handled," Cardozo said. "The record's been lost."

"I'm not surprised they'd want to lose that record."

"Do you remember the name of Eff's caseworker?"

"I'm never going to forget that woman. Her name was Ivy Melrose."

Cardozo made a note for the sake of realism. "What reason did she give you for removing Eff from your care?"

"She said it was regulations. You ask me, it was racism—they don't think a black can raise a white. That's B-U-double-L. I may not be rich. I may not be an educated person. But I have the common sense I was born with, and I know how to love a child. Plenty of whites adopt black kids, and some of them don't know how to love anyone. But you never see a black allowed to adopt a white."

"And had you tried to adopt Eff?"

"I *did* adopt him and I can show you papers to prove it. Of course, Ms. Melrose said the papers were no good—wrong date, wrong signature, wrong staples, wrong everything. They want to make you wrong, they'll find a way. So they took my little angel from me and put him in a white home."

It was mid-afternoon, but the trickle of light that came through the window grille was like the last vestiges of day.

"I hear the people they gave him to are working every city program for every dollar they can. I hear they go to Bermuda every year on vacation—own property down there. Some people wouldn't open their home to a kid without getting paid. They make their living off the problem, not the solution. No one ever paid me a cent. I loved that child. Still do."

"How long ago did the department take Eff from you?"

Her face tightened as though she still had trouble believing it had happened. "It'll be six years this July eighteenth. He was crying like a five-year-old when they pulled him out that door."

"And you stayed in touch with him?"

"Ms. Melrose tried to tell me I couldn't, but I got a lawyer to set her straight on that. I see my Eff once, twice a month at least. And every holiday. And he always remembers my birthday."

"How do you contact him?"

For just an instant, her brow seemed to pinch. "He wants to see me, he gets in touch."

"Do you have an address for him?"

The subject seemed to make her uncomfortable. She turned her cup 180 degrees in the saucer. "He's never in one place long enough. Matter of fact, he comes here to pick up his mail. He won't trust that foster home."

"I bet he gets a lot of mail."

There was wariness in her glance. "I wouldn't say so. Eff's had trouble making friends. But he has one pen pal. A priest sends him snapshots and letters."

"It's good that Eff has a friend like that. You wouldn't have this priest's name?"

"Eff never told me."

"You never noticed the return address?"

"There isn't any."

Cardozo broke the silence by picking up the Tiffany clock from the table. "I'll bet Eff gave you this."

"How did you guess?" She seemed pleasantly amazed. "He picked it up in a flea market. Most of my knickknacks are gifts from Eff. He has a real eye for quality."

"Very pretty." Cardozo wondered about the chalice on the piano, but he wasn't going to comment.

"Eff wants me to have pretty things." Mrs. Huffington rocked and smiled. "He says I'm his best girl. He says one day he's going to move me into an apartment in Peter Cooper Village. Maybe he's dreaming, but it's a beautiful dream. And what else have we poor folk got nowadays? You turn on the TV and look at the commercials and you feel like an exile from your own nation."

Cardozo stepped onto Highland Road. Two men in shabby clothes stumbled past, blinking as though daylight was physical agony to their eyes. They appeared to be addicts or beggars or out-of-work muggers.

Down the block, a neatly dressed little black boy was standing by the open fire hydrant where Cardozo had parked, just standing there and watching Cardozo approach. Cardozo was twenty feet away when the boy turned and ran into an abandoned building.

Ellie threw open the door of the Honda. "Will you look at the speed on that kid?"

Cardozo slid into the front seat beside her. "He keeps lookout and runs into that crack house when he sees cops. How much do you suppose he gets paid?"

"Eight hundred dollars a week." Ellie started the motor and pulled smoothly into the street. "How did you make out with Mrs. Huffington?"

"I don't think I fooled her, but I found out what I wanted. All we need to know now is when the next letter arrives."

The traffic light at the corner was red and Ellie slowed to a stop. "Do you realize that money's untaxed? By the time he's sixteen he'll have half a million dollars."

Cardozo's eyes came around. "Are you going to report me to Pierre Strauss if I order a tap on the line?"

"Vince, have I ever reported you to anyone for anything?" The light changed. "Where are we going?"

"Back to the dock. That's where Tod Lomax stayed and that's got to be where Father is getting his runaways. And he just got himself another one."

SIXTY-THREE

It was two-thirty in the afternoon and somewhere in America a bird must have been singing, but not on the Twelfth Street pier. The humidity was charged with chemicals floating downstream on the Hudson. Bumper-to-bumper traffic on the West Side Highway added its fumes to the mix.

A white kid was standing in the sun behind a rip in the chain-link fence. He was about fourteen, built like a sparrow, shirtless, and an easy, drugged goofiness played across his features.

Cardozo approached, smiling. In one hand he held a five-dollar bill; in the other, Eff's photo from the computerized rap sheet. "Wonder if you could help me."

The kid adjusted his flat blue gaze. His left ear was pierced and he had a small ring in it that looked like something from a hardware store keychain.

"Have you seen this guy? He hangs out around here."

The kid took the photo in a grimy hand. Luckily, the photo was encased in protective plastic. He examined it with uncaring eyes and handed it back. He reached for the five dollars. "Nell can tell you. Inside."

Sunlight fell through torn planking and shattered windows, dappling the dusty air. Cardozo threaded a path across the warehouse, through grave-size plots staked out by half-dressed children, through bedrolls and ripped-open garbage bags.

Nell sat by the northwest wall on a stained patchwork quilt, dealing herself a hand of solitaire.

"Nell. It's me again. Vince Cardozo."

Her eyelids came up and her eyes flicked to Cardozo and then back to her cards. She crossed her arms over the tank top that barely covered her adolescent breasts.

Cardozo hunkered down in a crouch. He laid Eff's photo on top of her queen of hearts. "They tell me you know Eff. I need to find him."

"Can't help you. Eff contacts the dock; the dock doesn't contact Eff." She laid a jack on top of the photo. "That's the way he does business."

"What kind of business?"

She lifted the back of a hand to wipe a ribbon of moisture from her upper lip. "Odd jobs."

"Has he ever done business with you?"

She didn't answer.

He took another five from his wallet and laid it on top of her jack of hearts.

She stared at the money. "I've worked with Eff."

"What kind of work?"

"What kind do you think? He's a pimp."

Cardozo laid down another five.

She picked up the money and tucked it into her tank top. "He gave me fifty dollars to do an Omaha chicken scene. Every now and then there's more money for a more specialized scene."

"Are there ever scenes involving a priest?"

She hesitated. Her eyelids dropped. "There's a priest that gets off giving confession and communion to sinners. But you have to pretend to be gay. I've never done one."

"When was Eff here last?"

"Yesterday. My friend Sandy did a scene for him."

"A scene with the priest?"

"I don't know. Sandy hasn't come back."

"When did Sandy leave?"

"Yesterday, around six—went to the Sea Shell to meet Eff."

The jukebox was crooning "I'll Be Seeing You" when Cardozo pushed through the door. There were only three customers in the softly lit bar: two men at a table by the window and a young man in a green sport shirt nursing a beer in the corner.

The bartender was arranging beer bottles on a mirrored shelf—

one of each brand the bar carried. Cardozo had an impression of an old man trying to keep things human and tidy in a time and place that weren't either.

Cardozo ordered a diet Pepsi.

"Want that in a mug?" The old man wore a plaid work shirt, sleeves rolled up over powerful biceps. Beneath snow-white eyebrows he had astonishingly blue eyes.

"In the can will be fine."

The bartender brought a chilled can and popped it open.

Cardozo laid Eff's photo on the bar. "Did you notice this kid in here yesterday, around six o'clock? He might have been with a friend." Cardozo began to take out his shield case.

The bartender gestured him not to bother. "I remember you." He put on reading glasses and frowned. After a moment he nodded. "Cocky kid . . . had a crucifix earring in his left ear . . . Nike high-tops, baggy black jeans . . . strutted around like he had five hundred dollars in his pocket. Called me 'my man.' He drank diet soda, but he bought tequila sunrises for his friend. Big spender."

"Tell me about the friend."

"A little older . . . dark-haired . . . scrawny . . . hopped-up. Looked like he came from the dock over there." The bartender nodded toward the plate-glass window with its front-row-center view of traffic clogging the West Side Highway. "Needed a shave, needed a shower, needed a lot."

"Any idea where they went?"

"They left together—around seven, seven-thirty." The bartender slipped his glasses back into his shirt pocket. "I heard the blond kid say something about catching a ferry."

The jukebox was blaring "Que Será, Será" when Ellie Siegel stepped into the bar.

"God bless air-conditioning." She daubed at her forehead with a fresh tissue. "That Gansevoort Street pier was a dead end. A very hot dead end. Vince, are you going to report me if I have a beer?"

"I'm not getting involved. It's between you and your conscience."

"My conscience can handle it." Ellie smiled at the bartender. "Rolling Rock."

He gave her a glass and a frosted bottle. "On the house."

"Thanks, but not allowed." Ellie put three dollars on the bar. She took her beer to a table near the jukebox.

Cardozo followed.

Ellie sat sipping at her foam. "If you didn't do any better than me, we wasted half a day."

"Eff was here last night. He had a kid called Sandy with him. Sandy hasn't been seen since."

Ellie set down her glass. A shaft of sunlight laid a weightless vibration across the Formica-topped table. "Any idea where they went from here?"

"The bartender heard them talking about a ferry."

"For once, I'm glad that New York no longer has a decent transportation system. There are two main ferry connections from the West Side—Staten Island and Hoboken." She took a long swallow of Rolling Rock and sighed. "Which do you want?"

Cardozo reached into his pocket for a quarter. "I'll flip you for Staten Island."

Cardozo calculated that Eff and Sandy couldn't have reached the Staten Island ferry before eight.

He made two assumptions. One: City transit employees tended to work the same shifts five days a week. Two: One of them might just possibly recall a kid with a blond ponytail and a crucifix in his ear and an attitude that stuck out like porcupine quills.

Cardozo made himself unpopular in two different token lines. Asked the clerk to look at the photo, received groans—"You gotta be kidding!" Flashed his shield to show he wasn't. Thanked the clerks for their stares of nonrecognition.

He rode the eight o'clock ferry from Battery Park and questioned the ferry personnel and scored marginally better: a man with a broom couldn't be sure, but he thought he'd had words with the little bastard on the subject of littering.

As the ferry pulled in to the Staten Island slip, the sky was darkening and pink-edged clouds were changing shape like a slow-motion kaleidoscope.

Cardozo joined the late commuters eddying down the gangplank. They were rushing to line up at the bus stop. No bus in sight. Two taxis waited at a cabstand, no customers in sight.

He surveyed the scene, putting himself in Eff's head, weighing options. *I have a date somewhere on this island with a priest. I have a stoned drunk in tow, so walking is out. What do I do?*

There was a rush of sirens from the west. Cardozo crossed to the taxi rank.

Ellie Siegel sat in front of a scarred wooden desk in the Third Street headquarters of the Hoboken Cab Company, smiling her prettiest smile while the dispatcher held a three-way argument with a telephone and a radio mike.

"Weehawken," he told the mike for the second time. This time the radio didn't talk back. He told the phone, "Three minutes." He slammed down the phone and grimaced at Ellie. "Sorry for the interruption. Where were we?"

"I was asking if any of your drivers might have picked that young man up at the ferry yesterday. Probably around eight or eight-thirty. He would have had another young man with him."

The dispatcher churned papers on his desk top and found the photo she had given him. He stared a long moment at the young man with long blond hair gathered in a ponytail. "What did he do? Kill someone?"

The dispatcher was wearing an imitation fifties Hawaiian shirt, khaki slacks, and loafers. Ellie knew he was wearing loafers because he had one foot propped up on the desk.

She made a sound that wasn't quite yes and wasn't quite no. "We'd like to question him."

"Any idea where he was headed? I could check the sheets."

"Possibly to church."

"Church?" The dispatcher fixed his brown-eyed gaze on her. "Nine o'clock at night?"

"It was a social call."

The dispatcher reached behind his ear and scratched. "How many of these photos can you give me? I'll show them around."

Ellie opened her purse. "How many can you use?"

In the armchair, Father sat drifting. The air conditioner gave a soft forward pulse to the silence. It was a long moment of floating contentment.

And then something prodded.

He became gradually aware of Sandy's hand touching his, reminding him. Father opened his eyes. "I just need a moment and I'll pull myself together."

Sandy's answer was silence.

Father tried to ignore the silence. He hated to be rushed. He raised his glass to his lips and drained the last drops of rum. A warmth spread through his body. He tried to enjoy the warmth. He wiped his lips with the back of his hand.

Again he felt the pressure of Sandy's fingers, that nagging urgency.

"Young people." Father shook his head. "You're a paradox. Nothing to live for—and always rushing." He wondered what it must be like to be Sandy—to be a generation shaped by material poverty, spiritual neglect, drugs, violence.

Thank God I'm not Sandy. Thank God I have an anchor.

The empty glass made a soft click as he set it back down onto the table. He pushed himself to his feet, centering himself. He gave Sandy's hand a squeeze.

"Okay, kiddo, I'm taking you home."

Father moved steadily now, down the stairs and straight to the van, undeflected, energized by a will that had added itself to his own. He swung open the van door. Hinges squeaked softly. He lifted the lid of the Styrobasket.

Sandy stared at him with quietly startled eyes, his mouth a little round O.

Father placed Sandy's hand with the other parts of him, neatly aligned with the forearms. He closed each eyelid, kissed each eyelid. His lips touched Sandy's mouth.

"God loves you," he whispered. "So do I."

SIXTY-FOUR

Cardozo reread the 1:30 A.M. entry. According to the log, Bonnie Ruskay came out of her building. She was in a hurry and she was wearing a raincoat. She crossed the street, engaged in a five-minute discussion with a security guard, and spent almost an hour inside the rectory. At 2:25 she returned to her apartment.

Cardozo phoned Empire Security and identified himself. "You sent a guard to St. Andrew's rectory on East Sixty-ninth Street at one-thirty this morning. Could you check that call for me?"

"One moment."

The phone broke into "New York, New York"—the Liza Minnelli rendition. Cardozo held it away from his ear till the woman came back on the line.

"That building was entered at 1:22 A.M. The security code was not transmitted. A guard was dispatched."

"And what was the matter?"

"No break-in. The lady forgot to reset her alarm."

Cardozo lowered the receiver. His ballpoint rapped out a bolero rhythm on the edge of an open desk drawer. After a moment he tapped a number into the phone and waited through seven rings.

"Henahan." The voice of a mean-tempered zombie.

"Did I wake you up, Jack?"

Cardozo took a swallow of lukewarm coffee while Henahan grumbled.

"Sorry. Look, I've been checking your log and I see a security man was dispatched to the rectory. The company says there was an entry but no break-in. Did you see anything?"

"I wasn't watching the rectory, Vince. I was across the street guarding Ruskay."

"It looks like someone had a key but didn't know the alarm

code. Did anyone come out with Ruskay when she went back to her apartment?"

"She was alone."

"What about later?"

"You didn't tell me you wanted the rectory watched too."

"I know, but did you happen to see anyone?"

Henahan sighed. "Let me think. It must have been an hour, three quarters of an hour later—the light was already out in her apartment—I saw that van drive out of the gate."

"A man was driving?"

"I don't know if a man was driving, but a man opened the gate."

"Can you describe him?"

"Sorry, Vince. It was dark and I didn't know it was important."

Cardozo phoned Harry Thoms at the D.A.'s office. "Any luck tracking down Father Montgomery?"

"Not a trace. What about you?"

"Nothing so far."

The gray morning promised rain. Cardozo pressed the doorbell. Through the curtained rectory window he could see a shadow approach and he recognized a gliding quality in the way Bonnie Ruskay moved.

She opened the door and something startled showed in her eyes. She covered with a smile. "Don't tell me you're still worrying about me."

"Always."

"Come in."

He accepted the invitation. "I don't suppose you've heard from Father Joe?"

She was busy tapping the code into the alarm box. "He hasn't phoned."

Cardozo realized that the question she'd answered was not exactly the one he'd asked. "Has he been here?"

"This is his home."

Cardozo had a sense she was playing with tiny verbal distinctions, like a lawyer. "Recently?"

"I don't stand guard over the manse."

"Is he here now?"

"I'd be very much surprised."

"Would you mind if I look?"

"Don't you believe me?"

"Unless you've looked yourself, you can't be sure."

"Can you do the job alone or do you need to call for a crew?"

"I can manage by myself."

She stepped aside with a kind of light dancing twirl. "Why don't we look together?"

The desk in Father Joe's office was bare except for the penholder and the blotter, the crystal bud vase with its single yellow hyacinth.

"A fresh flower," Cardozo said.

She nodded. "One of the cleaning woman's little rituals."

The coffee table was neatly stacked with books and current magazines. The air conditioner was running full blast, yet the air was warm, almost muggy. The window was open a crack, and he realized the machine had been set on exhaust.

"Airing out the place?"

"These old New York houses get musty."

There were traces of ash and curls of blackened paper beneath the cedar log in the fireplace.

She opened the closet door. "Well, he's not hiding here."

Cardozo followed her up the stairs. As he climbed he could feel that his white shirt needed a pressing. Today was the kind of muggy day where everybody's white shirt needed a pressing.

She clicked on a table lamp in Father Joe's room, and Cardozo had the momentary sense of standing in an immaculate hotel suite. The bed had been made and heaped with silk throw pillows. The air had a lemony smell of furniture polish.

"Someone certainly did a good job here," he said.

"I'm very happy with the new cleaning woman's work."

The tour ended in the garage.

"Where's the van?" Cardozo said.

"Today it's doing Meals-on-Wheels. Have you heard of them? Hot lunches for shut-ins."

Solomon Jones knew when he needed a break and he knew when his family needed a rest. So he took a sick day he had coming, and he picked up a bucket of arroz con pollo at the corner bodega and he brought his wife and daughter to the Ramble in Central Park.

It was a weekday, and it had rained that morning, so no one else had claimed the picnic table on top of the wooded hill. Solomon and Phoebe clinked iced cans of Coors and sat feeling the air and the sun on their skin.

He looked over to the woods where his little girl was exploring the bushes behind the oakwood gazebo. Mineola was wearing her birthday dress; she had just turned six, and she was a bright bouncing splash of yellow against the green foliage.

Solomon sighed. "This is it. This is what life ought to be. Except who is that bitch on the radio, and why is she making me listen to Beethoven?"

Before he could reach the portable radio and change to a rock station, Phoebe swung her hair off her shoulder and leaned to kiss him. She was wearing thin white pants and a thin white blouse knotted at her waist and they glided over her like silk, and Solomon could feel his mind taking another direction.

Over in the woods, something made a cracking-open sound and Mineola let out half a howl. That was funny—Mineola holding on to the other half of that howl.

Solomon opened one eye.

"What's she done now?" Phoebe murmured.

"Mineola," Solomon shouted. "Get over here."

The little girl came fluttering through the bushes. Her dress was smeared red.

"Damn it, honey," Phoebe said, "what have you done to your new clothes?"

The little girl stood twisting her fists, making the stains worse. "There's a box over there."

"Don't you be messing with other people's boxes."

Solomon felt something ripple through the trees like a whisper of alarm. He got up from the table and took Mineola's left hand. The girl was shaking badly. Her fist was jammed so tightly shut that he had to pry the fingers open one by one.

Her palm was smudged red. The red was dried blood, but it wasn't hers, thank God.

Solomon spoke gently. "Show me where you found this box, honey."

* * *

The usher unlocked the door to the grand tier box. The cardinal stepped in.

District Attorney William Kodahl and his guests had already arrived. Kodahl made introductions. The cardinal acknowledged each with a slight inclination of his head. No business with hands: the ring-kissing was too awkward in a small space.

A lady by the name of Samantha Schuyler tried to force him to accept a seat at the front of the box. "Please, your Eminence, I've been keeping it warm just for you."

The cardinal demurred pleasantly but firmly. "One of the burdens of office is that I can't be seen at the opera. If no one minds, I'll take the backseat—and move it a little further back."

Wallingford Amory, president of the Americas Trust Company, yielded the seat. "Think of the poor pope, your Eminence. He loves classical music, and he can't even go to the symphony." Amory shifted the position of the velvet-cushioned chair so that it was completely sunk in shadow. "For the sin of rising to the top of the Church, God has condemned him to hear the Vatican choir."

"Ouch." The cardinal sat.

The others sat.

The district attorney's wife turned around in her seat to hand him a book. "I hope you don't mind, your Eminence—I've taken the liberty of inscribing it to you."

The cardinal had an instant of wariness when he saw the cover. *Symphonie Fantastique: The True Love Story of Society's Most Enticing Heiress and Music's Most Fiery Maestro.* When he opened it and found neither imprimatur nor *nihil obstat,* he felt a jolt of alarm. By the time he reached the title page and saw that it was only a handwritten dedication, his brain cells had gone into a mild uproar. *Do I dare inscribe this book to Barry Cardinal Fitzwilliam? With deepest admiration, Pamela Proulx-Martin Kodahl.*

"Why, thank you." The cardinal put on his mask of smiling gratitude. "I look forward to relaxing with it. It's light fiction?"

"Light, I hope; but fiction, not at all. I've researched every word."

The crystal chandeliers, dimming to darkness, rose to the

golden ceiling. The Russian maestro hurried into the orchestra pit. Applause broke out. Jeweled wrists flashed in the blackness.

The conductor's baton flicked out a smart, sharp upbeat, and the Bolshoi orchestra thundered out the *Carmen* overture. The familiar music enclosed the cardinal like a comfortable rising tide. Thoughts drifted through his head. *Oh, that* Carmen. *Now, there's a piece of work. . . .*

He discovered that if he sat on top of Pamela Proulx-Martin Kodahl's book he could see beyond the ladies' hairdos. A gypsy-wigged Bulgarian mezzo stood framed in a Sevillian arcade. Shafts of light streamed in behind her.

The dark shadow of the madonna. Very dark. I'd swear she was Irish. In fact, I'd swear she was my sister.

During the habanera, the door to the box opened. A man in a dark suit leaned past the cardinal and whispered to the district attorney. Grave-faced, Bill Kodahl rose and beckoned the cardinal. They stepped back into the vestibule.

"What is it?" the cardinal whispered.

"Bad news. There's been another killing."

The cardinal felt himself sink into a freezing hollow at the heart of the moment. Behind him, Carmen was singing that love was a wild bird, that no one could trap it. "Our man again?"

"Our man again." The line between Kodahl's lips was as thin and straight as a blade. "This makes two since Father Romero died. We may not be able to keep this secret much longer."

SIXTY-FIVE

Dan Hippolito pulled back the black sheet, just far enough so Nell could see the face, not far enough for her to see that the head had been severed.

She took a moment preparing herself, and then she took two faltering steps forward. Her open-toed sandals clacked on the stone floor. She looked down into icy mist rising from the stainless steel tray.

Her face went from pale to white. She began trembling. She reached back and grabbed Cardozo's hand. A wordless whimpering sound came out of her, the sound a tethered and whipped animal might make.

Cardozo put an arm around her and led her away from the locker. He could feel her heart thudding. She turned her head, and her nose left a print of warmth on his palm.

He spoke to her quietly. "It'll be okay. It really will."

Those eyes with their meadow-flower blue irises misted over. She nodded, not saying a word. Her pain washed through him.

"Nell . . . is there anything I can do? Is there anything you need?"

Her teeth came down on her lower lip. "Could I have something to drink?"

"What would you like? Coffee? Soda?"

"Anything."

He took her to the soda machine in the corridor and bought a can of Coke and snapped it open for her.

They stood silently in nervous fluorescent light. He watched her take quick little sips.

"Could I ask a favor?" he said. "Would you allow Dr. Hippolito to examine you?"

"Why?"

"You said you did some scenes for a client of Eff's. He might have left marks on you. They might help us find the person who killed Sandy."

She stood thinking a moment. Her tongue curled over her upper lip in indecision. "Will it hurt?"

He couldn't help smiling. "Of course not."

She seemed uneasy, but in a way she seemed to like the attention. "Okay."

They went to Dan's office. Cardozo waited in the hallway, pacing, thinking of three quarters of a million kids growing up in the city without homes.

When Dan came out of the office, his face was grim. "Go easy on her, Vince. She's in terrible shape."

"I know that. What did you find?"

"She has the same marks as Sandy. The same marks as the others." Dan's tone was as hard as the edge of a steel ruler. "You can't let her go back to those docks."

Cardozo nodded. "I know."

"What are you going to do about her?"

"I'm thinking about that."

"I found something in Sandy's mouth."

It was as though a knot had been yanked tight in Cardozo's stomach. "The wafer? Finally?"

It was Dan's turn to nod. "She doesn't know it, but she's probably been in contact with the killer. And she's come damned close to winding up the same as her boyfriend. Put her someplace safe, Vince. She's not going to stay lucky."

"Who's the *s* that did those things to you?" Cardozo asked.

"I never saw him before," Nell said. "Eff set it up for me. I called him 'sir.' "

They were alone in the elevator, riding up to ground level.

"What did he look like?"

She had to think for a moment. "He was heavy . . . in his fifties . . . losing his hair."

"What color eyes?"

"I think he was wearing glasses. I only saw him that once. It was an Omaha scene. You're supposed to be new—you can't play it twice with the same john. I was pretty fogged out. He gave me a pill."

"What kind of pill?"

"Pink." She shook her head. "It sent me to Jupiter. I wish I had one of those pills now."

The elevator shuddered to a stop and the door slammed open.

"Hey," she said.

"What?"

"Thank you."

"Come on." He took her arm. A man was mopping the marble floor, and Cardozo guided her around the slippery area. The glass doors to First Avenue opened automatically at their approach. Night hit like a hot washcloth.

He'd parked the Honda beside a hydrant. A heavyset woman in

slacks was leaning on one of his fenders. She saw him and waved. "Vince! Thank God!"

The voice was unmistakable. His sister Jill. He felt a thick, dull pain like a toothache throughout his body.

"I had to track you down through the precinct." She'd tied her hair in a bandanna, but strands of pale brown were waving free. She kissed him and hair got tangled in the kiss.

"Jill, this is Nell. Nell, my sister Jill." He unlocked the passenger door. "What's the emergency?"

"I ran out of my prescription." She was wearing an enormous amount of makeup, and her face seemed to be trying to sweat it off. "The drugstore says I've used up my refills." She turned to explain to Nell. "If I don't have my prescription, I can't function, I can't sleep."

Cardozo sensed more than a touch of vodka in the white water rush of words.

"Vince, you've got to help me."

"Sure, but just let me handle one thing at a time. Nell was first."

"That's okay." Nell shrugged. "I'm not in any rush to get anywhere."

The druggist tilted the pill bottle into a cone of halogen light. "Sorry." He had a Chinese face and an American accent. "No way."

"They're for my sister." Cardozo handed his ID across the counter. "She puts a lot of faith in them, and she's run out."

"I'd like to help you." The druggist shook his shaved head. "But the law's very tough on these substances."

Cardozo lowered his voice. "You must have some kind of placebo pills—couldn't you just make up a fresh bottle, put a fake label on it?"

The expression of refusal melted into a smile. "It'll take me a couple of minutes."

Cardozo turned and looked across the all-night drugstore. Syrupy Muzak and pale chalky light drifted down from a honeycomb ceiling. Beyond the piled skyline of cosmetic and diet pill displays, Jill stood chatting with Nell, twirling a carousel rack of jokey greeting cards. They seemed to be getting along.

The druggist tapped a counter bell. "Okay, Officer."

"What do I owe you?"

"Forget it. On the house."

When Cardozo gave Jill the pills, she squinted at the label. "What are these?" Her face had a suspicious, childlike look.

"They're the generic. He says they're even better."

"Good." She dropped them into her purse. "I'll get a night's sleep."

Now she walked like a maharani, ruler of her own space. Cardozo held the door for the ladies.

Night was a growling gray shimmer over Second Avenue. When they reached his car, the radio was sputtering. He lifted the mike. "Cardozo."

"Just got a call from Staten Island." It was Greg Monteleone, patching in from the precinct. "A taxi driver picked up two kids at the ferry around 8:45 P.M. yesterday. Male teenagers. One was dark-haired, one was blond. He took them to Hylan Boulevard in Dongan Hills."

"What's there?"

"A church."

Cardozo slipped the mike back into its holder. He sat with the motor idling. "Problem."

"I'm listening," Jill said.

"I have to get going."

"What's the problem?"

"Nell needs a bed for the night."

Nell flicked him a defensive, chin-down look. "Is that so?"

"Yes," he said. "That's so."

"No problem." Jill's voice bubbled with an almost panicky good cheer. "Nell can stay with me. She can have Sally's room."

The driver brought his cab to a smooth halt. "I left them right here."

Cardozo stared out the window at a Mobil automated filling station, flood-lit like the Berlin Wall. He wondered if this could really be the place. "You're sure you brought them here?"

"Right. Two lowlife kids. One of them told me my English stank. That'll be four dollars."

Cardozo gave him five dollars and stepped out. He looked up

and down the darkened street. "Isn't there a church around here?"

The driver pointed. "Through the alley."

Cardozo didn't see the alley till he was five steps away. Two stores just beyond the filling station had been boarded up. A sign in one of the windows still advertised pet food.

A narrow cobbled lane ran between the stores. Beyond a neat row of garbage cans, a naked lightbulb burned above three wooden steps.

Cardozo climbed to the screened-in porch. He sidestepped a saucer of half-eaten cat food and pushed the buzzer. It was two minutes before a thin man with a mane of graying blond hair opened the door.

"Yes?" He was in shirtsleeves and wearing a clerical collar.

"I'm sorry to disturb you at this hour, Father." Cardozo showed his ID. "Vince Cardozo, Twenty-second Precinct."

"Where's that?"

"Manhattan."

"You're a little way off your beat, aren't you? I'm Father Henry Shea—rector of Redeemer."

"Could I trouble you for a little information?"

Father Shea had curiously bright gray eyes. "Certainly. What can I tell you?"

"Did two young men come to the church or the parish house the night before last?"

Father Shea didn't answer.

"Around nine?"

"Maybe you'd better come in."

It was a pleasant old kitchen, roomy and high-ceilinged, with wooden cabinets and an old-fashioned eight-burner gas range.

"The night before last was my mother's eightieth birthday. I was in Brooklyn celebrating with my family."

"Was anyone in the church or rectory?"

"The sexton was in the church."

An odd inflection caught Cardozo's ear. "Could I speak with the sexton?"

"I'm afraid not." Father Shea dipped two fingers into his shirt pocket and pulled out a packet of Marlboros. "I had to discharge him."

"Where he's gone?"

"I don't know." The tone of voice added, *And I don't want to know*. Father Shea offered a cigarette.

Cardozo shook his head. "When did you discharge him?"

"Yesterday."

Cardozo ran the chronology through his mind. "Could I ask why?"

It was obvious that Father Shea was uncomfortable talking about it. He lit a cigarette, drawing in a long pull. "He impersonated a priest."

"He pretended to be you?"

Father Shea exhaled. The smoke curled in every direction. "I don't know if he was pretending to be anyone in particular, but he put on my vestments and he celebrated Mass."

"When did he do this?"

"The night before last, while he had the church to himself."

"Did he give communion to anyone?"

Father Shea seemed surprised at the question. "Naturally. Communion *is* the Mass."

"Do you have evidence?"

"Evidence?"

"That your sexton gave communion two nights ago."

"Yes, indeed. There was clear evidence."

"Could I see it?"

SIXTY-SIX

At noon the following day, Father Henry stood watching the crime-scene team work. Uneasiness was obvious in his face.

"I'm sorry this is taking so long," Cardozo said. After three hours, technicians were still exploring the sanctuary of Redeemer, hunting down prints, hairs, skin particles, perspiration, saliva.

"It can't be helped," Father Henry said. "You're only doing

your work. If I'd done mine half as carefully, none of this would be necessary."

The church had become borderline hot and very soon it would be stifling. The windows were shut and the air-conditioning had not been turned on. Movement of the air had to be kept to a minimum so as not to disturb easily airborne evidence. Human skin prints lost their viscosity within seventy-two hours at room temperature, and cooling of any sort hastened the process. Without viscosity, the prints could not be made to fluoresce.

"This wasn't the first time he served communion," Father Henry said.

"When was the first time?"

"Last April. The nineteenth. I overlooked it."

"Why?"

"He's a veteran. He'd been hurt. Mentally hurt." Father Henry drummed the earpieces of his glasses against his wrist. "When I hired him I had no idea how deeply disturbed he was."

"Didn't the diocese have records?"

"Not on sextons—they're not ordained. And I didn't have time to check him out. It was an emergency situation. The church where he'd been working was in terrible upheaval. Draper had cracked once before, in the army, and it looked as though he was going to crack again. I detest the way our country has treated our veterans and I wanted to make some small sort of amends. I thought if he were moved to a less pressured environment, like Redeemer, he'd settle down again."

Two men and a woman moved abreast down the aisle. Father Henry stepped aside to let them pass. One was brushing the armrests of the pews with carbon powder. Another was aiming a high-intensity light. The third was handling a camera.

Another trio was examining the altar with the aid of a mercury laser. The beam of eerily pure white light caught minute deposits left by human contact and excited them to fluorescence. The oils in fingerprints showed purple. Saliva stains on the rim of the chalice showed rust. Wine residue showed blue, like bruises.

"What was the emergency at the previous church?" Cardozo said.

"The priest had been murdered. There'd been a nasty investigation and all sorts of innuendo."

"What's the name of the church?"

"St. Veronica's—over in Queens."

"Father Chuck's place?"

"That's right." Father Henry looked at him in wariness and surprise. "Did you know him?"

"He served with the American forces in Panama. I don't know exactly what happened there, but he came back suffering severe posttraumatic stress syndrome." Father Gus Monahan's expression was solemn. He was dressed in casually scruffy jeans and a priest's shirtfront. "Somehow he'd turned into a sort of pathetic church groupie. He wanted to be a priest and save the world. Failing that, he wanted some kind of work in a church. So Father Chuck took him on as sexton. In a way, Father Chuck adopted Draper."

"What exactly do you mean," Cardozo said, "adopted him?"

It was two-thirty in the afternoon. They were sitting in the scuffed leather chairs in St. Veronica's rectory.

"Took care of him—looked out for him—monitored his drinking—held his hand when he needed hand-holding—scolded him when he needed scolding—saw to it that he shaved and bathed. Generally steered him clear of trouble."

"It sounds as though Draper was a baby."

"Call him a child. Draper was highly dependent on Father Chuck for protection and guidance. And of course, when Chuck was murdered, Draper went to pieces. By the time I took over, his drinking and drugging were out of control. Frankly, and I wouldn't say this to anyone but an officer of the law, he'd become delusionary."

"What sort of delusions?"

"He'd wear a clerical collar—present himself to strangers as a priest." Father Gus seemed perfectly relaxed discussing his former sexton, except for his left foot. His legs were crossed, and the foot kept moving in a tight circle. He was wearing baby-blue socks and down-at-heel moccasins. They were obviously his comfy at-home shoes. "I even suspected Draper of using my vestments from time to time."

"What made you suspect that?"

"I found them rearranged in the closet."

"What reason would he have had to wear your vestments?"

"It could have been a dressing-up thing. Or it could have been more serious. He could have been celebrating Mass, right here in the church."

"Did you ever find any evidence of that?"

"Once or twice it seemed there were fewer consecrated wafers in the pyx than I remembered. And a chalice seemed to have been taken out and used. But there was never anything I could be positive of."

"When did this happen?"

"When I went away."

"How often was that?"

"I took a week's vacation every year. Other priests came in to celebrate Mass, but from sundown to sunrise the church was Draper's."

"And how often did Father Romero leave him in charge?"

"Father Chuck never took a vacation—but he did travel to church conventions."

"I don't suppose you'd have the dates of those conventions."

"The church bulletins would list them—if you have the time, I can look. They're in my office."

Father Gus's office, on the other side of the rectory, housed an IBM personal computer, a laser printer, and floor-to-ceiling bookcases. The shades were drawn and the air smelled of pipe tobacco and coffee simmered too long in a coffeemaker. Cardozo had the feeling that this was Father Gus's cave.

While Father Gus went through a stack of monthly bulletins, Cardozo studied the crayon drawings by children of the parish that decorated the walls.

In seven minutes Father Gus had the information. "Three years ago, Father Chuck was a delegate to the San Francisco convention from November seventh to November fourteenth. The following year he was a delegate to Lima from January twelfth to January twenty-second; and to New Orleans from March third to March seventeenth."

Cardozo jotted down the dates in his notebook.

"This is sad." Father Gus had come across a letter tucked inside one of the newsletters. "From Draper. I'd forgotten how unhappy he was after he left us." He handed Cardozo the handwritten note.

> Dear Father,
> I am not like you. I have become a loner—such a flop. I feel that God has forgotten me. If only I could do something splendid for God. How I yearn to risk my soul—lose it even—to serve His glory.
>
> Your friend,
> Collie

"He calls himself Collie?" Cardozo said.

"That's his nickname. I think the children gave it to him."

"Could you describe him?"

"Here, I have a picture." Father Gus took a photograph down from the wall. It showed a church picnic in a park. "That's Draper." He pointed out a lean, dark-haired man carrying a very happy little girl piggyback.

Cardozo's heart skipped a half beat. He recognized Bonnie's friend Collie, the man who chauffeured her children. "Could I borrow your phone?"

"Of course." Father Gus pushed the phone across the desk.

Cardozo dialed Bonnie's number. Her machine answered. He waited for the beep. "It's Vince. I'm not at the precinct—I'll call back. This is urgent. Make sure your kids are with your husband or with you—no one else. Do you understand? No one else."

When he hung up, Father Gus was watching him with a troubled expression.

"May I borrow that letter?" Cardozo said.

The precinct was screaming like a car alarm, so Cardozo shut the door of his cubicle. He brought the arm of the lamp down low to the desk and began comparing the dates of Father Chuck's absences with the time ranges that the M.E. had fixed for the murders.

The phone gave its I'm-about-to-ring-and-knock-your-ears-off rattle. "Cardozo."

"Sandy McCoy's clothes are saturated in the same incense as the other victims' clothes." It was Lou Stein over at the lab.

"Again, there are bits of generic acrylic gray shag carpet sticking to them, and again it means absolutely nothing."

"Except that it's the fifth time. What about the hamper?"

"Styrobasket, as usual. Same model as the other bodies were found in."

The light on the other line was blinking. "Thanks, Lou." Cardozo punched the button. "Cardozo."

"For the first time," Dan Hippolito said, "the victim's fresh enough for the wine to show up in the stomach."

"So he had communion?"

"Possibly twice. There were fragments of a second wafer lodged behind a molar."

"What caused death?"

"So far it's a toss-up. Asphyxiation due to C.N.S. shutdown due to overingestion of azidofluoramine, or massive blood loss due to severing of four major arteries with an electric saw. He had barely two quarts left in him. Hands were secured at some point with leather belts. Signs of beating within the last ten days and burning with dripped candle wax. Plus there's an injection mark on the inner left forearm, trace cocaine residue on injection mark. Plenty of alcohol and cocaine in the bloodstream."

"Same killer."

"You're the detective."

"I say it's the same."

"I'm with you."

Cardozo returned to his two lists of dates. The matches kept leaping off the pages.

"You shouldn't read in that light."

He hadn't heard the door open.

"You're going to ruin your eyes." Ellie stood watching him from the doorway. "You could buy yourself a new fluorescent bulb from the hardware shop and invoice the department. I could do it for you."

It was almost a minute before Cardozo pushed back from the desk, satisfied. "Father Chuck was away from his church when Richie Vegas was murdered. St. Veronica's was in the care of his sexton, Colin Draper. Ditto when Wally Wills was killed. Ditto when Wanda Gilmartin was killed. Colin Draper had the window of opportunity."

"In that case, you'll be interested in the preliminary crime scene results." Ellie handed him a slick sheet of faxed interdepartmental paper. "They've put Sandy at Church of the Redeemer an hour before his death."

Cardozo lifted the phone. Ellie watched him dial Bonnie's number.

This time Bonnie answered. "What do you mean, my kids could be in danger?"

"Where are they now?"

"With their father."

"Tell him to keep them there. And don't let Colin Draper get anywhere near them."

"But why?"

"I'll explain. I'm coming right up."

SIXTY-SEVEN

"**W**here can I find Colin Draper?" Cardozo said.

"He works at the Church of the Redeemer." Bonnie stood in profile beside her desk, slender in ice-blue. "On Staten Island."

"Is that your most recent address for him?"

"Yes."

"When did you last see him?"

The purring air conditioner created a climate like the air in a cave behind a waterfall. The blinds had been angled against the sun-dazzled day and the soft light of the desk lamp lit her from the side.

"I saw him last week when he brought my children over."

"When are you planning to see him next?"

"Next week when he brings the children here." She turned. "Unless there's a change in plans."

"When did you last speak to him on the phone?"

"Maybe two days ago. Maybe three. I forget."

"Did he mention anything out of the ordinary—any travel plans?"

She shook her head.

"Was anything bothering him? Did he sound odd—under pressure?"

"No more so than usual—Collie always sounds a little odd and a little pressured." There was a grace note of irony in the intonation. "You're awfully interested in Collie."

For a moment Cardozo did not speak. He felt like a man about to jump from an airplane, uncertain if the parachute would open. "Would you mind telling me exactly how long you've known this man, how you met him, what you know about him?"

A shadow slipped across her face. "We met when we were children. It was up in Mount Kisco, at a church-sponsored day camp run by Trappists. He played the organ. I was very impressed by him." She sat in the easy chair facing Cardozo. "I suppose it was a childhood crush. It never came to anything. We were like brother and sister. We confided everything to one another. I told him my problems, he told me his."

Something dreamy flitted through her eyes. She smiled. Only a half smile, but it was for her friend Colin, and it wounded Cardozo.

He knew some detachment was necessary. He was doing his best to detach and it wasn't working.

"Of course," she said, "he always had more problems than I did."

"What kind of problems?"

"Awful things. Life never quite seemed to work out for him."

"Why not?"

A kind of caution was stealing into her eyes. "Maybe because he got a rotten start. Maybe because he came out of a classic American dysfunctional family. His mother was an alcoholic and his father abandoned them when Colin was five. Anything he's achieved in life he's had to fight for."

"Is he unbalanced?"

She glanced across at him. In that split instant he could feel her alarm, hanging solid and tangible in the air between them. "Do you think I'd trust my children to him if there was the slightest question?"

"He wrote a letter to Father Gus." Cardozo handed her the letter.

She read it carefully. He could feel her trying to puzzle something out.

"Your friend Colin says he's willing to risk his soul or even lose it for God's sake."

Her eyes came up. "What's so odd about that?"

"Eff has been playing go-between in the communion killings." Cardozo kept his voice cool, measured, explanatory. "He collected the victims and led them to a man dressed as a priest. This man performed a sort of Mass—and then killed the kids."

She blinked and missed a beat. "And what does Collie's letter have to do with any of that?"

"The letter could mean that in some twisted way Colin Draper thinks that killing these kids is helping God."

She sat perfectly still, then she took in a breath and sprang to her feet. "No. That's not possible. Collie couldn't be doing those things. I *know* him. My *children* know him."

She strode to the bookcase. Then to the window. Just moving. No apparent purpose.

"You're misreading the letter. It could mean a dozen things."

"He's helping God."

She whirled. "God doesn't *need* anything, least of all help. You're not a trained theologian. Collie is. He wouldn't attribute deficits to an infinite, omnipotent being."

Cardozo wondered about Bonnie Ruskay. She had the intelligence to dissect a dot and yet she wouldn't let herself see that the undissected dots made up a picture.

"Have you heard from Father Joe?" he said.

"Since I last spoke with you? No."

"Aren't you worried?"

"I always worry about Joe." Her tone was just a bit too suddenly conversational.

"And is your van back?"

"It's back." She smiled and he couldn't quite make himself believe the smile. "Do you want me to show you?"

"When did it come back?"

"I don't know—the driver has a key to the garage."

"Who was driving it?"

She shrugged. "The Meals-on-Wheels drivers vary."

"You don't seem too curious about who's in and out of this building."

"Not as curious as you. I'm used to chaos."

Cardozo stood. For now, he had said all that he had to say to her. "Would you let me know if Colin contacts you?"

"All right."

"And if you leave the rectory, would you advise my office where you're going—or put your calls on call-forward?"

"Am I under your protection or your surveillance?"

"Let's just keep you safe and alive."

"You're wrong, you know. About Collie. He's a sweet, spiritual man."

"I know how fond you are of him. I'd love to be wrong."

After she'd let Cardozo out of the rectory, Bonnie hurried back to her office and phoned Collie at the Church of the Redeemer. After too many rings, a man told her that Collie was not there.

"Where is he?"

"Gone."

She recognized Father Henry's voice, but decided not to identify herself.

"Where can I get in touch with him? It's urgent."

"I have no idea." Father Henry sounded cold, angry. "He didn't leave a forwarding address."

Bonnie broke the connection. For a moment she had trouble drawing a full breath. She looked up a number in the directory and tapped seven digits into the phone. Three rings. Her fingers played with the phone cord.

"Pierre Strauss." A woman's voice.

"May I speak with him please? It's Reverend Bonnie Ruskay. Urgent."

She waited, fidgeting, staring out the window at sunlight streaking through the pear tree.

"Tell me you're not prosecuting my client," Pierre Strauss growled. "Please."

"I have an offer. I won't press the rape charge against Eff. In exchange, he has to meet me face-to-face. It can be alone. There

394 E D W A R D   S T E W A R T

don't have to be lawyers or police. He can pick the time and place."

"What do you want this meeting for?"

"I need the answers to some questions."

"What questions?"

"I can't tell you. But he knows."

Pierre Strauss sighed. "I'll have to get back to you."

The rectory door slammed with the sound of a cannon shot. A flight of pigeons stampeded into the sky.

Halfway down the block, behind the wheel of his double-parked Honda, Cardozo saw Bonnie Ruskay dash into the street. He started his motor.

Bonnie flung out an arm. A taxi screeched to a stop. She leapt in and the taxi took off.

Cardozo slammed his engine into gear and wheeled into traffic after her.

The taxi let her off on Broadway, south of Houston. The block was peppered with empty storefronts and FOR RENT signs and boarded-up windows. The glitzy boutiques and galleries that had moved in during the Soho boom of the eighties had moved back out with the hard times of the nineties.

Bonnie paid her cab and hurried into 474. It was a run-down loft building and several of the floors had wood planks nailed across the windows.

Cardozo double-parked and propped his placard in the wind-shield. He crossed the street and entered the tiny vestibule. Flyers and messages had been stickered to the wall: a Chinese take-out menu; a hand-scrawled *Mamie—will be back 5 P.M.—L.*; a typed plea to *Please keep the street door locked after 8 P.M. There have been incidents in the vestibule.*

The old-fashioned dial indicator over the elevator was pointing to *8*. He studied the building's directory.

There were ten floors and ten tenants. Most of the tenants had weirdly spaced gaps that made their names unpronounceable. Letters had obviously fallen off the board. The name ERBRO, however, was centered very neatly beside the numeral *8*.

* * *

"How's Beverly adjusting to your new work shift?" Cardozo asked. It was 9:30 P.M. and he was sitting in the cubicle that was Esther Epstein's office at the V.A. hospital.

"I can't say she's in love with these hours." Mrs. Epstein treated her moody Angora cat like a surrogate daughter, and the fastest way into her graces was to ask about Beverly. "But a job's a job, and in this economy, at my age, I'm lucky to have one."

"Esther, I need some information. Could you to look up the army record of a man called Colin Draper for me?" He spelled the name.

Her large, dark eyes examined him. "This is official?"

"It's official."

"Because we can't give out information for personal reasons."

"I don't personally know the man."

She flattened the front of her white cotton blouse and sat there. He was aware of a fierce, pushy decency in her; aware, too, that he was going to have to guilt-trip her.

"Do I need a court order to ask a favor from my own next-door neighbor?"

"Save your court order, I'm not a criminal." She sighed. "At least not yet." She stuck her head out of the cubicle and peered up and down the gray-carpeted corridor. Her hands tapped instructions into the keyboard. Little blips of light flashed and a column of amber print crawled up the screen. "Colin Draper served with the 32nd infantry in Panama."

"What rank?"

"He was a Catholic chaplain."

Cardozo frowned. "He was ordained?"

"Of course he was ordained, how else do you think he could have been a chaplain?"

Cardozo could recognize a fact when he was staring into an I.B.M. monitor at one. "What kind of discharge did they give him?"

The screen jump-cut to a new page of print.

"I shouldn't be telling anyone this without a court order. If you weren't a cop—"

"But I am a cop, Esther."

"Colin Draper was given a medical discharge. He had a psychotic break. He's still getting medication—Thorazine, fluorizan, methamphetamine, zilboacin . . ."

She stopped. The cursor flickered restlessly at the bottom of the screen. She frowned. "Your friend missed his last appointment. That was over a week ago."

"Colin Draper is not a friend of mine."

"Seems funny." She was shaking her head. "He couldn't get along without his medication. Maybe something's happened to him?"

"Could he be getting it under another name?"

"Possibly."

"See if you have anyone called Erbro in there." He spelled it.

She shook her head again. "No *Erbro* listed."

He ran it through his mind. "How often are these files updated?"

"This one's updated every time he comes in for medication."

"The minute he comes in—the minute he shows up on this computer—would you let me know?"

She gave him a tight-mouthed stare.

"I'll visit Beverly every night while you're out. I'll play with her."

"She likes being read to."

Cardozo kissed her. "Esther, I love you. And can you get me his fingerprints?"

SIXTY-EIGHT

"It's getting harder and harder to spring you," Pierre Strauss said as he and Jaycee Wheeler came down the concrete steps of the Lower Manhattan House of Detention. Police sirens and Con Ed drills jammed the air. "This last escapade cost two thousand cash."

Jaycee looked up at a sky swirling with pigeons. She rubbed her wrists. They were still swollen. "We'll sue them. They made me wear handcuffs even when I went to the john. The heteros didn't wear cuffs."

He shook his head.

"I'm serious. That's discrimination. *You* try wiping your ass with handcuffs on."

"I'm sure I'll get a chance one of these days. Can I give you a lift?"

"Sure."

Inside the cooled cavern of Pierre Strauss's Porsche he asked, "Where can I drop you?"

"St. Pat's."

"Christ, Jaycee—not again." The red light changed and he eased the blue Porsche across Canal.

"We're not going to ease up on the cardinal till he eases up on us."

Pierre Strauss didn't answer. He had never yet won an argument with Jaycee. That was why he liked her and that was why he bailed her out with his own firm's petty cash.

She was staring out the tinted glass at shop windows along Bowery. "Where do you suppose I can get a jar of dog piss?"

"I doubt the ASPCA sells it."

"Think anyone would know the difference if I used green Gatorade?"

A little after 6 P.M. that evening, Barry Ignatius Cardinal Fitzwilliam mounted to the pulpit of St. Patrick's Cathedral to read the lesson.

Turnout was small. There were no more than two hundred souls spread out in a space that was built to hold three thousand. Then the shouting began.

What most surprised the cardinal about the interruption was the sheer volume. There seemed to be thousands of protesters.

Yet, when he raised his eyes from the Bible and peered over his reading glasses, he saw only a dozen or so, scattered through the pews. Anger was burning and ugly in their faces. They raised bell jars of urine-colored liquid into the air. They began dropping communion wafers into the jars.

The cardinal felt shock and a sadness that went to the bone.

He watched plainclothes policemen and policewomen close in

to arrest the demonstrators. Over half tonight's congregation, he realized, were cops on duty.

He had to wonder: *Doesn't anyone come here to worship anymore?*

"I've heard from Father Damien again." Jonquil let a tease sneak into her drawl. "He wants to see me—badly."

"Are you going to see him?" Cardozo's voice asked.

"That depends." Jonquil stooped to check her reflection in the steel rectangle of the coin return. She adjusted the angle of her newly washed and spin-dried blond hair. "Are you still interested in meeting with him?"

"Very much so."

"If I set it up, what do I get—besides your eternal gratitude?"

"What do you want?"

"How about easing my parole so I'm free to leave town legally."

"I might be able to swing it."

"And—there's an *and*—how does a thousand dollars sound? We're talking cash, okay?"

"What's your phone number?"

"The George Washington is not that kind of hotel. I'll phone you in about an hour."

Jonquil placed the receiver back on the hook. She waited for the muffled clunk of the quarter dropping, then carefully worked the cylinder of paper napkin out of the coin-return slot. Her quarter was stuck to the Vaseline-coated tip.

Across the lobby, the desk clerk looked up from his falling-apart copy of the *Paris Review*. Under arched eyebrows, he shot Jonquil a mildly reprimanding glance. She slipped the napkin and the quarter into her change purse and blew him a kiss.

Her movements were swift now and resolved. She stepped into the elevator and pushed *5*. She let herself back into her room.

"Everything. The asphalt. The steel. The behavior." Father was still carrying on his half of the conversation.

"Sugar, you're so right." With a neat curtsying dip, Jonquil retrieved his glass from the floor. He had slouched so far down in the armchair that his ass was practically parked on the rug.

"Too much decay in this city."

"Mmm-hmm. Say that again." She dropped ice cubes into his glass and hers. She topped hers with iced tea and his with rum. Father had brought the bottle. He always brought the bottle. There was barely half an inch left in the bottom.

She held the glasses up to the light to be sure the colors matched. Father hated to drink alone.

"Too many people have fallen away from God." He tilted his head back and stared toward the elephant-shaped crack in the ceiling. "Fallen away from the sacraments."

"That's the trouble, mmm-hmm." She arranged mint sprigs between the ice cubes. Each glass got a lemon wedge neatly bisected on the rim. She crossed the room and placed his glass firmly in his hand.

"The sacraments could save this city." Father lifted his rum through a slant of lamplight and took two long, gulping swallows. "Communion and confession could turn New York around."

"Speaking of confession . . ." Jonquil arranged herself at Father's feet, her legs out to the side. "There's this cop that's been on my conscience. Vincent Cardozo?"

Father was silent for a moment. And for another.

"He's asking me a lot of questions about you."

A flick of Father's eyes held her. "About me?"

"About you, Daddy."

"Did you tell him what he wanted to know?"

"He thinks I did." Jonquil raised a manicured hand. The tip of her forefinger stroked the softening line of Father's jaw. "I pulled a little of the old wool over his eyes."

"You're good at that." Father diddled his fingers through the curls of her wig. "Awfully good."

"It's no trick. When a man likes you, he wants to believe you. He almost *has* to believe you." Jonquil sighed. "But my conscience hurts something awful."

"Why's that?"

"It's bad karma to lie. Maybe I should tell him the truth."

She gave Father's mind a moment to edge toward comprehension.

"Unless . . . unless you have some way of persuading me not to?"

Father's eyes locked on to hers. Suddenly they were icy and sober. "How could I persuade you"—he burped softly—"persuade you not to?"

Jonquil forced a dry swallow down the constricting column of her throat. God, how she hated moments of truth! "Maybe you could advance me a couple thousand?" She pressed Father's hand to the beating skin of her breast implant. "For services—to be rendered?"

"You're going to have to account for this money, you know." Captain Tom O'Reilly counted out twenty-five twenties on his desk top. Beside them he counted out ten fifties.

"I appreciate this," Cardozo said.

"You'll need something to carry it in." O'Reilly handed him a precinct business envelope. "I hope you do know what you're doing. Because your story's all over the place. Listening to you makes me feel I've been shot in the head."

Cardozo stuffed the bills into the envelope. They were old currency, wrinkled and faded and soft as laundered cotton. "You haven't been shot in the head, sir."

Cardozo returned to his cubicle. He phoned the George Washington Hotel and asked to speak to Jonquil.

"Sorry," the desk clerk said, "there are no phones in the rooms."

"Could I trouble you to go up and knock?"

"I can't leave the desk. Anyway, she's got a priest with her."

A starter's pistol went off in Cardozo's chest. "Don't let that priest leave."

"And who the hell are you?"

"My name's Cardozo. I'm a cop. I'm coming down there right now."

Cardozo grabbed his jacket. He was halfway out of the cubicle when he remembered the envelope of money. He dashed back and retrieved it.

He was halfway out of the squadroom when a phone began ringing.

"Vince," Ellie called. "Your phone."

"Take the message," he shouted.

Ellie exhaled slowly and walked into Cardozo's cubicle. The

desk looked as though a typhoon had passed over it. She lifted the receiver.

"I'm sorry, Lieutenant Cardozo isn't in the precinct at the moment. This is Detective Ellie Siegel—could I take a message?"

There was a hesitation and then a voice spoke with a nervous Irish brogue. "Could you tell him Mrs. Olga Quigley phoned?"

"With reference to what, Mrs. Quigley?"

"I used to clean house for Father Joe Montgomery and there's something I ought to tell Lieutenant Cardozo."

"I'm working on that case too. Could we talk about it?"

SIXTY-NINE

Cardozo knocked on the door to Jonquil's room.

No answer.

He tried the handle. It turned with a click and the door opened. He knew right away the dark was hiding something.

An Ice-T rap number pounded through the wall. Lemon-scented room deodorizer and patchouli cologne and peppermint breath-freshener layered the air in densities that would have asphyxiated a woolly mammoth. The shut window sealed in a temperature that must have reached ninety degrees.

He found the light switch beside the door. There was only one soft light, a lamp on the bureau with a scarf thrown over the shade.

It took him a moment to see Jonquil staring at him from the shadow. Her gaze was flat, empty. Part of her was on the chair, but most of her had spilled forward onto the floor. Blood had pooled in an oval around her knees.

In her nakedness she was a startling sight. At least she startled Cardozo. She had breasts too perfect to be nature's, and a penis, and a head of close-cropped hair that had gone a grandmotherly gray. He saw two stab wounds, one in the heart and one in the stomach.

He felt for a pulse. There was none in the wrist, none in the carotid in the neck. He found her room key on the bureau next to the spilled cologne. He locked the door and tore into the corridor.

The elevator was waiting and he thought it might be faster than the stairs. He didn't count on the woman who got in on the second floor with two squabbling children. It took three minutes to reach the lobby.

The desk clerk was glugging a Rolling Rock while he watched a commercial on a black-and-white Sony Watchman.

"You let Jonquil's visitor leave," Cardozo said. "I asked you not to."

The clerk thunked his bottle down. "There are three street doors to this hotel and I got one pair of eyes."

A very bloodshot pair of eyes, Cardozo noted. "Too bad for your hotel. He killed her."

"Shit."

"I need to use your phone."

Concentrating like watchmakers, the crime-scene crew performed their joyless ceremony. The still camera flashed; the videocam purred. The woman with the measuring tape measured distances and made notations on a crime-scene sketch. The man with the black powder dusted surfaces for prints.

Cardozo searched the bureau drawers, sifting through panty hose. "She wore an ivory cameo ring," he said. "I don't see it. So all of you keep an eye out."

His hand struck the edge of something solid. Three small leather-bound date books had been fastened together with rubber bands. He snapped the bands off and leafed through. The entries appeared to be straightforward listings of daily engagements.

"Now, what do you suppose that is?" The man from the medical examiner's office was shining a flashlight into Jonquil's mouth.

"Looks like a cocktail cracker. Maybe matzo."

Cardozo could see something white and paperlike lying on her tongue.

The tape woman came across the room and looked. "Communion wafer."

"How can you tell?" the medical man said.

"The shape. Priests break wafers into quarters—don't ask me why."

"My priest doesn't." The print man was using an atomizer to pump powder around an ashtray. "We get a whole wafer each."

"Pays to go to a rich church," the tape woman said.

Cardozo closed the door to his cubicle and sat at the desk and studied Jonquil's date books. They went back three years.

He sensed a cloud of whispers hovering over the pages, whispers he was only half hearing. There were errands to run, appointments to keep, part-time jobs, one-shot gigs. There was pain and solitude and at the same time a determination not to be crushed.

Back rent to pay, bill collectors to dodge. Doctors to consult, clients to service. A savings account, now totaling ninety-two hundred dollars, every deposit meticulously noted down to the cent.

She had listed the clients by first name—Bob, Tom, Jack, Abdul. Except for one—Wzn. Rzm. Mr. Rzm. showed up three times in the current year, and one of those was 4 P.M. today. Rzm. appeared to be the last person to see her alive.

And possibly the first to see her dead.

Time ticked by, and Cardozo became aware of a faint throbbing in his stomach and a not-so-faint throbbing in his head. He went to the men's room, dampened a paper towel in cold running water, and held the cool compress to his forehead for a slow count of ten.

He stared at himself in the mirror. He saw eyes like a beagle's and a lined forehead that looked as if Mother Nature had been doodling with a dull trowel.

Is this any way for the man in charge to look? Or feel?

He drummed his fingers on the edge of the sink, trying to empty his mind for just a moment of all the thoughts and questions that were giving it cramps. An idea came suddenly to him—a kind of double exposure inside his head. He saw a transparent calendar laid over an opaque one. Two sets of entries lined up. And then it hit him in the brain.

He tried to walk, not run, to his cubicle. He cleared desk space with a sweep of his forearm. He laid the list of runaways' known or estimated death dates next to Jonquil's date book.

He began with the most recent, Sandy McCoy. The date was known. May twelfth.

He turned to May twelfth in the date book. His finger moved down the page.

10 A.M.: Walk Sheba's dog.

1 P.M.: Audition for Club 82 sex show.

He skimmed to the bottom. No Mr. Wzn. Rzm. He turned the page.

10 A.M.: Walk Sheba's dog.

And there it was: *1 P.M.: Wzn. Rzm.—lunch/matinee.*

The death just prior to Sandy was Tod Lomax. Approximate date, first week in March. He flipped back in the date book to March first.

Walk Sheba's dog, but no Wzn. Rzm.

March second. No Wzn. Rzm. there either.

It was not until March tenth that he found *8 P.M.—Wzn. Rzm.—supper plus all-nightathon!*

Gilmartin's approximate death date: February or March of two years ago. In the date book on March twelfth: *1 P.M.—Wzn. Rzm.—matinee.*

Wills's approximate death date: January or February of two years ago. In the date book on January nineteenth: *1 P.M.—Wzn. Rzm.—matinee.*

Vegas's approximate death date: sometime between October and December of three years ago. In the date book on November fourth: *1 P.M.—Wzn. Rzm.—matinee.*

Cardozo sat tapping his ballpoint, wondering if it was a genuine pattern or just his coffee-fueled imagination imposing connections.

The phone jangled. He realized he hadn't heard the warning buzz. He snatched up the receiver. "Cardozo."

"Our young friend Sandy was hitting the drug smorgasbord," Dan Hippolito said. "His blood was loaded with alcohol, meth, Valium, crack, grass—and our old friend azidofluoramine."

Cardozo frowned. "What form does this drug come in?"

"It's a two-milligram pink pill."

"Nell says one of her johns gave her a pink pill. Says it sent her to Jupiter."

"The two-mil dose would send you at least to Jupiter."

"How would kids be getting this drug?"

"Possibly they all serviced the same john?"

"But where would he get it? You say there's not even a street analogue."

"The only thing I know of is the double-blind studies."

"Who are the doctors running those?"

"The FDA published the protocols yesterday. Let's see if I can access that on the computer. Okay, we've got Dr. Robles Milton in San Diego."

"Never heard of him."

"Join the club. We've got Dr. Randolph Blanca in Wichita."

"Never heard of him."

"It's a her."

Okay, Cardozo thought. *Randolph Blanca is a her.* "Anyone else?"

"One more. Right here in New York. Dr. Muller Vergil."

A ripple of electricity passed through the hairs on the back of Cardozo's neck. "Those names are reversed, right? The last name is listed first?"

"Right."

"So Muller Vergil is Vergil Muller."

"You say that like you know him."

"I sure do."

SEVENTY

"S he seems cheerful," Jill said, "but all she does is watch TV. I don't know if I should worry about her or be glad."

"Give yourself a break," Cardozo said. "Be glad."

There were changes in the apartment, little touches of tidiness that it took him a minute to put his finger on. No newspapers or clothing on the sofa. No coffee cups on the table. No drinking glasses anywhere. There was a new smell, too—pot roast—and he realized he hadn't smelled cooking in his sister's home since the predrink days before she'd started sending out for fast food.

"How's she eating?"

"Better than in the street."

"I'll bet you've put ten pounds on her."

"But she's still underweight." Jill looked away. Her hair was cut and neatly styled—no camouflage kerchief, no loose strands. He flashed that she was happy and embarrassed to show it.

"Go say hello." Jill gave him a push. "She's in Sally's room."

Nell Dunbar was sprawled like a pouting princess across the arms of a velvet-covered easy chair. She was wearing jeans and one of Sally's high school sweatshirts, lazily flicking channels with the remote.

Cardozo went and bent down to kiss her on the top of her head. "How's your new life?"

"The truth?"

"The truth."

"I miss getting high." A smile peeked through the tough-girl frown. "But I like having my own room and I love having my own TV."

"You and Jill getting along?"

"She's no trouble. I can handle her. Except I wish she'd get Home Box Office."

"Tell her to get it. Tell her it's your birthday." Cardozo lifted the remote out of Nell's hand. "Put on some shoes. You two need a change of scene. I'm taking you out."

On the dot of 6 P.M., Dr. Vergil Muller's spherical face came bobbing like a bespectacled buoy through the door of Delilah's pub. He saw Cardozo and smiled and pushed through the sea of loud, lubricated patrons.

"Lieutenant." He extended his hand. "What a pleasure. May I join you?"

"It's your regular table," Cardozo said. "I've joined you."

"In that case, be my guest." Muller dropped into a seat.

The hostess brought his martini—a double, straight up. He waved a finger at Cardozo's half-drunk diet Pepsi. "And another for my friend." He lifted his glass and clinked with Cardozo. "Health to us all."

"You're looking well," Cardozo said.

But Muller wasn't looking well: he was looking damp and red-faced, as though this was far from his first drink of the evening.

"Summer's truly the worst time." Muller daubed his forehead with a Delilah-embossed paper napkin. "Once that thermometer hits eighty-five, half the population of this town goes crazy."

Cardozo had put Nell and Jill at a table in the corner. Nell was making signals and he realized Muller had his back to her. She hadn't been able to get a clear look at his face. She stood up from her seat and began circling through the crowd behind him.

"Don't know how many evaluations I had to complete today." Muller shook his head glumly. "But I don't suppose summer's any picnic for you either."

"No season's a picnic," Cardozo said.

"Which is why I say, God bless happy hour." Muller took a long, savoring sip. "What brings you to this neck of the woods, Lieutenant? It couldn't be Delilah's vintage diet Pepsi."

"As a matter of fact, I happened to see your name in an FDA protocol."

"Really?" Muller looked surprised. "Don't tell me you have time to read those things."

"Not ordinarily, but azidofluoramine has been showing up in some of our homicides."

Muller fixed him with strangely blank eyes.

"Thought you might be able to help me."

"Gladly." Muller harpooned his olive on a toothpick and began nibbling. "But you have to realize that I only—"

"This is him." Nell stood beside Muller's chair, nodding. "I called him 'sir.' "

Muller looked around. He saw Nell and his martini went over. Understanding seemed to come in two punches—recognition of the girl, and then realization that she was with Cardozo. The second punch did it.

Muller sprang to his feet. The chair did a backward flip into a waitress. A tray of drinks catapulted into free fall and Muller began shoving toward the door.

Now Cardozo understood the wax on the victims' skin: Muller, not Damien. Eff had been supplying them both from the same pool of runaways.

By the time Cardozo pushed through the crowd to the sidewalk, twilight flowed through the street like a rising tide. His eye raked streams of homeward-bound office workers, cars parked legally and illegally at both curbs.

Muller stood at the intersection, fighting an old lady for a cab.

Cardozo went over and touched him on the elbow. "Come on. Be a gentleman."

"Don't do this to me," Muller begged.

"My car's down here." Cardozo guided him around the corner.

"It wasn't what you're thinking. It was research. They told me they were over twenty-one. They signed releases."

"Where would you be more comfortable talking?" Cardozo unlocked the passenger door. "Your place or the precinct?"

"Could I offer you something?" Muller said. "I'm going to make myself a martini."

"No, thanks." Cardozo looked around him. The decor of Vergil Muller's Fifth Avenue co-op was a glossy magazine's notion of an English lord's country home—all brocade and oriental antiques and broad inlaid tabletops and dark oil paintings of hunting parties and horses.

Muller went to a carved sideboard and fussed with bottles and ice and a crystal pitcher. The shelves behind him displayed bone china that looked as if it had been in someone's family since the Battle of Gettysburg.

He brought his martini glass around to the sofa, jittering like a nervous guest panelist on a TV talk show. "You're wondering how I happen to know Nell."

Cardozo nodded. "I'd be curious to hear your side of it."

"It goes back to a case that the district attorney called me in to consult on. A priest had been murdered. A juvenile by the name of Francis Huffington had been charged."

"Francis a.k.a. Eff."

Mueller smiled as though they had discovered a blood bond between them. "Then you know him."

"I know about him. I can't say I understand much."

"Eff has way-above-average intelligence, but he's a sociopath. He was never completely formed. Somewhere along the line, something was left out of him." Muller sank further into the sofa.

"Maybe the cause was genetic, maybe it was environmental. But he never learned to identify with other people—to feel their pain as his, their joy as his. He sees other living things as dead matter to be used and sold, punctured, burned—you name it. That's his problem."

"If it were only Eff's problem, I'd say let him have it. But it's also the problem of anyone unlucky enough to stand in his path."

"I take it then that you knew Father Romero?"

"I know a little about the case. I'd like to know more."

"It was my job to evaluate whether Eff was sane, and whether he was telling the truth."

"Was he?"

"Definitely sane."

"And telling the truth?"

"In my opinion, much of what he said . . . was truthful."

Muller looked away. Cardozo could see he was ashamed of this part of it.

"It came out—during the course of my examination of Eff— that he ran a sort of . . . employment agency. He provided young people to . . . customers who enjoyed that kind of thing. It so happens I'm doing research on juvenile prostitution. For the National Institutes of Health. The project is completely legitimate."

Muller had raised his voice and he seemed to realize it. His face flushed.

"Eff and I worked out an informal arrangement. He referred young people to me for my research—and in addition to paying his customary fee, I looked the other way when he stole azidofluoramine."

In other words, Cardozo translated, *you provided him with the drug and he provided it to half the runaways on the docks.* "And what kind of research did you do with these young people?"

"I interviewed them. We discussed the sorts of services they provided their clients."

"And did you ever ask them to demonstrate these services?"

"Once or twice—they volunteered." Muller set down his martini. "I've spent a lifetime researching human nature—yet there are still times I don't understand people, times when I don't understand the things they allow themselves to be put through."

"Do they always have a choice?"

"Yes. Always." Muller made a hollow of one hand and a ball of the other, and he socked the ball into the hollow. It was an angry, brutal, self-punishing movement. "And anyone who says otherwise is dipping deep into the well of psychobabble. Mind you, on the spectrum of paraphilia, what these young people allowed was barely middling-grade nastiness. Still, people progress to extremes. And often rapidly."

It bothered Cardozo that you could know as much about other people as Vergil Muller knew and still never take any responsibility for the truth about yourself. "How did Eff know which young people to send you?"

"He mailed me photographs and I returned the ones who looked—right for my research."

"Where did you return them?"

"To an address on Highland Road in the Bronx."

"Do you still have any of these photos?"

At nine-thirty sharp that evening, Ellie Siegel stepped into the Twenty-third Street Roy Rogers. About half the tables were taken, and six women were sitting alone, but none of them wore a yellow silk rose above her ear.

Ellie got herself a cup of coffee and was considering the hot apple pie when her conscience told her *absolutely not.* She took her coffee to a corner table where she could watch the door.

A woman who'd been sitting across the restaurant dropped into the chair next to her. "Lieutenant Siegel?"

Ellie turned. "Mrs. Quigley?"

The woman had graying dark hair, pulled back from the forehead and anchored with a barrette. She wore nothing else in her hair.

"I know, no yellow rose. I wanted a look at you before you got a look at me."

She was wearing a pup tent the color of autumn leaves, drawn in well above the waist with a knotted winter woolen scarf. Ellie wondered if that was a look or a necessity.

"Long day," Mrs. Quigley said. "Had to return some items I bought at a Canal Street closeout. *That* was a fight. And then a session with my chiropractor. My knees. Can't get down and clean a floor the way I used to."

"What about using a mop?"

Mrs. Quigley gave her a look that said, *No. Not now. Not ever.* "Mops can't scrub. You don't do your own housekeeping, do you?"

"I do when I have time."

"Most cleaning women take the easy way out. Spray polish. Spray 'n Vac. As long as I've been keeping house, I never used a spray anything. Not for Father Montgomery, not for Father Monahan, not for Father Romero. I hear Father Montgomery's new woman uses foam-rubber mops."

Olga Quigley's hand shot into her purse.

"It's Father Romero I'm here about. Did you know him?"

Ellie shook her head.

"Ever see any of his shows? They were terrific."

"Never saw one."

"He was a good man, even if he did drink. And he never touched those children. I'm not saying he was a saint by any stretch, but he never touched a child—or a teenager. Or anyone. All he wanted to do was help people. That Department of Law and that D.A. and what they did to Father Chuck's memory, it makes me sick."

Mrs. Quigley brought a plastic food bag out of her purse. It was stuffed with charred paper.

"When things started going wrong for Father Chuck, he began burning papers. His files—his calendars—his letters. His life. I saved what I could."

"What was he trying to hide?"

"I doubt he knew. But he felt he was being investigated. So he tried to hide everything."

Ellie opened the doggie bag and sifted through the blackened scraps.

"That one you've got there," Mrs. Quigley said, "that was the very first thing he ever burned."

Ellie looked down at a fragment of a card bearing the letters ALLY MANFRE. The address and phone were still legible.

SEVENTY-ONE

After dinner, Terri glanced across the space between their two easy chairs. "What's the matter, Dad?"

"Did I say anything was the matter?"

"You don't need to say it in words."

"I'm sorry if my body language is that transparent."

"It's your breathing. You hold it too long and then you grunt."

"I'm trying to figure something out. I think it's code. Wizzen Rizzem."

"Wizzen Rizzem?" When she stood it seemed to him she was already on the tall side of average for her age. She lifted the note-pad from his lap. "W - Z - N - R - Z - M. Where does it come from?"

"Somebody's date book. They had a few lunches and dinners with this guy."

She squinted, pursed her lips, gave the skin of her face an isometric workout. She ripped a blank piece of paper from the pad and folded the sheet lengthwise down the middle.

"What's this going to be, a paper glider?"

"This is going to blow your socks off." Her ballpoint moved rapidly, writing the alphabet in a column down the left-hand side of the fold. Then the pen came up the right-hand side of the fold. This time *A* to *Z* ran bottom to top. She began drawing horizontal arrows. The letter *W* on the left connected to *D* on the right. *Z* connected to *A*. "It's a reverse alphabet code."

Cardozo felt mild amazement. Amazed, first, that he had not remembered the code from his own childhood, when comic books had used it to encrypt messages from Superman and Captain Marvel. Amazed, secondly, that people were still entrusting their secrets to it.

Terri drew an arrow from *N* to *M*. When she drew the next arrow, *R* to *I,* he saw it.

"Damian—only misspelled."

Terri drew the last connection, *M* to *N*. "Anyone you know?"

"Not personally—but I'm becoming familiar with his work."

Cardozo crossed to Greg Monteleone's desk. "May I?" He opened the follow-log on Bonnie Ruskay. He ran his finger down yesterday's entries. "Who was following Ruskay yesterday evening—you or Henahan?"

Greg twanged one of his fire-engine-red suspenders. "Me—and unless my eyes deceived me, you. Henahan took over at eight."

Cardozo's finger stopped at 5:10 P.M., when Ruskay's taxi had left her at 474 Broadway. According to the log, she'd spent close to seven hours in the apartment of a W. Erbro on the eighth floor. "Who's this W. Erbro person?"

Greg shrugged. His lack of concern was not just breezy, it was monumental. "I looked him up in the phone listings. There's no such residence or business."

Cardozo frowned. His finger moved down. A little after midnight, Reverend Bonnie Ruskay had taken a taxi back to her apartment. "What kind of building is it?"

"A run-down old loft-building in Soho."

"That much I could see for myself. Who lives there, what happens there?"

"Artists and small manufacturing." Greg smirked. There seemed to be some kind of private little joke going on in the back of his mind. "The directory says eight is Erbro, but it doesn't say what kind of business he's in."

"Something strike you as amusing?"

Greg shrugged disdainfully.

Annoyance was like a wad of doughnut burning in Cardozo's throat. "Find out who Erbro is."

Greg snapped the other suspender. "I'm trying."

Cardozo went to his cubicle. He opened his briefcase and took out the photos Dr. Vergil Muller had surrendered. He spent a moment pondering each face in turn.

There were eight photos. He spread them on the desk top side by side, like playing cards. Five teenage girls, three teenage boys. Their names—or names that might have been theirs—had been block-printed in the lower margins.

Their charms had not been great enough to attract Dr. Muller. Which meant, possibly, that they had not yet been bound by belts or cut with knives or burned with hot candle wax. Possibly they were even still alive.

Now Cardozo arranged Father Joe's runaway photos in a line above Muller's.

The printing on the two series of photos was the same.

He could see only one difference: the names on Father Joe's were followed by a number. There was no number on any of Muller's.

He held a magnifying glass over the photo of a gap-toothed boy with the name Barry Bone. He examined the wall behind Mr. Bone.

At first his eyes had trouble focusing in the hard fluorescent light, and he saw nothing. Then he moved the glass a little further away, and a blemish appeared in the upper right-hand corner.

He moved the glass further and the blemish resolved itself into a lightning-shaped zigzag.

The seven other photos each had the same zigzag in the same place.

At that moment, sitting still was not one of Cardozo's talents. He lifted the phone and dialed Deborah Fairchild at the D.A.'s office.

"Fairchild." She sounded harried.

"Cardozo. Do I get a hello?"

She sighed. "Hello, Cardozo."

"Hello yourself. Have you got a minute?"

"No."

"Our friend Vergil Muller has been operating in a kind of ethical gray zone. While he was evaluating Eff Huffington for the D.A., he struck a private deal with him."

"Do I really want to hear what this deal was?"

"I doubt it. Muller hired Eff to provide him with teenage runaways for s/m games. He paid Eff in cash and an FDA protocol drug."

"I knew this was going to be awful."

"It gets worse. Eff sent Muller photos of the chicken-of-the-week candidates. The camera that took Muller's photos is the same camera that took the photos of the dead runaways in Father

Joe Montgomery's files. I have a hunch the D.A. is grooming Father Joe to star as the communion killer, and his case—if I'm not mistaken—rests on those photos."

"No, you're not mistaken. I wish you were." She was silent for a moment, putting it together. "I haven't been completely forthcoming with you."

"I didn't think you had been."

"I've been holding back one task force voucher—Fabrikant Gems on West Forty-seventh Street invoiced them twelve hundred dollars."

Cardozo scowled. "What did a D.A.'s task force need to buy from a gem store?"

"According to the invoice, a small gold-plated ring. I don't want to think what this one could mean."

"I'll meet you at Fabrikant in fifteen minutes."

Cardozo entered an arcade on West Forty-seventh, in the heart of Manhattan's block-long diamond district.

The space swarmed with sightseers, shoppers, the Hasidim who did most of the city's diamond dealing, delivery boys from nearby delicatessens. People were window-shopping, bargain-hunting, touting wares, arguing prices, disputing appraisals, and doing it all in shouts. The granite walls funneled a deafening babble of English, Hebrew, Yiddish, and Spanish.

If Deborah Fairchild hadn't waved to Cardozo from one of the shop fronts, he would never have spotted the tiny booth that was Fabrikant Gems, Inc.

"Vince, this is Aryeh Fabrikant."

A heavyset blond man in shirtsleeves, with traditional curls and a generic black yarmulke, sat behind a small jewelry-strewn worktable, talking into a phone in rapid Hebrew. He nodded to Cardozo, acknowledging the introduction. His body language was cool, minimal. Deborah had obviously outlined the situation and he knew he wasn't making a sale. What he didn't know was if he was facing any kind of accusation.

When he finally hung up the phone, Deborah laid an invoice on the worktable. "We need to know the details of this transaction."

Aryeh Fabrikant glowered at the invoice and took it to a steel filing cabinet against the wall. He pulled open a drawer and began thumbing through carbons of old receipts. He looked through three drawers and brought a flimsy sheet of yellow paper back to the table. He adjusted the arm of the jeweler's light and studied the faint tracks of handwriting.

"That was a rush order. They wanted me to duplicate a small gold-plated ring."

"What kind of small gold ring?" Cardozo said.

"Gold-*plated* ring," Aryeh Fabrikant said. "It was a trinket, a piece of junk—not even in good shape."

"Then why did it cost twelve hundred to copy it?" Deborah said.

The smile in Aryeh Fabrikant's eyes said there was no explaining human caprice, at least not in the jewelry business. "It had to be an exact copy, and it had to be done in twenty-four hours."

"Why twenty-four hours?"

"They wouldn't let me keep the original any longer than that. Why, they didn't say—I didn't ask. Frankly, I didn't want the job —I named a ridiculous price to discourage them. But they paid."

"Let me see the date on that order."

Aryeh Fabrikant handed Cardozo the yellow sheet.

The date of the order was four and a half weeks after the discovery of Wanda Gilmartin's body.

Cardozo moved the jeans, the T-shirt, the candle, the three-inch length of chain to one side of the counter, separating out the two small rings.

He swiveled the arm of the examining lamp. The tensor's bulb threw a wash of sizzling, almost blue light.

One of the rings flashed as though microscopic gem chips had been embedded in its gold plate. It was tagged 408-H-307-5 and it was the ring found in Martin Barth's knapsack.

The other ring, 408-H-307-1, did not flash when light played over it. It was the ring found in Wanda Gilmartin's left nipple, and there was hardly any gold plate left on it at all.

Cardozo stared at the two rings. Similar, yes. Identical, not very.

He placed the rings and the other items back in their manila file. He snapped off his disposable plastic gloves and returned to the property clerk's window.

The air-conditioning in the property room was still pumping out an arctic chill, and today the clerk was wearing a knitted ski sweater.

"I need to see the evidence logs from last year," Cardozo said.

The clerk vanished behind a storage rack, but not before giving Cardozo a glance that said he was a royal pain in the gazebo.

A TV set somewhere was blasting the fake kiddie voices of a *Sesame Street* rerun. Cardozo's beeper went off and it took him a moment to realize the beep-beep was not part of the *Sesame Street* backup band.

He crossed to the pay phone and dialed the precinct. The *Sesame Street* falsettos were bleating a number about a blue giraffe. The precinct finally answered. Cardozo had to shout.

The operator put him through to Ellie.

"The tap on Delphillea Huffington turned up another call from Eff," Ellie's voice said. "Where in the world are you? You sound as if you're talking from the bottom of a barrel of chipmunks."

"That about describes the situation."

"Delphillea says Eff has another letter from his priest friend. She recognized the handwriting on the envelope. Eff says he's on his way."

"When did the call come in?"

"We got the tape five minutes ago."

"Hey, Lieutenant." The propery clerk had returned with an evidence log. Cardozo said good-bye to Ellie and brushed a year's worth of dust from the binding.

He consulted the date on Aryeh Fabrikant's receipt—May third. He opened the log. A kind of darkness seemed to rush up from the pages. He flipped to 5-03 and studied an entry near the bottom of the page.

At 10:30 A.M., Harry Thoms of the D.A.'s office checked out item 408-H-307-1, the ring found in Gilmartin's nipple. He checked it back in at 4:20 P.M. the following day. Ten days later the ring from Barth's knapsack was registered with the property clerk as evidence item 408-H-307-5.

Cardozo slammed the log shut. He felt certainty within every cell of his body.

* * *

Cardozo parked behind a Dumpster, a block and a half from Delphillea Huffington's apartment building. He had a clear sight line on the front door.

The white boy with the blond ponytail didn't show.

The sun set. There was a flurry of movement—honest citizens hurrying home before the muggers and hookers and dopesters took over the street.

A little after nine, a bunch of kids came skateboarding by, giddy on crack, risking their lives as well as other people's, not caring.

Ten minutes later a junkie stumbled by and puked into a garbage can. He was a senior citizen and a gent of the old school—he put the lid back on the can.

Still no sign of Eff. No sign of any white boy.

A little before ten the radio in Cardozo's car crackled to life. It was Greg, at the precinct. "Bad news."

"Give it to me, I'm sitting down. I've been sitting down for five hours."

"We just found out the power source was down on that tap."

Shit, Cardozo thought. "How long?"

"A little over four hours. You know what I'm saying? We caught that call when power was restored, but it may have come in before the power break."

"I know what you're saying, Greg. He may have made the pickup four hours before I got here."

SEVENTY-TWO

"Here's the drill," Cardozo said. "We phone every Catholic church in the metropolitan area. Explain the situation, but keep it short and don't say *killer*."

"So what do we say?" Sam Richards asked. He was leaning against the file cabinet. Beside him, Detective O'Bannon was sitting on the edge of the desk. Ellie was standing beside the air conditioner, careful not to block the trickle of cool air.

"All they need to know is that a criminal is using empty churches. Find out which churches are going to be empty and unguarded tonight. Plead with them to put a priest on guard. If they can't do it, we'll put a cop on guard—but emphasize that's a last resort, because we haven't got the manpower. Ellie, you take the Bronx. Sam, Brooklyn. Tom, Manhattan. I'll do Queens. First one finished takes Staten Island. Okay, let's get on it."

It took less than an hour of nonstop phoning for Cardozo to begin raising a blood blister on the tip of his button-pushing finger.

"You don't suppose you could stay close to the church tonight?" He was talking with Father Malloy of Our Lady of Carmel.

"But it's bingo night down at St. Anastasia." Father Malloy's tone was desolate.

The other line began blinking. "Excuse me just a minute, Father." Cardozo switched calls.

It was Lieutenant Ross, who managed flack for Captain O'Reilly. "Your line's been busy."

"That's because I've been busy."

"O'Reilly needs to talk to you. Right away and in person."

When Cardozo stepped into O'Reilly's office, the coolness hit him like an ice block in the face. The captain's air conditioner was one of two on the floor that actually worked well.

"Vince, what the hell are you trying to do?" O'Reilly's sad, whiskeyed eyes added the footnote, *And why are you doing it to my pension?*

"I'm trying to save a kid's life."

"You're creating havoc. The diocesan press office says there's no communion killer. The D.A. says there's no communion killer."

"And between them they've kept the communion killer safely in business for the last three years."

"The commissioner says the mayor does not need this kind of panic."

"The commissioner seems to say whatever the mayor tells him to."

"The commissioner says no cops are to be assigned to guard churches tonight."

Cardozo let his breath out very slowly. "Trying to get any kind of job done under this administration is like barfing upwind."

"There's a chain of command here, Vince. Do you know what I'm saying?"

Cardozo's capacity to keep his mouth shut suddenly snapped. "I took an oath to uphold the law and protect citizens—not some bureaucrat's insecure ego. His Honor's scared that cops are going to offend someone. So we should go down with the first punch and take the count. Fine, and there may be enough cop-haters in this city to reelect him, but all he's going to be mayor of is a wall-to-wall riot."

O'Reilly just sat there and didn't speak. His anger was bright red on the skin of his face and neck.

"I'm sorry, sir. I didn't mean to lose my temper. I understand what you're saying. May I go?"

"You sure as hell may—and stop phoning those churches."

Cardozo showed his ID to the receptionist. "I have an urgent message for the cardinal. I'd prefer to deliver it personally."

"Do you have an appointment?"

"I'm afraid not."

She shot him a look through wire-rimmed glasses that said he had to be crazy.

He took a piece of paper from her desk and wrote in large, legible letters: *The communion killer will strike tonight.* He did not fold the note. He placed his shield on top and reversed the paper so the receptionist could read it. He slid it back toward her across the desk top.

She looked at the note and darted a glance back at him. "Just a moment, please." She vanished in a clatter of panicky heels.

The lights danced on her phone set. Visitors piled up behind Cardozo. Three minutes went by before she reappeared with a hefty-looking monsignor. He flashed a chummy smile and invited Cardozo to follow him.

They walked down a long, carpeted corridor hung with portraits of New York's last twenty-two cardinals. None of them looked like happy men. The monsignor tossed nods to two more receptionists and a uniformed private security guard. He paused at a paneled door. "Could I trouble you for your service revolver, please?"

Something in the manner of the monsignor's request startled Cardozo. It took him an instant to realize it was not the manner, but the eyes. The monsignor's left eye was pale brown and the right eye was pale blue.

Cardozo handed his gun over.

"Thank you." The monsignor knocked and opened the door. "His Eminence will see you."

Cardozo stepped into a Victorian chamber of high windows and heavy lace curtains. Most of the light came from a pair of lamps on the oak desk. They were carved and painted to resemble Black lady footmen in a Ruritanian operetta. Cardozo's note and shield lay on the desk top between them.

Barry Cardinal Fitzwilliam stood by a window adjusting his biretta. "It may not be appropriate to say thank you for a note as unwelcome as yours, Lieutenant—but thank you." When his Eminence turned, he looked no older than his photographs, but much wearier. "It was well-intentioned, I'm sure."

"Thank you for seeing me, your Eminence."

"I'm especially interested because, so far as we've been able to establish, the communion killer is largely a campaign of rumor."

"Rumor and five dead bodies." Cardozo placed the autopsies and photos on the desk.

The cardinal's robe made a whispering sound as he crossed the room. Gravely, he fitted a pair of reading spectacles to his nose. He sat at the desk. He studied the documents. He separated the photos into two groups: the three who had died before Father Chuck's murder—and the two who had died since. "You say one man is responsible for these crimes?"

"Yes, your Eminence."

"Do you know his identity?"

"No, your Eminence—but we believe he's a priest."

The cardinal hesitated. "An Episcopal priest?"

"We haven't determined that yet, but we know his pattern. He's using empty Catholic churches to give his victims communion. And he's going to kill his sixth victim tonight."

"Tonight?" The cardinal pulled back. "That doesn't give you much time to stop him."

"It gives us enough time if you're willing to help."

The cardinal fumbled the pictures together into a facedown stack. "Of course, anything in my power—but how?"

"Every empty Catholic church in the city has to be watched—and only you command the manpower to do that."

Cardozo parked in the alley beside the station house. The sun was a fiery smear sliding down the sky. He took two brown paper bags up to the squad room: Chinese takeout for Ellie, cheeseburger deluxe for Greg. They had agreed to stay behind to monitor the phones in case a church reported a break-in.

Greg made a face. "This cheeseburger's been cooked the way you clean pleated curtains—with steam."

Ellie ate her cashew chicken with chopsticks. She handled them with a deftness that surprised Cardozo. "Aren't you eating, Vince?"

"Not hungry."

"You still need to eat."

"I will." He stood at the window, watching the sky darken.

Phones kept ringing, but no priests.

Cardozo hated waiting. It was the one thing in life he hated most. He went to Ellie's desk in the squad room and checked the crime-scene logs on St. Andrew's rectory.

Ellie watched him. "What are you doing?"

"Killing time."

"If you told me what you're looking for, maybe I could help."

"Here. I found it." He showed her the entry. "The rectory wasn't secured until Pablo Cespedes died. That left it unguarded for eight hours after he was found. Anyone could have broken in and planted photos in the talent file."

"Hey, Vince," Greg Monteleone called over from his desk. "Radio message. Something's going down in one of the churches. It's on your phone."

"Holy Christ." Cardozo ran to his phone and jabbed the blinking button. "Cardozo."

A radio spat patched-in static. "Sorry, Lieutenant," the operator said. "False alarm. A cat got into St. Anne's in Queens."

A little after nine a full moon rose. By ten o'clock, cops were pulling crazies in off the street, and there were screams from the holding cage down on the second floor.

Ellie rapped on Cardozo's door. "Who says the photos were a plant?"

"They were taken with Eff's camera. There's a light leak that matches photos he sent to Vergil Muller. Believe me, Ellie, I've been through this with Lou."

She arched a skeptical eyebrow. "Okay, I believe you."

Cardozo was napping, head on his desk beside the telephone, when Ellie woke him with a cup of coffee.

"Are you sure you want this? You must have had two dozen since midnight."

"Did I ask for it?" He couldn't remember.

"Just a minute ago."

"Then I want it."

She handed him the cup.

He drained it in three gulps. Something sour rode halfway up his esophagus and lodged there.

She was watching him. "Why plant the photos in Father Joe's talent file?"

"To frame Father Joe. To bury the traces of a bungled investigation—and cover the D.A.'s ass—and get Harvey Thoms off the hook."

"Well, we've certainly changed our tune." She was staring with that expression he'd come to dislike, because it meant she was studying him and not the facts. "Okay, maybe there's a frame on Father Joe. But you're going way beyond the evidence if you're saying Thoms and the D.A. are behind it. And Eff's working with them? No way."

"Thoms is sure as hell behind something." Cardozo foraged through his briefcase. He slapped Aryeh Fabrikant's invoice down on the desk top. Beside it he slapped the Xerox of the task force's canceled check. "Four and a half weeks after Wanda Gilmartin's body was found, four days before Martin Barth confessed, Harvey Thoms checked Gilmartin's nipple ring out of the evidence room."

Ellie looked at the documents and then back at Cardozo. "So?"

"He hired a jeweler to make an exact copy."

424   EDWARD STEWART

She held Fabrikant's invoice up to the light. "Is this genuine?"

"Fabrikant says so."

Ellie did not speak, but her jaw tightened.

Cardozo looked at his wristwatch. "Did my watch stop?"

"It's only four. Feels later."

He handed her back the empty cup.

"Don't tell me you want another."

"I don't know what I want. Sleep." He yawned. "No word from any of the churches?"

"Nothing yet, thank God." She turned in the doorway. "One odd thing came in on the radio. Happened right here in Manhattan, Ninety-third Street, but it's not us. Someone broke into an empty Greek Orthodox church."

Cardozo's fist hit the desk. "I'm an idiot." He was erect in his chair, awake. "They recognize each other's orders."

"Beg your pardon?"

"The Catholics and the Greek Orthodox. In an emergency they can take communion from one another. He couldn't get into a Catholic church, so he went there."

SEVENTY-THREE

Father saw that his thumb and forefinger had left pink half-moons on the hamper.

He crossed the room and lifted the rotary saw out of the vulcanized iron washtub. He set it carefully on the cement floor. He turned the hot-water tap and held the cellulose sponge under the flow just long enough to dampen it.

He returned to the hamper and wiped the white plastic-foam surface clean.

Three fine strands of blond hair trailed out from under the lid.

He opened the hamper. The young face stared up at him, gentle now, gaze cool and beyond the reach of tribulation.

Father's finger traced the line of the lips. He separated them and eased the mouth open.

"God loves you," he whispered.

From the pocket of his smock he took a pyx, and from the small container he took a paper-thin white wafer. He slid the wafer between the lips.

"So do I."

He kissed the lips and then with his fingers he closed them.

At 6:32 A.M. a two-man patrol car was cruising east on the two-lane express road that cut through Central Park at Eighty-fifth Street. As the driver passed the police station just south of the road, he slowed.

"Something the matter?" his partner asked.

"Maybe not." The driver nosed the car up onto the curb, brought it to a stop, and stepped out.

He played the beam of his flashlight over the fieldstone walls of the one-story station house. It had been abandoned during the budget cuts of the eighties. The windows and doors were sealed with steel plate to prevent the homeless from breaking in.

He shined his beam up along the slate roof and down the rear of the building. Coming back to the pavement, the beam rippled over the edge of something that looked like a three-foot cube of dry ice.

The cop's hand checked that his gun was ready at his right hip. He stepped forward. The flashlight beam flattened on the side of an unmarked white plastic-foam basket. A dribble of red was slowly leaking from a dent near the base.

Above the cop's head, the starless night suddenly seemed charged with chemical poisons.

His fingers found the gap in the basket where the lid pressed down. He took a ballpoint pen from the evenly spaced row in his breast pocket. He jammed the pen into the gap and pushed.

It took ten more strategically aimed pushes, and the lid was loose. He raised it.

He looked into the basket and felt the blood drain sickeningly from his head.

He turned toward the patrol car. "Hey, Joey!"

* * *

Dan Hippolito inserted the key into the lock and turned. The steel door had a light powdering of frost. It swung open. He pulled out the body tray and lifted the black nylon sheet.

Light hit the dead woman in the face.

Cardozo looked down. He closed his eyes.

"You know her?" Dan said.

"I recognize her. Her name was Jaycee Wheeler."

"She's been dead less than ten hours."

"How'd she die?"

"She was strangled, then dismembered with an electric saw. The saw is similar to the one used on Sandy McCoy."

"She was alive when he did that?"

"I doubt she felt anything. There are no defensive wounds anywhere."

"I hope you mean unconscious."

"I'd say so."

"Did you find a communion wafer in her mouth?"

"I found something that sure as hell looked like one. The lab will tell us for sure."

"What about s/m markings on the body?"

"None."

Cardozo reached for the sheet.

Dan caught his arm. "Vince, you don't want to see. She's been cut up like an animal carcass, only not professionally."

"I want to see the hand."

"That's in here." Dan opened the neighboring locker.

The arms and legs had a tray of their own. In the shock of seeing them detached, Cardozo needed a moment to tell left from right. The ring finger stood upright and naked, extended away from the others.

"Wasn't she wearing a ring? A funny thing made out of flip-tops?"

Dan shook his head. "I didn't see it. But there were clothes folded in the basket with her—a blue chambray shirt and khaki pants. They had bits of gray acrylic shag sticking to them. They've gone to the lab."

"Sounds like she dressed up for him. And it sounds like he got her down on the same rug as the others."

Cardozo looked away from the limbs. He didn't want to remember them. His gaze went back to her face. Even dead she had that provocative, in-your-face, meant-to-be-noticed look.

He felt sad. He felt gravity pulling him down.

"Do me a favor, Dan. Let me know if there are any drugs or azidofluoramine in her bloodstream."

"Bad news," Cardozo said. "Very, very bad. Maybe you'd better sit down."

Scott Rivera's brown gaze flattened out, became guarded. "Jaycee."

Cardozo nodded.

"She's hurt?"

Cardozo was silent.

A wind of shocked disbelief shot through Rivera's eyes. He slid onto a stool. It rocked backward beneath him and he barely managed to keep it from tipping over.

Cardozo watched Rivera a moment. He was wearing a sleeveless cotton sweatshirt the color of Wheatena. He was hugging himself hard. For a build so slight, his arms were strong: long-tendoned muscles carried up to his shoulders. They were the gym-acquired arms of a convert to self-defense.

"How did she . . . ?" The question leaked away into silence.

"It was him," Cardozo said. "The communion killer."

"I told her not to go on that interview. Not alone."

"So why did she?"

"Her hustler friend said that was Damien's condition."

"And knowing what she did, she trusted him?"

"For Jaycee, life was like a ballgame. She had to take a swing at whatever flew over the plate."

"When was this interview? And where?"

"I don't know where. Her contact phoned yesterday, said to meet him at seven P.M. at some bar down by the docks."

"The Sea Shell?"

"Possibly. I didn't take the message, she didn't give me details."

"Who's this hustler contact?"

"I don't know the name."

"Have you ever seen him?"

"He came up here once—a white kid, blond hair—he wore it in a ponytail."

Eff, Cardozo realized, and his heart felt sick. *Eff was her informer. She died chasing down a scam.*

"The guy was a sleaze," Scott said. "A pimp. He procured teenagers for all kinds of sickos."

"How did Jaycee get him to open up?"

"Money. She topped Damien."

"How much was Damien paying?"

"The deal was two hundred dollars for each trick. In three years he delivered five tricks, and so he made a thousand dollars. Jaycee offered him five thousand if he would tell her about them."

"What did she learn?"

"She was extremely secretive about this story. It was going to be her breakthrough—the first investigative Pulitzer to a gay rag."

"Did she keep notes?"

"If you can call two Hefty bags of crumpled paper notes."

"Where are the Hefty bags?"

"Right this way."

Rivera wasn't kidding: the closet held two thirty-gallon black plastic garbage bags stuffed with torn, balled-up paper.

"I need to borrow your floor."

"Be my guest."

Cardozo emptied the bags in the middle of the loft floor. For the next two hours he combed through phone numbers, shopping lists, MasterCard charge duplicates, scribbled phrases that could as easily have been poetry as reporting.

A shadow fell across the sorted piles and Cardozo looked up. Rivera stood there holding a bag of audiocassettes.

"These were in her desk. I don't know what the hell they are, but she sometimes recorded her interviews."

SEVENTY-FOUR

Cardozo leaned back in the swivel chair and pressed the *play* button on his cassette player. He'd been working his way through Jaycee's tapes and this one was the third of eight, none of them labeled.

Nineteen minutes into an openly lesbian choreographer discussing AIDS in dance, a male voice interrupted. "I met him that September, in group therapy. I said I knew the gays that broke up a Mass at St. Pat's and he said he was a priest, and he would be interested in meeting them and helping them, could I arrange it."

Cardozo brought his chair upright, listening closely now. Jaycee had obviously recorded over the beginning of an interview with Eff, and this was the middle of the interview.

"I figured he was just another freak priest wanting to get his rocks off. I said these gays were whores and would do anything so long as there was money involved. He said he'd pay two hundred dollars. He was sentenced to group therapy for only eight weeks and he was leaving in a week, so I went to the docks and photographed eight people. I gave him the photographs. The deal was, he would send me a photograph of the gay he wanted, plus directions where and when to deliver the gay."

The voice that spoke next was Jaycee's. "And were any of these people actually involved in the St. Pat's zappings?"

The male voice said, "How the shit do I know?"

"Were any of them even gay?"

"For a price these kids would be anything you wanted."

"Can you introduce me to this priest?"

"Sure, if you turn that tape recorder off."

The blank hiss that followed had a horrible finality.

The phone rang. It was Dan Hippolito calling to report alcohol, but no drugs or azidofluoramine in Jaycee's bloodstream.

"Wine in her stomach?"

"You guessed it."

"So the bastard gave her communion."

"And then strangled her. A regular one-man church."

Cardozo replaced the phone receiver. Dan's wisecrack pushed his thoughts a little further in the direction that Jaycee's interview had started them. He angled the desk lamp closer to the spiral binder that she'd used for work notes. She had kept a running, updated record of cathedral zappings. As he leafed through the dates he realized that the media had reported only the zappings of the last twelve months. They had actually been going on for over three years.

The early dates interested him: Jaycee had first zapped St. Pat's on October 27, three years ago. The second zapping had occurred January 10, two years ago; the third, February 27, the same year.

There was no obvious pattern to the dates. Yet something about them disturbed Cardozo, some sense of the familiar.

Before he could home in on it, the phone rang again. "Cardozo."

"Jaycee's clothes were saturated in incense." It was Lou at the lab.

"Was it the same kind as the other victims?"

"It was the same and again, it tells us nothing. On the other hand, what *does* tell us something is the chalice from the Greek Orthodox church. The fingerprints match the prints from the V.A."

"Those are Colin Draper's prints."

"Do I know who Colin Draper is?"

"You do now."

As Cardozo hung up, Ellie stepped through the doorway. She was holding a sheet of fax paper. "Hot off the wire."

Cardozo glanced at the chemical analysis of the contents of Chablis's unlabeled cosmetics jars. "I was hoping someone on the crime-scene crew might have found that ivory cameo ring."

"Maybe she hocked it."

"I don't think so. It was her good luck charm. She said she always wore it." He handed back the fax. "Say, Ellie, do these dates mean anything to you?"

She frowned at the page of Jaycee's notebook. "Six dates. One's a Sunday—two are Wednesdays. You have a three-month gap, then a one-month gap, then a fifteen-month gap." She shook her head. "No, there's no pattern I can see. Maybe a computer could. Except maybe . . ." She was thoughtful. "What about the killings?"

"Those aren't the right dates."

"But they're the right intervals, aren't they?"

"If we're talking very approximately . . ." Cardozo picked up a ballpoint and flipped a blue departmental order form over to the blank side. He drew up two lists side by side: in one column, the dates of Jaycee's zaps. In the other, the approximate dates of death of the six known victims of the communion killer.

The connection struck him like a slap in the face. "He was getting even." He showed Ellie. "Within three weeks of each zapping, there was a communion killing. And Eff was providing the victims."

Ellie's eyes came around to Cardozo's, cool and inquiring. "How do you figure that?"

He wound back Jaycee's tape and played the segment where Eff answered questions.

"I don't hear *was* providing the victims," Ellie said. "I hear *is* providing. He hasn't stopped."

"How do we find him?" Cardozo sat tapping his ballpoint against the blue page.

"Pierre Strauss."

Cardozo shook his head. "No way. Civil libertarian. Better twenty more kids get killed than a single one of Eff's rights gets infringed."

After a moment Ellie said, "Sy Jencks."

"Jencks doesn't know where Eff is." The pencil stopped tapping. "But he said all his probationees are enrolled at Operation Second Chance."

"Paula Moseley."

"You're right." Cardozo snapped his fingers. "Paula."

The private security guard at Operation Second Chance asked if Cardozo had an appointment. Cardozo flashed his shield. The guard glanced dubiously at Cardozo's rumpled suit jacket and slacks but let him pass.

The elevator was busy, so Cardozo took the marble stairway

two steps at a time. He knocked and opened Paula Moseley's office door.

She was sitting at her desk in a dress the color of salmon mousse and her eyes shot him a glance of icy green.

"Mrs. Moseley, we've got to talk."

"Can't you see I'm busy?" She rose. Her voice crackled with impatience. "This is hardly the time or place."

"You've been treating Eff Huffington."

"What of it?"

"Where is he?"

An anorectic-looking black girl sat in one of the leather chairs. Paula Moseley tossed her a tight, reassuring smile. "I'll only be a moment, Sharlene."

She backed Cardozo into the hallway and shut the door.

"You have no right to barge in here." Her words were a whispered hiss.

"I'll leave as soon as you tell me where I can find Eff."

"I'm not going to tell you that."

"When's his next appointment scheduled?"

"There happens to be a tradition in this country known as civil liberties."

"You might be interested to know that during the time you've been treating Eff and safeguarding his civil liberties, he's raped a female Episcopal minister."

Cold sparks shot from Paula's eyes. "I can't believe that—he must have stopped taking his antidepressant."

"Do Eff's antidepressants explain why he was pimping kids for a priest in your therapy group? Or why those kids ended up dead?"

Paula Moseley reared back from him. "Are you crazy or just on drugs?"

"Who was that priest, Mrs. Moseley?"

"There's no way you can compel information from me."

Cardozo had had it with overpaid social engineers like Paula Moseley who thought there was no law or boundary they couldn't bend. "How well did Eff Huffington and Pablo Cespedes know one another? Were they partners in crime, or just fuck-buddies?"

Paula Moseley's eyelids came down, marking a pause, an indrawn breath. Cardozo sensed that they also marked a sort of class boundary.

"That's a vicious, homophobic slur. I refuse even to dignify the question with an answer. And you'd better get out of here, because I'm calling the mayor right now."

She about-faced and slammed the door behind her.

Three blocks away, Cardozo found a cigar store with one of its four pay phones still working. He dialed Sy Jencks's number. "Sy, it's Vince Cardozo. This is an emergency. Did Eff ever mention a priest who was in his therapy group for eight weeks?"

"I don't recall Eff ever talking about a priest. Anyone in Operation Second Chance has to go through the juvenile court system—but a priest sounds a little old for juvenile court."

"I need the priest's name. And fast."

"There might be a way." Sy's tone was thoughtful. "I could go through sentences and see who drew eight weeks in Paula Moseley's therapy group."

"Could you start right now? I'll be there in two minutes."

SEVENTY-FIVE

"**I** went through our Operation Second Chance records." Sy Jencks had his tie off, his shirtsleeves rolled up, and one foot on the open bottom drawer of his desk. "Eff joined his psychotherapy group three years ago. It's a twelve-member group. Over the last three years, what with dropouts and drop-ins, a total of fifty-one probationees have been assigned to that group. I've been over the list, and not one of them is a priest."

He leaned to punch up a file on the computer.

"But one offender—and only one offender—was sentenced to eight weeks in the group. A guy called Damien Cole."

"Damien Cole?" Cardozo sat forward to squint at the print

glowing on the monitor. "You're sure that's not *Father* Damien Cole?"

"There's no *Father* here and there's no mention of any profession. Which isn't unusual for our probationees—robbery and drug-running are not considered professions by the state labor board. Why, do you know a Father Cole?"

"No, but I've been hearing a lot about a Father Damien."

"Nothing here rules out his being a priest. For one thing, his age was thirty-one—thirteen years over the juvenile limit."

"Thirty-one and he was tried as a juvenile?"

"Says here. Obviously special treatment was involved."

"What was the crime?"

"He harassed a female gay activist."

Puzzle pieces began snapping together in Cardozo's head. "Was her name Jaycee Wheeler?"

"The file doesn't state the victim's name."

"Is that by any chance because the harassment took the form of rape?"

"The file doesn't state the nature of the harassment. This priest of yours raped a lesbian activist?"

"She didn't say he was a priest in so many words. But she did say he had church connections—and the sentence was a kiss on the wrist—eight weeks in a kiddie-therapy program."

"So it would fit." Sy Jencks scrolled the print up the screen. Despite the marine haircut, he looked like a playful monkey working the buttons on the computer. "Reading between the lines, the offense could have been a date-rape situation. But a priest wouldn't date."

"Not a normal priest. But your man Damien somehow sounds like a good possibility to me." Cardozo took out his notebook. "Why don't you give me his phone and address."

Sy Jencks shook his head. "There's no address, no phone. Damien came in on the honor system."

"Who's his probation officer?"

"There's no probation officer listed."

"Isn't that unusual?"

"Highly unusual."

"How the hell did a rapist get a deal like that?"

"Well, if he's a priest, he's connected, right?"

"Connected to who?"

"You have to ask?"

"I take your point." Cardozo thought for a moment. "Then the only way to Damien is through Eff. But Eff's not with his foster parents and Paula Moseley wouldn't tell me when he has his next psychotherapy."

"Tuesdays and Thursdays at three P.M. But he hasn't shown up in over a week. I have a hunch he's gone AWOL."

Barry Cardinal Fitzwilliam did not answer. He simply stood there staring out the window.

Cardozo said it again. "I know the name the communion killer is using."

The cardinal turned. "You say he's using a false name?"

Cardozo had a sense that everything the cardinal had ever wanted in his life was on the other side of that glass. "Yes, your Eminence. But your people would know his real name."

The cardinal crossed to his desk. He took a sheet of diocesan stationery from the drawer and a ballpoint from the marble pen holder. He sighed and looked over at Cardozo. "What name is he using?"

"Damien Cole."

"Lieutenant, I appreciate your zeal." The cardinal laid down the pen. "But that information is far too general to be of any use to you or to us. The name *Damien Cole* is an agreed-upon code. We use it to save embarrassment when a priest is put into detox. At any given moment, there are up to nine hundred Damien Coles affiliated with the church in this country."

"What do you do when you have a priest whose name really *is* Damien Cole?"

"The problem hasn't yet come up." The cardinal rose. It was a signal that the interview was over. "Thank you for your concern, Lieutenant."

"Thank you for your time, your Eminence."

As Cardozo left, the monsignor with different-colored eyes handed him back his revolver.

It was 4 A.M. Cardozo still could not sleep. Too much was running through his mind. When raindrops began falling on the air conditioner, pinging and ponging like a talentless neighbor rehearsing drum riffs, he got up and went into the kitchen and made himself a cup of warm milk.

He paced the darkened living room. Light from the street slanted through the curtained window, throwing a glow across the stillness. He stood a minute watching drizzle fall on the cars parked below him.

A car alarm somewhere started yelping.

He dropped into the easy chair and picked up the remote and flicked the TV on. A woman in a red beehive hairdo was selling a kitchen gadget. With the sound turned off, she seemed to be a mental patient mocking him. The image threw a flickering spillover onto the piano.

Cardozo's eye went to the music that Terri had left on the stand. She had laid a Chopin nocturne on top of another volume, and all he could read of the second cover was the right-hand half: *ubert / sitions / Four Hands* and beneath that a portion of an owner's label: *operty of / W. / erbrook*

Then he saw it—W. Erbro, hiding in plain sight.

He crossed to the piano and picked up the thick soft-cover album. *Franz Schubert, Compositions for Piano Four Hands. Property of W. Vanderbrook.* W. Erbro wasn't a person, it was a name on a directory with half the letters knocked off and never replaced.

Cardozo knocked and opened Terri's door. She moaned, blinking in the sudden spill of light from the hallway.

"Did Wright Vanderbrook have a place of his own?"

She sat up groggily. "Huh?"

"Did he have a loft on Broadway?"

She rubbed her eyes, shook her head. "He had a studio." She covered a yawn. "We used to practice there."

"What was the address?"

She pulled herself out of bed, brushing wrinkles from her nightgown. "Do you need it right now?"

"Can you find it?"

She switched on the desk lamp and pulled open a drawer. She sat, darkly pretty and silent, and searched through boxes of coins and bracelet charms. She held up a set of keys, frowning, and brought the tag into the lamplight. "The address was 474 Broadway."

"He gave you the keys?"

Terri shook her head at her father, smiling. "We were practicing piano duets—period."

"I need to borrow them."

SEVENTY-SIX

Overhead, dawn was beginning to streak the eastern sky. Except for two street people passed out in a doorway, the block was deserted.

Cardozo stood on the sidewalk across the street from 474 Broadway. He counted up from the shuttered window of the Mystic Bookshop to the windows of the eighth floor. They were both dark.

He crossed to 474. The outer steel door was locked. There were three keys on the ring Terri had given him. The first key that he tried was sticky, but it turned and he stepped into the little vestibule.

The smaller of the remaining keys got him into the tiny, clanking elevator. Its ceiling light threw just enough illumination for him to see the door at the end of the eighth-floor hallway.

He knocked. When there was no answer, he used the third key. He stepped into an unlit cave of undivided loft space. He stood listening. Something was breathing softly in the dark, with an occasional hiccup. It took him a moment to realize it must be a refrigerator.

Two windows were pale rectangles in the far wall. He closed the curtains, found the light switch on the wall, and flicked it. A lamp went on behind a decoupage screen, filling the loft with a lattice of light and shadow.

He surveyed the place.

Comforts were minimal. A Steinway concert grand stood lid-up against the wall. There was a set of four mission chairs grouped around a mission table.

He examined the closet that served as a bathroom. The toilet had an old-fashioned overhead tank, and the makeshift shower had obviously been built in by an amateur. There were towels, a washcloth, soap, a toothbrush, a razor—all recently used.

He explored behind the screen. There was a small bedroll, neatly rolled, and a waist-high refrigerator stocked with mineral water, yogurt, and salad greens. The greens had wilted, but according to the dates stamped on the containers, the yogurt had ten days to run.

Three books had been placed on top of the refrigerator: a book of common prayer in modern English, a book of common prayer in King James English, and a very tattered copy of *Winnie the Pooh*.

Beside the books lay a thick packet of letters bound with a pale pink silk ribbon.

Cardozo riffled through the letters. They were all in the same childish handwriting.

He untied the ribbon.

"Gracious me," a woman's voice said. "Are you a thief?"

The voice came from the shadows, and it took him a moment to recognize the Vanderbrook daughter crawling out from under the piano.

"I'm sorry," he said. "I knocked."

"I must have been dozing." Pierrette stood rubbing her eyes like a sleepy little girl who'd hidden all night in hopes of catching Santa Claus. "I see Mother gave you keys. She must trust you."

"Your brother gave the keys to my daughter two years ago."

"Really?" She came barefoot across the floor. "Why are you using them? And who are you?"

"Vince Cardozo. NYPD. We've met."

"Have we?"

"I thought Bonnie Ruskay or a friend might be here."

"That's no reason to housebreak."

"When you have keys it's not housebreaking."

"But it's still trespass. You must want to see Bonnie very badly to break the law." She was wearing a black silk shimmy and a rope of pearls so long that it almost tripped her. "I won't ask questions. But you won't find Bonnie here, because she only comes when Mother needs counseling."

"And how much counseling does your mother usually need?"

"Now, isn't *that* a personal question."

"You don't have to answer."

"But of course I'll answer. I love to gossip. By the way, I do remember you now. Nice to see you." She went up on tiptoes. Her lips brushed his cheek. "How much counseling does Mother usually need? Lately, a lot." She saw he was holding the letters. "Speak of the devil." She pulled one from his hand. "Mother shouldn't leave the family jewels lying around."

"Why does she?"

"Too much trouble to lock them up and get them out again. Besides, she likes to sit here in her pied-à-terre and reread them. They make her miserable. She loves being miserable. Did you enjoy them?"

"I haven't had a chance to look at them."

Pierrette pushed him toward a chair. "Then sit. Peruse the million-dollar epistles. Actually, Father only had to pay half a million to suppress them."

"Who did he pay?"

"Schuyler gave them to Samantha. Father paid Samantha. His gift to Wright's memory."

Cardozo began reading.

"Would you like a drink? It's only white wine." Pierrette went behind the screen. He heard her open the door of the refrigerator and yank out an ice tray. She came back with two glasses of ice and a bottle. "Not chilled, I'm afraid, but there's ice. I'm having another."

She filled both glasses.

"My use of the word *another* is not quite accurate. I've had an entire bottle already. I'm drowning my sorrows." She perched on the arm of a chair like a Prohibition-era chanteuse on the edge of a piano. "My lover has left me for a rich divorcée. But you know all that."

"No, I don't know anything about it."

"Really? It's in all the columns. Please, have a drink." She held out a glass. "It's very rude not to keep a drunk lady company and I know you're not a rude man."

He took the glass and set it on the floor beside him.

Pierrette was watching him. "I've always thought those letters were sweet. Repetitious but sweet."

"Then you must have thought your brother's affair was sweet too."

"It would have been sweet if he'd ever *had* an affair—but he was much more for thinking than doing. Especially in that department. The exact opposite of me."

"I heard he and the priest at St. Andrew's were lovers."

"To call them lovers shows very little respect for the meaning of that word. Bonnie was counseling him and they spent a lot of time together. Big deal."

Cardozo felt hollow when she said Bonnie's name. "I thought it was Father Joe they suspected."

"Suspected of what?"

"Seducing Wright and causing his death."

"Darling old Father Joe? Heavens, no. It was Bonnie. Modern, liberated, first-female-in-the-clergy Bonnie." She smiled with a drunk's caginess. "And the lawsuit never got anywhere. Our family has no luck in the courts. Which is sad, considering how much we pay our lawyers."

"Why's your mother meeting with Bonnie?"

"I suppose she wants to understand."

"Understand what?"

"What happened, and how to forgive. Isn't that all any of us need—just to understand and forgive?"

Bonnie opened the door wearing blue jeans and a lightweight sweatshirt with large blue letters that spelled *General Theological Seminary*.

"I've been trying to reach you all morning," Cardozo said.

"I'm sorry. I must have programmed the call-forwarding wrong."

They went to her office.

She looked at him. "Is something the matter?"

"Something's very much the matter. You were going to let my office know if you had to leave the parish house."

"Look, I don't think I can take that accusing tone right now."

"You know ten thousand ways of withholding, don't you? And you've been doing it from the start."

For an instant her mouth was a speechless O of astonishment. "What on earth do you think I'm withholding?"

"I've seen the letters between Wright Vanderbrook and his lover."

He could see she was shaken.

"How did you manage that?" she said.

"There's a collection of them in Wright Vanderbrook's studio at 474 Broadway."

"What were you doing there?"

"What were you doing there?"

"You've been following me."

"Yes, I've been having you followed."

"Why?"

"Originally, it was to protect you."

"And now there's another reason?"

"Why did you let me believe Father Joe was involved with Wright Vanderbrook—when all the time it was you?"

There was disbelief in her eyes and then resolve. "I never said it was Father Joe. No one was involved with Wright, not in the way you mean."

"Someone sure wrote a lot of sexy letters."

"I took notes of our sessions. Someone stole my papers."

Okay, he decided. *I can give her the benefit of the doubt. They were notes.* "Did you report the theft?"

"No, I did not."

"Why not?"

"I didn't realize the notes had been stolen till Wright's family produced them in the lawsuit."

"All the same, you misled me."

"Never."

"All right—you let me mislead myself. And if you let me mislead myself about Vanderbrook, how do I know you haven't let me mislead myself about everything else?"

The moment stretched out, endless and awful.

"What do you mean," she said, " 'everything else'?"

"I've asked you where Father Joe is."

"How can I tell you something I don't know?"

"You never exactly lie—you just give me enough truth to draw a false conclusion. Is that a technique they teach in seminary? Does it have a scholarly name?"

She drew in a long breath and held it.

"For all I know, you may even be hiding Father Joe. And your friend Collie too."

"Why should I need to hide them?" Her eyes were hard now and challenging. "Why should anyone need to? In a decent world, priests wouldn't need to hide."

She was using the same tactic again. *Not a lie at all,* he realized. *She does it all by implication.*

"You didn't tell me Colin Draper was ordained."

"You say that as though you think I was keeping it secret."

"Somebody was keeping it secret. Father Henry at Redeemer didn't know. Neither did Father Gus at St. Veronica. They thought he was a church groupie who put on vestments to make believe."

"It was none of their business—or mine—or anyone else's." She was staring across the room. Anger rippled out of her in tight pulsations. "Collie had a breakdown in combat. He was ashamed. He had the notion that a real priest wouldn't have come apart under gunfire. He didn't feel he could go on working as a priest and he never mentioned his ordination. So I never mentioned it either."

Suspicion kept nagging at Cardozo. She was extremely creative in covering her tracks, but the evidence never quite lined up on her side. "Did he give up the priesthood?"

"Not exactly." A sigh came out of her. "He removed himself from the directory of priests. I don't think he ever functioned as a priest again, except for . . ." She broke off.

"Except for what?"

"He's helped runaways from time to time—heard their confession, given them communion."

Cardozo rose from the chair and slowly circled the study. "Why runaways?"

"He identifies with them. He feels that in his way he's one of them."

"Is he?"

"He's had a very tough life. But so have we all."

Cardozo turned. "Where are Joe and Collie?"

"It's not them. It's not either of them. Father Joe's *blind*."

"Blind men have killed."

She didn't answer. She was somewhere else, some dark place in her mind.

"Are they together?" he said.

"If I knew, don't you think I'd tell you?"

God give me the gift of silence, he prayed. But God gave him words. "At this point, I don't honestly know what you'd do."

She looked up at him and her face was suffused with wondering and hurt. "You've never trusted me, have you?"

"That's not true," he said. "I trusted you till today."

"And now?"

"And now I don't. I'm sorry."

SEVENTY-SEVEN

Alone in her office, Bonnie paced. She was worried and she was scared. She knew she had to think clearly.

Her eyes fell on the photograph of her children.

She picked up the phone and dialed.

There was no answer. She broke the connection and paced.

An image leapt out at her from the wall: Father Damien preaching to the lepers. As she stared at it, the still air seemed to ripple.

She made up her mind and snatched up the phone again. She dialed another number.

"Pierre Strauss." That same woman's voice. His secretary.

"May I speak with him, please?"

"Of course, Reverend. Just a minute."

She wound the cord around her fingers and waited.

"What now?" Pierre Strauss grunted.

"I've got to meet with Eff."

"We've been through this. He's not afraid of the rape charge. He doesn't care whether you press it or drop it."

"I'll give him his money."

"What money are we talking about?"

"Just give him the message. I'll show up wherever he wants, whenever he wants. I'll have half the money on me in cash. He gets the other half after he answers my questions."

Pierre Strauss sighed. "I'll get back to you."

Cardozo's phone jangled. "Cardozo."

"I'm standing in a pay phone," Greg Monteleone's voice said, "and you're not going to believe what I just saw the lady reverend do."

"Tell me and I'll try."

"She just paid seven bucks and went into the Arcadia Cinema." It was obvious from the music of Greg's intonation that he was holding back something juicy.

Cardozo bit. "And where's this palace of the arts located?"

"Ninth Avenue and Forty-fourth Street."

Cardozo felt a spike of pressure just under his heart. "That's a porn location."

"Which is appropriate, because it's a porn movie house. Double feature. *Color Me Wow* and *Sophie's Choicest*."

"Was she alone?"

"Alone with a lunchbox. Obviously she's planning to have dinner in there."

"Obviously."

"Or could be it's her traveling kit, and she's giving communion to the lowly and humble."

Cardozo felt an overwhelming desire to punch Greg Monteleone's smile down his throat.

"Want me to go in after her?" Greg said.

"Give her twenty minutes. If she's not out by then, go in and get her."

The sign said seven dollars. Bonnie pushed the money through the opening under the bullet-proof window.

The woman selling tickets looked at her as though she had lost her mind. "You know what kind of a movie house this is, don't you?"

Bonnie's smile ached in her teeth. She knew it had that extra giveaway something that signaled nervousness, and she tried to tamp it down. "Yes, I know you show sex films."

"But do you know what *kind* of a movie house this is?"

"The sign says seven dollars. Here's my money. Please just give me my ticket."

"Okay, lady." A brass slot spat out the ticket. The woman shoved it under the bullet-proof glass.

Bonnie stepped out of the hot afternoon into a zone of pitch blackness that had the chilled damp of a rain forest. A turnstile buffeted her in the stomach. Somebody jostled her. She held the lunchbox tight against her side and waited for her eyes to adjust.

A stale smell of sweat rose like a gas around her. There was a hidden sting to the smell, something else that her nose didn't want to recognize.

She felt something waiting in the dark. Her body warned her: *Don't.*

A gray shifting light dappled the void in front of her. Gradually she made out shadows sliding against the darkness, the faint light-edged valley of an aisle. Rows of seats dimly outlined themselves. Heads floated above them, haloed in light sifting down from three primary-colored TV projector beams.

She hung back at the edge of the moment, trapped in a space of sudden uncertainty. The directions had been, *Eighth row from the rear, third seat in on the left.*

Inside the silence of her body she could feel her heart punching. She focused on that rhythm and moved forward, allowing two punches of the heart to each step of the feet. The important thing was not to show hesitation.

She adjusted her balance to the slight decline of the aisle and counted her way down eight rows. A man had passed out in the aisle seat. His trousers had a glistening reptile sheen and she realized he was urinating in his sleep. She squeezed past and tried to step over without touching him. She lowered herself into the third seat.

She waited.

The row rocked with each snoring breath of the man on the aisle.

She angled her watch again to catch the glow from the movie

screen. She could barely make out the hands. Eff had said three-twenty. It was already three twenty-five.

She checked the aisle. Shadowy men moved up and down. Some stopped and stared at her. Eyes in nodding heads were glazed points of light.

She looked to her left. Three seats down, a man was shooting a needle into his belted arm. She quickly turned her face. Her heart was tap-dancing inside her chest.

She wondered if Eff had set her up—if this was all some colossal practical joke.

No, he wouldn't walk out on five thousand dollars.

Not if he believed it was really five thousand.

Her arm tightened around the lunchbox, which she had stuffed with one-dollar bills and cut-up phone books. Her eyes went to the screen.

A huge, lumbering man in an American Indian headdress was straddling a woman in a police uniform. He handcuffed her wrists to the posts of a bed. She yanked and twisted sharply. He began garroting her with an athletic supporter.

The policewoman arched her back in a violent spasm. Purple glowing smudges appeared on her face.

Pounding rap music on the soundtrack urged the killer on: *Gonna kill me a pig, gonna bring me home some bacon, uh-huh, mmm-hmm. . . .*

Around Bonnie, there were stirrings in the seats. She saw manic grins and thumbs-up signs. She couldn't help but wonder if she was still in America.

She remembered the words of the theologican Martin Buber: *God can be beheld in each thing.* She wondered: *Where is the healing presence of God in all this?*

A sudden weight seized her by the hair and yanked her head back against the seat.

"Yo, bitch."

It was his voice, whispering. It was his smell, crashing in on her —the tunafish-and-cigarette stench of his breath, the sour heat of his sweat.

"Hand over my bread."

His body leaned over from the row behind, pressing all its

weight against her skull. His hand grabbed for the lunchbox. She
didn't let go.

"Give it up, bitch!"

Something cold and straight-edged and sharp pressed against
her windpipe. The salt taste of drowning flooded her eyes and
nose.

"Now!"

"I want"—she could barely push the words past the pressure of
the razor—"want . . . to know—"

"You want to die, bitch."

"Who . . . is . . . Damien . . . ?"

His grip eased on her hair but the razor didn't move. "What the
fuck you talking 'bout?"

"The man you've been leading the runaways to . . . Who is
he?"

Eff nudged her jaw around with the razor. "A dude tells me his
name is Damien, his name is Damien." Chemically fired eyes
blazed into hers. "You tell me you got my money, you got my
money."

"Is he a priest?"

"The dude says he's a priest, he's a priest."

"Is he Joe Montgomery?"

Veins pumped up in Eff's temples. "Give me my money, bitch!"

"Is he Colin Draper?"

Eff's hand swooped down again and grabbed for the lunchbox.
When she didn't let go, the razor flew up from her throat and
arced down and twisted into her wrist.

It was as though a jet of water had scalded her.

Eff grabbed the lunchbox and slammed it into the side of her
head. Sparks perforated her vision. She pitched sideways across
the seat.

SEVENTY-EIGHT

It was late afternoon by the time Bonnie left the emergency room. When she opened the door to her office, the red message light on the answering machine was blinking. She switched on the desk lamp and pressed the *play* button.

The first six calls were from parishioners. And then:

"Hello, Bonnie—this is Collie—"

His tone was urgent, childlike. She knew that tone, and fear skittered on her skin.

"Just wanted to hear your voice. Need to ask your advice. I'm kind of confused. I guess the trouble is, I'm in trouble. There's a deep analysis for you, right? If you're there, pick up please. . . . Guess you're not. I'm calling because I'm afraid of what's happening to me and the things I'm doing. This is kind of hard to say. I'm . . . uh . . . I had a drink."

Oh, no, she thought, sinking into a chair. *Please, God, no.*

"I guess that means I've started drinking again. Bonnie—you there? I wish we could talk about it. I'll call back."

The machine cut off. The silence hit her like a ricocheting bullet. She took a moment to breathe deeply, focusing herself, and then she picked up the phone. The fingers of her bandaged hand managed to tap in the number of her brother's direct line at work.

"Ben, it's me."

"No kidding." His voice smiled. "How's my reckless, feckless little sister?"

"Collie left a message on my machine. He's drinking."

"Oh, Lord."

"Do you know where he is?"

"Isn't he usually at Redeemer this time of day?"

"They fired him."

"Oh, no. Why?"

"I don't know."

"Poor guy."

"You have church contacts. Could you ask around? Maybe somebody knows where he is. Maybe they're hiding him somewhere."

"Why would they be hiding him?"

"They've hidden him before—when he's had emotional problems."

"Look, Sis, isn't this something that a lawyer would know how to handle? What about David Lowndes?"

"This isn't about getting his job back. I have to see him myself."

"You worry an awful lot about that guy."

"Next to you, he's my best friend."

"He's an adult, just like you and me."

"But that's the problem. He's *not* like you and me."

Ben sighed. "Okay. I don't approve, but if it will make my little sister any happier, I'll try to locate Collie. I'll call you back."

"Ben—no. Not on the phone. I'll come to you."

"You're acting as though your phone's tapped."

"Let's just be careful. Other people are—looking for him too."

"Someday," Ben said, "you're going to have to stop rescuing Collie. It never does any good."

"Please, Ben," she said.

He smiled wryly, accepting that Bonnie was exactly what she was. "What did you do to your hand?"

She glanced down at the lump of bandage. "It got . . . caught."

A stillness flowed through Ben's office. The room had a few touches of personal comfort, but not many: a storm-at-sea painting, a small table of knickknacks and photos of Bonnie's children, a wall of books, the bentwood rocker that Bonnie was sitting in. A faint, pleasant scent of potpourri hovered.

"Did you get a tetanus shot?" he said.

She nodded.

"You're running yourself ragged, Sis. You've got to slow down."

She sensed him steering conversation toward brother-and-sister things, comfortable and familiar, like the words of an old song.

"I'll slow down someday—when there's time. Have you found out anything?"

Ben sat there behind his desk. No reaction. No reply. His desk top was a neat and tidy domain, like Ben himself, papers categorized and stacked, pencils in one cup and ballpoints in another, everything visible at a glance. He moved a pencil into the ballpoint cup. She could feel disapproval radiating from him like energy from a heat lamp.

"Where did you get your tetanus shot?" he said quietly.

"Don't baby me, Ben—and don't evade me." Blood rushed to her face and her gaze dropped to her lap. "I'm sorry. I don't mean to take it out on you. I'm in a mess and I don't know how I got myself into it." Her eyes lifted. "That's not true. I do know. I know exactly."

She felt too restless to sit. She walked to the window.

"One day I looked up from my knitting and thought God wanted me to be a priest."

"And he does."

She went to Ben and leaned over and kissed him on the bald spot on the crown of his head, thanking him for his blunt certainty. "But what chaos that simple decision has made of everyone's life."

"Stop being responsible for the whole world."

She couldn't help smiling. "All right. As soon as I've saved it."

He stared at her, shaking his head. "I spoke with Father Henry's bishop."

She knew instantly by the set of his mouth that he had news. "And?"

"He thinks Collie may have been placed in St. Kerry's."

Bonnie pulled her Mazda just clear of the gate and stopped. She got out and went back to swing the rectory gate shut and lock it. Her heels clicked quickly against the sidewalk.

She slid back into the small green two-door sedan and angled onto the street. She looked to the left and to the right.

A dark blue Pontiac was double-parked halfway down the block, its turn signal blinking. There was a faint light inside the car, as though the glove compartment were open, and she could see the shadow of someone moving around behind the steering wheel. She waited to see what the Pontiac was going to do, and when she realized it was just going to sit there, she pulled into traffic.

Wheels squealed behind her. She flicked her eyes up to the rear-view mirror. Three cars back, the Pontiac had nosed ahead of a checkered cab.

A horn blared.

At the corner of Madison she looked again in the rearview. The Pontiac was still behind her. She turned north on Madison.

The Pontiac made the same turn.

The situation felt off-centered and unreal. She took the next right. A sanitation department garbage truck was collecting trash. She steered around it.

At the end of the block a PARKING AVAILABLE sign blinked like a theater marquee. She slowed.

"Hi. My name is Mel." A heavyset man in a Panama hat bent down to the driver's window. "And I'm your favorite street singer." His voice was teasingly high, as though he were imitating a cartoon character. "I really am."

He held out a paper cup, rattling the change in it, and began singing the Mickey Mouse Club theme song.

She opened her purse and with her left hand took out a ten-dollar bill. "Mel—there's a blue Pontiac trying to get around that garbage truck. He's following me."

"Is that the truth?"

"Could you do me a favor? Jump on his hood, fall down in front of him, do whatever it takes—but delay him till I get away."

"I'll sing him all four verses." Mel delicately lifted the bill from her fingers. "From the top."

Bonnie swung down the ramp into the parking garage. She took the blue ticket from the ticket-spitter. A moment later the barrier gate rose. The garage went through the block and she drove straight to the exit on the other side.

The man in the booth looked at her ticket. "You sure didn't stay long."

"Changed my mind."

"It's still a seven seventy-nine minimum."

She took another ten from her purse and she didn't wait for change.

Cardozo had dozed off in front of a Channel Thirteen foreign affairs special when Terri called to him. "Dad—phone call for you."

He turned down the TV and went to the hallway. She handed him the receiver.

"Cardozo."

"I lost her," Greg Monteleone said.

"Don't tell me you lost her in the porn theater."

"No, she came out of the Arcadia and went to St. Clare's Hospital."

"You lost her in the hospital."

"No, she came out two hours later with a bandage on her right hand."

"What happened to her hand?"

"I don't know. She went back to the rectory and about a half hour later she went to a midtown hunting-and-fishing shop."

"Hunting and fishing?"

"The Fish and the Fox."

"The Fish and the Lamb."

"Right. She spent about a half hour there, and back to the rectory again. About an hour later she comes out in her car."

"Where was she driving?"

"I don't know—I got stuck behind a garbage truck and this nut started serenading me with the Mickey Mouse song and I lost her."

"That's the dumbest excuse I ever heard."

"It's not an excuse, it's what happened."

"Find her and call me when you do." Cardozo slammed the phone down.

He spent the rest of the evening in front of the TV, waiting for the phone to ring and brooding.

Terri was used to his moods. She didn't ask what was wrong, didn't try to cheer him up. As he was turning off the eleven o'clock news, she set a cup of hot milk at his elbow and kissed him good night.

"Get some sleep," she said.

He tried. At two in the morning the phone still hadn't rung. He made himself another cup of hot milk. It didn't work any better than the first had.

At 4:30 A.M. he heard someone knocking and buzzing at the front door.

"Did I wake Terri?" Esther Epstein, crackling with urgency, walked into the apartment. "I only wanted to wake you."

"That's okay. Terri's asleep and I wasn't."

She was wearing a pale pink dress that looked as wild on her as a brilliant red dress would have on a younger woman. "Vince, you'll never guess what. That mix of medications your friend is taking—Colin Draper? I had the computer search to see if anyone new started the same mix when Colin Draper dropped out."

She opened her purse and took out a lace-edged handkerchief. She daubed at her lips for a long, teasing moment.

"Esther, this is the wrong time of day for drama. You wouldn't be here if you hadn't found something."

Her smile slid out from behind the hankie. "Just before I got off my shift, the computer found one. He's at the V.A. hospital in Mount Kisco. He started two days ago—first time ever in our records. No previous medical history, which is possible. No armed services history at all—which is impossible. He's taking the exact same mix, plus benzetac."

"What's benzetac?"

"A generic. It aids withdrawal from alcohol."

"Are you going to tell me this man's name?"

"I think it's a phony name."

"What's the phony name?"

"I could be wrong. Damien Cole. Doesn't that sound like a phony name to you? It does to me."

"Esther, you've saved my life."

"Good." She took his hand and laid it against her cheek. "Maybe you'll get some sleep now."

Two minutes later Cardozo was telephoning the V.A. hospital in Mount Kisco. They confirmed that Damien Cole was a patient, but said they could give out no further information till office hours.

SEVENTY-NINE

At five minutes after nine in the morning, Cardozo was standing at the reception desk of the V.A. hospital in Mount Kisco, trying to charm a woman whose name tag said Ms. Sheridan. "You have a patient here by the name of Damien Cole." He laid his ID and his shield on the countertop. "I'd appreciate it very much if you could let me visit him."

The lobby smelled of ammonia, and Ms. Sheridan was having none of Cardozo's charm or his ID. "As the sign says, visiting hours begin at two P.M." She pushed buttons on a keyboard and referred to a computer screen. "Besides, Damien Cole isn't here."

"I was told he was."

"You were not told right. Damien Cole's an outpatient."

"Do you have any idea where I'd find him?"

"Well, since you're a cop . . . He's over at the monastery—St. Kerry's."

Cardozo looked at Ms. Sheridan blankly.

Her forefinger played with a coil of blond hair, slowly pushing it back from her brow. "You mean to say I have to draw a New York City cop a map?"

"It would help."

St. Kerry's—a two-story half-timbered building on eight wooded acres at the edge of town—looked new, as if Disney had built it last year as a monastic theme park. Cardozo pushed the buzzer and a recorded bell chimed.

The short, stocky, middle-aged man who opened the door was not Cardozo's idea of a religious brother. No brown robe, no tonsure, no clicking wood rosary at the belt. Blue jeans and Nike high-tops and a T-shirt that said *Gold's Gym*. He looked as though he not only worked out with weights, but binged on steroids.

"Hi. I'm Brother Tom. Can I help you?"

Cardozo showed his ID. "I'm looking for Damien Cole."

Brother Tom took a moment to reflect. "No, we have no brother by that name."

"He could be here as a sexton, or in some service capacity."

"No, certainly not in any service capacity." Behind his bifocals, Brother Tom's eyes were deep blue and bloodshot. "But has he possibly been here as a retreatant? We're very popular for retreats."

He led Cardozo into a small, tidy office. A menu of options glowed on the screen of a desk computer. He punched keys and peered at the result. "I'm sorry, I don't see any Damien Cole on our list of past retreatants. Am I spelling it right?"

Cardozo angled himself to read over Brother Tom's beefy shoulder. There was no Cole, but at the bottom of the screen he noticed C. Draper—home address, care of B. Ruskay, Queens. "You have a retreatant by the name of Colin Draper?"

"Yes, indeed. Often."

"Is he here now?"

"Colin cut short his retreat. He left last night after the ten o'clock news." Brother Tom shook his head. "Retreatants shouldn't watch TV. They had another zapping at St. Pat's."

Cardozo's heart fell like a dropped stone. "*OutMag* zapped the cathedral again?"

"Yesterday. In memory of Jaycee Wheeler. It was on Channel Five."

"I missed it. I was watching seven."

"Five's a little livelier."

"Do you know where Mr. Draper went?"

"He said he had to go home."

"I notice that home is care of B. Ruskay—do you happen to have that address?"

"Certainly." Brother Tom scrolled down the list of retreatants till he reached the *R*'s. "That's 810 Spellman Drive, Russell Gardens. As a matter of fact, Ms. Ruskay picked him up."

"Bonnie Ruskay? Last night?"

Brother Tom nodded. "That's right. The reverend."

* * *

Cardozo called the precinct from a pay phone. He told Ellie to put a twenty-four-hour live monitor on Delphillea Huffington's phone tap. "Damien's going to be lining up another communion killing."

"Maybe we'll stop him this time."

Cardozo hoped Ellie was right. "Has Bonnie Ruskay showed up yet? Greg lost her last night."

"Wait a minute, I'll ask." There was a silence, and then Ellie came back on the line. "O'Bannon's watching the rectory. She's still missing."

The Ruskays' two-story colonial home was set back from the wooded lane on a lushly landscaped lot. Lawn sprinklers arced lazily in the evening light. Rhododendron leaves gleamed as though they'd just been waxed.

Cardozo parked in the drive and rang the front doorbell. A uniformed maid opened the door.

"I'd like to speak with Colin Draper, please."

She admitted him to a hallway smelling of furniture polish. The chairs had gilt legs. The maid glided away and in a moment glided back and asked him to follow her.

In a living room crowded with cut crystal and cut flowers, a white-haired lady in blue rose from a sofa. She walked toward him with the help of a silver-knobbed ebony cane. "Are you a friend of Collie's? I've never met a soul who knows him—aside from my children. He's their big brother. A self-appointed big brother, perhaps. But they've accepted the appointment." She was silent, and her silence said she had not accepted it.

"I'm a police officer." Cardozo showed his shield. "Vince Cardozo."

"Really?" She stared at him, green eyes shining with curiosity. "Is something wrong?"

"I'd like to talk to Mr. Draper. It's urgent."

"That sounds a little ominous. He's not here right now. Would you care to sit down?"

"I don't mean to trouble you. When are you expecting him?"

"With Collie that's hard to say. He was never one to file a flight plan."

Cardozo smiled. "What time did you last speak to him?"

"What *time*? I haven't spoken to Collie in years."

"But he lists this address as his home."

"He lists the chauffeur's apartment over the garage. He uses the address for his New York benefits. He's on state assistance. Janitor's pay doesn't go far in today's economy."

"Is that where he's living now?"

"I really don't know. He has a key and he enjoys fiddling with the roses, but I haven't seen him in ages."

"Would it be too much trouble if I had a look at that apartment?"

"It would be if you expect me to show it to you. I have trouble with stairs."

"I could manage by myself."

She took his hand and suddenly he became her walking stick. She steered him into the pantry. She peered at a pegboard of keys, holding her spectacles in front of her without putting them on, like an artist examining detail work under a magnifying glass. She plucked a key off the board and handed it to him.

"I warn you. It's bound to be a mess. No one's been up there for years."

EIGHTY

Violet shadows slid across the lawn, and above the trees the darkening sky flowed with cawing birds. Cardozo didn't want to risk Collie's returning and seeing lights in the apartment. He went back to his car and took the flashlight from the glove compartment. He crossed to the garage.

The sliding door was down, and the key Mrs. Ruskay had given him didn't fit.

Around the side of the building he found another door with a bush of pink-and-yellow roses blooming next to it.

Hello, Linda Porter, he thought.

The key turned easily in the lock. The door opened with a mousy squeak.

A damp smell pooled just inside. He turned on the flashlight. Motes danced brightly in the beam.

He aimed the light in a slow arc around him. The beam wriggled across gardening tools, hoses, stacked lawn furniture, a tall pile of boxes covered with a tarpaulin.

Just beyond the boxes, a van had been parked close to the garage wall. The beam picked out a New York license plate. His footsteps echoed on the concrete floor. He walked around to the side of the van.

The beam moved across a teardrop-shaped window. It swung over to a smiling sun painted on the driver's door. Beneath the sun, the beam picked out the words, GOD LOVES YOU—SO DO I.

The quiet thickened.

He walked back to the stack of boxes. As he touched the edge of the tarpaulin, a faint chemical smell floated up. He lifted the canvas.

A blinding reflected white struck his face. He angled the beam lower. It played across a surface that had the faint dents of pockmarks in snow. His fingertips recognized the brittleness of plastic foam, and he saw that the boxes were jumbo hampers, stacked one inside the other like cups in a giant's cupboard.

The flashlight caught the shadowed indentations that formed the four letters K A L A. He lifted the canvas and saw M A Z O O.

The beam groped along the floor. A rust-colored stain led from a drain to a doorway. Beyond the open door was a stairway, and beyond the stairs, a second chamber. The flashlight played across enormous twin sinks joined by a ribbed drain board. Old-fashioned washtubs. Rust-colored stains ran down the sides.

He raised the enameled steel lid. Hairs and skin particles had caught on the drains. He turned away quickly and moved up the stairs, one foot after the other on the bare steps, pushing through dead air.

At the top of the flight the elliptical wafer of light spread over rose-patterned paper. His lungs pulled in the thick fumes of incense residue. The beam of light hit a bookshelf.

He opened St. Augustine's *Confessions*. The flyleaf bore an inscription: *To Damien—Love, from Damien*. He opened *City of God* and *Hound of Heaven*, *The Seven-Story Mountain* and *Jesus, Are You with Me?* All had the same inscription: *To Damien— Love, from Damien*.

The beam reached across gray shag carpet and struck the bottom of a closed door.

He rose and pulled on the door handle. The door was fastened. There was no key in the keyhole, but it was a primitive-looking lock.

He explored. The flashlight found a hallway. A wet glow at eye level jumped out at him. His own face stared at him, reflected in glass.

Behind the pane, fragments of Gothic lettering came together: *Bring me young sinners.* Behind another pane, *Suffer the little children to come unto me.*

The beam leapt to the opposite wall. *My kingdom is not of this world.*

In the bathroom, another framed Gothic placard: *The kingdom of God is within you.*

In the kitchen, two more: *You must become again as a child. He who dies with forgiveness of sins . . . wins!*

He opened a drawer and searched through kitchen utensils and found a thin, sturdy-looking knife. He returned to the living room and inserted the blade in the crack of the locked door. He worked it up and down and sideways. The lock clicked and the door swung open and he was staring into a closet.

The flashlight began at the top. Boxes and bric-a-brac crowded a narrow shelf.

The beam traveled down to the hanger rod, along overcoats and raincoats and men's suit jackets. Down to slippers and tennis shoes and galoshes and something else winking through dust.

He stooped and recognized a half-dozen empty Bacardi rum bottles. And something else. A small Minolta camera and the antique piggy bank from Bonnie's study.

As he lifted the piggy bank, something clunked.

He shook it. There was a rattling in the cash drawer. He frowned and then reached into his pocket and found a penny. He dropped the coin into the slot.

A silvery snatch of "Swanee River" tinkled.

There was a squeak, as though a bat had been impaled on a needle, and the drawer popped open.

He shined the flashlight into it.

Besides his penny, there were four small objects inside. Three of them sparkled, and he saw that they were rings.

One was an ivory cameo. As he held it to the light he could make out a carving of a peacock.

Another had been fashioned out of flip-tops from soda cans and coated with bronze.

The third, too small to fit any finger but a newborn baby's, was a circle of slightly tarnished gold.

The last object in the drawer was a lock of dark Caucasian hair fastened with a rubber band.

Cardozo took a small plastic evidence bag from his pocket. He lifted the bank and emptied it into the bag.

Now he felt deeper under the galoshes. His hand struck the edge of something rectangular and solid. He pulled out a photograph album.

The first dozen pages were New York sights—the Statue of Liberty, the Chrysler Building. Then came a group of photos of the ceremony at Vanderbilt Garden. One showed two young men dragging a large picnic basket from the bushes. The remaining photographs were flash portraits of young people, each of them asleep or passed out in a wing chair slip-covered in parakeet chintz.

Cardozo stared at their faces, bleached and dumb as driftwood. They touched an aching nerve in his memory. He recognized the dead kids from Father Joe's talent file.

He turned the page. Three sheets of paper had been tucked between the leaves. He teased them loose. They were stationery with an engraved letterhead: *St. Andrew's Rectory.*

Line after line of block letters had been carefully printed and neatly crossed out. He read through them slowly:

THE DEAD THE MURDERED CHILDREN DEAD TEEN-AGERS THE PHOTOGRAPHS OF THE DEAD RUNAWAYS WILL BE FOUND ARE IN THE DESK THE RECTOR'S THE BOX IN THE SHOE BOX

And then, finally, not crossed out:

THE MURDERED RUNAWAYS ARE IN THE SHOE BOX IN
THE RECTOR'S DESK.

A sheet of stationery slipped from his hand. As he bent to pick
it up, the flashlight beam struck the edge of a chair. A wing chair
—slip-covered in parakeet chintz.

He stood there, hearing no sound but his own heartbeat. It was
as if the world had dropped away and he had entered a space
completely apart.

He played the flashlight beam upward across the closet. It
caught the mirrored brightness of a second clothes rod behind the
first. He reached through the jackets and touched a fold of linen.

He pulled it into the light and recognized a priest's white chasuble. Blossoms of dried blood dotted the lace trim. The cloth was
stained and smeared like a butcher's apron where hands had
wiped themselves on it.

At the bottom of the closet, in the very rear, cassocks and stoles
had been balled into a pile. He crouched down to feel them. The
black cloth was caked and crusted.

His ribs pulled violently together. A taste of bile shot into his
mouth. He lunged for the bathroom, caromed off a wall, found
the toilet and vomited.

He stayed there, braced against the wall, eyes stinging. The
spasms passed. He groped for the sink and cupped running cold
water into his mouth and spat it clean. He carefully rinsed his face
and hands and shook his hands dry.

"Is that you, Collie?" a voice said.

He swung the flashlight.

Father Joe Montgomery stood in the doorway. One eye was
covered in gauze. The other was blinking rapidly. "I was sleeping
—I heard sounds. Are you all right?"

"It's not Collie," Cardozo said.

Father Joe tightened the sash of his robe. He seemed to reach
out with all his available senses, listening, sniffing. "Who are
you?"

"Vince Cardozo."

Father Joe pondered for a moment. There was something
deeply baffled in his face. "What are you doing in the dark?"

"Looking for you."

* * *

Cardozo phoned Ellie at the precinct. "Have you got a pencil?"

"Right in my hand."

He gave her the address. "Send the crime-scene crew with a search warrant—and a four-man backup to secure the scene."

"What have you found?"

"Scene of six homicides."

Ellie gave a low whistle.

"Has Eff contacted his grandmother yet?"

"Not yet," she said. "But Reverend Bonnie Ruskay's flock can breathe easier. She's back at the rectory."

EIGHTY-ONE

Above the rectory, clouds crowded a sunless sky. Cardozo leaned his full weight on the door buzzer. The cleaning woman opened the door. He pushed past her down the corridor to Bonnie's office.

She looked up from her desk, startled and angry. "If you don't mind, we're having a private discussion." She waved him away and he saw a white bandage on her right hand, thick as a mitten with the fingers cut out. "Would you please wait outside?"

A pale woman, wraithlike and jeweled and tall, rose from one of the armchairs. "No, Bonnie. It's time we got this into the open."

"Irene—don't say one word."

Cardozo recognized Irene Vanderbrook.

"You've shielded me long enough." Irene Vanderbrook turned to Cardozo. "Are you going to prosecute Bonnie?"

"The D.A. decides that, not me."

"Bonnie's not responsible. I'm the responsible person."

"You don't have to tell him anything," Bonnie said.

"What's left to tell?" Irene Vanderbrook said. "He's seen the notes my son and Mommy wrote."

"That's not why I'm here," Cardozo said.

"I was Mommy." Irene Vanderbrook's eyes, deep-set and green, fixed him. "That's why Wright went into pastoral counseling. That's why he took his life. I'm prepared to go on the record. Bonnie can't defend herself. She's bound by the seal of the confessional. I've thrashed this out with her, and she's aware of my decision."

Cardozo had a paralyzing sense of embarrassment. "Mrs. Vanderbrook, we're not prosecuting your son's death."

She glanced from him to Bonnie, confused. "But you came to the house—you were looking into it again."

"Yes, I looked into it, but believe me, the reverend isn't in any danger on that score."

Irene Vanderbrook looked down at the floor. Her shame was palpable. "In that case, my conscience is a little lighter on one small point. I'll be going."

The minute the door was shut, Bonnie whirled. "How could you do that to that poor woman?"

"What happened to your hand?"

"My hand is my concern."

Cardozo watched her put all the elements together: the righteous rage, the finishing-school carriage, the womanly vulnerability, the borderline-haughty speech mannerisms. "You said those letters of Wright Vanderbrooks's were notes you'd taken."

"I did not. I said I took notes and the notes were stolen."

"Then you misled me."

"You misled yourself."

"You really have it down to a science. You play with words. You withhold. You do whatever it takes to protect your technical innocence."

"I'm sorry if that's what you think of me after one misunderstanding."

"Not a misunderstanding, and not just one. You knew I was looking for Father Joe. You knew he was in the apartment over your mother's garage."

There was a startled reflex in her eyes. "What have you done with him?"

"He's back in the hospital—under guard."

She gathered a careful neutrality into her expression. "I didn't lie to you."

"But you and Collie hid him."

"I'll be damned if I'll justify my actions as a priest to you or anyone else."

"There was a warrant for Father Joe's arrest."

"It was an immoral, illegal, invalid warrant and he left the hospital before it was issued."

"How did a blind man walk out of a hospital?"

"Sonya Barnett helped him."

"Then you're all accomplices."

She cocked her gaze up, defiant now. "David Lowndes doesn't happen to agree with your interpretation of the statute."

"At least you've had the good sense to consult your lawyer. When did you do that—when you realized I was looking for Collie?"

"I did nothing to obstruct you."

"You knew he was at St. Kerry's and you withheld the information."

"I didn't know."

"For the love of God—you drove up there and brought him back!"

"I didn't know till my brother traced him."

"Your brother just happened to trace him?"

"I asked him to. I was worried sick. When Collie lost his job he started drinking again."

"And do you know why he lost his job?"

"He's not making any secret of it. He celebrated Mass for a runaway and the rector discovered it."

"Doesn't it seem odd to you—celebrating Mass for a lone runaway?"

"Maybe it is odd and whimsical—maybe Collie's odd and whimsical. He chooses to help runaways—just as Father Joe chooses to help them. Is it a crime to help the helpless? To bring God into their lives?"

"It is if you kill them afterward."

"He didn't!"

"We got Collie's fingerprints from the VA. They were on the same chalice as Sandy McCoy's. They were on the same chalice as Jaycee Wheeler's. Sandy and Jaycee were both dead within hours of taking communion."

"First you say it's Father Joe and then you say it's Collie. Why not toss a coin and just choose between them? Or are you so greedy now you want them both?"

"Who's Damien?"

She looked over at him, confused. "Damien ministered to the lepers."

"Not that Damien—the Damien who gives books to himself. Collie has a whole collection of them."

"Damien is a name priests use when they're being treated for embarrassing problems like alcoholism."

"And it's a name Collie uses when he's off his nut. And when he's off his nut he kills runaways because he thinks they've been bashing the Church—and I wonder how long you've known that?"

"You don't know Collie. I do. He's never harmed a soul."

"Then why did you warn him I was looking for him?"

"Because he's innocent and you won't believe it."

"What does it take to shake your faith? There are bloody vestments hanging in the closet. There are souvenirs from the victims sitting in your piggy bank—photographs of the corpses in the scrap book—drafts of that anonymous note blaming Father Joe—and to you he's still innocent and you're still hiding him."

"He *is* innocent and he's *not* hiding!"

"Then where is he?"

She hesitated. "He went to St. Patrick's."

"So he can sit in on another zap?"

"He never—"

The phone rang. She crossed the room to answer. "Rectory . . . Yes, he's right here." Frowning, she held the receiver out to Cardozo.

"Cardozo."

"Eff just phoned his grandmother," Ellie said. "She says a letter came for him this morning, Federal Express. He's on his way now to pick it up."

"Then we're into countdown. Wait for me." Cardozo hung up the phone. He turned to Bonnie. "We'll have to finish this later."

EIGHTY-TWO

By the time Cardozo collected Ellie and Greg Monteleone from the precinct and negotiated traffic up to the Bronx, the sun had begun to slip down the sky and shadows were creeping up the face of 322 Highland Road. He pulled the Honda into the space beside an open hydrant, near enough to see the front stoop, far enough not to be noticed.

Heat shimmered over the street like ripples in a pair of cheap sunglasses. Boom boxes and backfires echoed in the dead air.

"I forgot to mention the bad news," Ellie said. "The crime-scene crew can't go out to the garage till tomorrow."

"Why the hell not?" Cardozo said.

"They don't want to run up the overtime."

"Who doesn't?"

"Some bean counter in the Puzzle Palace."

"What about the guard? Can we at least protect the crime scene?"

"No money for them either. Which reminds me—the captain yanked Reverend Bonnie's guard. She's on her own."

"I don't believe the incompetence of these watch-your-assers!"

Greg spat a mouthful of orange pips out the window. "Believe it."

"What if Eff decides to attack her again?"

"The captain says he won't."

"The captain could have his head up his gazoo."

"That would be bad news," Ellie said. "On the other hand, Eff's got his priorities, right? And right now his priority is his grandmother, not the reverend."

"Let's hope he keeps his priorities straight," Cardozo said glumly.

"And let's not forget the good news," Ellie said. "I've got a search warrant for the garage."

"That's really helpful," Cardozo said.

At that moment a blue baseball cap came around the corner. It was wagging a blond ponytail and it was bouncing straight toward 322.

Cardozo nodded. "That's him."

Ellie double-checked the rounds in her revolver. She looked over at Cardozo and Greg with a falsely bright smile. "You never know, guys."

Grammaw opened the door wearing a blood-colored shawl. Eff was standing with one elbow against the doorjamb, New York Mets cap pushed way forward over a mock-streetwise scowl.

Grammaw pushed a smile onto her face and kissed him. He sauntered into the apartment. He picked up the oversize Federal Express envelope from the table.

"Must be awfully important," she said.

He grinned. "I doubt it."

She watched him tear the envelope open. There was a second envelope inside. He didn't open that one.

"Do you have time to visit? I was just making some coffee."

"How about some ice water? And could I use the bathroom?"

"Of course you can."

Eff went into the bathroom and quietly turned the key in the lock. He opened the second envelope. It contained a photo of a teenage girl sunbathing topless on the dock. He stared at the photo a moment, at the splash of freckles across her breasts, and then his eye went down to the name and numeral printed in block letters below the picture.

He lowered the toilet seat cover, stepped up onto it, and reached into the opening in the sash. He pulled up the stash bag and retrieved one of the special pink pills.

When he returned to the living room, Grammaw patted the sofa cushion beside her. "Come sit. Let's talk."

"In a minute, Grammaw. Can I borrow your phone?" He felt the soft pressure of her concern as she watched him lift the receiver and dial.

A young female voice answered.

"Hi," Eff said. "That little job we discussed? Better get yourself ready—it's come through."

"How soon?" she said.

"Right now. I'm on my way to get you." He hung up and met the troubled glow of his grandmother's eyes.

"Honey," she said, "I'm serious. We have to talk."

"Next time, Grammaw. I'm in a rush."

She held out his glass of ice water. Her eyes commanded him. He sat.

"When you raise a kid, there are some things you never know for sure." Her gaze was sad. "Some things you never want to know for sure. Some things you have to know for sure."

"I don't know what you're talking about, Grammaw."

"A cop was here, a white man, pretending to be from foster care. He was asking about you, and about your priest friend. What are you doing, honey, what have you got yourself into?"

"You know what I'm doing, Grammaw—I'm earning money, putting it away so we can move you out of here into Peter Cooper Village."

Grammaw shook her head. "This is my home right here, Eff—I don't need to move."

Eff hugged her. "I don't want my grammaw having to step over junkies and crackheads and dodging bullets every time she comes home."

She didn't seem to have heard him. "Eff, I have a bad feeling about that man. I'm scared for you."

He laughed. "Don't worry about your little Eff. He's got the juice. He's gonna take care of himself."

Bonnie had no idea how much time she spent pacing, just walking the same tight circle around her office. Refusal pumped through her. She didn't want to think. Tried not to think.

It was no good. The beat of her blood slowed down and the thought went through her head like the melody of a hated song: *I know the truth now.*

She could see day dying through the window, shadows of dogwood and pear tree seeping across the brick courtyard wall.

I know who, I know why. God forgive me.

She hurried to the garage. She slid into the car, fastened the safety belt, and shoved the gearshift into reverse. The nerves in her bandaged hand screamed.

A rap station boomed from stereo speakers. She killed the radio. She ignored the pain that shot again through her hand. *No time now for pain. I'm fine. Every little ache in place.*

She backed into the courtyard. She waited for the garage door to creak back down before she opened the gate and pulled into the street.

Today there was no dark blue Pontiac in her rearview mirror. No screech of wheels behind her as she angled into traffic. No one guarding her, no one tailing her.

In her mind she saw Vince Cardozo's grim dark eyes and she felt compassion. *Poor soul. He really believes he has the answer.*

EIGHTY-THREE

Ellie gave Cardozo a sharp nudge. *"There he is."*

Eff Huffington, supercool, came boogying down the steps of the graffitied, dust-caked stoop, fingers snapping, ponytail flipping.

"Mr. Wonderful," Cardozo muttered.

Eff hailed a cruising gypsy cab and hopped in. The cab took off in a crazy screech of rubber, its rear end fishtailing like a catfish out of salt water.

"Seat belt alert," Cardozo advised.

"Mine doesn't work," Greg Monteleone grumbled from the backseat.

"Sorry about that. Just grab something that isn't Ellie's or my neck and hold on."

Cardozo gunned the motor and the Honda shot forward.

Eff's cab ran three red lights, hooked two illegal turns, and sped west on a one-way east-bound street.

"Eff must have promised him a hell of a tip," Ellie said.

Cardozo busted the same lights and made the same turns, but he drew the line at the one-way street. He whipped south and then west on the next legal street.

"You're losing him," Ellie warned.

"I think we can guess where he's headed."

Cardozo picked up the cab on the entrance ramp to the West Side Highway. The ride south was a horn-blasting nonstop lane-hop.

He lost the cab when it ran another red light on Forty-second Street. He spotted it again at Twenty-third, hooking a wild left against oncoming traffic.

"He's not going to the docks," Ellie said.

"Unless he knows a new way of getting there." Cardozo used the horn, not the siren, and cut the car sharp into the left east-bound lane. A chorus of horns exploded. Somewhere behind him metal bongoed into metal.

Eff's cab executed a dizzy weave around ambulances and moving vans and pimpmobiles. Ellie frowned. "Where the hell is he going?"

At Fifth Avenue and Madison Square Park, Cardozo had no idea. When the cab careered across Second Avenue he was beginning to form a notion, and when it pulled to a shuddering stop at the north edge of Peter Cooper Village, he was sickeningly sure.

Ellie scanned the neat redbrick apartment buildings rising catty-cornered to the street. "Isn't that where your sister lives?"

"No way I'm going to let this happen." Cardozo snapped his seat belt off and was out of the car in one movement. He cut across the lawn toward Jill's building. He was halfway to the door when he heard a voice call: "Eff! Over here!"

He whirled and saw Nell Dunbar, waiting on the other side of Twenty-third Street, waving.

It was too late to stop her, too late even to shout. The cab nose-dived into a U-turn and came to a screeching two-second halt. A door slammed, and when the cab shot west, the freckle-faced girl in jeans and straw hat was gone.

He ran back to the car and slammed into gear.

The cab, almost a full block ahead now, turned north on Third Avenue.

"How did Eff know where she was staying?" Ellie said.

Cardozo swung north. "Nell must have contacted him to get drugs."

"What's wrong with the girl? Her boyfriend went with Eff on

one of these jobs and that was the last anyone saw of him. Can't she put two and two together?"

"Maybe not. Where Nell's been living, boyfriends disappear every week."

Storm clouds were gathering and day had shrunk to a band of embers over the New Jersey skyline when Eff's cab crossed the Willis Avenue Bridge into the Bronx.

"I never met a teenager yet," Greg said, "who didn't think they were immortal."

Cardozo followed the cab onto Willis Avenue. Rain exploded.

Ellie shook her head. "Funny he's not going on the Bruckner."

The cab swung right onto 132nd Street into an area of mostly burned-out buildings.

At Brown Place a fire truck cut in front of Cardozo. He slammed on the brakes. "Screw!"

It was thirty seconds before the fire truck cleared the street, and by then the cab had vanished.

The rain was falling steadily now, like thin sheets of crinkled plastic wrap.

"The church has got to be near here," Cardozo said. "They wouldn't have gotten off the avenue if they weren't close."

Ellie peered out the windshield. "I don't see a steeple."

"Better ask at that bodega," Greg said.

Cardozo eased to the curb and waited while Ellie went into the shop. She came back with three cups of Italian ice.

"Straight ahead two blocks, take a left, go four blocks to the busted traffic light and never mind the police barrier. One block further and you can't miss it." She handed Cardozo and Greg a cup each. "Hope you guys like lime."

A streetlight caught a rising smiling sun painted on the door of a dark blue Toyota van. The van had parked in front of a small church with boarded-up windows. The street dead-ended in a field of rubble.

Greg squinted to read the lettering. *"God loves you—so do I."*

"That's our man." As Cardozo slowed the car, the church door opened. He braked gently to a stop a half block away.

On the church steps, three figures stood silhouetted against a dull red glow. A heavy mist was falling through the air, but Cardozo recognized Eff and the girl. The tall man with them wore a priest's cassock. His hand rested on Nell's shoulder.

She looked confused and uneasy. She was wearing a raincoat now and she moved with a kind of leggy lack of control that was practically stumbling.

"They gave her something," Cardozo said.

Ellie nodded. "She's stoned."

Crossing the pavement, Nell almost fell. Eff helped her up. She was shaking her head violently. The priest opened the van door and Eff was trying to push her inside.

As Cardozo pressed the accelerator, the motor went dead. "Damn. Ellie, take the wheel. Block the street and don't let them get by." He hit the pavement at a sprint.

There was a slam and a backfire. Stripping gears shrieked. The van lurched toward the dead end. Behind him, Cardozo heard the Honda kick into a high, spinning whine.

The van began a turn, but instead of completing the U, it veered behind the church. Cardozo shot forward.

Ellie brought up the headlights and they caught Eff standing alone on the sidewalk. He froze. He glanced right and left, evaluating the best route of escape. He took a half second to decide and that was a half second too long.

Cardozo hit him with a body-block and the impact spun him around. Greg was there and ready when Eff crashed into him. His right fist caught the boy full in the face. Eff tried to cry out, but Greg followed with the left and slammed another punch. And another. Eff crashed down into the street and came to a sitting-down stop with his mouth open, like a clown.

Cardozo grabbed him from behind, a full nelson hold under the shoulders and around the neck. He lifted the kicking body and dragged it to the Honda and pitched it into the backseat.

Eff was panting like a winded dog.

Cardozo slid in next to him. "Where's that van going?"

Eff gave him a defiant glare. "I want my lawyer."

"Greg—help me."

Greg grabbed Eff's legs and Cardozo frisked him. From the left trouser pocket he pulled a wallet stuffed with charge cards. From the right pocket, a plastic bag of pills and rolled joints. From the left sock, a razor. He tossed them all into the front seat.

"Talk to me, Eff. Tell me where your friends are going." Cardozo drew his service revolver out of the holster.

"I don't know!" Eff screamed. "I don't know where they're going!"

Cardozo spun the chamber of the revolver. It made a clicking sound like a rhythm instrument in a rumba band.

"They're going south!" Eff screamed. "Manhattan!"

Ellie slipped the motor into forward. "Which bridge?"

"Eff, which bridge?"

"Triborough!"

"We'll head them off," Ellie said.

"Hey, Eff, let's talk about the rectory," Cardozo said. "The first time. Why did you break in?"

"Who says I broke in anywhere?"

"The first time, Eff. Why did you go in that very first time?"

Streetlights flashed by, striping Eff's face.

"Was it to put those photos in Father Joe's file?" Cardozo gave the gun barrel another twirl.

"Okay, okay. It was to leave the photos."

"Who told you to do it?"

"Nobody."

"Come on, Eff. You just decided to give Father Joe a present? Don't give me shit, Eff." Cardozo cocked the .38. "Was it your friend Damien?"

Eff considered for a moment. "I don't remember."

"Come on, Eff."

"I don't remember his name."

Cardozo nuzzled the barrel of the gun into Eff's ear. "Who was it?"

"Okay, it was Damien."

"Who's Damien? What's his real name?"

"All I know is, he calls himself Damien."

Cardozo slammed the gun into the seat beside Eff's head. "Tell me the name, punk."

"Cole. His name is Damien Cole."

Ellie steered the Honda over a head-banging bump in the road, then swerved onto an entrance ramp to the Triborough Bridge.

"How'd you get into the rectory?"

"The window upstairs."

"You numbered the photos. Why?"

"Damien wants people from *OutMag*. So I said this is the number one guy, this is the number two guy."

"Why did you bring Pablo?"

Eff didn't answer. Bridge lights whipped past the window.

"You'd better tell me why, Eff."

Eff tried to smile. "Too much good stuff for one person to carry."

Cardozo moved the barrel of the gun up to Eff's temple. "Why did you go back and leave Pablo's photo in the desk?"

A fine line of sweat broke out on Eff's cheekbones.

"Pablo wasn't one of your kiddie hookers." Cardozo stroked the gun along Eff's hairline. "Why'd you go back and leave his photo?"

Eff's mouth opened and for one panicky instant nothing came out but the labored sound of lungs pulling in gulps of air.

"Why, Eff?"

"Because . . ." Eff's voice dropped. "Because he was dead."

Approaching the line of tollbooths, Ellie slowed and steered toward an exact-change lane. "Vince," she said. "Over there."

Two lanes over, the blue Toyota van waited in line. Burps of smoke curled from its exhaust.

"How did Pablo die?" Cardozo said.

"He walked into a booby trap and it killed him." Eff flinched from the next anticipated blow. "Man, I couldn't let it lead back to me. I'm on probation. They were going to suspect that faggot priest anyway. Let them suspect him for one more."

The van passed through the tollgate. Shadows of three passengers slipped across the side window.

"Then you knew those other kids were dead."

"Hell, no!" Eff yanked away. "I don't know anything about that!"

But Cardozo could see the answer ugly on his face. "The evidence says you killed Pablo."

"No way! Fuck you!"

Ellie allowed the van a ten-car lead, then began following.

"The evidence shows the booby trap only wounded him." Cardozo took hold of the ponytail and pulled with a steady pressure.

"A witness heard Pablo screaming. You were afraid the neighbors would call the cops. So you killed him."

"Let go! Ow! You got it wrong!"

"And then you broke a windowpane to make it look like he broke in."

"Fuck no, you got it all wrong."

Cardozo gave the ponytail a jerk like a toilet chain.

"Come on, man," Eff howled. "That's my hair!"

"Tell me the truth."

"That booby trap fucked his skull, man. He was begging me to put him out of his misery—it was a mercy killing."

"Mercy killing?" Cardozo tsk-tsked. "My, my. You are one kindhearted guy, Eff."

Ahead, on a midtown Manhattan street, the van slowed to the curb.

"Pull over here," Cardozo told Ellie.

EIGHTY-FOUR

A tall man stepped out of the van, followed by a girl. They both wore raincoats.

Ellie and Cardozo got out of the Honda.

Fifty feet away, the man and the girl were heading down the sidewalk with swift buoyant strides, raincoats bouncing. They turned a corner.

Cardozo and Ellie broke into a run. They reached the corner just as a door halfway down the block closed behind two raincoats.

They sprinted.

When they reached the building, the man was just locking the mailbox and the girl was holding the inner door. As the man passed beneath an overhead light, Cardozo recognized Bonnie's friend Colin Draper. Colin and the girl went into the last apartment on the right.

Ellie pushed buzzers for apartments on the higher floors.

A voice came over the intercom. "Who is it?"

"Pizza," Cardozo called.

A buzz let them into the building. They moved quickly to the door at the end of the corridor.

Footsteps approached on the other side—soft muffled treads on carpet; a hard, rushed pattering on tile. Metal clicked as a lock bolt snapped into place. The steps went away, their hard-soft pattern reversed.

A man's voice spoke. Cardozo could not make out the words, but there was a shouted resonance to them. A woman's voice yelled something.

Ellie glanced at him, eyes wary.

He put his eye to the peephole. The wood was dark and shiny with old coats of varnish. The tiny curved lens gave him a tunnel view into nothingness.

The voices kept going. Two people could have been carrying on a conversation from opposite ends of the apartment; or they could have been arguing, building up to an explosion.

There was a blast of raucous music with a hypermanic TV sales pitch babbling over it. Footsteps clacked and the sound was quickly lowered.

The man shouted again. The woman shouted back. It was different this time. Cardozo could feel something happening.

Some kind of heavy object made a deep thud on the other side of the door, more vibration than sound. There was a split second of stillness. And then the woman let out a scream like a car alarm.

Cardozo yanked his revolver from its holster, took aim, fired two rounds. The lock jumped out of the door. He threw his full weight against the wood. It slammed inward.

Ellie advanced, gun raised and steady in both hands. "Police!"

A smoking wok trailed a comet spill of chopped vegetables across the kitchen floor of a gentrified railroad flat. A woman had taken crouching cover behind the refrigerator. In the room just beyond, Colin Draper was hunkered down behind an old wing chair.

Cardozo held up his shield. "Who screamed?"

"I did." The woman's eyes were fearful beneath pale brown curls.

"Why?"

"Is it against the law to scream?" She stood. She was wearing a man's T-shirt with a Yale Divinity School seal and both arms ripped off. "I burned myself with the wok."

Cardozo had seen the face before, in a photo on Bonnie Ruskay's desk. "You're Ben Ruskay's fiancée." *With ten years tacked on,* his mind added.

"If that's a crime," she said, "I'm innocent."

"Anne and Ben were never engaged. Ben just liked to say they were." Colin Draper came forward with his hands raised. "What's this about? Are we under arrest for something? Because we have a right to know what you think we've done."

"I pray to God you haven't had time to do anything yet," Cardozo said.

Ellie came back from the other rooms. Her eyes told Cardozo that something was wrong.

"Did you find Nell back there?"

Ellie shook her head. "There's no one else here."

Cardozo's heart gave a jump. "I saw you get out of the van with Nell. You brought her in here. What the hell have you done with her?"

"I got out of the van with Anne," Colin Draper said. "Nell stayed in the van and went with Ben."

"Ben Ruskay was in the van too?"

"Of course."

"What's he doing with Nell?"

"Ben's reaching out to runaways." The woman's voice was impatient now.

"Reaching out with what?" Cardozo said, but already in that one exploding instant he understood.

A shadow flicked across Colin Draper's face. "Ben brings runaways to me and I give them communion."

"And what's your part in this?" Cardozo asked the woman. "Acolyte?"

She stiffened. "Communicant. I happen to love the Eucharist."

"Come on," Cardozo said. "The girl was doped to her eyeballs.

What the hell did you think was going on? Didn't one of you ever suspect something was happening besides communion?"

"Drugs are an important part of the runaways' lifestyle," Colin Draper said. "That doesn't have to come between them and God."

"How can you people be so goddamned naive? I just don't understand what you thought you were doing."

"Helping the helpless," the woman said.

"Don't you realize what's been happening to these kids?" Cardozo shouted. "Don't you know what that man's going to do to Nell?"

Colin Draper looked sincerely baffled. "All he's doing is taking her home."

Nell Dunbar closed the bathroom door. A wave of nausea buffeted her. She knelt at the toilet, bracing her elbows against the icy white porcelain.

Spasms ripped her.

She opened her mouth. A yawning reflection flashed up at her from the toilet bowl. She shut her eyes, blotting it out. Darkness rushed up around her.

Sweat was running down her face and arms. She could feel her heart beat with a furious drumming. Her tiny hammer-and-sickle silver earrings tinkled like a pair of wind chimes.

A fit of retching took her, but nothing came up. She tried and she tried till she was choking on her own tears.

She opened her eyes and pushed herself to standing. She still had a buzz on from all the drugs—especially that pink pill that Eff gave her. What the hell was that pink pill?

She promised herself never to take one of those again.

Three wobbling steps brought her to the sink, breathless. She swung the cabinet door open and found a bottle of Brut aftershave. She dabbed some behind her ears and on her wrists and then under her baggy Georgetown sweatshirt, between her breasts.

She stumbled back into the other room. A wall hit her broadside. She found herself staring at parchments covered with Gothic lettering. She tried to focus. The word *blessed* came swimming at her.

A hand reached over to touch her shoulder. "Tell me, my child," Father said, "how long have you been a runaway?"

She had to will her brain to communicate with her tongue to produce the words. "Awhile."

His vestments were streaked in red. He was lighting incense in a small copper bowl and already the room was drowning in the sweet honeyed stink of it.

"Tell me, my child, how long have you been taking drugs?"

"Eight or nine years."

"And how long have you been prostituting yourself?"

"I don't know . . . since I was . . ."

She tried to say "ten," but something inside her sealed off and died and she pitched forward onto the sofa.

Father's hand supported her under the nape of her neck. Every ten seconds or so the breath came out of her in a sigh and he felt the warmth of it against his face. He felt such love and sympathy and joy for her that it made his eyes sting.

He laid her in the washtub. The ribbed drain board was her pillow. She was looking up at the ceiling now, eyes unfocused and unseeing.

He relaxed the naked hips, tilting them so the knees reached over the edge of the tub. The legs swung lazily in the dark, damp air. The legs of a bored little girl.

His footsteps echoed against concrete. He was in no rush. He was absolutely still inside himself, absolutely at peace with the rhythms of the ceremony. He opened the tool chest and lifted out the chain saw. He worked the three-pronged plug into the wall socket.

The outlet and the tubs were on opposite sides of the empty room. As he crossed back, carrying the saw, he let the loops of electric cord uncoil from his hand.

He pressed the *start* button, testing the current. The small motor growled. The blade blurred. A fine mist of rust-colored dust fell in her face.

He heard her breath sigh, a shuddering sigh this time. A muscle worked in the pale blue of her irises. Her uncomprehending stare fought to focus itself.

He lifted the whirring saw and there was a snap of recognition in her eyes.

The tendons in her neck made a wrenching effort.

"Relax," he urged. "God loves you. So do I. We both love you very much. You could not be more loved than you are at this instant."

With her eyes half-turned in their sockets she had the cunning, evasive look of a guilty child found out.

Her throat pushed out a bubble of protest.

He pressed the *fast* button. The saw's whining became a shriek.

With one hand he turned her head sideways, just so. A tiny shadow pulsed at her jugular.

He raised the saw and carefully brought it down in a measured arc. He would begin with the throat. He always began with the throat. He angled the blade.

The shriek of the motor dropped to a squeal. The squeal dropped to a moan. The moan dropped to . . . *silence.*

And then a voice.

"Ben—what are you doing?"

EIGHTY-FIVE

The voice spun him around. At first, all he saw was a woman standing on the stairway, holding the three-pronged plug of an electric cord.

"I'm doing my duty." Somewhere in his mind he knew why he was here with a saw dangling at his side, but in the shock of seeing her he had to struggle to recall the reason. "I'm doing God's will."

"Remember when we were children?" Gray light spilled down and outlined her. "Remember how we made believe we were Father Damien? We gave one another presents and signed them 'to Damien, from Damien.' But I'm not Damien—I'm Bonnie. And you're not Damien. You're Ben. You're my brother. And I love you. And you're not a priest."

"But I'm a deacon of the Church. I can't give communion or hear confession, but I can perform marriages. I can assist at Mass."

"Ben—what are you doing with this child?"

"I'm sending her to God while she's still in a state of grace."

"And how did you choose *this* child?"

"Because she's one of them."

"One of *who*?"

"They bashed the cathedral—they interrupted the cardinal and threw consecrated hosts on the floor."

She let the plug fall to the floor. "But it wasn't her. She wasn't one of them." She spoke with the voice he remembered from childhood—the voice of admonishment—chiding but carrying no malice. "Eff's been tricking you. None of the youngsters he brought you were activists. They were just runaways. They were never even inside St. Patrick's."

The concrete floor swayed like a rope bridge beneath him. "But they told me—"

"They were lying. They were doing it for money."

He looked into her eyes. "Then I'm the sinner?"

Her eyes did not look away.

"Not them?" The terror of certainty hit him. "How has God let me do this?" He seized her hand. "You're a priest. Help me. *Please.*" He sank to his knees. "Hear my confession."

"Ben—no."

He held tight to the hand. "I confess to Almighty God and to you, his priest, that I have sinned."

She gave a long, surrendering sigh. "When did you make your last confession?"

"I haven't made a true confession since . . . I can't remember. Years. I confess that I broke the commandment against murder. I killed six young people. But I did it for them, out of love. They died in a state of forgiveness of sin. I gave them Christian burial. I took flowers to their graves."

He watched his sister's face. It did not change. Yet it looked so tired—so remote. Panic washed through him.

"I committed sins of envy and anger. After your ordination, I raped a woman."

"Why?"

"Because she opposed Church teaching. So many people are opposing the Church—an example has to be made."

"Don't you think God can make his own examples?"

"I confess that I doubted that. I confess that I broke the commandment to be truthful. I said I'd stopped drinking. But I never stopped. When you thought I was in detox, I was in court."

"For the rape?"

He nodded. "The judge made me pay her. She used the money to bash the Church and profane the cathedral. I couldn't stand by and let that happen, could I?"

His sister didn't answer.

"She made sinners of young people—but I saved their souls. She sinned against me—but I forgave her—and sent her to God too."

His sister probed him with disbelieving eyes.

"I confess that I maligned Father Joe. I had photos put in his desk and I sent an anonymous note on your letterhead."

"Why, Ben? Why Father Joe?"

"Because of what he was doing to you and to young people."

"He was only trying to serve."

"With *condoms*?"

His sister took a step away from him. He clung to her hand.

"But my greatest sin was malice. The birthday presents that you asked me to pass along to Mother—the books . . . the rose clipping . . . the piggy bank . . ." Tears stung his eyes. "I confess that I kept them—because I was jealous of you. In my heart, I hated you, because you were what I could never become—a priest."

He bowed his head in shame. A deep pool of silence closed over him.

A light fell across the stillness, and he heard the sound of his sister's voice pronouncing the formula of forgiveness.

"Ego te absolvo."

I absolve you.

* * *

Cardozo stepped through the door at the side of the garage. He heard voices. He approached the second doorway, gun drawn.

Bonnie stood in profile, absolutely still. A man knelt before her, head bowed. Even with his black shadow of beard stubble, Cardozo recognized Ben from the religious goods shop.

His body stiffened into firing stance. Gripping with both hands, he raised the revolver to eye level. He lined up the front sight on the kneeling man.

He said one word. "Freeze."

Ben got to his feet.

Cardozo brought the sight up with him. "I said freeze."

Ben was holding an electric saw. "Kill me," he said quietly.

Cardozo stood motionless, holding Ben in his sights.

"Kill me now!" Ben screamed.

Bonnie half-turned to look over at Cardozo. She was shaking her head. "Vince . . . no . . ." She moved into the sights. Now she was standing between the gun and Ben.

Cardozo spoke very slowly. "Bonnie . . . step aside."

"Kill me." Ben's voice cracked into a high, keening quaver, and then it dropped. "Or I'll kill her." He swung the saw up into the air. The blade caught a ricochet of light.

"Bonnie . . . step away."

She glanced behind her and then quickly back at Cardozo. "It's not plugged in!" she shrieked.

It didn't need to be. Ben brought the saw crashing down. It struck with the force of a serrated sledgehammer, tearing into the side of her head.

A *crack* echoed.

For one moment she stood absolutely still, her mouth open just a little. And then a slanting line in her temple split open and blood spurted across her eyes and face.

The impact carried her to the side and for an instant Cardozo had Ben clear in the gun sights.

He fired.

White light shot from the barrel. A clap of thunder rocked the concrete walls.

The bullet tore a third eye in Ben's forehead. The saw clattered to the floor. He staggered backward, spun, and toppled.

EIGHTY-SIX

Cardozo stepped into the hospital room holding a dozen red roses. He could see they weren't needed. The room was so packed with flower arrangements it looked like a florist's shop window.

A private nurse was seated in a chair beside the window reading a medical suspense paperback. She looked up, laid the book facedown on the table, and rose from her chair. "May I help you?"

"How's she doing?"

"I'm sorry—the doctor doesn't wish the reverend to see visitors."

In the hospital bed, Bonnie opened her eyes. Her head was wrapped in a turban of white gauze and a bandage slanted down over her left eyebrow. An IV fed into her arm. The bed had been raised to a half-sitting position.

"Bonnie," he said.

Bonnie's gaze moved across the room by deliberate degrees, as though it had to draw support from each object it grazed before it could limp on to the next. Her eyes finally met his. They were weary, sedated, beyond shock, beyond grief. Yet their beauty struck him with the force of a blow from a sharpened instrument.

"Please," the nurse said, and Cardozo could feel her ready to oppose him.

"Do you suppose you could find a vase for these?" He pushed the flowers at her and stepped around her to the bed.

"Vince." Bonnie's voice was weak.

He pulled up a chair. "How are you feeling?"

"I've caused so much trouble for everyone."

Her hands lay on top of the thin blue hospital blanket, side by side, thumbs touching. He took her right hand. It rested in his, then squeezed.

"If only I'd seen how Ben was suffering—and drinking—and using the people around him—" She turned away and looked toward the window.

"We're human. Sometimes we let ourselves be deceived. You loved your brother. It was natural to believe what he told you. It was natural to believe in *him*."

"I loved him—but I knew the truth. I knew when you said Collie gave communion to the murdered boy—Sandy McCoy." Her hand slid from Cardozo's. "The only people Collie gave communion to were Ben's runaways. I should have spoken out then. Ben might still be alive. That little girl might still be alive."

"Nell's alive. She's in the hospital and she's recovering."

"Thank God." Bonnie's eyes did not move from the gray of the window. "But I've hurt so many others."

He felt something wounded and self-wounding in her. "Stop blaming yourself. Look at me. Look at the hell I put Father Joe through."

"You were doing your work. He understands."

A silence fell.

"Have you spoken with him?"

She nodded.

"How is he?" Cardozo said.

"Wonderful—and amazing—as always." Her eyes came around. "He's worried what will happen to Eff."

"With a plea bargain, Eff will get three years for killing Pablo. It's not much, but when he's out he'll be an adult and the next crime he commits maybe they'll give him life."

"Poor child."

"I guess there are certain subjects you and I are never going to agree on."

She smiled. "Never in this life."

He felt the nurse's touch, firm on his elbow. "The doctor's here. You have to go now."

He kissed her on the forehead, beside the bandage. He backed away from the bed. Bonnie's eyes followed him.

He stepped into the corridor, suddenly exhausted. His legs could barely carry him.

The nurse came clattering after him. "There are no vases left." She was holding his flowers. "Not even a pitcher."

"You keep them."

"We're not allowed—" she started to say.

"I'll take them." Ellie Siegel glided smoothly between them and rescued the bouquet. "These will brighten up my desk. Thanks, Vince. It's been six years since a man's given me flowers on my birthday."

"It's your birthday?" Cardozo gave her a long glance, wondering how she'd found him and why.

"Every July—regular as clockwork."

An elevator was waiting. They got in. The door hissed shut and the elevator dropped eighteen floors through whispering silence.

"Vince—stop brooding." Ellie took his arm. "You had to fire. Any cop would have done the same. I was there—I saw what was about to happen."

"She was there, too—and I don't think she agrees."

"That's why people like her need people like us."

He looked at Ellie with her mild dark eyes, with her hair catching flashes of fluorescence from the light.

"Happy birthday," he said. "Sorry I didn't remember."

They walked to his car and piled in.

"Where to?" he said.

"I know a terrific Chinese place on Forty-ninth—they have a lunch special for families. Think we can pass?"

"We can damned well try."

They were driving west on Forty-ninth when Ellie said, "The D.A. hid and falsified evidence. He should answer for it."

"Don't look at me. I'm only a cop." Cardozo steered around a disabled cab. "It's up to Fairchild. She says she can prove indictable fraud."

"Will she?"

"Wouldn't do much good. Kodahl would claim he didn't know. He'd say the cover-up was Thoms's brainchild."

"And if Fairchild doesn't go public?"

"That's the interesting alternative. If that happens, somewhere not too far down the line Kodahl will take early retirement and Deborah Fairchild will make D.A."

"Think she'd be any good?"

"A hell of a lot better than what we've got now."

Ellie pointed. "Slow down. There's a parking place."

* * *

All New York must have heard about the Chinese lunch special. Chattering diners at tiny tables jammed the narrow, brightly lit restaurant.

"Look who's over there." Ellie tossed a nod.

Cardozo peered over bobbing heads and galloping chopsticks. He saw Terri sitting at a table by the far window. Suddenly it felt like a setup: Ellie's birthday, which he'd never heard of happening in July before; this restaurant, Terri just happening to be here.

Ellie sidestepped flying trays and mandarin waiters and led the way to the table. They were standing close enough to count the pieces of chive in the wonton soup when Terri looked up. "Hi, Dad."

"Didn't know this was one of your lunch hangouts," Cardozo said.

Terri was sitting with a friend, a slightly older girl with dark hair and studious-looking glasses. The friend broke into a big grin and there was no question—she was grinning at Cardozo.

Okay, he thought, *I'm funny.*

The friend pushed up from the table. "You look great." It was a voice that struck memories. "Really great, Uncle Vince."

That word *Uncle* hit with almost physical force. "Sally?"

She stepped into his embrace. *This is my sister's little girl?* he wondered. He arms told him that this was nobody's little girl, this was no little girl.

"It's really you?"

"It's me." She kept grinning. "Really."

"You're all right?"

"Sure, I'm all right."

"I hate to nag, but where the hell were you?"

She stepped away from his arms and sat down again. "Sawyer's Island, New York."

"That's an island?"

She nodded.

"Where?"

"Lake Erie."

"Why? Why didn't you write? Or phone?"

"I don't know why. I just kept putting it off." She was poking a chopstick at a mound of brown rice. "And after a while I couldn't, because I hadn't."

That poking movement recalled something. Cardozo remembered a mound of frozen yogurt and a sixteen-year-old girl with a dessert spoon.

"I can't even explain it to myself," she said. "I knew what Mom must have been going through. I felt guilty because I didn't feel guilty. If I'd heard from Mom or you maybe I would have felt guilty enough to phone."

"You don't hear from people unless you leave a forwarding address."

She gave him a look that was almost mischievous. "But Uncle Vince, you're a detective."

"I thought I was." He felt his eyes filming and then things wobbled a little. "How did Ms. Sherlock here find you?"

Ellie pulled out a chair and sat. "How does any case get broken after six years? A lucky break. A witness came forward. Kind of."

Cardozo flexed his memory, trying to match now to then, trying to see his niece with long hair, without the glasses, the face a little less full, the figure a lot less full. "Sally—can you tell me—why did you go? Why didn't we hear from you?"

"I was pregnant."

It was a simple statement of fact. Didn't seem to matter who else was at the table. No embarrassment at all.

Cardozo dropped into a seat. "So that was it. And Father Joe helped you disappear."

She shook her head. "Father Joe told me to go back to Mom. Father Chuck said, have the baby and then decide. He gave me the money and the address."

"What did you do with the baby?"

"He's still with us. He's five years old."

"Us?"

"I'm married."

"To a fireman," Terri said. "Sally's been telling me everything."

"And we have a two-year-old girl of our own." Sally opened her purse and brought out color photographs of two children playing in a backyard.

A delayed shock hit Cardozo. The words pouring out around the table seemed to have no relation to reality. The pictures in his hand had no connection to his life. He could have been watching a television screen, listening to a bunch of chirpy newscasters reciting the weather.

"I work for the fire department too." There was a quiet sort of pride in Sally's voice. "I'm a firewoman."

He didn't know whether she had actually said that or he was hallucinating it. "That so? I thought you looked . . ." He searched for a diplomatic word.

"Big." She laughed a no-regrets laugh.

To Cardozo's ear there was something about that laugh, about the very act of letting herself laugh that freely—something that wasn't exactly hayseed but almost. She was no longer a Big City girl. He didn't know how he felt. Happy for her, definitely; sad for himself, maybe.

"I had to get big to pass the physical," she said. "The guys hate me. I'm the first woman on the force."

If this was the truth, there some some part of him that was going to fight it. "Can you be a fireperson and wear glasses?"

She twirled the glasses. "For menus."

"What happened to acting?"

She looked down at the brown rice. Just a dipping glance down, then back up. "Life got real. I had to get real."

"We'd better think about eating," Ellie said. "The orders have to be in by one P.M. to get the special."

"Your mother would like to hear from you," Cardozo said.

Sally hesitated. "I'm kind of rushed this trip. I have to be back on Sawyer's Island tomorrow. I have the afternoon shift."

"You've got time to drop in and hug her, let her know you're alive."

Sally's eyes were big dark question marks. "I don't know, Uncle Vince. If Mom starts nagging the way she used to—she'll drive me crazy all over again."

"Your mom's changed. She's got Nell to worry about now."

"Who's Nell?"

"A lost little girl your mom's decided to save. In my opinion, the savee has saved the savior. It's a long story." Cardozo reached across the table for Sally's hand. "Just take a half hour and say 'Hi, Mom, I'm alive.' "

"All right." Sally smiled uncertainly. "A half hour."
Ellie raised a Chinese teacup. "Here's to welcome home."
"Welcome home," Cardozo said.
Four cups clinked.